Acclaim For Jennifer Colt's McAfee Twins Series

The Hellraiser of The Hollywood Hills: A McAfee Twins Novel

Finalist, Amazon Breakthrough Novel Award

"You can't teach someone to write like this; you are either born able to generate such wit or you'll never be able to learn it. I got a big kick out of this story, and only hope there will soon be another madcap crime spree in Hollywood for the McAfee Twins to solve."

—**Elizabeth Gilbert**, bestselling author of *Eat, Pray, Love*

"Fans of Janet Evanovich's 'Stephanie Plum' series would be entirely at home with level-headed Kerry, wannabe-stuntwoman Terry, and their assortment of odd-ball friends and ~~~~~~~~, from a trio of helpful prostitutes ~~~~~~~ Lance Manley. Lively characters ~~~~~~~ make this mystery more than wc ~~~~~ ng."

D0873217

~eekly

The Con Artist of Catalina Island: A McAfee TwinsChristmas Novel

"*The Con Artist of Catalina Island* is not only a good mystery, it's also a hilarious screwball comedy... Recommended for those who have already stumbled upon Colt's fantastic series, and for new fans who will undoubtedly finish this book only to run to the nearest bookstore to find the rest of the adventures of the McAfee twins."

—Curled Up with a Good Book

"Jennifer Colt has an outstanding comedic talent plus an ability to create larger-than-life characters that draw in the reader instantly. The McAfee twins are a pleasurable change from run-of-the-mill sleuths, and the constant antics of Reba, Robert, and Jacques add to the fun. The McAfee twins series is a rollicking good time!"

—Midwest Book Review

The Vampire of Venice Beach: A Novel

"Colt's lovable detective duo, redheaded twins Kerry and Terry McAfee find themselves on security duty for a group of vampire wannabes at the Venice Goth Parade. The last thing they expect is to end up with an actual dead body on their hands, but that's precisely what happens... [W]ill have mystery lovers reading rapidly to reach the exciting conclusion. "

—Booklist

"Prowling Venice Beach are two flame-haired detectives, Kerry and Terry McAfee... They're identical twins who spout snarky dialogue while solving murders in Malibu, Venice Beach, Beverly Hills and Catalina Island. Author Jennifer Colt created these engaging characters for a series of light and escapist mysteries full of cutting social commentary and wit."

—NPR.org

"The far-out plot features entertaining characters like a really gross vamp named Shatán, but the standouts are the wisecracking sisters on their shocking pink motorcycle."

—*Publishers Weekly*

"*The Vampire of Venice Beach* is a fun little mystery full of quirky characters, slap-happy comedy, and a touch of social commentary. It should be a staple in every vampire romance lover's beach bag."

—*Vampireromancebooks.com*

The Mangler of Malibu Canyon: A Novel

"The second installment of Colt's engaging series opens with the McAfee twins, Kerry and Terry, stopping an attempted terrorist takeover of an L.A.-bound plane. Things don't slow down when the pair arrives home: their Aunt Reba has found a woman's body rolled up in a rug at her Malibu home, and her son, Robbie, who is supposed to be in rehab, shows up disoriented and carrying the woman's head... A wild, entertaining romp anchored by its very different but equally likable heroines."

—*Booklist*

"Kerry (the boy-crazy twin addicted to law enforcement types with big guns) and Terry (the twin who goes for leggy ladies) provide plenty of laughs."

—*Publishers Weekly*

"A nice mix of fun, a bit of romance, just enough danger and two feisty PIs who can take on the bad guys and gals. This is one you can take to the beach."

—*WHRO Radio, Norfolk, VA*

The Butcher of Beverly Hills: A Novel

"What if Stephanie Plum had an ex-cokehead for a sister? Gorgeous twin crime fighters battle a bunch of shady dudes in screenwriter Colt's vivacious debut...a fast-paced, gum-snapping, snarky chick-lit mystery with sparkle to spare."

—*Publishers Weekly*

"Colt's smart writing, amusing plot twists, and glamorous Hollywood setting make this mystery a true original."

—*Pages Magazine*

"Fast and furious, and the laughs keep coming."

—*Barnes and Noble Editors*

"The Butcher of Beverly Hills sparkles like a Beverly Hills diamond, and is fast and flirty as a pink Harley-Davidson. Colt has a winner with this series of zippy, screwball, and ultra-hip mysteries."

—*Julie Kenner, USA Today bestselling author of Carpe Demon: Adventures of a Demon-Hunting Soccer Mom*

"Entertaining from start to finish, The Butcher of Beverly Hills is [a] murder mystery masterpiece. Starring the ultimate in private detective teams, twin sisters Terry and Kerry McAfee, the story is hilarious, smart and fun."

—*Empowerment4women.org*

"If you like Evanovich...then Colt should be on your list. "

—*Crimespree Magazine*

The Hellraiser of the Hollywood Hills

A McAfee Twins Novel

Jennifer Colt

Tessera Books
Santa Monica, California

**Other books featuring the McAfee Twins
by Jennifer Colt:**

The Butcher of Beverly Hills: A Novel
The Mangler of Malibu Canyon: A Novel
The Vampire of Venice Beach: A Novel
The Con Artist of Catalina Island: A McAfee Twins Christmas Novel

Published by Tessera Books
Copyright © 2010 by Tessera Productions, Inc.

Published in the United States of America by Tessera Books, a division of Tessera Productions, Inc., Santa Monica, California.

"Copacabana (at the Copa)" © Music and lyrics by Barry Manilow, Bruce Howard Sussman, and Jack A. Feldman
"Rock Around the Clock" © Written by Max C. Freedman and Jimmy de Knight

Library of Congress-Cataloguing-in-Publication Data
Colt, Jennifer

The Hellraiser of the Hollywood Hills: a McAfee Twins Novel / Jennifer Colt. — 1st ed.
        p. cm.

Summary: Terry and Kerry McAfee, identical twin proprietors of Double Indemnity Investigations, must protect an unbalanced teen pop princess from the dangers of fame.

1. Women private investigators—California—Los Angeles—Fiction. 2. Murder—Investigation—California—Hollywood—Fiction. 3. Sisters—Fiction. 4. Twins—Fiction. 5. Hollywood (Calif.)—Fiction. 1. Title

[Fic]—dc22   2009943783

ISBN-13: 978-1-43926-788-2
ISBN-10: 1-4392-6788-X

10 9 8 7 6 5 4 3 2 1
First Edition

The Hellraiser of the Hollywood Hills

Prologue

he following is a true crime story set in Hollywood. Only the names have been changed to protect the ~~litigious~~ innocent. I'm Kerry, the better half of a private investigation duo known as the McAfee Twins.

If you're joining us on our adventures for the first time, I'll give you the thumbnail sketch: Terry and I are identical females, twenty-five years old as of this writing, orphans who live on North Beverly Glen Boulevard in West Los Angeles. We stand five feet eight; we have long, red hair and more freckles than there is sand in Afghanistan; and we drive a hot pink Harley when we're fighting crime, which is all the time.

I'm straight, she's gay. I'm sane, she's certifiable. I try to keep a roof over our heads, she's the human hurricane who keeps trying to blow the roof off.

Next life I'm coming back as an only child. Count on it.

erry banged on the wheel of the Rent-A-Wreck Chrysler Imperial. "Nuts!" she yelled.

"Is something wrong?" I said, knowing I shouldn't have asked.

"I'm *bored.*"

"Boring is good, Terry."

"Since when?"

"Since we're not under threat of death, and the tax assessor has his check, and it's not going to bounce."

We were broke again, but at least we were honest broke. No ill-gotten gains, no blood money staining our hands. Terry had accepted a cash tip from a killer on our last case, and I'd made her donate it to a women's shelter. She'd been sulking ever since.

It was true that our client had killed someone who really needed killing, but that didn't tip the scales of justice in her direction. You're not supposed to take the law into your own hands, and there's a very good reason for that, as I'd tried explaining to Terry.

"What if one day somebody decided *you* needed killing?" I'd said. "What if they decided that you were such an ungrateful, selfish, obnoxious she-devil that they put their hands around your neck and squeezed and squeezed and squeezed until your big, green eyes popped out of your bloated, purple face?"

She'd shrugged off the argument and went right ahead being an obnoxious she-devil with no regard for who might want to kill her for it.

Now she was staring out the dirty windshield, spoiling for a fight. "You know your problem?"

"Please. Tell me what my problem is." I knew what she was doing, but I took the bait. Truth was, I was bored, too.

"You demand too little from life."

This was a new one. "A roof, food, clothes...? Seems like a lot to demand with our finances."

"See? The basic necessities. You can't think past the end of your nose. That's why I'm poor and doing stupid stakeouts, because I'm hemmed in by *your* consciousness."

The "stupid stakeout" was our current job. We own and run a private investigation firm called Double Indemnity Investigations. On this occasion we'd been hired to get evidence of an extramarital affair, which is why we were sitting down the block from the target's apartment in the trashed-out Chrysler. We hadn't even bothered trying to be inconspicuous after the first day of surveillance. In this neighborhood no cops would hassle us if we sat here for hours; no well-meaning citizen would demand our ID. We'd be taken for harmless crackheads or hookers making an honest living. Lots of people around here lived in the streets or their cars, so we fit right in.

"Excuse me?" I blinked in the glare coming off the hood. "How is this about my 'consciousness'?"

"I'm a victim of your limited thinking. You reap what you sow, you know. Your thought creates your experience—"

"And your point is?"

"*You* think small; therefore I reap small potatoes 'cause my fate is tied up with yours."

This wasn't Terry's usual rant. Terry typically complained that I was a "bossy cow." Secretly, I was giving her points for novelty. "Where are you getting this?" I asked.

She pulled a dog-eared paperback from beneath the driver's seat and tossed it to me. The cover was a radioactive orange with big block letters screaming across the top: *Sky's the Limit! Think Big! Be a Millionaire!*

"How many titles does this book *have*? And when did you buy it?"

We'd been on this stakeout for three days, inhaling each other's burger breath, squirming in the seats to get circulation back into our butt cheeks, occasionally answering the call of nature in the bushes. There'd been precious little time for personal development.

"It was under the seat. I read it when you went to get lunch."

"You read a whole book while I was at In-N-Out Burger?"

"It's written in a very readable style."

Terry is dyslexic. There was no way she'd read a full-length book while I was out fetching cheeseburgers. But she had the uncanny ability to absorb a book by reading random passages and filling in the blanks intuitively. That's how she got through school—that and buying the answers to exams.

I turned the book over to look at the author's photograph. He had a lot of letters after his name: PhD, MFCC, DC. He also had receding, kinky hair, a russet potato nose, and Coke-bottle glasses. Bozo goes to college. It was only a headshot, but I just knew the guy had food stains on his tie and walked on the balls of his feet. And he was going to tell *me* about self-improvement.

"Let me get this straight. You find a book under the seat of a thirty-year-old, bashed-up Chrysler, no doubt left by the last loser who couldn't afford to rent anything better..."

"Maybe he traded up for a Jaguar, ever think of that?"

"And you decide to make it your life philosophy?"

"Why don't you read it before you judge?"

If I didn't humor her, I'd never hear the end of it. And when I say never, I mean *never*. We'd go through endless cycles of death and rebirth, working off Terry's karma while she blamed all of our problems on me. I could hear it now: "We wouldn't be in this mess if you'd read that self-help book ten lifetimes ago!"

I sighed and opened the book to the introduction.

> Thinking creates your experience. Everything begins with a thought; thought precedes every action. What you dwell on in consciousness becomes your experience. Allow your thoughts to get bigger and your good experiences will expand in scope and frequency.

"Okay." I chucked the book into the back seat. "You didn't read much."

"I think I got the message."

"Which is?"

"Think big."

"Right." Terry smiled at me. "So what are you thinking now?"

I let my voice go dreamy. "I'm thinking of a palatial home in the Hollywood Hills."

She nodded. "Good, good."

"I'm thinking of *hundreds* of *millions* of dollars."

A thumbs-up, indicating how pleased she was with my perspicacity. "Excellent!"

"And I'm thinking they belong to Ryan Seacrest."

Terry groaned, falling back in her seat. "I hate my life. Wake me when it's over."

We were indeed in Hollywood, but not in the exclusive hills where the celebrities holed up in their mansions. This was down and dirty Hollyweird, a block up from Sunset Boulevard. Here there were runaways living in refrigerator boxes, senior citizens cashing in their Social Security checks to buy beer and Lotto tickets, and people of every age, gender, and hue out on the streets plying the sex trade.

Terry was right. It was not only boring sitting outside these low-rent apartments, it was depressing. But it was a paying gig, and it was not life threatening—two big pluses in my book.

"Three whole days of this!" Terry moaned. "I don't even believe this guy has a young girlfriend. You saw him. He's a pig."

"Maybe he's a pig who *thinks big*."

"And even if he is playing around, why would his wife care? It'd be good riddance as far as I'm concerned."

"The ways of the heart are mysterious."

Terry yanked her feet down from the dash. "Mayday. Mayday. Babe alert, one o'clock."

A slender young woman was heading our way, walking with an athlete's bounce on black and blue Pumas, casting surreptitious glances at the ground floor apartment of the piggish Paul Fellows.

"About time!" I dug the digital camera out of the In-N-Out wrappers on the floor and aimed it at the sidewalk. The girl wore a long-sleeved, baggy T-shirt in the toasty September weather, a fringed scarf wound around her lower face, and a racing cap pulled down over reflector shades.

I zoomed in on the target. "She's definitely *incognito.*"

"Chiquita incogni-*taaaaaa.*" Terry rubbed her hands together. "Walkin' right into our trap."

Click. She slows near the apartments. *Click.* She checks a piece of paper to confirm the address. *Click.* She stuffs the paper into the pocket of her ripped-up jeans. *Click.* She looks around to see if anyone's watching. *Click, click, click.*

Terry grunted, annoyed at being left out of the action. "Lemme do some!" She scooted over in the seat, grabbing for the camera, simultaneously jabbing her elbow into my left boob.

"Owww!" I yelled.

The girl heard me cry out. She hesitated, then turned toward us to stare. She was only a few yards away.

"She made us." Terry shoved the camera back at me. "Let's book."

"Why couldn't you stay on your side of the seat?"

"If you'd *ever* let me do any of the good stuff...!"

She slid behind the wheel and cranked the ignition, the eight-cylinder clunker roaring to life. But Incognito Girl was on the car in a flash, thrusting her arms into the window.

"Stinking paparazzi!" She clawed at the camera in my hands.

I slapped at her grasping hands. "Hey! Get off!"

Before I knew it, she had a vise grip on the camera, and it was all I could do to hold on. The camera cleared the window, and I found myself being pulled out of the car by my arms.

Terry jumped out of the driver's side. "Leave her alone!" she yelled.

The window glass was cutting into my triceps. I was afraid it would shear off and amputate my arms above the elbows. I did a quick mental calculation and decided that a two-hundred-dollar camera wasn't worth going through life as a double amputee; I let it go.

Incognito Girl toppled backwards into Terry, who'd just come up behind her. The girl lurched away, then spun and around and bashed Terry on the side of the head with the camera. Terry toppled over on the grass. The camera flew into the air, plummeting to the ground a few feet away.

Next the girl pounced on Terry with a banshee yell, pinning her to the ground. The two of them fought, hands locked, snarling, practically spitting in each other's faces as they strained for advantage.

"Girl fight!" someone yelled from a passing car. "Woo-hoo!"

I leaped out of the Chrysler, raced over to them, and threw my arms around the girl's waist. I yanked with all my might, pulling her up and off of Terry. Her body was slim but made of solid muscle. She kicked. She flailed. She squirmed around in my arms, knocking the hat off her head and sending her sunglasses sailing. Blond hair tumbled down around her shoulders.

I dug my feet into the grass and shoved her as hard as I could. She staggered away, tripped on a sprinkler head, and dropped to her hands and knees with a loud exhalation of air. Only then did I look back to see if Terry was all right.

She lay on the ground with her mouth open in shock.

"You all right?" I asked her.

Terry pointed behind me and her lips moved, but nothing came out of them. I spun around, prepared to fend off another attack, and then I saw what Terry had seen, and I knew at once what had taken her breath away.

There, panting like a dog, grass stains on her knees and murder in her large blue eyes, was the world's biggest pop music phenomenon.

I gaped at her. "Bethany?"

"Duh." The teen idol bent over to retrieve her shades, slapping them on her nose. She stuffed her hair back into the racing cap.

"I'm...Gosh, I'm sorry." I tried to brush some grass off her arm, but she wheeled back as if to slap me.

"Touch me again, and my people will bury you."

I raised my hands in surrender. "There's been a big mistake. We're private investigators, licensed. We were on a stakeout, waiting for someone else."

Terry scrambled to her feet as she continued to make excuses for our behavior. "It's a matrimonial issue. A man in that building has a young—" She stopped mid-sentence, staring at Bethany, her brow creased in confusion.

Bethany glared back, hands on her hips. "What's that got to do with me?"

I moved between them before fists could fly again, holding them at bay with outstretched arms. "Nothing, obviously. The whole thing was one giant mistake."

Just then something caught Bethany's eye. She jerked her head towards the apartment building, and Terry and I swung around at the same time, watching as the curtain dropped in Paul Fellows's window.

Great. Fellows had seen everything. Not only had we opened a can of whoop-ass on pop's reigning princess, but we'd blown our cover as well.

I looked back at Bethany. "Listen, we're sorry. We didn't know it was you. We were just doing our job."

Terry strained to get her mind around this scenario. "What are you doing here, anyway? " she asked Bethany. "Why would a celebrity like you be bumming around this neigh—"

Bethany looked over at camera lying on the grass and made a sudden dive for it.

"Not so fast." Terry kicked the camera out of Bethany's reach.

Bethany straightened up slowly. She and Terry locked eyes as something passed between them, grudging admiration for a worthy foe or abject loathing, I couldn't tell which.

"It's none of your business what I'm doing here, you douche."

Terry winced. "You kiss your mother with that mouth?"

"Helllooooooo!" Bethany waved her hands. "Read *Us Weekly* much? I am *emancipated* from my mother. I haven't seen the witch for years."

"Lucky mom," I mumbled.

Bethany shot hate vibes in my direction. "You have no right to judge me, you *nobody.*"

She spun on her rubber soles and headed up the sidewalk the way she'd come, brushing off her pert behind. "If I see those pictures on *TMZ*, you're gonna wish you were dead. I'll sue you for everything you're worth!"

We stood there a moment speechless, reeling from a dustup with the girl who'd sold more records than Elvis. "If she gained some weight, she could be a major star on the Sumo circuit," Terry said, rubbing her shoulder.

"What's she doing on foot?" I watched Bethany disappear up the block. "Doesn't she have a fleet of limos?"

No sooner were the words out of my mouth than a white stretch limo with tinted windows screeched up to the curb next to her. The back doors flew open. Two muscled goons in golf shirts and khakis jumped out of the car and ran toward Bethany.

She tensed like a cornered rabbit, head whipping around in panic, and then she took off toward the apartment building. The thick-necked men were on her in seconds. They grabbed her arms and started dragging her back toward the limo.

Terry turned to me, wide-eyed. "Holy cats, Batman. She's being kidnapped!"

But before we could move, the tables were turned. Conditioned by years of gyrating and thrashing her hair, Bethany was able to twist around in her captors' grip and nail one of the men with a swift kick to the groin.

He yelped and doubled over, hands between his legs. Bethany then swung back and clocked the other man in the face with a right hook. He pinwheeled backwards, blood streaming from his nose.

She turned and ran in our direction, screaming, "Help me!"

I yanked open the back door of the Chrysler. Bethany dove inside. I jumped in after her with the soles of my feet on the partly closed door. One of the men ran up to the car, scrabbling for the door handle. I kicked out and slammed the door into his torso.

He fell back over the curb, legs in the air. When he tried to sit up, I winged the self-help book at him, whacking him on the forehead.

"Think big!" I yelled, as he fell back on the lawn.

Terry hopped into the driver's seat. She jammed the car into reverse, just as the other kidnapper jerked open her door. She stomped the gas at the same instant, and we plowed into the car behind us. *Crunch!*

The second goon went flying, knocked on his keister by Terry's door. He sprawled on the asphalt, then rolled to his hands and feet as Terry jerked the wheel in his direction, laying on the horn. The man crab-scuttled away from our front tires, diving headlong onto the lawn across the street.

Terry rocketed down the block, fishtailing around the limo, tires squealing as we cornered around the stop sign at the end of the block. The movement brought the back door within my reach. I grabbed the armrest, slamming it shut. Bethany crawled to the other side of the seat to hunker against the door, blue eyes round and terrified.

Halfway down the next block, Terry zipped into an alley, then swung around a dumpster and screeched into a carport, slamming to a stop just before we plowed into a group of stumblebums passing a bottle in a brown paper bag. The bums sat frozen in fear for a moment, and then, all at once, they skittered to the corners like kitchen roaches fleeing the light.

The three of us girls sat in the Chrysler without uttering a word. After a moment, we let out a collective breath.

Terry's eyes caught Bethany's in the rearview mirror.

"You guys do stuff like that all the time?" Bethany turned to look out the back windshield.

"All the time," Terry bragged.

I rolled my eyes, then looked around in time to catch sight of the limousine speeding down the street perpendicular to the alley.

"Didn't catch the license number," I said to Bethany. "Did you see it?"

"It's not really the kind of thing I pay attention to."

"It's okay," Terry said. "We got a good look. We could identify them."

"So could I. They're my bodyguards."

"Your *what*?" Terry and I shouted in unison.

Bethany covered her ears with her hands. "Do you mind? I need my eardrums for recording sessions."

"Wait a minute," I said. "We thought you were in trouble! What was that all about? You were running away from your own bodyguards?"

Bethany stuck out her chin defiantly. "I *said* it's none of your business."

The nerve of this girl!

"Well, you've got us there. It's just *our* smashed rental car, guaranteed on *our* credit card..." I leaned over and aimed a finger at her pert little nose, causing her to flinch. "And just *our* lives that were almost snuffed out by two giant bruisers we thought were kidnappers, but it's none of our freakin' *business*?"

"Look, I'm, I'm...*sorry*. Okay?" Bethany choked on the word as if it were an inhaled bug.

I folded my arms over my chest. "*Not* okay. Start talking, honey. What's going on here?"

"I can't tell you. I would if I could, honest. But I really appreciate your help."

Gratitude took a lot out of her, to judge by the pained expression on her face. I decided not to press the issue. It appeared to be pointless, and would only make matters worse. "You're welcome. What's done is done. Now, where do we drop you off?"

"Oh, uh..." Bethany gave me a pitiful look. "I might need you to help me a little more."

Terry perked up in her seat. "What do you mean, help you?"

Uh-oh. Not good. This was the most action Terry had seen in days, and she was chomping at the bit for more excitement. I didn't want her getting any ideas about riding in to the rescue of this distressed little damsel. I blinked Morse code at her with my eyes: *No... no...no...*

Of course she ignored me.

"Would you...take me someplace safe?" Bethany begged.

I cut in before Terry could answer. "You're not safe with the people whose job it is to keep you safe? Maybe you should pay 'em more."

Bethany looked down at the hands twisting in her lap. The bling on her right hand would have made Snoop Dogg whimper, a ring that spelled out the word *Cute* in diamonds. Some of the bodyguard's blood was stuck between the stones.

"Don't you understand?" I said, exasperated beyond all reason. "We assaulted those guys! They could press charges! And we're gonna have to pay for the busted bumper on the car! Make that *two* cars!"

"I'll pay for it, I swear...I mean, when I can get to my money."

"We can take you to a bank," Terry offered, "no problem."

Bethany looked up from beneath long lashes. "No, I...I don't have my own account. I get a couple hundred bucks allowance, but I spent this week's already. On ice cream."

I slapped my forehead. "You get an allowance? I don't believe this. You have to be worth at least half a billion!"

"I don't know." Bethany chewed on her cuticle. "I've never seen any bank statements or anything."

"Trust me, you are. Who pays your bills?"

"My manager, Claude. He's also my producer."

"He's the one who gives you an allowance?" Terry asked.

"Yep. He's been in charge of me since I was fourteen. Four totally sucky years. But I'm gonna turn eighteen next week, and then I can get my life back."

"Back from who?" Terry wanted to know. "From this Claude guy?"

Bethany let out a musical sigh. "From the whole world."

The whole world, huh? If having millions in the bank and just as many screaming fans didn't mean she had the whole world in *her* hands, I wasn't sure what did.

This girl was a real piece of work. She didn't seem mature enough to be eighteen. She reminded me of someone who'd been kept in a basement her whole life—completely bereft of social skills and common sense, and probably even table manners.

"Isn't there someone else you can stay with?" My voice came out as a whine, a sure sign I was losing control. "Any relatives or friends?"

"I *told* you. I haven't been in touch with my mother-the-witch since I was fourteen. I never even knew my father-the-bastard."

I was getting tired of her mouthiness. "So, when they say 'honor your mother and father,' you take that to mean 'talk trash on them'?"

"Real cute," she said, biting off the T. "Maybe your father didn't abandon you at birth. Maybe your mother didn't rip you off. You're *lucky*. It doesn't make you better than me." She tugged down the bill of her racing cap, sniffling.

Terry glared at me. "She's right, Ker."

"Sorry," I muttered.

Perhaps I'd been too harsh. Okay, I'd been downright mean. But I noticed that Bethany hadn't addressed the issue of friends, which I guessed meant that she didn't have any. Right. Now I was feeling like a complete jerk. No friends, no parents. I guess it's true that money can't buy happiness.

But wait—it appeared she didn't have any of that at the moment, either.

"You need enough to last the week?" Terry said. "Shouldn't be a problem. If you need a loan, we could help you out."

I shot Terry a look—*Help her out with what?*

Bethany chewed her lower lip. "It's not just that. I have to...lay low until I turn eighteen."

"Why?" I asked. "What's going to happen to you in the next few days?"

"Trust me. I have to stay out of sight."

Trust the girl who beat up Terry, threatened to sue the crap out of us, and then got us mixed up in a free-for-all with her own bodyguards.

"They'll be looking for you," Terry said. "You can't hide. There's nowhere you can go without being recognized. Everyone with eyes in his head knows who you are."

Bethany nodded glumly, and then sat up with fresh inspiration. "Hey, could I hang with you guys?"

Terry raised her eyebrows. "With us?"

"Yeah, it'd be fun. You kick ass, for paparazzi."

"We're not paparazzi!" I fished out my wallet, waving my license in her face. "Private investigators, remember?"

Bethany glanced briefly at the license, shrugging. "Whatever. So can I stay with you? Come on, *pleeeeee-ase?*"

She gave me the kind of look you get from a kid who wants a new toy and will promise you anything—keeping her room clean, feeding the fish, doing her homework—to get it. I realized with a sinking feeling that I had lost this round. And I suspected there'd be guppies floating belly-up in the tank before we were through.

"What would we do with you for a week?" I was still hoping there was some way to wriggle out of this.

"I know!" Bethany said, eyes alight. "Let's get a sleazy motel room and watch porno and get drunk!"

I looked over at Terry. "Gonna be a long week."

Someone knocked on the window. The stumble-bums were pressing themselves into the car, smudging the windows.

"Hey, it's Bethany!" one of them mouthed through the glass.

They started banging on the sides of the car, the hood, and the trunk, hooting and hollering.

"Your public," Terry said, shoving the gearshift into reverse.

Bethany wrinkled her nose. "Yick."

Terry blasted the horn and gunned the engine, scattering the bums to the corners of the garage again. One toothless oldster put his arms behind his head, bumping and grinding in urine-stained pants, belting out Bethany's signature tune: "*I ain't your baby, now...I ain't no baby no more...*"

"Don't give up your day job, Gramps," Bethany mumbled.

Terry ripped out of the carport, executed a two-point turn in the alley, and headed back down towards Sunset. We motored along in the filthy heap, bumping our way over potholes and past reeking trash cans with a billionaire brat slumped in the back seat. I glanced back and saw Bethany stick her thumb in her mouth.

She sucked.

he Starlight Motel graced the corner of La Braig and Sunset, a Pepto-Bismol-colored stucco box sitting sideways on the boulevard. The paint at ground level was sooty with car exhaust. The balcony on the second level canted inward as a result of faulty construction or earthquake damage. The plastic sign advertised a mind-boggling array of amenities: air-conditioning, color TV, free adult movies.

Does it get any better than this? I thought, as Terry pulled into one of the parking slots next to the ground floor rooms.

"You'd better stay with Terry," I told Bethany. "I'll go check us in."

Terry tossed me a Dodgers cap. "Here. Cover the hair."

"Right."

Whenever we were identified by witnesses, it was always as "flat-chested redheads." Here in the Land of Enhancement, small-breasted women are about as common as two-headed goats. If you want to get noticed, go around Los Angeles with the chest you were born with. You'll inspire pity, but you *will* stand out.

There was nothing I could do about the ironing board figure, short of stuffing socks in my bra, but the hair was a red flag. Hiding it would be prudent. I put on my shades and stuffed the ponytail under the blue cap.

The glass-enclosed office sat under a rickety portico. A window to the right of the office had a sign that said "Night Check-in." There was a money drawer like those you see at drive-thru bank tellers, and bulletproof glass as thick as the bubble on the Pope-mobile. Very reassuring.

I hit the button and was buzzed into the dank vestibule. It smelled like the place mildew goes to die. A clerk sat behind yet another bulletproof window playing video games on a discolored PC. He was an overweight, oily man, with sweat stains that began under his arms and spread out under his man-boobs. It looked like someone with a cheese grater had mistaken his face for a lump of Parmesan.

He finally came to a stopping point in the game and looked up at me with hooded eyes. Then he leaned closer to the window in order to take in the length of my body.

"Help you?" His breath steamed the window.

"Checkin' in," I said in a breezy southern accent— *Suzie Tourist goes to Hollywood*. "How much, please?"

"How long you stayin'?"

I hoped it was only a short while, until we could regroup and decide how to talk Bethany into going back to her life. "Um, just a couple hours."

Big mistake. He took me for a pro. His eyes narrowed to glinty little slits, wet lips turning up in a smile that looked like a worm squirming on hot asphalt.

"You gonna need extra maid service during your stay?" He waggled his furry eyebrows.

"Uh, no."

He leaned back, clicking his dirty fingernails on the armrests of his chair. "You look kinda new at this sort of thing, so let me give you some advice: Your customers will appreciate good hygiene. Clean sheets make a happy john. How you fixed for prophylactics?" He whipped a box of rubbers off of the counter, rummaging around like someone searching for his favorite tea in an assortment box. "We got your glow-in-the-dark, your chocolate, your French tickler..."

Ewwww. "Could I just get a room, please?" My voice came out more hysterical than I'd intended.

He waved a lubricated Trojan in my face. "Just trying to ensure that your stay here is pleasant and disease-free."

"Thanks, but...I know what I'm doing."

"Is that a fact? Maybe we could talk about getting you a discount on the room—"

"No!" I felt myself turning purple. "I mean, I have a very tight schedule."

Tight schedule? I smacked myself mentally. *Way to throw gasoline on the fire, Kerry.*

"Bet you do at that. Nice 'n' tight. Heh heh heh heh heh." The man-boobs bounced in his shirt as he laughed. I stared in morbid fascination at the fleshy mounds that should have been mine by birthright. "By the way," he said, giving me a *gotcha* wink. "What happened to your southern accent?"

Oh yeah, I was supposed to be Suzie Tourist. Well, it was too late to resurrect her now.

"Here's what I would really like," I said, dropping the southern drawl. "I would like for you to rent me a room. No extras, no insinuations. Okay? Think you can do that? Or do I need to take my business elsewhere?"

He glared at me for a second, wiping the sheen off his forehead with a meaty paw. "Fifty bucks. Visa or MasterCard."

If he handled my credit card, I'd have to soak it in alcohol before I could touch it again. That would probably wreak havoc with the magnetic strip. "I have cash." I emptied my wallet and shoved the money under the window.

"Cash. Of course."

He flicked a knowing smile at me and pulled on some reading glasses that were repaired with fraying adhesive tape, holding the bills up to the light as if he were some big undercover agent for the U.S. Mint. He licked his finger and made a show of examining each bill, and then marked them all with a yellow pen. I decided that if he owed me any change, I was going to leave it lying there in the drawer. I was not going to touch *anything* that had come into contact with his slobber-coated fingers.

He stuffed my money into a cash drawer and slid a key under the window. "I think number thirteen will suit your needs."

Thirteen. I stared at the diamond-shaped plastic tab with the unlucky number on it. I'd never been a triskaidekaphobic, but now seemed like a good time to start. "Do you have anything else?" I asked in a nicer tone. "I'm a little superstitious."

He sniggered. "Not unless you want to share my room."

"Thirteen is great! My lucky number! Thank you so very much!" I pulled my sleeve down over my fingers and grabbed the key, bolting for the exit.

"I can send you a lot of business if I can recommend you personally," he called after me. "Let me know if you can *squeeze me in.* Heh heh heh heh heh."

Tasting bile, I slammed myself against the push bar, spinning out of the door in a circle and toppling off the curb in the drop-off zone in front of the motel. Then I tore across the parking lot to the Chrysler and rapped frantically on the window. "C'mon, we're in!"

Terry and Bethany piled out of the car. Bethany was concealed in her sunglasses, hat, and scarf, but she couldn't hide her excitement as she took in the fleabag motel.

"It's so cheesy!" she cried, practically skipping up the stairs.

"No singing!" I glanced back to see if the clerk was watching us.

Sure enough, he was craning his neck around the window to catch the action. Terry had covered her hair with a beret she'd brought along for the stakeout, but we must have made for an intriguing sight: three young *incognito* chicks checking into a room together, two of us identical.

Identical twins are big-time fantasy material for big fat slobs, I knew from painful personal experience. And the tag-along adolescent, well...I could only imagine the *bacchanal* going on in his filthy mind.

We won't stay long, I thought. *Just long enough to watch the news to see if there's an APB out on us.*

If the coast was clear, we'd contact Bethany's handlers and make a deal for her return—the deal being that they wouldn't press charges and we wouldn't reveal what a little beast she is to the world press.

I held out the key to Terry at the door. "Here. You open it."

She looked down at the key, gripped in my shirt-sleeve. "Did he blow his nose with his hand or something?"

"No! Just...I want you to open it."

"Nuh-uh, that key's been slimed." She stepped back. "*You* open it."

I grasped the key with the tips of my fingers to minimize exposure, shoving it into the lock.

"You touched the snot key," Terry sang. "Neener, neener, neener—"

"Shut up." I opened the door and hustled Bethany through. Terry and I followed her inside.

We took off our sunglasses, pupils slowly adjusting to the dark interior. The room had all the charm of the inside of a Porta John. There were unidentifiable stains on the wall, the carpet, and the lampshades. It reeked of nicotine, with subtle notes of rat droppings.

Bethany looked around with the expression of someone seeing the Sistine Chapel for the first time. "This is the jankiest pit I've ever seen! It's totally sick!"

She ran to one of the double beds and jumped on it, trampolining and screaming, "Yippeee! Look at me!"

Terry grabbed Bethany's hand, yanking her off the bed. "Don't do that! We don't want to draw attention to ourselves by crashing through the floor into the room below."

A half-empty bottle of Jack Daniels sat on the dresser beneath a portrait of a toreador. Bethany saw it and lunged for it, but Terry got there ahead of her.

"Whoa, hold on!" Terry whipped the bottle out of her reach. "You're underage."

"I drink all the time," Bethany declared with a little pout.

"Maybe," I said, "but we need this for disinfectant."

Terry tossed me the bottle, and I took it into the bathroom, setting the whiskey on the sink next to a sticky blob that had once been a bar of soap. I plunged my fingers into the glop, trying not to think about who'd used it last, and lathered my hands under the tepid water.

I poured some of the whiskey on the toilet seat and used most of what was left of the rough roll of tissue paper to wipe it clean. I might end up smelling like our friends with the paper bag refreshments, but good ol' Jack would put the kibosh on any nasty organisms clinging to the surface. No single-celled creature could stand up to eighty-proof whiskey. Not that many humans could stand up to it.

"Pardon me." I closed the bathroom door.

I could hear their voices in the other room—Bethany's high-pitched wheedling, followed by Terry's gruff responses.

"Come on, let's check out the adult movies!"

"No! You're too young. Besides, they're disgusting."

"How would you know? I bet you watch 'em all the time. I just want to see *one*."

"No!"

"Come on, I'm paying for the room! I mean, when I get my money."

Did I say *long week*? This was going to be the longest afternoon in history. I washed my hands again and walked out of the bathroom, wiping them on my jeans. "Look, Bethany, we have to talk—"

"My turn!" She dashed past me into the bathroom and slammed the door behind her.

I turned to Terry. "How did we get here?"

She fluttered her eyelashes. "Limited thinking?"

"Don't start with that again. You volunteered to keep her for a week. Are you insane?"

"She's under a lot of pressure. I think she just wants to bug out of her life for a while, like Audrey Hepburn in *Roman Holiday*. One afternoon in this place and she'll go running back to her limos and mansions, you'll see."

"But the girl's out of control."

Terry chuckled and fell down on a twin bed, hands behind her head. "If you think she's out of control now, wait till she guzzles the Jack Daniels you left in the bathroom."

"Yikes!"

I threw myself against the door, wrenching the knob. But the door was locked. I banged on the wood. "Bethany, listen. Don't mean to intrude, but could you just hand me that bottle of whiskey through the door?"

"One second. I'm peeing."

"I know, I just need that bottle—"

"Okey dokey. Almost done..."

The toiled flushed and the door opened. Bethany held out the Jack Daniels bottle to me, completely empty. She swayed on her feet, an idiotic smile on her face, and then she fell into my arms with a rumbling belch and passed out.

"Great!" I wailed, dragging her to the other bed. "Now we've contributed to the delinquency of a minor!"

Terry laughed. "You ask me, that minor was born delinquent."

"I'm glad you're so amused."

"Oh, lighten up, Kerry."

"I'll lighten up when she's out of my sight." I slumped Bethany onto the bed. "I'm telling you, Terry. I've got a very bad feeling about this."

Bethany's loose limbs flopped all over the place. Terry lifted her legs and straightened them out, tugging on the frayed cuffs of her jeans. I undid the laces of her running shoes and pulled them off her feet. "What do we do now?"

"Let her sleep it off, I guess."

"But what if she's got alcohol poisoning or something? Shouldn't we take her to the hospital?"

"She's not the first teenager to get wasted. She'll have a little snooze and wake up with a wicked hangover. It'll put her off whiskey for life. Meanwhile, we can discuss what to do with her."

I gazed down at the girl and was hit with an involuntary wave of sympathy. Lying there, Bethany looked like a sleeping angel—long lashes brushing her porcelain cheeks, a perfect little nose, and full pink lips. She breathed through her mouth like a congested infant.

"I think she's troubled," I said.

"Troubled doesn't begin to cover it. She's psycho."

"But she looks so sweet like this."

Suddenly, Bethany lurched up and spewed a stream of Jack Daniels over the side of the bed.

"Yahhhh!" I sprang back, but my boots had been coated with upchuck.

Bethany fell back on the pillow and was immediately snoring again.

"She never even opened her eyes," Terry said in awe.

I ran into the bathroom to wash off my boots. "Do they have exorcists in the phone book?"

"If not, maybe we can try the Archdiocese or something."

I jumped into the shower and spun both knobs to full blast. As I sat on the edge of the tub and yanked the boots off to soak, I wondered if I'd have to write off a pair of perfectly good biker boots on top of everything else. This day was really beginning to bite.

When I was done with the rinsing, I padded back into the bedroom in my stocking feet and found Terry lounging on the bed across from Bethany's, riveted by a skin flick on TV. The onscreen couple was going at it atop a bed just like the one Terry currently occupied. The action, such as it was, could have been in this very room.

Note to self: Do not go near bedspread unless wearing human-sized rubber.

I put my hands on my hips. "What are you doing?"

"What? They're free."

"Don't you think we'd better check out the news?"

"Oh, right."

I grabbed up the remote to change the channel, and there it was:

Breaking news.

The news was not good. The police had issued an "Amber Alert" for Bethany. They'd used a younger photo for the announcement instead of her recent publicity shots, probably because the sex-kitten-in-a-transparent-beaded-outfit look wouldn't set the right tone for a child abduction.

CHPS had been scrambled along the highways, signs flashed the alert along thoroughfares, and regular programming had been interrupted to notify the public of a high-profile crime in progress.

"Pop superstar Bethany has been kidnapped by two women described as redheads in their twenties, tentatively identified as private investigators Terry and Kerry McAfee..."

A picture of us flashed up on the screen, grinning like fools, helmets in hand, leaning against our shocking pink Harley. The Harley's our trademark, recognized by every enforcement agency in the county since Terry led the LAPD on a televised slow-speed chase last summer.

I vowed to take an ax to it next chance I got. And to dye my hair blond or black or green, and to emancipate myself from Terry. I'd change my name to Barbie, have some plastic surgery, and move to Barbados. "Hi, I'm Barbie from Barbados. No, never heard of anyone named Terry McAfee! Who's *she*?"

"Holy schneikes," Terry said. "We're America's Most Wanted Twins. Where'd they get that picture?"

"The stations probably keep it on file in case you pull one of your colossally stupid stunts." I stomped around the room, wringing my hands. "We never should have driven off with her!"

"What else could we do, under the circumstances?"

"And we never should have checked in here. We should have called someone. Her management company."

The announcer came back on screen. "Bethany's manager and legal guardian, Claude Sterling, made this impassioned plea to the kidnappers outside of Bethany's Hollywood Hills mansion."

They cut to the image of a man with too-black hair woven on top of his head. He had big, wet eyes in a tanning-parlor face, shirt open to the sternum, gold chains glinting on a chest like a jewelry display made out of fur. A woman in a shark's tooth mini-suit stood at his side with a comforting hand on his shoulder. Her face was obscured by large, black sunglasses, and she wore her bright purple hair in a mannish cut.

"Bethany belongs to all of us," Sterling said between sobs. "She's an American treasure."

I glanced over at the vomit-stained thing on the bed. "Yeah, she's a real peach."

Why did she pass out so quickly? I wondered. *Did she already have drugs in her system when she drank the whiskey?*

Sterling was winding himself up for the cameras. "Bring her back or I will hunt you down like the animals you are. There's nowhere you can go, nowhere you can hide. The whole world will be demanding your red heads, and I will personally see that you pay for this outrage!"

Sterling broke down, burying his face in his hands. The purple-haired woman pushed the microphone away and helped him stagger between two stone lions up the stairs to his mansion.

"And there you have it," the announcer said. "The chief of police has promised whatever resources are necessary to find America's pop princess, dedicating a hundred patrol officers on the streets in the vicinity of the kidnapping."

"Uh-oh," Terry said. "We may be in trouble."

I was pleased to hear that the gravity of the situation was beginning to penetrate her thick skull. "The bodyguards must have told the cops we kidnapped her."

"But she jumped in *our* car!"

"Maybe they missed that part. One guy took a shot to the groin, the other guy got a bloody nose. Under those conditions, maybe it looked to them like an abduction."

"This is whack!"

"We have to call the cops and tell them what happened, Terry. We have to get them to call off the dragnet before the media blows this even more out of proportion. That Claude guy, he knows she's a handful. He'll back us up."

"Back *us* up? No way. They're going to want to pin this on someone, and they won't want Bethany tarnished. They can't admit she beat up her own bodyguards and jumped in our car. Who would believe it, anyway?"

"Okay, so we call Eli," I proposed. "Get him to be the go-between."

Eli Weintraub was my former boss and Terry's criminal attorney, the reason she was not still in prison on drug charges and was free to fulfill her potential on the outside as an upstanding-citizen-slash-celebrity-kidnapper.

Someone pounded on the door. I spun around and stared at it, as if trying to penetrate the wood with X-ray vision.

"Who is it?" I called in a quavering voice.

"Maid service."

I looked around the room and decided that "maid service" wouldn't cover it. Maybe a crew in HAZMAT suits with high-pressure hoses.

"No thank you!" I yelled back, and then whispered to Terry, "The clerk thought I was a hooker. He offered to change the sheets."

"What?"

"Long story." I listened for the maid, but didn't hear anything more. "I think she's gone."

BAM BAM BAM.

I jumped a foot in the air.

"Maid service!" the woman shouted again.

"Probably the only English words she knows," Terry muttered, rising from the bed.

I had an instant premonition of doom. My stomach froze over like a puddle in a blizzard. "Terry, don't open it!"

She threw me a look—*What am I, stupid?*— and then said slowly and emphatically, "No thank you, *no maid...!*"

And that's when the battering ram demolished the door, splintering the wood into a million matchsticks. Five men in SWAT uniforms charged into the room, automatic weapons flashing. Terry flew backward, her arms flailing as she stumbled toward the bathroom. Black-suited, jackbooted men in helmets all screamed at once.

"Police! Get down! *Now!*"

I threw myself to the floor.

A knee slammed into my upper back. My arms were yanked upward, and cuffs were slapped on my wrists. I heard Terry yelling on the other side of the room.

"You don't know what you're doing! This is a big mistake!"

"Terry, don't resist!" The sound of my voice was lost in the mayhem, muffled by the filthy shag carpeting.

The cops fanned out through the room, the vibrations of their boots bouncing me on the floor. After a few moments, I was jerked upright, lifted off the ground by the wrists, my shoulders shrieking as my arms almost left their sockets. I saw that Terry was also being cuffed and whisked to her feet.

Then I noticed a sixth member of the team: a man with a hand-held video camera, the light pointed straight in my eyes. I flinched and jerked my head away in shame. *The police tape their busts now?*

Probably due to lawsuits for excessive force, I realized, like the cameras mounted in the front of cruisers to record roadside arrests.

Well, this struck me as a tad excessive—five SWAT officers to bring down two unarmed women and an unconscious teenager? We had a humdinger of a lawsuit, if you asked me.

But no one *was* asking me, and I had no breath to speak. It had been crushed out of me by the knee in my back, and by the shock and pain and fear.

I glanced back over at the bed and was hardly surprised by what I saw.

Bethany had slept through the whole thing.

"You're under arrest." The SWAT commander sounded Darth Vader-like behind his face shield.

"What's the charge?" Terry demanded.

"Kidnapping."

"We didn't kidnap her!"

Two paramedics rushed past us to check on Bethany. One of them took her pulse while the other readied an oxygen tank.

"With an aggravator of sexual enslavement," the commander added.

"*What?*" I yelled. "Where'd you get that idea, from the motel clerk?"

"All we did was check into a room," Terry protested. "We've broken no laws!"

"I wasn't done yet. Giving a controlled substance to a minor and corrupting said minor with pornography. You're in a heap of trouble, little ladies."

How did they know all this? Had they been listening at the keyhole?

The cameraman zoomed in on Bethany's inert form. "Is she gonna make it? Looks pretty bad."

The SWAT commander agreed. "Yeah, we might be looking at a charge of attempted murder, too."

"Oh sure, pile it on," I snapped. "What's another false accusation?"

A storm trooper shoved his gun at my nose. "Shut your freaking face!"

I complied at once.

The paramedic looked up from Bethany's side. "Pulse is normal, breathing regular. Looks like she's just inebriated."

"Could you please wake her up?" Terry begged him. "Throw some water in her face or something? She'll tell you what really happened here."

"Hey, Bethany." The cameraman moved in, aiming his camera at her face. "Wake up, sweetheart. Give us a little—" he belted out Bethany's signature song, "*I ain't your baby, now...*"

Bethany's eyes blinked twice and then opened wide in surprise. She came fully awake, jerking up in the bed, fury washing over her as she took in the scene around her. She slammed a hand into the camera. The filter went flying, and the cameraman stumbled sideways, crunching it underfoot. "Owww! She broke my nose!"

"Don't take my picture!" Bethany yelled. "What's going on here?"

I tried to get her attention around the broad back of a SWAT officer. "Bethany, please! Tell them what happened!"

"They think we kidnapped you," Terry told her. "They said we brought you here to sexually exploit you. You have to tell them the truth!"

Bethany's mouth hung open as she looked from Terry, to the sniffling cameraman, then back over at the SWAT commander. She seemed confused, groggy from her mini-bender—either that or calculating her response. Finally she jumped up from the bed and ran to the commander, throwing her arms around him with her slim little hips pressed into his manly thigh.

"Thank you for rescuing me!" she simpered.

The holding cell was a big improvement over the room at the Starlight Motel. It smelled much better and had the advantage of a toilet where the infectious organisms were in plain view. I'd let my bladder explode before I'd go near it.

At the moment it was occupied by a large black woman with her spandex shorts down around her feet. Her long brown hair was teased high on her head. Light blue eye shadow glimmered from her thick, false lashes to her finely plucked brows, and her full lips were painted gold. Large expanses of breast strained the chartreuse tank top.

Terry sat next to me on a bench, apparently asleep. She was leaning back against the wall, eyes closed.

I'm so glad you're able to relax, I thought.

There was some comfort in knowing that Eli was on his way down to try to bail us out, though I was beginning to have my doubts as to whether he could. This was a felony kidnapping charge, not to mention sexual enslavement, corruption of a minor, and all the assorted cherries on top of the main charge. The bond would be sky high.

We might even have to break our long-standing rule and ask our rich aunt Reba for a handout.

Actually, now that I think of it, I'd rather rot in jail.

Terry had used her phone call to contact Lance Manley, our dog-sitter. Lance was an actor turned bodyguard turned Malibu sheriff's deputy, and was under the impression that he owed us his life. Actually, he'd sort of saved *us* and got himself shot in the process, suffering a scalp wound. Though minor, the injury left a scar that started at his hairline and zigzagged through his spiked blond hair. Lance stood six feet six, with a blocky head atop three-foot-wide shoulders. The new scar kind of suited him, enhancing the overall Frankenstein motif.

I must have spaced out, because the next thing I knew, the woman on the can was looking in my direction, glaring at me with open hostility.

"What you staring at?"

"Nothing." I looked down, but out of the corner of my eye I saw her rise and pull up her shorts, loose thighs squeezing into spandex like chocolate toothpaste going back in the tube.

"You want to give a lady privacy? Just 'cause I in here, don't mean I ain't a lady."

"Oh, I *know* you are." I tried to defuse the tension by going for an instant sister connection. "That's really great eye shadow, by the way. What is it, Maybelline?"

"Maybelline!" She headed toward me, spoiling for action. I made matters worse by continuing to babble as she headed in my direction. "Fine makeup," I said. "*Sensibly* priced..."

"It *ain't* Maybelline, you dumb cracker! It's Estée Lauder!"

I nodded furiously. "Even better! Say, I think I have a coupon for a free Estée Lauder gift—"

"You wasn't admiring my eye shadow." She stood over me, blocking out the light. "You was disrespecting me."

A Latina in a studded white leather skirt and spike-heeled sandals sidled up next to her, oozing attitude. She was beautiful, with large, saintly eyes and a rose-bud mouth, but her expression was deadly. The anti-Madonna.

"Thinks she's better than us," Miniskirt said, sneering at me. "Thinks she don't belong in here with us lowlifes." She flexed her fingers in front of my eyes, as if dying to dig those long, red nails right into the sockets.

Blue eyelids stepped up ran a finger down my cheek. "Think you better than us, Strawberry Shortcake?"

"N-no...no *way*..."

"You just as white as the snow, ain't you?"

"I tend to burn easily—"

She shoved me in the chest, slamming me against the wall. I looked over at Terry, who was still asleep. What's the point of having a pugilistic sister if she snores through your assault in a holding cell?

"You didn't answer my question," Blue eyelids said. "You better than us, little Miss Strawberry?"

"Shut it," Terry said behind closed eyes.

The woman's mouth flew open. She wheeled around at Terry, shrieking, "Telling me to shut it?"

"Who you telling to shut it?" Miniskirt yelled.

"She was talking to me!" I waved my hands around frantically. "She's...she's got bad PMS, makes her cranky. But she's one of the girls, just like me and you! We were probably all caught in the same bust!"

The two women were joined by a white creature in an orange chiffon party dress, cowering behind the others as if they were her protectors even as she towered above them. Her striking features were too hard to be called pretty. She had large hands and bony knees, and I was fairly sure she'd never had an ounce of thigh cellulite in her life.

"I'll give her PMS," Blue Eyelids said, lunging for Terry.

Terry's hand whipped up with a stiff-fingered jab to the woman's breastbone. Blue Eyelids stumbled back, gasping, as Miniskirt grabbed her by the wrist to keep her from toppling over on her copious behind. The tall, white one in the orange dress squealed, pulling her skirt up to her face like it was some kind of invisibility cloak.

Yep. Hundred percent fat-and-cellulite-free thighs. Just as I'd suspected, a shemale.

"Look," Terry said in her *You don't want to mess with us* voice. "We won't be here much longer, and we don't want any trouble in the meantime."

"Oh yeah?" Miniskirt said. "How come you won't be here?"

"Yeah, how come?" Blue Eyelids said, rubbing her sore breastbone. "How come you so sure you gettin' out?"

"Because we've got a kick-ass lawyer named Eli Weintraub," Terry told her. "He's on his way now."

"Jewish boy?" Blue Eyelids said.

Terry nodded.

"They the ones to have," Miniskirt agreed.

"You lawyer need any more clients?" Blue Eyelids wanted to know.

"You don't have one?"

"Honey, I got a worthless pimp. He supposed to send some shyster to pay our fines, but do you see him here?"

I looked around, shaking my head. Not a shyster in sight.

"Probably out of his mind right now. Man's a methhead. Your lawyer do drugs?"

"He drinks a little scotch and smokes a cigar," Terry said. "Far as I know, those are his drugs of choice."

"And he can get you out?"

"He always has in the past."

"Tell him he got some more clients," Miniskirt said.

I didn't know if Eli wanted a stable of ho's in his care, but I wasn't about to antagonize them just as they were warming up to us.

"We'll talk to him about it," I said. "You're all interested?"

The three of them nodded enthusiastically.

"I'm Shotanya," my nemesis said, suddenly all sweetness and light. We shook hands and she introduced us to the other two. "This here's Raquel." Miniskirt gave us a nod, then Shotanya pointed to the shemale in chiffon. "And this here's Bob."

"It's Bobbi, if you please. With an I." She had a sultry voice and a posh English accent. *Was Hugh Grant back on the boulevard?*

"What you in for, anyway?" Raquel asked. "Solicitation?"

"That was the original idea," I told them. "But now they've got us for kidnapping."

"Kidnapping!" the hookers said at once, looking at us with new respect.

"Yeah, but we didn't do it."

Shotanya gave me an exaggerated nod. "Course not."

"Whom did you allegedly kidnap?" Bobbi asked excitedly.

"Bethany," Terry said.

"Bethany, works down by Pink's Hot Dogs?" Shotanya asked.

"No. Bethany the pop singer."

Shotanya reared back in surprise. "The no-butt white skank with all the hair?"

Terry and I nodded.

"Why you want to go kidnapping her?" Raquel asked. "Was it for ransom?"

"Tell, tell!" Bobbi squealed, her voice going up an octave.

"We didn't kidnap her," Terry insisted. "She jumped into our car. She said she was fleeing some kidnappers."

Shotanya looked over at the other two hookers and began to nod again. "Uh-huh, uh-huh...and you know what? Same thing happened to me. Exact same thing. Fleeing a kidnapper...no a *rapist*...and I jumped into a car, and that sick pervert just pulled out his thang! I be the victim, here!"

"Happen' to me, too!" Raquel said, getting in on the act. "Jus' like that! Running away from some bad men, and along come a car and I try to escape, and this john—I mean, this man—he jumped me!"

"Me, too!" Bobbi sang. "I was running from my pursuers and leapt headlong into a passing truck. How was I to know my rescuer was a sexual deviant? All I wanted was succor!"

Everyone turned and stared at Bobbi.

"It means *help*," she explained.

"Uh-huh," Shotanya said. "I'd leave that part out. Don't sound quite right." She clapped her hands together. "Dang, girl, this be one fine defense!"

And suddenly the cell was ablaze with the righteous indignation of two falsely accused women and one falsely accused prom queen with an Adam's apple. Bars were rattled. Someone clanged on the communal toilet with her shoe, using it as a gong. Hollers and wails rang through the air.

"We the victims! We need us a lawyer! False arrest!"

Terry threw me a look. "Don't incite a riot, okay?"

The clatter and clamoring rose in volume as a woman sergeant swaggered up to the cell—a fan of capital punishment to judge by the look on her face. "Keep it down in here or I'll turn the hose on you!" She jerked her thumb at me. "Hey, Norma Rae, your lawyer's here."

She unlocked the door and swung a baton in the air. "Get back!" she yelled at our sister detainees, who backed up against the far side of the cell. Terry and I ducked out the door, and it slammed behind us with a clang. The girls ran up and threw themselves against the bars.

"Don't forget us!" they called.

"We'll be in touch," Terry assured them, waving good-bye.

"Yo," said Shotanya.

"Hasta luego," said Raquel.

"Toodle-oo!" Bobbi sang.

Terry leaned over and whispered to me, "*That's* the way to make friends and influence people."

"Next time, could we make friends somewhere other than the holding tank?"

"Snob."

The sergeant led us to an interview room with a two-way mirror. Eli sat at the table, his ancient briefcase open in front of him. It looked like something unearthed at an archeological dig, covered with centuries of dust and camel dung. Eli himself didn't look so good, either. He was sixty-five years old and carried an extra sixty pounds on his tall frame, most of it around the middle. He sweated profusely and chewed on an ever-present, unlit cigar (when he deigned to abide by smoking regulations, that is). Never the poster boy for senior health and vigor, his complexion looked unusually ashen.

But he was undeniably cheerful. Something about finding us in custody always gave him a lift.

"You've really outdone yourselves, girls. We're not just talking national coverage. There are newscasters in Sri Lanka talking about you. They're calling you 'Telly and Kelly.'"

We plopped down in the molded plastic chairs across from him.

"I don't suppose you're interested in hearing our side of the story," I said sullenly.

"Sure, this oughta be good." He sat back and crossed his arms over his belly. "G'head."

"We were on a stakeout," Terry began. "We were waiting for the alleged lover of this guy named Fellows when a girl came by, and we took her picture."

"It was Bethany," I continued. "We didn't recognize her because she was all covered up in loose clothing and a hat. But she attacked us and threatened to sue us. Next thing you know, a stretch limousine screeched up to the curb, and some big guys started dragging her in—"

"And you thought what?" Eli interrupted. "She was being kidnapped?"

"I know it sounds crazy, but she was kicking and screaming, begging us to help her. We couldn't know the men were her bodyguards."

"So you took her to a motel and plied her with whiskey?"

"No!" I came up in my seat, but Eli waved me down.

"Just giving you the cops' version."

"She said she wasn't safe with them," I went on. "We didn't know what to believe, so we pretended to help her hide. Once we got to the room we were gonna call her manager and straighten things out—"

"But she went nuts," Terry interjected. "Grabbed some leftover whiskey that was on the dresser and chugged it in the bathroom. Then she threw up all over Kerry's boots."

I lifted my leg and wiggled my canvas jailbird shoes. "I had to take them off in the shower. It was a mess. Next thing you know, a SWAT team busted in and we were arrested."

Eli nodded, a smile playing on his lips. "Ever wonder how they got onto you so fast?" he asked, looking back and forth between the two of us.

Terry gave him a quizzical look. "Fine footwork by the boys in blue?"

He shook his head in response.

"The motel clerk thought we looked suspicious, and called it in?" I guessed.

"Wrong again," he said with a devilish chuckle. "The room was wired. The clerk put you in number thirteen 'cause he thought you were working girls. Hollywood Vice was running a sting operation out of the motel for a reality TV show. They got everything, sound *and* video. The footage is worth millions. Bethany's people are negotiating to get it back right now."

"*What?*" Terry and I yelled.

Eli shrugged his pudgy shoulders, equal parts philosophical and amused. "Hey, think of it as your fifteen minutes of fame."

I sank my head onto my arms. "Is the whole world just one big reality TV show now? How are you supposed to know what's *real* anymore?"

"We can discuss the evils of modern culture some other time. For the moment, it's working in your favor."

"How so?"

"The charges against you are being dropped."

Terry grinned and thrust her hand toward me for a fist bump.

I didn't return it. "What's the catch?" I asked Eli.

He opened his hands in a magnanimous gesture. "They'll be satisfied if you accept a monetary payment for your trouble and sign an affidavit to the effect that the whole thing was a publicity stunt, in addition to signing a waiver on any damages. Also, you agree not to go to the tabloids with your side of the story."

Now I came all the way out of my chair. "Forget it! That unholy brat jumped in our car, abused our good intentions, and got us arrested and beat up, and then she tried to frame us!"

"She apologizes for that."

My cheeks were steaming. "Says who?"

"Says her manager, Sterling. He claims she panicked. All she could think of was the news media screaming the story all over the place, which would have been the end of her career."

I paced the room, practically bouncing off the walls. "Oh, really? She's worried about her career? Then by all means, swear out a lie against *us*."

"Yeah," Terry said, matching my tone. "What about *our* careers?"

"Well, she came clean about what happened. And she says she's sorry. Don't you owe it to her to try to work things out?"

"I owe her zip!" I pounded my fist on the table. "And I sure don't owe her a sworn statement that's a lie! You know, we could sue *her*. We'd probably win. Right Eli?"

"Yep. That's probably why they're willing to pay you ten grand to forestall a lawsuit."

"Ten grand?" Terry's eyes widened and she leaned forward in her chair, eyebrows leaping up to her hairline. "That's what *I'm* talking about. A little compensation for the pain and suffering."

"Uh-uh," I said. "Nothin' doin.'"

Terry made a face at me, and then turned to Eli. "Don't worry, I'll forge her signature. I got it down pat."

I pointed at her. "You sell your soul to the music industry if you want to. I'm having nothing to do with it. They'd drop the charges anyway. There's absolutely no evidence of a crime."

Eli cleared his throat. "There *is* the little matter of the car you crashed into..."

My righteous indignation left me in a rush. "Oh. How bad was it?"

"Couple of thousand. I offered to cover the damages."

"Thanks. We'll pay you back."

"Forget it, that's not the point. They can charge you with leaving the scene. That's a hefty fine and a misdemeanor charge. They can probably even jack it up to felony endangerment." He nodded at Terry. "Strike *numero dos* for our girl, here."

Despite my best efforts, Terry was always inching closer to her third strike and life in prison.

"What are you saying?" I asked him. "The police are willing to forgive the car crash if we cooperate with Bethany's handlers?"

"They're gonna look like idiots, bashing down the door to arrest three unarmed women, especially now that Bethany denies any coercion. They don't want to see the whole *mishegoss* come out on TV."

Did I say something about this day biting the big one?

"What a world." I sighed and held out my hand to Eli. "Let me see the affidavit."

He produced it from his briefcase. A tissue of lies from start to finish, it claimed the "kidnapping" thing was a *Punk'd*-type stunt done as advance publicity for

Bethany's new album and tour scheduled for two weeks from that day.

I signed the affidavit as Eli took a check out of his briefcase for ten thousand dollars. Terry reached for it, but I slapped her hand away.

"We'll endorse it, and Eli will give it to a women's shelter."

"We already gave!" Terry wailed.

"Okay, he'll give it to the homeless. Look, Terry, this thing could have unforeseen ramifications. Criminal or civil charges, who knows? We can always claim we signed the affidavit under duress if something comes up later, but that's out the window if we take their money. It's kind of hard to claim someone coerced you into depositing their check."

Eli smiled proudly at Terry. "What can I say? I taught her well."

"Thanks loads," Terry said.

I endorsed the check on the back, and then handed the pen to her. She scribbled her name.

"I think you misunderstood the concept of *thinking big*. You have to be grateful for money that falls into your lap. You can't be a money sieve and expect the universe to keep ponying up."

Eli gave her a baffled look.

"She's been reading spiritual self-help books," I explained.

"You might want to help yourselves by leaving town for a while," he suggested. "Just a thought."

Terry handed the check back to Eli, who stowed it in his polyester jacket pocket. "How'd Bethany's people get to you so quickly, Eli? Or did you call *them*?"

"Remember Louie the Lip?" Eli said. "Mob enforcer...?"

"Oh yeah. Good ol' Louie."

"He was at the sports bar and saw you two on the tube when they interrupted the game to make the announcement. He called me, then I got in touch with Sterling and told him I could guarantee Bethany's return."

"So we have *you* to thank that this all of this worked out," I said.

"Yeah, unfortunately the SWATs got there before we could hash out all the details. If that hadn't happened, we'd have made the trade and everything would have been handled *sub rosa.*"

Somehow I doubted that. It seemed like any contact with Bethany guaranteed you a spot in the freaking limelight.

"Incidentally, there're some working girls in the tank who need representation," Terry said to Eli. "Can you help them out?"

"How many?"

"Three, and they're all innocent. They were fleeing rapists when they jumped into the johns' cars."

"Hey, great story. I haven't had any streetwalkers on the client rolls in a while. They're always fun."

"I hope they're good for it."

"I'll consider it *pro bono.* They're public servants, really."

"Thanks."

"Okay, I'll go confirm the deal with the captain and we're set." Eli reached into his briefcase. "But there's a bunch of media types surrounding the building. I figured you'd want to cover up like last time. Got your disguises right here."

He held up a couple of full-face latex horror masks. One was Michael Myers from *Halloween*; the other was Jason's hockey mask from *Friday the 13th*.

"Where'd you get these?" Terry said, claiming Jason's mask for her own.

"Priss bought 'em on sale at Costco. Good thing for you she went Halloween shopping early."

"Yeah, good thing." I poked my fingers through Michael's hollow eyes. "Now we can be known as the Texas Chainsaw Twins."

We ran the gauntlet of media types down the steps of the police station on the way to Eli's waiting car. The questions flew at us like bullets.

"Are you the kidnappers?"

"What's up with the masks? Are you serial killers, too?"

"Why did you abduct the teen queen?"

We clambered into the back of the gold Ford LTD with the white vinyl roof, slamming the door behind us. Eli turned to face the members of the press, holding them at bay while he announced to the throng, "The whole thing was a stunt, ladies and gentlemen. Publicity for Bethany's upcoming tour. It was an ill-advised ploy that had unintended consequences. Bethany's spokesman will have more to say on the subject at a press conference this afternoon. That is all."

He knocked on the window, and I cracked it open. "Check you later. I got to go consult with my new clients. Get 'em home, Priss."

Our driver, Priscilla, was Eli's receptionist and legal secretary, a punked-out babe with white and purple striped hair extensions and a fondness for vinyl boots in all the colors of the rainbow. She screeched away from the curb, heedless of the press types clinging to the car, who were whisked off like flies from a horse's tail. One microphone-toting brunette fell backward into a cameraman, and the two of them tumbled down on the lawn in a tangle of legs and video equipment.

"Go, Speed Racer!" Terry cheered.

Priss gave her a thumbs-up in the rearview mirror and gunned it through a yellow light. Once we'd reached a safe distance from the reporters, Terry and I pulled off our disguises.

"Perfect theme for our lives," I said, looking at the mask in my hand. "One long horror show."

Priss said, "It's only fifteen minutes, don't forget."

"People always say that, but our fifteen minutes keep turning into endless night."

"We gotta pick up our rental car at the motel. Sunset and La Braig," Terry told her.

"Okey-doke," Priss replied, speeding around a corner.

I sat back in the seat and sighed, trying to remember how we'd gotten there. Oh yeah, it had been Terry's idea. She just had to come to the pop princess's rescue, out of boredom or perversity or a combination of the two. I looked over and saw that she appeared to be completely relaxed. She thrived on this kind of thing and was actually enjoying the fact that we were being treated like pariahs by the same media who had made national heroines out of us only weeks ago.

Wonder Women one day, serial killer-kidnappers the next. It didn't matter that we were stone innocent; they'd spin it however they pleased, whatever made for a more sensational story.

"How is Eli these days?" I asked Priss.

She glanced at me in the mirror. "Same as always."

"He looked a little gray, I thought."

"Yeah. I've noticed that, too."

"Has he been to a doctor lately?" Terry asked.

"Are you kidding?" Priss wagged her head to the tinkling of chandelier earrings. "Calls 'em death mongers. Says it's their job to find something wrong, and then kill you trying to cure it."

"How about his social life?" I asked, changing the subject. "Is he seeing anyone?"

"He's been spending all his time at the sports bar. Maybe that's the problem. At least when he was with your aunt, he got one meal a day that wasn't a chili dog or a Sausage McMuffin, and I doubt she let him smoke in the house. Probably made him cut back on the scotch, too."

Eli and our great-aunt Reba had met a while back and had gone at each other like a couple of sex-crazed bonobos. There had been talk of marriage but relationship troubles began to surface almost immediately. They even tried couples counseling for a while. However, the great romance ended in break-up before it even got off the ground. Reba had made the fatal mistake of trying to make over a guy who was set in his ways like feet set in concrete, and she'd paid the price of losing him.

She'd been married on five previous occasions, each time to a man who was filthy rich and on his last legs. It left her wealthy but unfulfilled. I suspected she'd never really been in love with anyone before Eli. She was completely transformed around him, going all giggly and flirty, just like a fifteen-year-old girl (minus the good muscle tone).

After the end of the affair, Reba tried living the bohemian life in Venice, devoting herself to helping the homeless. The homeless showed their appreciation by throwing her into an oilcan fire. (I guess she'd been a little haughty.) Then she and our recently sober, would-be artist cousin Robert had moved back to Beverly Hills and were currently living in Reba's Tudor mansion on Palm Drive.

We hadn't seen them since the move, and I felt a little guilty about that. But it was hard keeping up with those two. They were always chasing some kind of perfect lifestyle, not realizing that if you don't like being by yourself in a room, it doesn't matter where that room is located or how much you paid for it.

Priss pulled up to the curb next to the motel. The parking lot was packed with news vans. Cameramen were shooting footage of the broken door while reporters recounted the story of the bogus kidnapping of the teen idol for their live-cam feeds. I could see through the gaggle of reporters to our former parking spot. The Chrysler was gone.

"It's not there!" I wailed.

Terry shrugged. "Must have been towed. Taken into evidence."

"Oh, perfect!" I lowered my face into my hands. "This is just the perfect capper for a perfect day."

"Coulda been worse," Priss volunteered.

"How?"

"Give me a few hours." She pulled away from the curb. "I'll think of something."

5

*P*riss dropped us in the driveway of our house on North Beverly Glen. It's a tiny, shingled cabin jammed up against the canyon wall, rickety and lopsided and barely habitable, but our beloved homestead. We inherited the place from our mother's father, Pops, who built it after WWII. Property values have skyrocketed in the decades since, and we could probably sell it and live like queens in Arizona or someplace, but that would be like selling the happiest moments of our lives.

One day when we get the money, we'll cover over the gaps in the outside walls and put in some proper insulation so that it's not freezing during most of the year. And we'll tear up the curly linoleum in the kitchen and rewire the whole place so the lights don't fade in and out as if they were powered by poltergeists. Until that time, it's a bit like living in someone's fishing cabin in the woods.

We waved good-bye to Priss, and I ran to the house, my anxiety ebbing with the knowledge that, on the other side of the door there were eight little feet scrambling to meet us.

Terry and I are the adoptive mothers of a pug and a Pomeranian, Muffy and Paquito. They had recently spawned a litter of hybrids we called *Pompugs*. Not the most auspicious breeding experiment, a fireplug with a smashed face coupling with a hairy rat; but the puppies came out adorable in a butt-ugly kind of way, kind of like doggie troll dolls. They had all been placed in loving homes just as soon as they were old enough to leave their mama.

The embarrassing thing was that we hadn't known Muffy was in heat, or that she and Paquito hadn't been fixed, so we missed all the horseplay going on right under our noses.

I opened the door and they came running, the canine loves of our lives. They jiggled their behinds excitedly and licked us as if we were covered in bacon grease.

"Sorry we didn't come home," I said to them. "We were in jail."

They stared at me, uncomprehending.

"It's the dog pound for people," I explained.

More blank looks from the pups.

"I'm always forgetting where they're from," I told Terry. "Beverly Hills lapdogs don't know the seamy side of life. They're used to being carted around in designer leather totes."

Our little dogs had led a pampered existence before they came to live with us here in the canyon—living, breathing fashion accessories for the very rich. Paquito had even done his share of *eating* the rich, but that was a gruesome story best put behind us.

"We're home now," Terry cooed, scratching their chins. "Don't fill their pretty little heads with your sordid stories."

I looked around the house for a sign of our dog-sitter. "Where's Lance?"

"Maybe he went out to dinner."

I headed upstairs for a change of clothes. My bedroom is a six-feet-by-eight-feet platform built into the eaves of the cabin, with half a wall and a skylight. Terry sleeps on a mattress on the floor of a bay alcove. She uses the alcove's window seat she for a dresser, and has an accordion door for privacy.

Jail smell wafted up to my nostrils. "Boy, do I need a shower."

"And I don't?"

"I called it first."

"You didn't dibs it."

"The dibs was implicit!"

She gave in. "Don't hog all the hot water."

I found evidence of Lance in my upstairs bedroom: three huge pairs of cowboy boots docked against the wall like pontoons. There was one gray lizard pair, one pair in black leather, and one pair in green ostrich skin that resembled the plucked hide of an alien. His uniforms were neatly hung in the closet, and the bed had been made with military precision. I took a quarter out of my pocket and bounced it on the cover. It *pinged* off onto the floor, rolling out the door and down the stairs.

"Hey," Terry called from below. "You're leaking money again!"

I opened my underwear drawer and found Lance's professionally laundered, lightly starched boxers stacked next to my panties. They were printed with bucking broncos ridden by Marlboro Men swinging lassoes in the air. I guessed Lance was really getting into the Wild West theme out there in the Malibu sheriff's department. These might have even been department-issue shorts.

I headed back down the stairs. "Lance has certainly made himself comfortable. He's got enough clothes to last him a month."

"And enough eggs to last him a week," Terry replied.

"Huh?"

"Take a look."

When I arrived in the living room, she pointed to a box on the floor next to the couch. There was a goose-neck lamp trained on it for heat, and inside of it was a blanket cradling five light brown, speckled eggs.

"He's not going to eat those. He's hatching them!"

"Oh." Terry peered down into the basket. "What are they?"

"Some kind of bird, probably."

"Duh."

"Well, they could be snake eggs."

She gasped. *"Snake eggs?"*

"It's a possibility."

Muffy and Paquito trotted over to look into the box with us. Terry suddenly became concerned for the eggs' welfare. "You think the dogs'll eat them?"

"They've been known to eat some strange things. Maybe I should remove temptation."

"Good idea. Meanwhile, I'll call impound, see if we can pick up the car. What's the number?"

"1-877-CAL-LAPD."

As she flopped on the couch and picked up the cordless to make the call, I gingerly lifted the box of eggs, moved it to the buffet against the wall, and positioned the heat lamp over the box, aiming it at the eggs again.

"I hope we don't end up with a living room full of writhing vipers," I mused. "That would kind of suck."

Terry spoke to a clerk for a minute, describing the car and giving the address of the motel.

"Are you sure?" She was frowning. "Okay. Thanks."

She hung up and turned a baffled face to me. "The cops didn't impound the car."

"So, what happened to it?"

"Beats me. Maybe it was stolen."

"Acccchh! What did we do to deserve this?"

Terry merely shrugged.

"Let me rephrase that. What did *you* do to deserve this?"

"Let's not play the blame game." Terry *always* said that when the blame fell squarely on her head. "Think we should we call the cops?"

"Are you *daft?*"

"Okay then, let's go have a chat with the motel clerk. Maybe he saw something."

I shuddered to think of another encounter with that amorphous, sweaty blob. "I can't go back there tonight."

"But we're chalking up more rental fees as we sit here!"

"We've already eaten the rental for today. Let's go in the morning, please?"

"Oh, all right."

I heard a key in the front door. It swung open, and Lance stepped over the threshold. He saw us and jumped back, squealing in fright.

They just don't make Marlboro Men like they used to.

"Hey Lance!" I called. "It's only us!"

Cowboy boots hit the hardwood, sounding like boulders raining down on the roof. He trotted into the living room with a plastic bag from PETCO in one hand, the other covering his heart.

"You scared me to death!" he said. "What are you doing here? You get bailed out or something?"

"Charges dropped," Terry told him. "They had nothing anyway, but they could have made trouble for us. We agreed to pretend the whole thing was a promotional stunt."

"Oh, good." He looked over at the couch. "Omigosh! My eggs!"

I pointed to the buffet. "They're over there. Safe and sound and out of the dogs' way."

His small blue eyes popped. "You think the dogs would eat them?"

"You never know," Terry said. "They're cute little things, but they're descended from wolves, predators at heart."

Lance hovered over the eggs. "Wouldn't that be horrible? Their mother taken away from them before they're born, and then being eaten before they even have a chance at life."

"Um, what *was* their mother?" Terry asked. "She wasn't a snake by any chance?"

"A duck, I'm pretty sure. We got a complaint about some kids drinking beer out at Cross Creek. When we broke it up, we found the nest abandoned—" His voice cracked, and he looked down at his feet. "I saw feathers strewn around and *blood*. I think the mother duck was a meal for a coyote. I must have scared him off before he could come back for the eggs."

Terry and I shook our heads sadly.

Lance perked up, his natural optimism reasserting itself. "So I figure I'll hatch the little guys, and when they're big enough, I'll take them back to the creek and release them. Maybe some other mother duck will adopt them."

"Or maybe they'll be coyote appetizers," Terry muttered.

Lance and I glared at her by way of response.

She raised her hands in the air. "I'm just saying... it's only animals doing what comes naturally. They're always killing each other for food or over territory..."

We continued to glare at her.

"Oh for crying out loud, I don't *want* them to get eaten. I want them to grow up and paddle around and mate for life, okay?"

"I'm glad to hear it," Lance said. "I was beginning to think you were some kind of duck-hater."

"Not true! I love ducks. I had Peking Duck just two weeks ago at Chin Chin."

Lance threw his hands over the eggs. "Please! Children in the womb can hear their mothers. I bet it's the same for eggs."

"Number one, genius, the eggs don't speak English," Terry retorted. "Number two, if you guys want to live with your heads in the sand, be my guests. I live in the real world, not some fairyland where ducks and bunnies have no natural enemies. It's called a *food chain*, all right?"

"I'm never eating meat again," Lance whispered to me. "This has been a wake-up call for me. I'm going vegan."

"Do you know what *they* eat?" I asked him.

"What kind of parent would I be if I didn't know?" He nodded to the PETCO bag on the couch. "I got some bugs from the pet store. I'm gonna crush them up and put them in distilled water and feed it to them with a sterilized eyedropper."

Terry headed for the kitchen. "I'm going to go look for something for us to eat. Do we have any sausage pizza? Or aren't we consuming toppings from the animal kingdom anymore?"

She slammed through the kitchen door and opened the freezer noisily.

"Looks like we're ordering Chinese!" she hollered.

I turned to Lance. "So what are your plans? You're welcome to hang out here if you want."

"Thanks, but I don't want to move the nest right now. It might be traumatic, taking them away from the heat lamp."

"We certainly wouldn't want to traumatize your eggs." I opened the junk closet near the front door. "I'll get the air mattress."

Later, the kitchen table was littered with Chinese take-out cartons of exclusively vegetarian dishes. No pork, no fowl. I was trying to pick up the remaining peanuts from the Kung Pao Tofu box with wooden chopsticks.

"So, what's our next move, boss?" Terry asked, as Lance got up to rinse the dishes.

I'd just come to a conclusion about that. "We call Deirdre Fellows and drop the case."

Terry looked at me slack-jawed. *"What?"*

"Who's Deirdre Fellows?" Lance asked.

"The woman who hired us to spy on her husband. We were staking him out when we picked up Bethany."

"Did you hear that, Lance? Did you catch that word 'hired'? That's why Kerry wants to drop the case. She's developed an allergy to money."

"No, I want to drop the case because we blew it. Fellows saw everything that happened on the lawn. He's not going to be meeting his cutie at the love nest anymore, not after the Amber Alert. We've put *him* on alert, and we owe it to the client to fess up."

"But we could still follow him. It'd be tougher, but we could do it." Terry chewed on the end of her chopstick. "We can't let the client down. It's not her fault Bethany was walking past Paul Fellows's apartment and everything went bananas."

"Give me the cell phone." I held out my hand for it. "Come on, fork it over."

"One day it'll be a fork in the eye." She tossed the phone at me.

I scrolled down to Deirdre's number. I got a "no longer in service" notice.

"Disconnected," I said.

"Try again."

I did, with the same result. "Still disconnected."

Lance sat down at the table. "Go by her place tomorrow."

"We don't know where she lives." Terry said. "She gave us a money order, dropped it off in the mailbox. The envelope had no return address."

We'd never even seen the woman who'd hired us to spy on Paul Fellows. We'd outlined the terms of our contract to her on the phone, and she agreed to them by delivering a retainer of a thousand dollars.

Lance furrowed his big brow. "Didn't you think that was kind of...funny?"

Terry gave him a withering look. "Yes, Mr. Rookie Cop...*Mr. I-found-blood-at-the-scene-of-the-ducknapping*...we did think it was 'funny.' But guess what? A lot of people get funny about spying on their mates."

"It's humiliating for the one cheated on," I explained to him. "They want to know what's happening, but they don't want to look you in the eye and tell you about their suspicions."

"And spying makes you look like the kind of person someone would want to cheat on in the first place," Terry added. "A jealous Klingon."

This was certainly a strange development.

Terry sat there for a moment, a frustrated look on her face. Then all at once, she smacked the table next to me. "It was a set-up!"

I was taken aback by her ferocity. "What was a set-up?"

"Everything!" She jumped up from her chair to pace the floor. "Think about it, Kerry. This alleged 'Deirdre Fellows' hires us to spy on her alleged husband, and then Bethany shows up and they stage the kidnapping. And the next thing you know we're unwitting pawns in this whole *Punk'd* scheme. I can't believe I didn't see it before!"

My head started to throb. "Whoa, whoa, Conspiracy Queen. You're saying Bethany *knew* we were going to be there?"

"It's the only thing that makes sense. Everything was too neat. We pick her up, we check into the motel, the SWATs are there within minutes...Bang-bang-bang. That doesn't just happen, Kerry. It was like it was choreographed, or scripted—"

"Just like 'unscripted' TV," Lance chimed in.

"But the SWATs were there within minutes because of the hidden cameras," I reminded her. "If this was all a set-up, how could they know we'd take her to a motel rigged with cameras?"

"Maybe they figured we'd go to the closest motel. Come to think of it, it was Bethany who suggested that place, wasn't it?"

I thought back and decided that she was right. "I hate to admit it, but I may be starting to believe you."

Terry gave me a twisted smile. "Welcome to the dark side."

"But why would they do it?" Lance asked. "What's in it for them?"

"Publicity. The kind money can't buy. Bethany's got a tour coming up. Maybe the ticket sales weren't all they could be, and they decided to take drastic measures to pump them up. Maybe her CD sales aren't all that great, either." Terry hit her palm with a balled-up fist. "Boy, if we were incarcerated to shore up Bethany's record sales—"

"That would be evil," Lance said, completing her thought.

6

Within twenty minutes of some online research, we had a good idea of the direction Bethany's career was taking: straight down the tubes with a bullet.

"Wow," Lance said. "She's gone from selling ten million copies a few years ago to only two hundred thousand on the last release."

"She's still worth a ton of money," I said.

Terry wasn't so sure. "Maybe, but she's no longer on top." She clicked the keys to access more Web sites, searching for clues.

"How long has she been at this?" I asked her.

"About seven years."

"That's a long career. Most people flame out in half that time."

"You really think she got you arrested just to get her face on TV?" Lance asked, looking at the screen over Terry's shoulder.

"Not to be cynical," I said, "but consider the world we live in. People would sell their mothers to get on TV."

"They do worse than that; they swap mothers," Terry muttered while continuing her search. "They'll probably even eat their mothers when Fox TV airs the first-ever cannibal family hour."

I poked her shoulder. "You'd look sweet roasting on a spit."

She licked a finger and put it to her hip. "S-s-smokin'!"

"Speaking of mothers, see if there's anything there about Bethany's mom."

"Why?"

"I don't know. Just curious about this falling out they had."

We got a lot of hits on the woman in question, whose name was Andie Sue. The mother of a superstar, she was fair game for the paparazzi, and the cameras had not been kind. The photos showed a woman looking older than her years, a face ravaged by alcohol and possibly drugs that couldn't be reclaimed with an obvious facelift. She had fried blond hair, tons of makeup, store-bought cleavage. She looked like a trophy wife for the state bowling champ.

Andie Sue had been Bethany's manager, but there had been a huge lawsuit over her handling of Bethany's affairs, brought by the pop tart herself. Fraud was alleged. Andie Sue lost.

She got drunk and drove her BMW off Laurel Canyon Drive, but by some miracle she survived. After she was released from the hospital, she moved to a trailer park in Palm Desert. Broken financially and emotionally, the poor woman drank herself to death. The mother of one of the world's richest celebrities had died indigent.

My stomach felt hollowed out. "How sad."

Lance whistled through his teeth. "Yeah. Riding high as the mom of a famous singer one day, dead the next."

"Hey, wait a second." Terry tapped the computer screen. "Look at this!"

She'd hit on an article on the *Weekly World News* site with the headline: "Bethany's Mother Kidnapped by Aliens."

I gave Terry a look. "Why do I doubt the veracity of that story?"

"You're missing the point. Here's a woman who claims she saw Andie Sue coming out of the ShopRite in Reseda two weeks after she supposedly died."

"So the aliens dropped her off to do a little shopping?"

She rolled her eyes. "The point is, she's supposed to be six feet under, not shopping for sundries."

"I'm not sold on the journalistic integrity of a paper with stories like "I Was Raised by Wolverines." Anyway, there's no telling when that picture was taken. Coulda been before she died, and they saved it for a slow week."

"Hold on." Terry back paged to the article on the death of Bethany's mother. "When did she die?"

I pointed to the date. "A year ago."

"So why does Bethany talk about her mother in the present tense?"

"Huh?" Lance said. "What do you mean, present tense?"

Terry looked up at him. "Bethany said, and I quote, 'I am emancipated from my mother-the-witch.'"

He mulled it over. "Maybe she's in denial about the whole thing."

Terry cocked an eyebrow. "Or maybe she doesn't *believe* her mother's dead."

I left Terry and Lance downstairs watching a true-crime program showcasing the illustrious careers of Jeffrey Dahmer, Ted Bundy, and David Berkowitz. The two of them sat on the couch hugging their knees, huddled together like two kids listening to campfire stories. The dogs were curled up at their sides, happily snoozing away through all the TV mayhem.

I slipped under the covers just as the phone rang. My heart skipped when I looked at the caller ID. I grabbed up the phone before Terry could answer.

"Hello?"

"Hey lady, what'd you do with the Lindbergh baby?"

"Hardy har har."

It was my main squeeze, John Boatwright. Gorgeous specimen of manhood and public servant, he was a homicide detective in that world-famous enclave of people too rich for their own good, Beverly Hills. I'd met Boatwright when Terry and I were investigating some murders there. He and I had been trying to get together in a biblical sense ever since.

He was sensitive to my situation, being Terry's *de facto* probation officer and only sibling; and to show he wasn't going to come between us, he'd invited her along on all of our dates for the past few weeks. Movies, dinner, everywhere we went, the jolly threesome. But I could tell he was getting impatient. He felt he'd done his bit being supportive, and it was time to pay the piper.

"You want to go out to dinner tomorrow and tell me all about it?"

"No."

"No?" He sounded hurt.

"I mean, I want to go to dinner, but I don't want to talk about it."

"No problem. I'll ply you with liquor and get it out of you."

"You can try."

"So this is just us, right? You and me? A romantic burrito dinner for two?"

Nothing says romance like refried beans. "Yeah, I think I can manage it."

"Good. I want some quality time."

Ooooh. Something in that harmless phrase sent a zinging sensation all the way down my spine. "Hey, what would you do if I bleached my hair blond and had a boob job?"

"Probably smile a lot."

He heard my sharp intake of breath.

"I'm kidding. If you so much as remove a freckle or change a hair on your head, I'll strangle you. Why would you ask such a boneheaded question?"

"I was just fantasizing about not being recognized everywhere I go, not being the other half of the red-headed menace."

"Yeah, I hear ya. That's why I called to invite you to dinner. Judging by your record lately, it may be your last meal on the outside. Wouldn't want to miss my chance."

I tried to laugh, but his joke sounded too much like prophecy to be amusing. "See you tomorrow night."

"I'm looking forward to it," he said. "More than you know."

Ooooh. Another zing.

I hung up and lay back on my pillow, thinking about Boatwright and how thrilled I was at the prospect of finally hooking up with him.

Are you? said a voice in my head.

Sure I am.

Then why do you keep thinking about the one that got away?

Hey, who's that in my head? Get out of there!

The person that the annoying voice was referring to was one Dwight Franzen, special agent for the FBI, a.k.a the Eagle Scout.

I had almost forgotten what he looked like. I mean, I could tell you he had blond, short-cropped hair. I could tell you he had a ramrod-straight, very erect... posture (what did you *think* I was going to say?). With a killer body and hazel eyes, he was all-around perfect except for a couple of endearing flaws, namely a broken nose and teeth that overlapped a millimeter in front.

He was the straightest of arrows, deliciously corruptible. But I couldn't conjure up an image of the whole man, and it was making me nuts. His image was slipping away from me like a will 'o the wisp. And the harder I tried, the more my heart ached. Had I turned Franzen into some unattainable ideal in my mind after he disappeared to hunt terrorist cells in the San Fernando Valley?

I'd met him after Terry and I encountered some hijackers on a flight from Hawaii. We participated in bringing the terrorists down, and the plane landed safely. Afterward, we'd tried to keep our identities from the public, but eventually people found us out. The mayor of LA even gave us citizenship medals.

Now we'd squandered that heroine status by getting involved with Bethany.

My next question: Was I going to squander my chances with a hottie like Boatwright because of one night under the moon with an FBI agent? One kiss and what I imagined to be some kind of soul connection?

You haven't even heard from the guy, Kerry.

Yeah, but he's undercover! He's probably working with high-tech listening equipment and can't use a mobile phone in the vicinity.

Undercover agents never pass a 7-11? Can't drop 35 cents into the phone?

How should I know how they work? How would you know?

I know, trust me. Forget about him. Concentrate on Boatwright. One in the hand, Kerry. One in the hand...

Whoever that was talking in my head, she had a point.

That settles it, I thought. No more Cinderella fantasies about a dashing knight in shining armor, keeping the world safe for democracy. No more psychic energy spent on someone who simply wasn't around. I was going to put all my romantic stock in Boatwright.

I snuggled under the comforter and fell asleep, satisfied with my resolve.

And I dreamt of Franzen.

he next morning, Lance had taken off before we got up. He had the early shift at the sheriff's office in Malibu and a long drive up PCH to get there. He claimed he didn't mind the commute, though. He loved driving past the glittering bay as the sun was coming up. And let us not forget the other perks of the job—cowboy boots and bucking bronco boxers.

Terry and I sipped our coffee as we checked on the duck eggs. She held one up to the light. We could see the outline of a baby bird, curled up in his little calcium condo.

"Isn't it cute?" I whispered.

"Cuter than a coiled reptile, for sure."

"I think they're gonna come out soon. He looks ready to pop. I hope we don't miss the big event."

"Yeah, and if it happens when we're not here, I hope they stay in the box and don't tempt the dogs."

"Thought your attitude was anything goes, as long as it's natural."

"Yeah, but I wouldn't want nature to take its course in our living room. How long before they can be let out in the wild?"

"Who knows?"

"Think we're gonna have them till then?"

"I'd be more worried we'll have Lance till then."

Terry grinned. "I like having Lance around. He's like the little brother I never had. After the serial killer show last night, I had to tell him stories before he could sleep."

"Goldilocks and the Three Bears?"

"You were listening?"

"Lucky guess." I gulped down my coffee. "You ready to rock?"

"Yeah," she said, draining her own mug. "Let's go locate the Rent-A-Wreck."

We hopped on the motorcycle and drove down the canyon road and took a left on Sunset, my favorite street in the whole of Los Angeles.

Sunset Boulevard *is* LA to me. I love to pick it up from the beach and take it all the way to the east side, or just the reverse. It passes through areas that are stately and gorgeous, other parts that are garish and engorged with commercialism. You start at the glamorous castles of the Palisades and end up a half-hour later in some of the sceeviest parts of town.

We traveled east toward the Hollywoods. First, there's West Hollywood, a.k.a. Boytown, an incorporated city that is home to half of the area's gay population. (They always have the best parades and street festivals.) Then there's Hollywood proper, home to half of the area's drug dealers and prostitutes, who get rounded up and locked away like batty relatives in the attic when the Academy Awards come to town. To the northeast is North Hollywood, which is home to half of the area's gun and pawnshops. (To its credit, it's trying very hard to catch up to its gentrifying cousins.)

Soon the lush green trees of the UCLA campus and the landscaped mansions of Bel Air give way to the commercial strip that runs past Sunset Plaza in Beverly Hills, a collection of fancy clothing stores and pricey restaurants, the median strip flowering no matter what the season. After that you hit the stretch of road that winds past cultural landmarks like the Laugh Factory, the Rainbow Room, the Viper Room, Tower Records, Carney's railroad car restaurant, and the famous Chateau Marmont Hotel. (Celebrities take turns dying in all these venues, which makes them perennial stops on the city tours.)

I looked up from the motorcycle and saw the advertisements looming over the boulevard like geological formations in some weird parallel universe. The side of a ten-story building was painted with an ad for a rap group, a Mt. Rushmore of hip-hoppers. Billboards hulked over the street like the white cliffs of Dover painted with the latest movies and TV shows.

This was LA at its "company town" crassest, and I loved it. Around the next curve, a thirty-foot ad featuring Bethany herself loomed above us, promoting the upcoming CD and tour. Her pouty lips were lipsticked in shiny peach, her taut midriff bore a diamond navel ring, and a discreet tattoo of a candy conversation heart on one ankle said, "Be Mine."

Blond hair streamed around her head in a wind-blown corona. Enhanced breasts strained at the crystal-beaded cups of her bra. Curvy hips angled up to the level of her outstretched arm. The not-so-subliminal message: "I can't wait till I'm no longer a professional virgin. Buy my CDs, and it could be *you*."

It looked like they were spending good money promoting Bethany's tour. Probably a last-gasp effort to rescue her career before the sound of flushing was heard worldwide.

We passed through Little Armenia and Little Saigon, which looked suspiciously like California rather than Central or Southeast Asia, and finally arrived at the Starlight Motel.

The news vans were gone. The on-site journalists had taken their act somewhere else.

Terry parked next to the office, and we climbed off the bike.

The clerk hulked behind the desk playing video games. *I'd like to blast his big ass out of the sky with a laser weapon.* Terry knocked on the door and he looked up, waving to us from behind the bulletproof glass. He buzzed us in.

"Hey, I've been expecting you. Got your money right here."

He shoved a stack of bills under the window. It was more than the fifty dollars and tax we'd paid for the room. *Did he have an attack of conscience for setting us up?*

"What's this?" I asked.

"Your cut from the Chrysler."

Terry squinted at him through the glass. "What do you mean 'our cut'? What'd you do with it?"

"I sold it on eBay."

I started pounding on the side of my head to dislodge the beans from my ears. "Excuse me, what did you just say?"

He spoke slowly, as if I were hard of hearing or maybe just stupid. "I *sold* your *Chrysler* on *eBay*."

"How could you do that?" I screeched, sounding like a wounded macaw.

"Easy. You just put it up for auction, and the rest is cake."

"Okay, *why* did you do that?"

"It was the car Bethany was abducted in, dummy. You shoulda seen it. The bids went through the roof in five minutes."

"How much did you get?" Terry asked him.

I wheeled around, shouting at her, "Who cares how much? It's grand theft auto!"

"Three thousand dollars," the clerk said. "Probably a lot more than the blue book value of the car, if it even has a blue book."

Terry took the money and started to count it. "He's right, it's a good deal. He gave us half."

"Wait a minute, wait a minute!" Had we all boarded the bus to Crazy Land? "You can't *do* that!"

"What's your prob?" The sleazeball pointed to Terry. "Your little twin here is okay with the transaction."

"Her opinion doesn't count! She's a felon!"

Terry was still thumbing through the bills. "I'm a *rehabilitated* felon," she said.

I turned back to the clerk. "I'll tell you my *prob*, fella. It's not even our car; it's a rental. That's why you can't sell it!"

He sat there with the unmovable gaze of a bullfrog squatting in mud. "Well, I did."

"Well, you can't!"

"Well, I did."

"Well, it's illegal!"

"So call the law. Look, I couldn't wait for you to get out of jail. You gotta strike while the iron's hot."

"But you're the reason we were in jail in the first place. You deliberately put us in room thirteen!"

"A door closes," he said philosophically, "and a window opens."

I smacked my forehead. "Could I maybe have five minutes where somebody isn't spouting New Age BS at me in this town? Could we pretend we're in Nebraska, or someplace normal for a while? You know, the kind of place where people don't set you up for a televised police sting then sell your car out from under you while acting like they've done you a favor?"

I got the unblinking toad eyes in response.

"We were back in five hours," I railed. "How did you auction the car in five hours?"

"Bethany's Amber alert was all over the news, and I immediately recognized a money-making opportunity." He permitted himself a smile, proud of his toady initiative. "The motel was shown on TV with the Chrysler out front, so all's I had to do was post the pictures and the bidding took off right away. Fortunately, a guy in LA placed the winning bid. He came over, towed the car, and *presto*. Everybody makes out."

"But he doesn't have the pink slip or the keys; he can't drive it!" Why was I still arguing with this unreasoning blob?

"He's not going to *drive* it. He's Bethany's number one fan. His whole house is a shrine to her. He's going to park it in his back yard and charge admission to see it."

"Admission?" I slumped forward, banging my head against the bulletproof glass.

"What's our alternative?" Terry said. "Report it to the cops? You want to deal with them again?"

"No, but—"

"What's done is done. We'll go to Rent-A-Wreck and give them a sob story about how it was stolen. We can pay for it out of this." She flashed the cash. "It's bound to be enough to cover the replacement value."

"Looks like we have no choice." I balled up my fist and punched the glass, causing the clerk to jerk back in his seat. "But next time you sell somebody's car, ask for it first!"

"Next time you kidnap Bethany," he said sullenly, "sell the car yourself. It's not like I got nothing better to do."

Then he lopped his beefy hand on top of the computer mouse and went back to zapping aliens.

The scrawny guy behind the counter at Rent-A-Wreck was in his early twenties, with black hair plastered down on his forehead and a soul patch on his chin.

"Did you file a police report?" he wanted to know.

"We couldn't," I said testily. "We were under arrest."

"Yeah, that happens with a lot of our customers."

"And then when we got out of jail, the car was gone," Terry explained. "It disappeared from a motel on Sunset Boulevard."

"You're liable for the replacement cost." His fingers raced over the computer keys. "It'll be five hundred dollars, plus what you owe for three days' rental, plus a tank of gas."

"A tank of gas?" I protested. "There's no tank to put it in!"

"Is that my fault? Forty bucks for a refill."

Terry took out the wad of bills from the eBay sale and peeled off the amount in twenties, tens, and singles. When she was done, there was still a good amount of ill-gotten gains in her hot little hand.

"It's *not* going to a shelter," she said, shoving the remaining bills in her pocket. "Somebody's gotta shelter us, you know."

"If you got cash, you should buy your own heap next time." The guy gave me a form to sign. "It's way more cost-effective."

"Would everyone quit saying 'next time'! There is not going to *be* a next time, okay? You got that? No *next time*!"

He smiled at me. "Hey, babe. Chillax. It's all good."

How good *would it be if I yanked your soul patch out by the roots?* I thought about saying, but signed the form instead.

I took stock of our lives as we walked back to the bike: falsely accused of kidnapping a pop star, forced to lie and say it was a stunt, our rental car sold out from under us, bugged out on the only paying job we'd had in weeks.

"Our lives are a shambles," I muttered.

"Hey, at least we've still got the bike." Terry patted the pink leather seat.

"Yeah."

"And the pups."

"Yeah."

"And each other."

"Don't push it."

She hopped on the hog. "All right. What now?"

"Let's get some lunch. I feel a headache coming on."

"Your wish is my command."

We decided on Café 50's on Santa Monica Boulevard in West LA, a monument to malteds and poodle skirts and Formica booths covered with atomic designs. The walls were plastered with old movie one-sheets and actors' headshots. Some of them were stars, some were one-film wonders. I found myself envying the women in the B-movie posters. They had wonderfully pointy bras and perky, sprayed hairdos; and the copy underneath their billowing skirts said things like "She was a wide-eyed innocent until she was... *Shamed!*"

Being shamed by fifties standards sounded pretty tame. She probably did something horrible, like making out with a boy, and got a...*Reputation!*

I wished my problems were so simple.

We ordered burgers and shakes. Terry put a quarter in the jukebox. "Rock around the Clock" bopped out of the tinny speaker.

"Mom told me she was conceived to this song," Terry said, singing along. *"Two o'clock, three o'clock rock..."*

"She did not."

"Did so!...*Four o'clock, five o'clock, six o'clock rock...* Grandma and Pops did it in the back of a fifty-seven Chevy while this song was on the radio."

"You are such a liar."

"We're gonna rock... around... the clock tonight! It's true, I swear!"

"Really?"

She slugged me. "Chump."

"When will I learn not to trust you?"

"Give it up...ba baddy ba..."

"It *is* kind of a fun image." I laughed in spite of myself. "Grammy went out to the Chevy with Pops and was...*shamed!*"

"Gonna rock, gonna roll...a-round...the clock tonight!"

The burgers and milkshakes arrived as the song ended. The waitress set them down, applauded Terry's performance with a stony expression. Then she walked away.

"Hey, I figured out where they got our picture on TV." Terry slurped chocolate ice cream through a straw.

"Where?"

Her eyes suddenly exploded from their sockets, and she bounced up and down up in the booth, smacking the sides of her face. "Oh, oh, oh...!"

"Brain freeze?" I grimaced in sympathy.

"Accchhhh!" She jumped out of the booth, sucking in big gulps of air, hopping around in a circle. Finally the frostbite on her cerebellum subsided, and she lowered herself back down in the both.

"Wow." She was rubbing her temples. "I wonder if the Pentagon knows about brain freeze. It'd be better than dragging people around nude in dog collars. I'd tell them everything if they brain froze me."

"And I suppose if they put a dog collar on you, you'd just prance around naked?"

"No, I'd pee on their leg. That'd show 'em."

"You were saying? About the pictures...?"

"Oh yeah, the camera. We lost it at the stakeout. It fell in the grass, remember? They must have found it."

I stirred my malted, nodding. "One of the Bruces took our picture next to the bike when we were testing the new camera. You never downloaded them?"

"I figured I'd do it when the chip got full. Never got around to it."

"So who has it now? The cops?"

"Probably."

"I guess we write it off."

"Write it off?" She gave me a look of astonishment. "Ms. Cheapo wants to write off a two-hundred-dollar camera?"

"It's got the pictures of Bethany on it. It's probably been stolen from the evidence locker and sold on eBay."

She gave me a sly look. "We might want those pictures one day."

"What for? You thinking of selling them to the tabs? Stooping to blackmail, perhaps?"

"It'd be a good insurance policy, is all I'm saying."

"Nuh-uh. We don't want those pictures for anything. We signed a release, and everything's all hunky dory with Bethany and her handlers. We're going to forget the whole thing."

Terry grunted in frustration, sipping her shake. Then she stopped, and her eyes widened again.

"If you keep freezing your brain, it's gonna break up into little gray ice cubes and rattle around in your skull."

"No, it's not a brain freeze. It's a brainstorm!"

"What?"

She picked up her burger, ripping off a bite. "We don't know where our dear client Deirdre Fellows is. We don't know if the whole thing was a setup. But there is one way we can find out."

"How?"

"It's obvious! We go talk to *Mr.* Fellows."

"We can't do that."

"Why not?"

"It's unethical! We were hired to find out about his extramarital affair. We can't go barging in on the subject, asking him questions."

"Helloooo?" She waved the burger in front of my face. "The client's disappeared. We don't even know if it was a real job to begin with, or if Fellows and his alleged wife set us up!"

She was making no sense. "If he was in on it, why would he talk to us? How do we even know his name *is* Paul Fellows? They could all be using fake names."

She jabbed a french fry in the air. "That, my girl, is what we're going to find out." Then she bit into the fry with the gusto of Ozzie Osbourne beheading a bat.

When we parked on Sunset near the corner of Fellows's block, who should we see back in business, strutting their stuff on the streets? Our new best friends, Shotanya, Raquel, and Bobbi.

Good ol' Eli, friend of the working woman.

Shotanya gave us each a high-five. "Hey, girlfriends. You clean up nice."

Terry smiled at the compliment. "Thanks. How'd things work out for you at court?"

"Righteous defense. You girls oughta think about lawyering. Judge let us off with a fine."

"Mr. Weintraub is the nicest man I ever met," Raquel said. "An' so smart."

"He's not going to charge us either," Bobbi said, fluffing her long, strawberry-blond hair. "I offered him a little something for his trouble, but he said no thanks." She leaned in and whispered confidentially, "He told me about his problem."

Terry's eyes bugged. "What problem?"

Bobbi smirked. "Nothing a little Viagra couldn't cure."

Terry gave me a puzzled expression.

It was just an excuse, I beamed to her.

"Say, you not working, are you?" Shotanya wanted to know. "'Cause this our block." Shotanya let her big, brown eyes sweep across their territory. "Don' mean to be pushy or nothin' since you helped us out, but we missed a lot of action when we was locked up."

"Actually, we're not hookers." I handed her a business card. "We're private investigators."

All three women huddled together to read the card.

"Double Indemnity." Shotanya looked up, indignant. "You lied to us?"

"We took a little license," I confessed. "We've got a case going, and the man in that apartment down there has information we need."

Raquel looked around. "Which apartment?"

"That one." I pointed to the ground level apartment. "Do you know him?"

Shotanya nodded. "Oh yeah, I seen him. He's not a customer, though. He keep to himself."

"Have you seen a woman going in there? Older? Maybe in her forties?"

"What she look like?"

"We don't know. We never saw her, just heard her voice," Terry explained.

"I ain't seen no older woman go in there today." Shotanya looked at Raquel and Bobbi. "You?"

Her cohorts shook their heads.

"How about the last day or so?"

"Girl, we was in lockup, same as you," Raquel reminded us. "But it sure don't look like he's home."

We thanked them for their trouble; then Raquel and Shotanya sashayed over to negotiate with a potential customer through the open window of a red pickup truck.

Terry and I wandered up to Fellows's porch. The curtains were drawn. Circulars advertising everything from Thai restaurants to Vietnamese massage parlors littered the stoop. A scraggly bush stood next to the porch, a dirty sock hanging from one branch.

Terry banged on the door, then listened for movement inside.

"Mr. Fellows! We need to speak to you!" She tried the knob, but it was locked. Then she noticed the mailbox, which was full to bursting. She pulled out a magazine and some bills.

"Addressed to Paul Fellows." She showed me an envelope that bore the name. "At least *he's* real."

"But not at home." I pointed to the magazine in her hand—*Inside Stunts*, a monthly from the Stuntman's Association. "Check it out. Mr. Fellows is in the business."

She read from the cover, "Anatomy of a Stunt... High fall basics...*cool!* I always wanted to be a stunt person."

"Or you could put your skills to work as a stunt driver: Eval Twin Knievel. It'd be a perfect job for a thrill-seeking sicko such as yourself."

She flipped open to the article on falls, accompanied by photos of lunatics with death wishes sailing through the air. "Look. You got your face-off, your header, your back fall, and your suicide."

"Suicide sounds like your speed."

"This looks easy."

"Yeah, so does going over Niagara Falls in a barrel. But you'd have to be mental to try it."

"Hey, let's go by the association's office." She ripped off an inside corner with the address. "Maybe we could kill two birds with one stone. Get the dirt on Fellows and see about getting me a union card."

Bobbi was gone when we headed back to the bike. Raquel and Shotanya were steaming with resentment.

"Bobbi got the catch?" Terry asked.

Shotanya huffed, "What we need around here is some *real* men."

"Listen," Terry said, "I wonder if you guys could do us a favor."

"Anything," Raquel responded. "As long as it's legal."

I decided to let that one go by.

"Could you keep an eye on that apartment?" Terry asked. "The one we were talking about before?"

"What you want to know?" Raquel said.

"We want to know when the guy who lives there comes back. Also, if a woman comes to call—young or old—we want to know immediately."

"One of us is usually here," Shotanya said. "We'll keep an eye out."

"That'd be great." Terry peeled a few twenties off her cash wad. The girls tried to refuse it, but Terry wouldn't budge. She held the bills in her outstretched hand until Shotanya finally grabbed them, stuffing them down her cleavage.

"Great," Raquel griped. "Now it's lost *forever*."

Terry handed our business card to Shotanya. She chased the twenties with it. They promised to call if they saw any activity around Paul Fellows's apartment.

"That's how the real cops do it," Terry said as we headed to the bike. "They have street informants on the payroll."

I pulled on my helmet. "Terry?"

"Yeah?"

"You *do* know we're not cops, don't you?"

She bonked me on top of the helmet, causing my teeth to clack together.

"Don't be so friggin' literal," she said.

We headed back up Laurel Canyon Drive, winding along in bumper-to-bumper traffic. I looked down over the side of the road into the chasm below, picturing poor Andie Sue sailing out into the air in a BMW. The result of flying too close to the sun, seduced by fame and money. Most people think money is the answer to all of life's problems, but frequently it's just the start of them.

We crested the mountain, then dipped down the other side into the Valley, taking a right on Ventura Boulevard. The Association office was located in an anachronistic collection of businesses that looked like a Czechoslovakian village set down in the middle of suburban America.

The headquarters was a small anteroom with chrome chairs with black leather upholstery. The décor was standard for all industry-related businesses: movie posters and actors' headshots on the walls. Two larger offices opened off of the main room, their doors closed. A buffed-out woman smiled at us from the reception desk. She wore a sleeveless, leather vest and a short skirt, revealing biceps, quadriceps, and calves that would make the governator weep. Her fingernails were frosty white, her face, tanned.

"Help you?" Her high voice was strangely at odds with the impressive musculature.

"Hi," Terry said. "We're producing a small, independent film. We need some information on stuntmen."

"Surely." The woman reached into a drawer and pulled out a binder of headshots. "Would you like to see some of our members?"

"Thanks."

I took the book and flipped through to the F's while Terry chatted up the receptionist. "We're looking for someone who's a little older. In his forties, kind of shlubby-looking. Do you have anyone like that?"

I'd just come across Fellows's headshot in the binder. I turned it around to face the woman. "This guy would be perfect."

"Paul Fellows. Nice guy. Had some problems, but he's in AA now and doing great." She slapped a hand over her mouth. "Oops, it's supposed to be anonymous."

"No such thing in this town," Terry joked. "Is he available?"

The woman pulled up a file on her computer. "No, sorry. He's working on a show at Paramount."

"Oh really? How long is the job?"

"It looks like he'll be busy for another couple of weeks. *A Night at the Circus.*" She reached for the binder. "Let me see if we can find you someone else—"

"But he's exactly what we want," I wheedled. "We don't start production for a month. Maybe he'll be free by then?"

"Why don't you give me your card, and I'll make sure it gets to his agent."

"That's okay. We'll call him ourselves." I pulled out my small notepad and wrote down Fellows's number.

"By the way," Terry said, snapping the notebook shut. "I have a cousin who wants to be a stunt person. How would she go about it?"

"She can't actually join the association until she has some experience, and there's really no way to learn the craft except by doing it. That's sort of the catch-22. But if she's physically right for a show, someone may hire her and teach her the stunts. Obviously she has to be in good shape and completely fearless. Is she fearless?"

Terry cracked a grin. "Yeah. Fearless as all get-out."

"Incidentally," I said. "Is there a *Mrs.* Paul Fellows?"

The sculpted blond looked at me curiously.

"It's just that I know a *Deirdre* Fellows whose husband works in the business. I wondered if he might be the same one."

"I'm pretty sure Paul's wife left him some years ago. You know, when he was having his problems. But I think her name was Molly, not Deirdre. I guess he could have remarried."

Or maybe there is *no Mrs. Fellows.*

Once we were back outside, Terry began to envision her new career move.

"I can't wait to get started doing stunts. Would I look hot behind the wheel of a Formula One racing car?" She mimed steering a wheel. "Or how about falling out of the window of a fifty-story burning building?" She leaned back on one leg, waving her arms, mouth open in an *oh no!* fake scream.

"What about *our* business? You going to abandon crime fighting?"

"You'll carry on the great tradition."

"Okay, then. I'll take your name off the masthead."

"Hey!" She punched me on the shoulder. "Don't be in such a hurry to get rid of me."

"Hurry? I've been waiting all my life."

"Bite me," she replied.

It took us a half-hour to get home. When we pulled up in our driveway, we came upon a surreal sight. The porch was covered with dozens of red roses, maybe even a dozen dozen. I could smell their perfume, wafting to us over the exhaust of the motorcycle.

I climbed off the bike. "What is that, a gross of roses?"

Terry appeared awestruck. "Boatwright wants you *bad*. I can't believe how bad."

I gave her an indignant look.

"I mean, you're the greatest. But you're not *that* hot. No offense."

"We're identical, moron."

"Oh yeah. I keep forgetting that."

I was pretty stunned myself by this extravagant display. I had never been wooed with expensive flowers before, except for the time Brent Graebner gave me a wrist orchid for the prom. And on the occasion of our television debut, Boatwright gave me some of those roses wrapped in plastic that they sell on freeway on-ramps. But that's the closest I'd ever come.

"We have a date tonight." I tried to suppress a smile that was pure gloat. "He's probably trying to get me in the mood."

"Any chance I'm invited on this date?"

"The chance a mouse fart has in a wind tunnel."

"Thought not."

I grabbed a card from one of the arrangements. What would it say? *My freckled goddess, I worship you.*

Wrong.

It was a one-word message: "Sorry."

I showed the card to Terry. "What's he apologizing for?"

"Look, it's signed with initials 'C. S.'"

"What?"

She grabbed another of the note cards and ripped it open, then turned to me. "This one says sorry, too." We whipped up more cards. On each one was the one-word apology followed by the initials C. S.

Terry finally made the connection. "C. S....*Claude Sterling.*"

"Oh." My heart sank. "I guess he's trying to apologize for the arrest."

Terry gave me a pitying look. "That's disappointing, huh?"

I unlocked the door and threw it open, storming into the house. "Well, you can leave them out here. I don't want his lousy flowers."

Even as I spoke, I realized my irritation was actually aimed at Boatwright. How irrational was that? It wasn't Boatwright's fault the flowers were from someone else.

The phone was ringing. I picked it up and barked out a greeting. "Hello?"

"Is this the McAfee residence?"

"It's Kerry. Who's calling?"

"Claude Sterling. You get my peace offering?"

I took a deep breath to get my annoyance under control. "Yes, we did. And it was totally unnecessary."

"I felt terrible for what happened to you two. I'm glad I caught you. Your sister there?"

"We're rarely separated," I said sardonically as Terry picked up the extension. "So...thanks for the flowers, but there's nothing to worry about."

"That's not why I called. I got a favor to ask."

"What?" Terry said. "We signed your affidavit. And we haven't been to the tabs..."

"Yeah, I appreciate that. Very refreshing, these days, to find somebody who's not on the take. I heard you donated the money to a shelter."

"We didn't want it in the first place," I told him. "We didn't want *any* of what's happened."

"I understand that, and I want to make good. That's why I'd like to hire you."

What was this fresh horror?

"For what?" I managed to say.

"Bethany needs some looking after. And she liked you two."

Yes, she does need looking after. By people in white coats with big needles full of Thorazine.

"Sorry," I said, "you've got the wrong girls. We've had nothing but trouble since we met your little client.

"Imagine what it's like for me. I have her full-time."

Terry mimed playing a tiny violin while I tried to get my mind around this situation. Why, if the whole thing was a setup, would he be trying to hire us again? One big scene was enough to accomplish what he wanted: global publicity.

"Would you happen to know if Bethany has any connection to a man named Paul Fellows?" I asked him.

A pause. "I don't think so. Why?"

"He's the man we were watching when we ran into Bethany and the whole Amber Alert mess happened."

Another momentary silence.

"What does this guy do?" Claude wanted to know.

"He's a stuntman."

He coughed up a laugh. "I think you can rule it out. She doesn't usually hang with the 'below the line' types." By that he meant people who weren't movie stars or directors or producers.

But I'd heard something...a hesitation in his voice.

"So what do you say?" Claude said. "Want a job or not?"

"What are you paying?"

"Five thousand a week for two weeks. If things work out, we can talk about taking you on the road with the tour."

Shoo. Ten thousand dollars for a two-week babysitting gig and possibly several weeks on the road—I looked over at Terry and saw her practically drooling at the prospect of all that cash.

"I gotta have an answer now."

"Why the urgency?"

"I'm...short-handed. The two guys you beat up quit on me. No notice, nothing."

"But surely there would be people lining up for the job..."

"To tell you the truth, I'm thinking maybe what Bethany needs is a little female companionship. You know, girlfriends she can talk to, instead of a bunch of muscle-bound goons."

Sounded like he wanted us to do therapist duty. I wasn't sure I was up for that.

"Let me put it this way: I need to keep her in line long enough to get through the tour. Once she's fulfilled her contractual commitments, I'm outta here. Life is too short. All you gotta do is keep an eye on her, make sure she goes to rehearsals, and don't get into any more monkey business."

Terry flashed ten fingers at me over and over, mouthing the words, *Ten thousand smackers. Ten thousand smackers.*

"Would you give us a second to discuss it?" she said to Claude.

"I got a second, but no more. I'm up against a wall here."

"Thanks."

Terry put her hand over the phone and raised her eyebrows at me.

"No fricking way," I whispered.

She squinted at me. "No funky waves?"

"You know what I said."

"I also know the guy can't hear us, so why don't you talk like a human?"

"I don't want to do this."

"Well, I do!"

"I thought you wanted to be a stuntman."

"*Person.* Stunt *person.*"

"Whatever. There's something very strange going on here, Terry. I don't know what it is, but it goes deeper than drumming up publicity. I think Bethany was actually on her way to meet Fellows. And Claude denies knowing the man, but I don't buy it."

"So, maybe Fellows is her drug dealer or something. Maybe she's into some bad stuff, and Claude knows about it. As far as I'm concerned, the best reason for taking the job is to find out what's really going on, that and the bodacious bucks. We can solve a mystery and maybe even get back our dignity after what happened with the SWATs. Meanwhile we line our pockets."

Seeing my indecision, she hit me with the ultimate challenge: "Are we detectives or not? Don't you want to *know* what's been going on? Or do you want to be made out to be the fool?"

I stared at her for a moment, and then brought the phone up to my ear. "We're back."

"So. What's the word?" Claude asked.

"We'll do it."

Terry jumped in the air, pumping her fist, and came down hard on the floorboards. It sounded like an elephant parachuting into the living room.

"You guys have a quake over there?"

"Yeah, about a three-point-four," I lied. "Are you sure this is the best idea after that business at the motel? I mean, there was a lot of adverse publicity—"

"Girly, I know something about it, and there's no such thing. All publicity's good publicity. If you two are seen with her, it'll give credence to the stunt story. This way no one suspects she had a meltdown."

"And what if she has another one?"

"You don't need to worry about that. What do I pay her shrink for? Pack your clothes. I'll send the limo right over."

"Whoa!" I said. "We can't start today. I have...I have a very important function to attend this evening."

That wasn't what Claude wanted to hear. "Okay, I'll give you one night to get the function out of your system, whoever he is. Pick you up at eleven tomorrow morning."

"All right. Our address is—"

"What do I look like, a *schmuck*? I got the address when I sent the roses."

He hung up before I was tempted to answer his rhetorical question.

I winced at Terry. "Are we really going to work for someone who calls us 'girly'?"

"We've done worse," she replied.

Boatwright arrived for our date ten minutes early in his souped-up, vintage Ford Gran Torino. This baby sang on eight cylinders and never let you forget who was boss, rumbling down the street sounding like a fleet of choppers. As we left the house, Terry and Lance stood on the porch with their arms around each other, waving like proud parents sending their daughter off on her first date.

"Our little baby's going out with a man, Pa," Terry sniffed, burying her face in Lance's shoulder.

Lance hugged her to him. "If you love something, Ma, set it free."

Boatwright laughed, and I set my middle finger free, flipping them off behind my back.

"You gonna tell me who sent the roses?" Boatwright asked with more than a hint of jealousy.

"Oh, just an admirer. Someone who wants me *bad.*"

He held open the car door for me, giving me a steely look.

"For a job." I elbowed him in the ribs. "Wants me for a job. I'll tell you all about it over dinner."

We drove straight to Don Antonio's restaurant on Pico. They seated us in a courtyard that was choked with hanging geraniums and trailing cactus plants, the brick walls covered with posters featuring Cantinflas and other Mexican stars. The small forest of twinkling, light-entwined ficus and flowering plants took me far away from LA. Fiercely romantic lyrics came from the speakers—"*Yo te amo,*" "*Tu eres mi vida,*" and "*Sin ti, me moriré.*" Would anyone ever tell me that he'd die without me?

Boatwright clinked my iced tea glass. "To quality time."

"Cheers."

I flashed on a vision of Franzen's face.

Would you cut that out? I yelled at myself. *You're clinking with one man and thinking of another.*

I looked up and saw Boatwright regarding me quizzically. His eyes were blue, with dark blue circles around the lighter irises. Laugh lines framed his mouth. A grainy beard was visible beneath the smooth skin of his cheeks, and his thick, dark hair was cut short.

He was a dream. How dare I daydream about someone who wasn't there?

Boatwright tapped me on the hand. "You disappeared on me. Where'd you go?"

I grabbed a chip from the basket in front of me, dipping it in the zippy salsa. "Sorry, zoned out for a second. It's been an insane couple of days."

"You doing okay with everything?"

"I guess so. But you know, it's exhausting being Terry's twin. I sometimes wonder what would happen if I decided to be the wild child for once. Would she suddenly spring into shape and become civilized?"

"Don't know why you can't both be civilized."

"That's our dynamic, always has been. She Tarzan, me Jane. Maybe it was some past life deal that we made with each other. I was the one who made her pull her hair out last time around, and she swore she'd get even with me in this life."

"She does seem determined to complicate things. Maybe if she had a girlfriend...?"

"Yeah, I thought she was gonna go for this girl named Angie, the tattoo artist? But she pulled back at the last minute. I think she broke Angie's heart."

"What was wrong with Angie?"

"Not sure. Might have been the cobra tattooed on her neck. It's cool looking, but I think Terry wants a lifetime commitment. The idea of a saggy, baggy snake hanging down from an old woman's chin is kind of unappealing."

"That's funny. I wouldn't have guessed Terry was looking for a serious relationship."

"Oh, yeah. Don't you know the joke? What does a lesbian bring on the first date?"

He shrugged.

"A U-Haul."

"Ha."

"Women are nesters. Even if they *are* dykes."

"And what about you?"

"Me? No U-Hauls up my sleeve."

"But you want to get married some day, don't you?"

I was not particularly big on the idea of commitment, let alone marriage. My eggs could afford to get a little older before I made that kind of life-altering decision.

"Eventually," I said, hedging my bets.

"And what do you want in a mate?"

"I'm looking for longevity, too. Someone to visit the Grand Canyon with on his 'n' hers HoverRounds when we're ninety."

"And does the old guy on the HoverRound in this scenario have a seventy-year-old tattoo?"

"Makes no difference to me."

"Good."

"You have one?" I'd seen everything that wasn't covered by his briefs in a tent on Malibu beach, but I hadn't noticed any tattoo.

"It's on my hip. It says 'Sexy Charlene.'"

My jaw dropped open.

"I'm lying. I don't have a tattoo."

"Oh. I'm such a dope. I believe everything people tell me."

"Would you believe it if I said I loved you?"

"Uh—" I drew in a breath to respond, and a piece of chip lodged in my windpipe. *"Haaaaccckkk!"*

Boatwright jumped up and ran to my side of the table, slapping me on the back. "You all right?"

He pounded away as I choked and hacked and gagged and wheezed for what seemed like hours, checking the table periodically to see if I'd coughed my lungs up onto my plate. Finally, I felt something give, and the dastardly taco chip shot into my napkin. I grabbed a glass of ice water off the table, chugging the freezing water as if my life depended on it.

Boatwright made his way back to his chair and sat down, never taking his eyes off of me. I flicked the killer tostada remnant out of my napkin, wiped my eyes, patted my lips, and put on my most charming smile.

"Sorry about that. Now, where were we?"

He didn't respond. He leaned back in his chair and stared at me like I was a freak.

Oh come on, I thought. *Cut me a break. It was an accident. An esophageal mishap that could have happened to anyone.*

Sheesh, a girl doesn't nearly choke herself to death to get out of an awkward moment, does she? A girl wouldn't put her life in jeopardy just to avoid giving someone an answer, right?

A girl might talk about herself in the third person like a raging psychotic, but that's a whole different problem.

Eventually Boatwright loosened up, and the rest of dinner passed without further incident. We ate enchiladas in green tomatillo sauce while I filled Boatwright in on the situation with Bethany (leaving out the part about accepting a job from her manager). But as we talked, I sensed a little coolness in the air. No more *yo té amo* talk from him. I guess I *had* sort of stepped on his romantic moment, but his reaction still struck me as unfair.

After he paid the bill, we sauntered back out to the parking lot.

"Where to?" I wanted to get back in his good graces. "Want to go necking up on Mulholland?"

Mulholland is a road that winds along the mountains separating the San Fernando Valley from Los Angeles proper. At night there's an amazing view of the basin, dotted with twinkling lights for miles and miles. It's a famous spot for parking, famous also as a body and weapons dump. After blowing their parents away, the Menendez brothers disposed of their shotguns at that very spot.

I know. I'm a hopeless romantic.

"I'd love to go necking, but I'm afraid of heights," Boatwright said. "If I went up to Mulholland, there'd be no kissing. I'd be grinding my teeth, and you'd have to pry my fingers off the steering wheel with a tire iron."

"Really? You have a sissy streak? I never even suspected."

"I stick to the flatlands as much as I can."

"Okay then, want to neck in the parking lot of Don Antonio's?"

"I wouldn't want to be responsible for the valet walking off the job. Want to go to my place?"

I swallowed hard. *Could I say no?* Of course I could say no. And then I could forever wonder why I blew it with this stone cold hottie. Guess Terry wasn't the only one with a self-destructive streak.

"Sure. I'm dying to see what kind of window treatments you have."

He laughed. "Interior decorating is not my strong suit."

"Thank goodness. I was beginning to think you were gay."

"*Oh, really?*" He pushed me up against the car, pressing his hips into mine. Then he grabbed the back of my neck and covered my lips with his, his tongue going into my mouth.

My knees collapsed. He caught me with an arm around the waist. Every cell of my body was electrified. I was sure the two of us had lit up like a Christmas tree, spreading holiday cheer for miles. It was closer to Halloween than Christmas, but so what? 'Twas the season for hot monkey love, whatever the calendar said.

A valet walked up beside us and cleared his throat. "Um, want your keys?"

Without breaking stride, Boatwright pulled the wallet out of his back pocket and tossed it to him. The guy took a couple of bucks and handed it back.

By this time, I was trembling and going liquid all over. I literally ached for him. I was measuring the back seat of his car in my mind. I didn't think we'd make it all the way to his place. As I was turning it over in my mind, his phone chirped.

He gave me an apologetic smile, moving a few feet away for a short conversation.

I was slouched against the car, my arms frozen in the air in front of me like those of a store mannequin, reaching for him long after he had stepped away.

The valet returned. He dangled the keys in front of me. I forced my fingers to close around the pieces of cold metal, and their icy hardness snapped me out of my spell.

I closed my mouth and straightened myself up just as Boatwright ended his conversation.

He returned the phone to his jacket. "Duty calls," he said.

Nooooooooooooooooooo! My scream echoed off the walls of the restaurant and down the block. Cars screeched to a stop in the street, drivers craning their heads out of windows to see who was being murdered.

Not really. The scream was only in my head.

Outwardly, I gave him a casual shrug and tossed him the keys. "Can't win 'em all."

When we arrived at the house, I suggested to Boatwright that we say goodnight in the car. I didn't want a repeat performance by Lance and Terry on the front porch.

"Sorry about this," Boatwright said. "I'll make it up to you."

"Yes. You will."

He leaned over to kiss me, and I drank in his wonderful scent. The kiss wasn't as prolonged as the one in the parking lot, but that was okay. I didn't want to go back in the house all blurry with desire, having to answer a bunch of questions about the *datus interruptus*. When he pulled away from me, I noticed that the back of his hair was cut in a straight line, a sprinkling of tiny hairs on his collar. I realized with a breaking heart that he'd gone for a haircut before picking me up.

"How about tomorrow night?"

I almost said *Sure!* Then I remembered our plan. "Uh, I won't be available tomorrow night."

"No problem. Day after that?"

"That's out, too. In fact, I'll probably be tied up for a week or two. Maybe longer."

"I thought we were past playing hard to get."

"I'm not playing, I swear. Terry and I have a job as bodyguards for Bethany."

"*What?* You're joking, right?"

"Nope. Her manager just hired us."

He flopped over on the steering wheel, shaking his head. "You took the job, knowing what you know about this girl?"

"We have our reasons."

"That's crazy, Kerry."

"It may be crazy, but it's not as stupid as it looks."

"Convince me."

I resented his tone, but gave him the rationale anyway. "Bethany was trying to escape her handlers for some reason, which has something to do with getting control over her life. Her manager says he's ready to dump her as soon as she's done with her new tour, but he seems determined to keep her on a tight leash until then. Meanwhile, we were hired to spy on a man by his wife, a man that Bethany may have been going to see on the sly. Then the alleged wife disappeared on us right after we were arrested.

"Bottom line, working next to Bethany may be the only way to solve all these mysteries."

He rubbed his weary eyes. "That girl is a curse. If you need work, I could get you a position with the best private investigation agency around, Mickey West and Associates."

I crossed my arms. "I *have* a private investigation agency. I like being my own boss."

"It's a free country. I guess I have to let you shoot yourself in the foot."

"Gee, thanks."

I got a quick *I may be changing my mind about you* kiss good-bye. I threw open the door and let myself out, slamming it behind me.

Boatwright took off down the driveway, and I watched his taillights disappear into traffic on Beverly Glen before dragging myself into the house.

"If I hear *one word*," I said, anticipating a slew of obnoxious remarks from Lance and Terry.

"Shhhhhhh!" They hovered over the box on the buffet. Pieces of wet eggshell were lying on a saucer.

"They're here!" Lance announced in an excited whisper.

Sure enough, there were five tiny, yellow, squeaking lumps in the box, wiggling under the heat lamp. Their feathers were all puffed up, making them look like popcorn balls with beaks. The babies cheeped and pecked at the rose petals lining their box.

"They're adorable! Can I pet one?"

"Better not," Lance said. "You might be carrying bacteria."

"Right."

"Let me introduce you. This is Huey, Dewey, Louie, Terry, and Kerry."

I smiled at Terry. "Awwww, we have duckling namesakes. How sweet."

"It's the least I could do," Lance declared. "You saved their mother's life. If it wasn't for you, they'd never have been hatched."

I stood there, confused. Wasn't the mother killed by a coyote? Then I realized he was talking about the time we allegedly saved *his* life. Lance was the mother duck in this scenario.

"That's about the most special thing that's ever happened to me," I told him.

"Me, too," Terry said.

Lance dipped an eyedropper into a small glass that was filled with blackish goo dotted with exoskeletons. Bug stew.

"Can't you give them some kind of feed?" I asked. "Might be a little less repulsive."

"This is the best thing for them when they're first born. We'll move up to feed later on." He dripped some bug slop into one of the suckling mouths while the others cheeped anxiously for their share.

"They do seem to be enjoying it," I said.

"Of course the witty bitty duckies enjoy it," Terry said, wagging her fingers at them, making smoochy noises.

The tender side of Terry. Enjoy it while you can.

"Hey, we didn't expect you back so soon," Lance said. "What happened to your date?"

"I'm saving myself for marriage," I answered breezily, heading up to my loft. "Don't forget to pack your stuff, Ter."

I glanced back over my shoulder and saw them standing next to each other, shaking their heads as they watched me mount the stairs.

"Our little baby can't get laid to save her life, Pa."

"Well, Ma, there's more important things in life than great sex."

I rounded the corner of my loft and threw myself down on the bed, fully clothed. I thought about crying, but passed out instead. I slept dreamlessly until morning, for which I was grateful to the Sandman or Sigmund Freud or whoever was behind those strange after-hours movies that had been my nightly torment.

L ance took off the next morning with the baby ducks in their box. He'd stayed up all night petting them and feeding them, and was considering asking for family leave from work. Terry'd advised him against it on the grounds that he'd only been on the job for a couple of months, and it wouldn't be wise to take time off to be a neonatal duck nurse.

Lance planned to leave the box in the office while he made his rounds. He was sure some of the clerical staff would enjoy feeding the babies their bugs. Meanwhile, he offered to stay at our house and continue dog sitting while we were off working for Bethany.

At eleven o'clock the doorbell rang. I opened the door to see an older man with a gray mustache wearing a chauffeur's uniform. I saw the white limo in the drive, the same one used in the bogus Bethany abduction.

"I'm Harold, your driver."

"Is Bethany with you?"

"We're going to pick her up, now. Mr. Sterling wanted to take advantage of this time to brief you on the job."

He stuffed our suitcases into the trunk, then opened the back door for us. We slipped in across from Claude, who was talking into two cell phones simultaneously. He wore a pinky ring with his initials in diamonds, a blue shirt with French cuffs and gold links engraved with C. S., and just in case he should still forget his own name, the initials were stamped in gold on the notebook computer case sitting next to him and embroidered in dark blue on his breast pocket.

He held up a manicured hand. "Be right with you girls. Are you friggin' nuts?" he yelled into the phone. "I said no magazines with less than a hundred thousand circulation. What are you, deaf?" He put the other phone to his ear. "Okay, how about I cancel the venue and sue you for breach? Thought so. Sell those tickets or we're gonna have a *big* problem!" He hung up.

"Good morning," I said.

"Putz!" he yelled at the air, and then he took a breath. "Sorry. Morning. Okay, we're picking Bethany up at the temple. Afterwards, she goes straight to Paramount for rehearsals, understand?" Yet another phone rang. "Yeah...? Hold on."

Back to us. "She gets *one* ice cream break every two hours. Make sure she throws up afterwards. She's gotta get into a skimpy costume in two weeks." Into the phone: "No, not you. You make *me* throw up. Yeah, hold on." Back to us again: "After rehearsal you go straight home. She does *not* leave the house under any circumstances, understand? Lupe will make you dinner." He popped a Tums into his mouth and chewed. "Give me five seconds, wouldja?" he growled into the phone. "And no sharp objects," he said to us, covering the microphone with his hand. "Keep her away from all sharp objects. Don't even let her have paper or she'll give herself a paper cut. She's gotta wear a see-through outfit on this tour. I can't afford to have her all nicked up."

And so it went. Screaming at people, hanging up on them, taking other calls to curse at yet another person. In between, we got a pretty clear idea of Bethany's day: rehearsal, ice cream, regurgitation, costume fitting, self-mutilation, ice cream, and so on.

"I was right," Terry whispered to me. "She's majorly disturbed."

"Is it any wonder?"

We were approaching a Jewish temple on Robertson, near the 10 Freeway. A whole line of limos snaked around the block. I thought it must have been some sort of publicity event, maybe a fundraiser. Expensively dressed people began to pour out the doors.

"What's this about?" Claude banged on the privacy window. "We don't wait in line. Get up front!"

Harold stepped on the gas and jerked out of line, screeching up to the front door to double park in front of the temple.

Terry gasped. "Look who's here!"

Coming down the stairs was our own great-aunt Reba. She wore a scarf on her head, and her face was solemn, her carriage reverent. She had the look of someone leaving a funeral.

"I wonder who died," Terry said.

"Nobody died." Claude scoffed at the suggestion. "It's Kabbalah class."

Terry gave him a bewildered look. "What?"

"Jewish mysticism. Where you been, babe? It's all the rage."

Our family had been spotty on church attendance, but when they went, it was to Sunday services at normal churches. All other religious weirdness—Inquisitions, witch-burnings, crusades—was in the past, and now they were about people going to listen to a sermon, mouthing hymns and throwing money in the plate, and handing out their business cards over donuts in the gym. The closest we came to mystics was a couple of Masons two generations back. But they mostly tossed back beers and wore funny hats with their brethren at the lodge.

"Excuse me a second," I said, jumping out of the car.

"Hey," Claude called after me. "Where you going?"

Terry followed. "Back in a sec. We need to speak to someone."

We caught up to Reba in the parking lot just as she was getting into her mint-green Mercedes SL 500.

"Reba!" I said. "What are you doing here?"

She spun around with her keys in one hand, the Torah in the other. I noticed a red string tied around her wrist.

"Darlings!" she greeted us. "Have you become truth-seekers, too?"

Terry shot me a worried glance. "Uh, no. We were just passing by and saw you. It was pure coincidence."

"There are no coincidences, dear. That's one of the first things you learn in the Kabbalah."

"So...you're truth-seeking?" I said.

"Just between us, I'm thinking of converting to Judaism. It occurred to me that Eli might be holding back because we're not of the same faith."

Hello? Are we talking about the same Eli Weintraub here?

Eli had faith in his ability to get his clients acquitted. The sports bar was his temple. The Lakers, his gods. But Reba was obsessed with him. She'd try anything she could think of, even changing religions, to get him hooked. I was sure this latest, desperate ploy of hers was doomed to failure.

"But why this Kabbalah stuff?" I said. "If you want to be Jewish, why not go to Hebrew school?"

Reba gave me a patronizing smile. "All the celebrities are into it. Can you imagine them trotting over to Temple Beth-El to get instruction from some dowdy little rabbi?" She shuddered at the mere thought of it. "No, this is where the action is."

Well, if you were going to convert, of course you'd want *designer* Judaism.

"How are you liking it so far?" Terry asked her.

"It's a lot to take in," Reba sighed. "I understand it takes *years* to plumb its mysteries. I'll give it a couple of weeks and see what it does for me."

Terry stifled a laugh. "At least you're really committed to it."

A horn honked, and I looked back at the limo queue. Claude's hand was waving to us from a partially opened window.

"Gotta go," I told Reba. "See you later."

"Why don't you girls come for dinner?"

"We'll be tied up with work for a couple of weeks. We'll call you when we're done. Meantime, don't sign over all your worldly goods to them, promise?"

"Not to worry!" Reba hopped into her Mercedes. "Shalom!"

Terry and I hurried back to the limo and scooted in next to Bethany on the back seat.

"Who was that?" she wanted to know.

"Our aunt Reba," Terry said. "I guess she's into this Kabbalah thing, too."

"It's *The Kabbalah*," Bethany huffed. "Not 'this Kabbalah thing.'"

"Whatever," Terry said. "So how do you like it? Is it interesting?"

"It's my connection to the mysteries of the ages. It's totally awesome."

We dropped Claude off at the Capitol Records building on Sunset, a Hollywood landmark designed to resemble a stack of records. Looking at it made me nostalgic for an age I never really knew. Our parents played old vinyl records when we were kids, but we were always making fun of them for it. I made a mental note to find some of those old recordings and listen to them again. If we could locate a turntable, that is. It would please mom and dad to no end if we did, provided they were still around somewhere.

"I gotta take a meeting." Claude was reaching for the door handle. "I'll meet up with you at rehearsal. You got my cell phone numbers?"

Bethany held out her hand to Terry. "I've got 'em memorized. Give me your phone."

Terry tossed Bethany the phone. She clicked the buttons with amazing speed, popping in the numbers with the facility of someone who'd used a cell phone from the crib. She hit the ringer and made a face when she heard the "William Tell Overture."

"Weak ring tone. You should get one of mine. Only costs a few dollars."

"Sure thing." Terry checked out the new speed-dial listings as I looked over her shoulder: Claude one, two, three.

Claude pointed a finger at Bethany. "No crap outta you today!"

She stuck her tongue out at him, and he slammed the door. Then the driver took off down Hollywood Boulevard.

"You guys have a good relationship, I see," Terry remarked.

"He's such a loser," Bethany said. "I can't wait until I'm eighteen so I can fire him."

Claude might be a bit of a *schmuck*, but Bethany was no walk in the park, either. "Seems to me you owe him a lot. He did make you a star, didn't he?"

She looked out the window, pouting. "Sure he did. Just ask *him*." She flicked the intercom on the armrest. "Stop at the Pink Spot, Harold."

"Yes, madam." The limo cornered right and headed down toward Sunset. The Pink Spot is a convenience store painted purple with a large pink circle above the door.

"Are you allowed to go to the Pink Spot?" I asked her.

Bethany scowled at me. "We're *outta* ice cream."

"Can't you send somebody to get it?"

"If I wanna *wait*. But I don't *wanna* wait."

Oh boy, is this job ever going to be fun.

Bethany leaned back in the seat and looked us over. "So, Claude hired you guys to watch me." There was a hint of amusement in her tone.

"He told us your other bodyguards quit," Terry said. "I guess they couldn't take the abuse."

Bethany suddenly went contrite. "Hey, I'm sorry about what happened the other day. You know, telling the police you kidnapped me and all. I just wigged, you know? I knew I was in big trouble."

I didn't think it wise to trust her little mood swings. She might be sorry in this moment, but she could come out duking like a prizefighter the next.

"What made you run away in the first place?" I asked, trying the gentle approach.

Bethany flipped her hair behind her shoulder. "I dunno! I just went psycho, know what I mean?"

"Uh-huh." I knew exactly what she meant.

Terry refused to let her off the hook. "But you were very specific. You said you had to lay low until you were eighteen. That's still a few days away, right?"

"But obviously I can't 'lay low.' I mean, I've got rehearsals and everything. And a twenty-city tour, right? I can't just flake."

"And yet you did."

Bethany stared directly into Terry's eyes. "I *told* you," she said slowly. "I tweaked. People tweak sometimes, it doesn't mean anything."

The limo pulled up at the store. Harold spoke over the intercom. "What flavor would you like, madam?"

"I'll go myself." She reached for the door handle.

"Madam, I don't think that's a good ide—"

Bethany was out the door. Terry and I jumped out after her.

"Are you crazy?" Terry grabbed Bethany's arm. "You'll cause a riot if you go in there!"

The driver got out of the limo. "She's right, madam. Better let me go."

A head popped up from the Taurus parked next to us.

"It's Bethany!" someone yelled.

"I thought she was kidnapped!"

"No, that's Bethany!"

"Look, there she is!"

And then the most extraordinary thing occurred. Out of nowhere, a huge crowd materialized in the parking lot. It was as if a magician had tossed out some magic powder, and *whoosh*—there they were, closing in on us like a blanket of giant equatorial insects. I had to fight against mounting claustrophobia.

Harold opened the limo door for Bethany. "Get back in the car, madam, please."

Bethany spun around and blew kisses to the crowd. "Hi, everybody! I'm back! Whassup?"

Cheers went up from the crowd. Napkins and shopping lists and shoes were thrust in her direction with demands for autographs.

"Sor-reee," Bethany singsonged. "My merchandising company won't let me sign autographs! Go to my Web site and place an order!"

"Harold," I said to the driver. "You go inside. We'll wait for you out here!"

Harold squeezed through the throng as Terry and I inserted ourselves between Bethany and the crowd, trying to push them back. But they continued to press forward like a giant amoeba with multiple probing mouths.

"Bethany has a rehearsal to go to," I shouted. "Sorry, everyone! Step back, please!"

They got more riled and angrier by the second, one step away from bloodthirsty Romans.

"You can catch her tour in two weeks," Terry told a guy in a muscle shirt who was trying to get past.

He pushed her. "Let me through!"

"Get off, man!" Terry shoved him back.

Bethany finally wised up, jumping into the back seat. When I was sure she was safe inside, I grabbed Terry's shirt, pulling her away from the belligerent fan.

"Come on. Let's lock ourselves in."

I turned toward the limo and opened the door, throwing myself in just in time to see Bethany scooting out the opposite side. She slammed the door in my face.

"No!"

Terry bounded in after me. "What's the matter?"

"She bolted!" I dove towards the opposite door and threw it open. It slammed into the thighs of a woman outside who shrieked, stumbling backwards.

"Sorry!" I yelled, piling out of the limo.

I saw the door slam on a maroon Ford Escape. Seconds later, the SUV peeled out of the parking lot with Bethany in the front seat. A car on Sunset laid on its horn as the SUV wheeled out into traffic. The car slammed on its brakes; then a whole line of cars behind it came to a screeching, blaring halt. The Escape took off west on Sunset.

Cute. Fleeing in an Escape.

"Hey, that's my car!" the woman with the thighs yelled. "I just got out to see what all the commotion was. I left the engine running!"

Terry was tearing around the parking lot looking for Bethany. "She's not here!"

"She stole that SUV!" I ran for the driver's side door of the limo. "Come on, we have to catch her!"

I'd never driven a limo before, but it had wheels and a steering column and an accelerator and a brake and in many other ways resembled a car. So what if the sight in the rearview mirror looked more like the stern of a luxury yacht? *I can do this. Nothin' to it.*

"Tell me if I hit anything!" I said as Terry hopped into the passenger seat. Then I wheeled the behemoth back into traffic.

There's something about a limo. People make way for them. The cars on Sunset stopped to let me into traffic, surprised by the sight of the glammobile coming out of the tacky convenience store parking lot.

I fishtailed out into Sunset Boulevard, going west.

"Where'd she go, Terry?"

"How should I know? I don't see her up ahead."

"She took a side street. Keep a look out for the car!"

"There it is!" She pointed down the next block. "Where?"

"You passed it!"

I veered over into the right lane, horns screaming behind me. But no one slammed into the back. I cornered right on the next street and barreled to the end of the block. A car was idling at the corner stop sign. I honked the limo's horn, and the guy flipped me off as he turned into traffic.

Who cared? I wasn't going for Considerate Motorist of the Year. Being considerate in LA traffic is tantamount to suicide, anyway. It's the law of the jungle here: Mow them down before they can mow you.

I have to catch that evil brat. I stomped the pedal, winging a right to reach the side street Bethany had taken. *Ditched again.* More horns were blasted at us as I angled the boat onto a narrow residential street.

Parked cars lined both sides of the street. A convertible Humvee approached us from the opposite direction, and the two of us slammed to a standoff. We couldn't go forward; the Humvee wouldn't back up. Another car came up behind us, and then we were completely stuck. A gum-chewing, pony-tailed blond sat behind the Humvee's wheel, laying on her horn.

I rolled down the limo's window. "Back up!"

"Back up yourself!" She popped a bubble.

"It's a friggin' off-road vehicle!" Terry shouted out her window. "Go over the grass!"

"Kiss my ass!"

"Fine!" Terry jumped out of the limo, headed for the Humvee with fire in her eyes. The girl hurriedly locked her door. Terry came down with two fists on the Humvee's hood. The girl made a horrified face, jerked the Humvee back over a curb, and then jammed it into drive and ripped across the apartment lawns all the way down the block before bumping off the curb into traffic.

Ponytailed blonde in modified Army vehicle: zero.

Skinny redheads in limousine: one.

Terry raced back to the limo, and we sped down the block. There was no sign of the Escape. I pulled to the curb in the red zone so the car behind me could pass. Again, our friendly fellow motorist honked at us.

"What should I do?"

Terry pointed down an alley. There was the Escape, abandoned next to a Dumpster. The door to the Escape was ajar, but no one was visible inside. "She's on foot."

"She could be on the floor of the car."

"Right." Terry hopped down and ran over to the abandoned car to scope it out. She came jogging back, slightly out of breath.

"Rabbit hunt?"

"Did she leave the keys in the ignition?" I asked, and Terry nodded. "Then I think our first priority is to return the stolen car so that Bethany doesn't go up for grand theft auto."

Terry sighed. "This is the shortest job anyone ever had."

"I'll alert Guinness." The car phone rang in its cradle. I picked it up. "Hello?"

"Hello, madam. It's Harold the chauffeur."

"Hi, Harold."

"Are you planning to return the limousine, madam?"

"Yes, I am. And then I'm planning to quit this job."

"A wise decision, madam. When shall I be expecting you?"

"Five minutes."

"Is Miss Bethany with you?"

"I'm afraid she's in the wind."

There was a silence on the line. "Very well. I'll inform Mr. Sterling."

"Thanks. And please tell the woman whose car Bethany borrowed that we're bringing it back unharmed."

"Yes, madam."

Terry retrieved the Escape. I pulled to the corner, put on my left blinker, and watched the cars speed by on Sunset, waiting for my chance to enter the stream of traffic. I was still steeped in adrenaline after the chase, seething with frustration that Bethany had eluded us again.

Suddenly and almost unconsciously, I put the pedal to the metal and gunned it into the middle of the street. Cars screeched to a stop to avoid hitting me. Hundreds of horns blared, like the brass section of hell's own philharmonic.

I smiled, feeling much better. Why hadn't anyone ever told me that road rage was so cathartic?

*B*ethany's house was a study in conspicuous consumption, old Hollywood grandeur that rambled over half an acre. No doubt it was built sometime in the thirties for a movie star making thousands a week playing a destitute waif on the screen. The house was composed of pink granite, with snarling stone lions that guarded the steps leading up to the front porch.

"See, here's the power of the spoken word." Terry gazed up at the mansion as we exited the limo. "We're at a palatial home in the Hollywood Hills, and the person who owns it is worth hundreds of millions of dollars. That's exactly what you said."

"Pure coincidence." Though I wouldn't admit it to Terry, I did find it strange.

"Next time you're *thinking big*, specify that the things you're talking about belong to *us*."

"Shall I unload your suitcases?" Harold asked us.

"Uh-uh," I said. "We won't be staying long."

"What do we say to Claude?" Terry asked as we mounted the stairs.

"Improvise."

We arrived at the large oaken door with a brass woodpecker knocker. I was about to bash his beak against the door when it swung open. A uniformed butler greeted us, looming in the doorway like Lurch. He was tall and gaunt with cropped white hair and blue eyes that were professionally blank, focused on a point somewhere beyond us.

"Good afternoon."

"Hello," we replied in unison.

He turned wordlessly and led us through the airy main room, which featured twenty-foot ceilings with skylights. One wall of windows faced a pool surrounded by towering palm trees. The bookshelf was crammed with albums, plaques for gold and platinum records, and biographies of musical artists from Billie Holiday to the Rolling Stones.

In the study, we found Claude with a phone jammed in his ear, pounding on a notebook computer as he talked. The guy never did one thing at a time. His eyes traveled up to our faces, and there was no smile of welcome. Not even a nod of acknowledgment. He pointed to two wooden chairs in front of the carved Spanish table that served as his desk.

Terry and I waited while he finished up his conversation.

"Yeah, they're here now. I'll get back to you...of *course* I'll let you know. What am I, a *schmuck*?"

There it was again. The rhetorical question that just begged for a *Yes, you are a major schmuck!*

He hung up the phone. "Good news. No camera phone pictures have shown up on Defamer."

We'd learned from Harold on the way over that he had offered monetary compensation to the woman with the purloined Escape. No theft charges would be forthcoming.

"You're not getting paid for today," Claude informed us. "I hope you realize that."

"Money is the least of our worries," I lied. "We're sorry she got away from us."

"I don't need your apologies! I needed competent bodyguards today, and I got bupkis! I needed a little sharpness, a little professionalism. Boy, did I ever make a mistake, hiring you."

Terry deflected the tirade with an obvious question. "Why is she so determined to run away?"

"How should I know?"

"You *must* have some idea."

"Let me tell you something, girly." He aimed a pudgy finger at her nose. "You been in the business as long as I have, you stop asking yourself why they do what they do. You'd lose your mind." He leaned back in his chair, swiveling around to look out over the lawn. "You just try to keep them half-sober and showing up for recording sessions and tour dates. That's all you can do."

"But you're her guardian," I said. "You're more like a parent than a manager. You have some responsibility here."

He waved a hand past his face. "It's a financial arrangement, no parenting express or implied. The court wouldn't let her be emancipated at fourteen without assigning me, but we both know who's boss. She runs *me*."

It sure didn't sound that way in the limo. It sounded like he controlled her every move, including when she should revisit her ice cream.

"Is it the stress of being a star?" Terry asked him. "Think it's getting to her? The childhood she never had?"

"Beats me." He turned back to us, pinching the flesh between his eyebrows as if to stave off a headache. "Jeez, you make someone rich and successful beyond her wildest dreams, and this is how she thanks you."

"Maybe she's rich enough now," I said. "Maybe she'd like to give up the business. Have some kind of life. Get a boyfriend and be normal..."

Claude tugged on his toupee, urging it closer to his forehead. "Actually, now that you mention it, that *may* be part of the problem."

"*What* may be part of the problem?" I asked. "Boys?"

"She had a little flirtation with one of her bodyguards," Claude said wearily. "I don't know how far it went, but I put the kibosh on it as soon as I found out."

"But what would it hurt if she had a serious romance?" I asked. "She's almost eighteen. I don't understand."

"She's a role model! I already get hate mail from parents whose daughters are screaming for ankle tattoos at the age of five. Bethany has to watch what she does."

I had been pretty wild about Madonna when I was a kid. But when Mom caught me dancing around the house wearing her lingerie, singing into a hairbrush, and rolling around on the couch suggestively, that was the end of that.

"You said all publicity was good publicity," I reminded him.

"All publicity except for sex and drugs. When she turns twenty-one, she can do anything she wants. Until then, as far as the public is concerned, she's a clean and sober virgin."

"That's three years away," Terry said. "She can do a lot of damage in that time."

"Don't I know it." Claude looked to the ceiling. "She's gonna ruin me. Give me a heart attack and then ruin me."

I had no sympathy for him. He was an opportunist who'd been squeezing every last exploitable ounce out of Bethany while denying her all normal rites of passage in the interest of profit. His anguish was real enough, but it was all self-pity.

"What are you going to do?" Terry asked.

"I thought having you two around would help. Obviously I was wrong."

"What happened to the bodyguard she got involved with?"

Claude slapped the desk with his palms. "I fired him!"

"Good move," I said. "It sounds like he was her first love. That means a lot to a girl. I'd bet you anything she's over at his place right now."

Claude's eyes widened. "You think?"

"Sure. You could go over there and pick her up, but you'd have to keep coercing her to keep her captive. A few days from now, there's going to be nothing you can do. She'll be an adult."

"I can sue. I may do it. She squirrels out of this tour, it'll cost me millions. I put my own money into this one."

"You can sue an adult for something she did as a kid?" Terry said doubtfully.

"She's an emancipated child. That means she can enter into a contract and be held to it. But you can run into trouble with judges sometimes. They let the kids off the hook out of the misguided feeling that they're not fully responsible for their actions."

"Why did you put your own money into the tour?" Terry asked. "I didn't think you entertainment types *ever* put your own money into projects."

"Profit. Ever heard of it? Return on investment?"

At least he could admit it out loud.

"Look, I've known for a while that Bethany and I were parting ways after this tour. It was my last chance to make a big score. I need something to show for all the years I put into her, all the heartache. My cholesterol level is in the stratosphere. She's killing me, I tell ya."

I stood up from my chair. "Sorry we let you down. We just wanted to explain our side of the story. Good luck."

Terry and I started for the door.

"Whoa! Hold on!" Claude's hands fluttered through the air like overfed pigeons. "I need you now more than ever."

Terry turned to him, hands on her hips. "I thought we were incompetent."

"Yeah, but maybe...maybe it wasn't all your fault she got away."

I shook my head. "Hire someone else. We're done."

His tone turned desperate. "Here's my problem, okay? If word gets out about this latest episode, the insurance company will back out of the tour. To say nothing of the record company, who'll be suing me at the same time I sue her."

Terry gawked at him. "The record company doesn't know about the situation?"

Claude gave a derisive laugh. "I fed them some bull about how we'd staged that whole kidnapping thing. They thought it was brilliant. Gave me some grief about not letting them in on it, but agreed it was great publicity."

I narrowed my eyes at him. "You *didn't* stage it, did you?"

"How would I do that? I didn't know she was going to spin out. And I sure didn't know you two were gonna be there." He was trying hard to persuade us. Maybe too hard. "I made the best of a bad situation afterwards, but I never in my wildest nightmares thought I'd have to deal with this kinda thing, let alone twice in two days."

"There are many reputable investigation firms that can help you," I said, parroting Boatwright. "I can give you the name of one right now: Mickey West and Associates."

"I can't hire the usual goons. It won't work. You two know how to think like her. You got the boyfriend angle. I can't believe I didn't think of it, myself. I didn't know he meant that much to her. Guess I'm kinda clueless, huh?"

Terry looked over at me. "Do we have anything else on the burner, boss?"

I gave her a shrug.

"Okay, we'll do it," Terry said. "Cash up front."

"What? You don't trust me?"

"Your own ward doesn't trust you," I pointed out. "It's not much of a recommendation."

"*Touché.*" Claude spun around in the chair and worked the combination to a safe. He pulled open the door and reached in for a brick of money, and then turned around and tossed it on the desk.

"Five thousand. Count it."

Terry licked her finger and flipped through the hundred-dollar bills. She seemed to be satisfied with the amount. "Okay, where do we start? Write down some addresses that mean something to her."

"Bethany doesn't know addresses. She's gets chauffeured anywhere she wants to go."

"She may be more observant than you give her credit for," I suggested. "She might be able to make her way over to the boyfriend's place. Let's start with that."

Claude opened a file on his computer and pulled up an address for a man named Kyle Hearn.

I jotted it down in my notebook. "Any friends or associates she would turn to?"

"She's doing rehearsals at a sound stage on the Paramount lot. The choreographer's a Chinese *fegallah* named Darius Hu. They're thick as thieves. You know how it is with women and gays."

I made a note of that name as well.

"The only thing is, I called and told him she was indisposed due to female troubles. They cancelled rehearsal for this afternoon."

"What about tomorrow?"

"Yeah, they'll start around ten in the morning. Go talk to Darius and see if you can dig anything up. I'll call afterward and make more excuses."

"Unless we find her today."

"From your lips." Claude shot a finger to the ceiling.

"Tell this Darius person that we're reporters doing a profile on Bethany," Terry said. "We'll say we're there to get background for the article."

"That's good. I'll call and get you a pass onto the lot. Stage number fourteen."

"Now we need to see Bethany's room," Terry said.

"Her wing, you mean. How come you want to see it?"

"Clues."

"Clues?" Claude rose from his desk with a grunt. "Friggin' Nancy and Nancy Drew I've got here."

He led us out of the study and across the living room. Over the stone fireplace was what looked like an original David Hockney painting—a swimming pool in pixilated pastels depicting the fabled Southern California good life. On another wall hung guitars that had doubtless belonged to famous dead musicians. One was a Cadillac red; another was M&M candy blue. I was curious about them, but now was not the time for a trip down memory lane. I kept my silence.

The three of us passed through a kitchen big enough to feed a platoon, decorated in Spanish tile with brushed stainless steel appliances. A Latina in a white uniform shredded lettuce in a colander, watching us as we crossed into a living-and-sitting area on the other side, which was clearly Bethany's domain. The walls here alternated pink and yellow. There were overstuffed couches in a cowhide print, covered with stuffed toys: pigs, bears, bunnies, a giraffe, an elephant, a zebra, and even something that looked like a porcupine.

Posters of every heartthrob you could name hung on the walls above the couches: Ashton Kutchner, Jay-Z, Jared Leto, the Jonas Brothers—all of them signed personally. I guess she could have her choice of boyfriends if Claude ever permitted it.

He directed us to a room off the sitting area. "That's her bedroom. Knock yourselves out." Then he padded back through to the kitchen, leaving us on our own.

We wandered into the bedroom, which was white on virginal white. The four-poster bed was piled with a mountain of baby dolls. Eyelet curtains fluttered on the windows. Terry went to the side of the room and pulled back one of the panels.

"Check it out. Bars on the windows."

The bars were molded in a floral design, but they were still forbidding.

"You think that's to keep people out, or to keep her in?"

"If they don't open from inside, it's a total hazard. She'd be trapped in here if there were a fire."

Terry opened one of the casement windows and then felt around the bars for a release. She didn't find one. She grabbed the bars and shook them. "They don't open."

"Maybe this tendency to run away isn't a new thing."

The closet took up an entire wall. The doors slid open on a walk-in the size of our living room. Multiple rods climbed the walls, stuffed with designer clothes, some still bearing the price tags. I glanced at some of the prices and almost fainted. "If I ever pay six hundred dollars for a T-shirt, shoot me."

"If you ever pay six hundred dollars for a T-shirt, I won't be able to shoot you. I'll be on the floor, dead from shock."

Shelves covered the back wall up to the ceiling, reminding me of the warehouse from *The X-Files*. The shelves held hundreds of pairs of shoes, from slinky little red stilettos, to running shoes with lights, to plastic sunflower sandals. Terry and I began sifting through lingerie drawers.

I held up a leopard print thong. "And if I ever pay two hundred dollars for a thong—"

"I'll nuke you and feed you to the dogs. What are we looking for, anyway?"

"I don't know. See any papers or anything?"

"No, it's all clothes."

After a few more minutes of rummaging around, I turned to leave and came face-to-face with the cook. I stifled a gasp.

"You looking for Miss Bethany?" She kept her voice low.

"Yes. Any idea where she might have gone, Ms...?"

"Lupe." She held out her hand for me to shake. I felt a piece of paper pressed into my palm. Her eyes flicked up to the corner of the closet, then back to mine. "I hear a noise, so I come to see if there is a problem."

"Uh, no problem." Terry came up beside me. "We were just testing the windows. Do they open from the inside?"

Lupe didn't answer, but turned and walked away without another word.

I pretended to be stretching my back, slipping the piece of paper into my front jeans pocket as I looked up into the corner of the closet. There was a tiny camera lens trained directly on us, but I didn't linger on it. Instead, I made a show of turning my head all around the closet.

"Like I said...nothing to see here."

Terry took her cue. "Yeah, let's go."

We walked over to the king-sized bed and ran our hands under the mattress, looking for hidden stash, then opened up the drawers of the bedside tables.

I found an empty prescription drug vial. According to the label, Bethany was supposed to take three tablets daily as per Dr. Marietta Kirby, "for vomiting."

I showed the vial to Terry.

"I didn't know they made pills that could keep you from sticking your finger down your throat," she said.

I stuck the empty vial in my bag, scanning the bedroom for another camera lens. I didn't see one, but that didn't mean it wasn't there. It might have been a nanny cam, hidden behind the unblinking, glass eyes of one of those creepy baby dolls, or secreted into a tiny pinhole in one of the bedposts.

After ten more minutes, we gave up. As we left Bethany's lair, Terry gestured at the couch full of stuffed animals. "If she isn't with the boyfriend, we might try Toys'R'Us."

"Or the Häagen-Dazs factory."

Claude met us at the front door of the mansion. "Find any clues? Her diary, maybe? 'Dear Diary, today I'm gonna go shack up with my boyfriend and give Claude a heart attack.'"

I ignored his schtick. "No such luck. You mentioned a psychiatrist when we spoke on the phone. Could Bethany have gone to him?"

"It's a woman, Marietta Kirby. But she's in Geneva for some kinda conference."

That was the name on the vial in my purse.

"Any chance she'd go see her mother?" Terry asked.

"You mean go to her mother's grave?"

Terry gave me a sideways glance. "Uh, yeah."

"No chance, it's in Nashville. There's no way she'd try to go cross-country. She's got no money and besides, she hated her mother."

Harold dropped us off at the house, depositing our suitcases on the front porch.

"What will the neighbors think?" Terry said, as the limo pulled out of the drive. "Men coming and going at all hours, limos picking us up and dropping us off?"

"We're celebrities?" I wheeled my suitcase to the front door.

"That's better than what I had in mind."

Once inside, I pulled out the piece of paper that Lupe had slipped to me. It was covered with Bethany's signature, written over and over in pink. Her full name, apparently, was Bethany Jo Kopalski.

Terry leaned over my shoulder to look at it "What's that?"

"Looks like Bethany's been practicing her signature."

"Why would she do that?"

"Maybe it's just a teenage thing. You know, writing her name over and over because she's self-obsessed."

"Or maybe someone *else* was practicing her signature."

"You think?"

"I don't know, but the way the cook sneaked it to you, obviously *she* thought there was something funky about it."

"We'll ask Bethany about it if we see her." I stuffed the paper back into my pocket.

"Yeah, *if* we see her. For now, let's go check out the boyfriend."

Kyle Hearn lived a block north of trendy Melrose Avenue in a small, mustard-colored Spanish house with a red-tiled roof. The lawn was green, and the grass had been recently mowed. Sage and succulents bloomed in the garden patch next to the porch. Sheers covered the lower half of the arched windows.

I gestured to the front of the house. "You take the door, and I'll go around back in case they make a break for it. Give me two minutes."

Terry nodded and stood to the side of the door, out of the line of sight of anyone inside.

I went up the driveway past a shiny new, black Lexus SUV with luggage racks on the roof. I came to a white gate that was chest-high, and that's when I heard the sound of toenails hitting the concrete—toenails sprouting from some very large toes.

Two Rottweilers trotted around the corner from the back yard and meandered up to the gate. Their tongues were dripping. Their ribcages poked through their shiny black coats. They appeared very hungry.

I backed away slowly.

They moved forward, closing the gap in front of the gate. They could have easily jumped over it and snared me in their massive jaws.

"Good doggies. Sweet doggies. I'm leaving now. I'm going straight to PETCO. I'll be right back with some Beggin' Strips. Back before you can say 'aarf'..."

I was still cooing promises at the beasts as I rounded the corner. They were no longer visible, but I was sure they could still smell the fear wafting off of me like a dinner invitation.

"Dogs?" Terry whispered when I caught up to her.

I let out my breath. "Big, mean ones with lots of teeth. Ribcages poking through their coats. He keeps 'em hungry."

"I hate him already." She raised her fist to the door and gave it a sharp rap.

We heard heavy footsteps inside. After a few seconds, the door opened, and a man appeared.

Mamma mia. Adonis in jeans.

He was half-dressed, his bare chest tanned and ripped and hairless. My eyes made their way up from his washboard abdomen, past the flat, muscular pecs. Before I could stop myself, I'd envisioned trailing the length of his torso with my tongue, licking him like a salty lollipop.

What is up *with me*, I thought. Must be Boatwright's fault, getting my hormones all stirred up.

His face was rugged yet soulful. Light brown, pillowhead hair. Eyes that were large and golden brown, like a spaniel's.

"Met the dogs?" he said smugly.

Speaking of spaniels.

"Uh, yeah," My voice was a little hoarse from the extra saliva. "They're very friendly. Didn't bark."

"They're trained to attack silently."

"Oh."

"Don't you feed them?" Terry squinted at him. "There are people at the Humane Society who would like to know if you don't."

"They're not starved. I keep 'em trim. Most people let their dogs get fat. It gives them kidney and joint problems. Check the charts on your vet's wall some time. My dogs are perfect the way they are."

Oh, good. He wasn't an animal abuser. I could go back to my illicit fantasy with a clear conscience.

"Anyway, Bethany's not here," he said, closing the door in our faces.

Terry pushed back. "How do you know we're not with the Lottery commission, here to deliver her winnings?"

"Like she needs it."

"Okay, then how'd you know it's about Bethany?"

He gave her a quick smile. "I caught your action on TV. Pretty stupid little stunt, that kidnapping."

"It wasn't a stunt," I told him. "Bethany was running away for real, and we got caught in the middle. Now she's gone again."

"If she keeps running away from you, why don't you take a hint and stop chasing her?"

"She's not running away from *us*," Terry said. "She's running away from her responsibilities. It's gonna get her in trouble."

"Well, I don't know where she is. And if I knew, I wouldn't tell you." He started to close the door again.

Terry was blowing it with this guy. It was time for some of my inimitable tact.

"I'm Kerry McAfee," I said, stepping forward. "This is my sister, Terry. We were hired by Claude Sterling to bring Bethany home, but we're also personally concerned about her. We know she's troubled, and we want to help."

He opened the door a few inches. "If you know Claude, then you know why she's gone. *And* you know why she's troubled."

"He's pretty obnoxious," I agreed, "but we don't know why that would have sent her over the edge all of a sudden. Can we talk to you for a few minutes? We're harmless, I swear."

He looked me over for a second, gauging my sincerity. I gave him a face full of it.

"Okay," he said finally. "Give me a second to put on a shirt."

"Oh, you don't *have* to—" I started to say, but Terry kicked me in the calf. "I mean, if you're more comfortable like that, it doesn't bother us."

He gestured for us to enter. "I'll be right back."

The house was typical Bachelorland. There was a black leather armchair situated in front of a large-screen TV the size of a handball court. A six-foot poster of Bethany was hung on the wall, advertising her shimmering, come-hither sexuality. Some high-end skiing equipment leaned against a corner in the dining area.

Kyle disappeared down a short hallway and came back a few seconds later, pulling on a golf shirt. It mussed his hair some more, but he didn't do anything about it. I guess it was his style. *You want tousled hair?*

I'll gladly come over every morning and tousle it for you.

Terry and I sat on the couch, and he took the large, black armchair, swinging his bare feet up on the coffee table. They were slender and graceful, neatly manicured.

"Can I get you something to drink?" He trained the spaniel peepers on me.

"Thanks, no."

"You get dry on that motorcycle, don't you?"

Not when drool is pooling in my mouth.

"We're all right, thanks anyway. So we heard Claude fired you. Are you still out of work?"

"Yeah, he canned me two weeks ago. I could have gotten other work, but I just didn't feel like it."

"He told us about you and Bethany," Terry added. "That's why we're here. We thought she might have run away because of her crush on you."

He let out a sardonic laugh. "She's not crushed out on me."

"But Claude said—"

"We hooked up for one night. She came after *me* if you want to know. I mean..." His eyes traveled over to the poster. "I had feelings for her; that's why I didn't resist. But for her it was just scratching an itch."

"Why do you say that?" Terry asked.

He looked down, embarrassed. "She told me afterwards she had just wanted to lose her virginity. Anyway, it never happened again."

I wasn't surprised to hear that Bethany would use someone like that and toss him away afterwards, but it was still distasteful to hear. Sometimes I don't like being right about people. "You didn't have any qualms about being her first?"

"I didn't know, I swear. By the time I figured it out, it was too late. She was coming on pretty strong, and I guess I thought...I don't know. I thought I was special to her or something."

"Wow," Terry said, "she really used you, didn't she?"

"Not only that, I got a big payoff for going away. That's why I haven't looked for more work." He twisted his hands together so hard the finger bones showed through his skin. "I'm not feeling so good about things right now."

"Would she come to you if she was in trouble?" Terry asked him.

"Nah, this would be the last place she would come. I don't think she wants to face me again. She barely wanted to face me at the time. She jumped up and locked herself in the bathroom as soon as we were finished." He looked away. "I think she was crying."

We paused a moment to let him have his feelings, and then Terry spoke up again. "Claude told us he caught you at it. Was that just an expression or did he actually walk in on you?"

"No, he confronted Bethany and she confessed. Apparently there's a moral turpitude clause in her contract or something. He could have enforced it if he wanted to, but he let her off with a warning."

"You mean her management contract with Claude?" I was baffled. "Which is he, her guardian or her manager? It seems like a conflict of interest for him to be both."

"How so?"

"I mean, as a parent figure, you're in charge of your kid's moral development, right? If the kid does something bad, like getting involved with drugs or alcohol or shoplifting, how does that nullify the parent's responsibility toward the kid? It doesn't seem right."

"What can you do? It's Hollywood."

Even so, moral turpitude would have to be pretty narrowly defined these days. It couldn't be the use of recreational drugs or a romantic fling. This wasn't the fifties. It was hard to believe, whatever Claude said, that Bethany's career would tank just because she was... *Shamed!*

"Any idea where she would go?" Terry asked him. "What's she gonna do out there with no money?"

"She has money. I gave it to her."

Terry sat bolt upright in her chair. "So you *have* seen her!"

"No, this was before all that other stuff happened. She asked me for a loan."

Terry and I exchanged glances.

"How much?" I asked him.

"A few hundred."

"Why?" Terry still didn't trust him. "Did she tell you she was going to run away?"

He shook his head. "She told me she wanted to go shopping for new shoes."

Shoes she'd never wear, apparently, added to the thousands piled up in her closet, gathering dust until they went out of style. I wondered if Bethany had a shopping compulsion on top of everything else. More likely, the reason she asked for the money was not to add to her collection, but to have ready cash for her getaway.

"She could live a long time in Hollywood with a few hundred," Terry observed. "Especially with her preference for janky motels."

"What?" Kyle laughed. "She's never stayed in anything but five-star hotels. I know; I stayed in plenty of them with her. She loves being pampered. She gets the massages, the in-room pedicures, room service ten times a day."

"Maid service to clean up after the room service," Terry added pointedly.

Kyle tacitly acknowledged the bulimia diagnosis. "She has a lot of stress. I don't know if I could handle it as well as she does."

"She's not handling it at all these days," I said. "She's flipping out for some reason."

He looked thoughtful, but didn't advance any theories on the reasons for Bethany's erratic behavior.

"Do you know why she was so anxious to lay low until she turns eighteen? She told us that was the reason she was running away. She had to stay out of sight until she was an adult."

"For all practical purposes, she's been an adult since she was fourteen. That may be part of the problem."

"But she said she could get control of her life at eighteen," Terry pressed him. "We figured she was talking about her business life. She didn't know much about her own finances, not even her own net worth."

"Let's face it, she's not the brightest bulb in the vanity. Maybe you should talk to her accountants or her lawyers or somebody about that."

I was sure it wouldn't do us any good to approach Bethany's business managers. Besides, Claude would probably want to keep them in the dark about this latest development, causing as little panic as possible in the money machinery of Bethany's life.

"Do you know a man named Paul Fellows?" I ventured.

"Never heard of him. Why?"

"Bethany was outside his apartment when we first met up with her. We thought she might have been going to see him for some reason."

He cocked his head curiously. With the big, honey-brown eyes, he was now firmly in spaniel territory. "You got me."

"Can you give any personal contacts for Bethany?"

"Why don't you ask Claude?"

"The truth?" Terry said. "We don't know if we can believe him. Anyway, yours is the only name he volunteered."

"You must know the people around her," I insisted. "Did she have a teacher on tour?"

"Oh yeah, she did. Glen Adler. Kind of creepy, if you know what I mean."

"Not really. What do you mean?"

"If I had a kid, I wouldn't leave her alone with him."

"Do you know how he can be reached?"

"Phone book?"

"Know where he lives?" Terry asked.

He shook his head again.

This was frustrating. "Do you know anything about Bethany's mother?"

"I know her mother stole money from her. I know Bethany wouldn't speak to her the last few years."

"So she's definitely dead," Terry said.

He gave her a strange look. "Yeah. Why?"

"Just asking."

"What about her father?" An idea was forming in the back of my head, an intuitive hit that I couldn't quite get a hold of. Could Paul Fellows have been connected with the absent father somehow?

"What about him?"

"Bethany claimed she never knew him. Called him 'the bastard.'"

"Never mentioned him to me."

"By the way..." I pulled the paper out of my pocket. "Would you know Bethany's signature if you saw it?"

He glanced at the paper. "She never signed anything around me. Never had to. Somebody was always trailing behind her with a stack of credit cards."

"She told us Claude gives her a weekly allowance of two hundred dollars."

"Yeah, I guess he has to give her *something*. If he never let her touch her own money, she might start making noise."

Terry jumped on that. "Making noise about what?"

"About how he spends it."

"Are you saying he's ripping her off?"

"I'm not saying anything for the record, except... I mean, money doesn't always bring out the best in people."

"Including Claude?"

He held her eyes for a moment, and then nodded ever so slightly.

"Just tell us straight up. Is there any danger in bringing Bethany back to Claude? Does she have anything to fear from him?"

He waved a hand in the air. "No, no. Nothing that sinister. It's just a messed-up situation. I'm glad to be out of it myself." He stood, glancing at the front door.

Terry and I reluctantly took our cue and stood to go.

I tucked the signature paper into my pocket. "Any other ideas you can give us?"

He bit down on his lower lip. "It's just a thought..."

"What? We're open to anything."

"Every time we drove through Hollywood she'd point to things and say, 'I wanna go there! I wanna go there!' Like she was dying to hit all the tourist spots."

"What tourist spots?"

"You know, Ripley's Believe It or Not Museum. The Roosevelt Hotel. The Chinese Theatre."

"She's never been to any of those places?" Terry looked surprised. "She lives a mile away."

"I guess she never got a chance. Claude never stops the car, and Bethany's always on her way somewhere. Rehearsals or recording sessions or whatever. I guess she never gets the chance to go out and play."

I looked over at Terry. "We could try combing some of those spots."

"I don't know. She'd be mobbed if she showed up in them."

"Unless she disguised herself," Kyle said. "She's pretty good with hair and makeup. She's been doing it since she was eight."

erry and I drove to an Internet café on La Brea that provided online access to the clientele. We ordered coffee and then logged onto Glen Adler's Web site. He advertised instruction for child actors and claimed to be certified by the Screen Actors Guild. He appeared to be a small man with pale eyes, thinning brown hair, and a big, bushy mustache. The Web page contained a glowing testimonial from our girl.

"Glen totally taught me everything I know!" Bethany ☺

"That must have taken all of two weeks," Terry quipped. "Hey, I've been wondering. Why did you bring up Bethany's father when we were at Kyle's?"

"I got an intuitive hit out of nowhere that maybe she's looking for her father. I mean, wouldn't you want to know who your daddy was, especially if your mother was dead?"

"A father quest, huh?"

"What if Fellows contacted her and said *he* was her father? And that's why Bethany was going to see him."

"Anybody could step up now and claim to be dad. The mother's not around to confirm or deny."

"Paternity can be proved with DNA."

"Yeah." Terry sipped her mocha latte. "But if that were the case, why the secrecy? And why would Claude and the bodyguards try to prevent her from seeing him?"

"Maybe Claude doesn't want the competition from another father figure. Oh, no." I'd had a horrifying thought. "What if *Claude* is her father?"

Terry choked. "Ewwwww!"

"Can you imagine having a fantasy image of your dad your whole life—like he's George Clooney or something—and it turns out you were sired by *Claude?*"

"I think you're way off with this."

"Why?"

"Because *I'm* the intuitive one, and we both know it. You're too left-brained. And my Spidey senses do not tell me this is about fathers."

Before I could respond, Terry's phone rang in her pocket. She answered and listened for a second; then she grabbed the computer and began searching for something online, the phone between her ear and shoulder.

"Okay," she said excitedly. "What's the address?"

She typed in an URL and brought up a page with a photograph of a Hollywood street.

But it wasn't a photograph. It was a Web-streaming camera at Hollywoodcam.com. The camera captured only a couple a frames per second, so the vehicles in the street appeared to move in and out of the intersection with jerky motions, like toy cars being juiced along an electrical track. On the right was a hotel that resembled the Roosevelt. On the left was a big, red sign. Behind it was a tall building painted with some kind of mural.

"What are we looking at?" I whispered to Terry.

She shushed me then spoke into the phone again. "Yes, I'm there. What am I looking for?"

As we watched the screen, a tiny figure darted out onto the sidewalk, beneath a street sign in the lower left hand corner. The figure waved its arms in the air, jumping up and down. The stop-motion effect of the video gave the impression of a marionette bouncing on a string. Then the marionette bent over and pulled down its pants, aiming its derriere at the street.

On the street a second later, a toy car crashed into the bumper of the one in front of it. The next image showed a toy-car pileup. I could only imagine the din from their toy horns.

The figure finally straightened back up and ran down the sidewalk, ducking into an alley and disappearing from view

I couldn't believe my eyes. "Was that Bethany?"

"Yes!"

"She's mooning people on the street?"

I caught a flash of color nosing out of the alley on the screen. A green Jeep was inching into the traffic and heading west with staticky little movements.

Terry took the phone away from her ear and looked for the return number. "Blocked ID."

"What's she trying to do? Get arrested for indecent exposure?"

"I wouldn't worry about that." Terry chuckled. "I'm sure she was wearing a two-hundred-dollar thong."

At first no one at the café could pinpoint the location of the Webcam. The coffee server and the cashier tried looking at the screen, but couldn't say exactly what they were looking at. Finally, a goateed guy stood up at the back of the room and sauntered over. He was a Hollywood denizen, right down to the square black glasses and vintage seventies clothes.

He immediately came up with the coordinates. "It's just south of Hollywood Boulevard around Highland. Parallel to the Hollywood sign."

"Thanks!" Terry threw down a five on the table. "Have one on us," she told the goateed guy.

We ran outside and hopped on the bike, and Terry jammed into the eastbound traffic. After taking a left onto Highland Avenue, we were mingling with the cars in the intersection we'd seen on the screen, the drivers unaware that they were at that moment streaming worldwide. The famous Hollywood sign rose on our left, only partially obscured by smog. I spotted the red sign I'd seen on the screen, as well as what I'd thought was a mural. It turned out to be an ad for Campari.

Terry pulled into the alley. We parked next to a Dumpster under a *No Parking* sign and then dashed out onto the sidewalk. When we were underneath the street sign, Terry's phone rang again.

She pulled it open and listened, looking up into the sky and waving. "Yeah. You, too." Then she laughed and hung up.

"What? Is she here?"

"No, she's at the Internet Café. She's watching us right now. Apparently she'd followed us there in the first place and got the idea to mess with us via the Webcam."

I gestured at the camera with my fist. "Hey Bethany! This is for you!"

Terry yanked my arm down. "That's no way to act with a client."

"How about the way she's acting? What is her *problem*?"

We rushed back to the Internet Café, but Bethany was long gone. The cashier told us a woman had come in, logged on for a second, and made a phone call, after which she paid up and left.

"What'd she look like?" Terry asked. "I mean, did she resemble anyone famous?"

"Famous?" The cashier looked at a server. The two of them shrugged.

"I guess she looked kind of like Tina Fey," the server said. "She had dark hair, and she was wearing square glasses."

"Okay," I said. "Thanks a lot."

We went out into the street and stood next to the bike, parked at a meter.

"She had a getaway vehicle, a disguise, and several hundred dollars stashed away," I said. "This was all premeditated."

"Guess so." Terry plopped her pink helmet onto the meter, sleeve-buffing the purple flower-power daisy on its side.

"What do we do now? Is there some way to track her location by the phone?"

"Sure, if you have a subpoena from a law enforcement agency."

"So we just keep getting *Punk'd* by her over and over?"

"Let's talk to the teacher," Terry offered. "See if he has some insights."

"Beats waiting around for another stunt, doesn't it?"

"That it does, girly." She opened her phone to make the call. "That it does."

14

Terry devised a clever story to get us a meeting with Glen Adler, the instructor for child actors. She told she had a "special needs" sister who required tutoring. Guess which part I was supposed to play?

"Just be yourself," she told me.

"At least we know he's not harboring our little fugitive. He wouldn't let anyone come over if he was."

We took off for Adler's apartment in Park La Brea, a collection of beige apartment buildings that advertised itself as Art Deco splendor but looked more like an East German housing project. It sprawled over two blocks on West Third Street, just south of The Grove, housing thousands of residents. Terry parked at the curb, and we wandered around the complex until we found Adler's name on an intercom board.

His voice came over the speaker: "Adler. Who is it?"

The man sounded drunk.

"It's Terry McAfee. We spoke on the phone?"

"I know who you are. I looked you up. You're a liar, and I'm not talking to you."

The intercom went dead.

"Dang," Terry said. "I shouldn't have given him our real names." She hit the buzzer again.

"Adler. Who is it?"

"It's Terry and Kerry McAfee, and we would greatly appreciate five minutes of your time."

"I don't talk to liars."

The line went dead. Terry stood there for a moment, stumped. Then she buzzed again.

"Adler. Who is it?"

"UPS," Terry said.

The release buzzed and the bolt clunked. Terry ran to open the glass door, shaking her head in disbelief. "And he's teaching *children*. Scary."

We took the elevator up to the fourth floor. Adler stuck his comb-over out into the hallway. His eyes widened in panic when he saw that we were not wearing brown uniforms, and he slammed the door.

"Liars!" he yelled from inside.

We stood there for a moment, wondering what to do next.

"Forget it," Terry said. "He's not going to talk to us. Let's bounce."

"Give me a chance to sweet-talk him." I stepped up and knocked on the door. "Oh Mr. Adler! Please open the door. We'll only take a moment of your time."

"You kidnapped Bethany!" he shouted.

"No, we didn't. We've been hired for a private matter that your former student would not appreciate us yelling about out here in the hallway."

The door opened on a chain. "What do you want?" His breath carried the rank tang of fermentation.

"Information," I said. "Information that will help your former student."

After a few seconds, he closed the door and took off the chain to let us in. I stepped over the threshold first. "Thank you, Mr. Adler. I understand your jumpiness considering—"

I stopped when I saw the gun pointed at my stomach. Terry gasped and lunged for the door.

"Hold it," Adler growled at her. "One more move and I'll shoot your little doppelgänger here."

We slowly raised our hands in the air. The gun was a pearl-handled .22, a "chick's weapon." But I didn't delude myself that it wasn't lethal just because it was cute. I doubted that Adler had any real expertise with firearms, and that made the situation all the more dangerous. A nervous newbie with a gun can kill you as easily as look at you.

Adler stepped forward to pat me down. I tried to remain calm.

"I don't carry a gun. I'm not licensed to." *Read: I am a good girl who would never break the rules, skip class, talk back to the teacher, that sort of thing.*

"Didn't stop you from kidnapping a girl in broad daylight." The alcohol smell was overpowering up close. The man could start a bonfire with one sneeze.

I watched as he patted Terry down. She cocked one foot on its toe, ready to kick Adler in the groin. I gave her the *Don't* signal with my eyes and she reluctantly lowered her foot to the ground.

"Later," I whispered to her.

"No talking!" Adler motioned in a crazy circle with the gun, causing me to duck. "Over there!" he commanded.

He prodded me into the living room with the gun barrel in my back. There was a large desk next to a chalkboard across the room, hung with a poster of the ABC's: apple, boy, cat. Facing the large desk were four tiny children's writing desks.

Adler gestured to the desks with the gun. "Sit."

"We can't sit in those," Terry protested. "They're for midgets!"

"Do it!"

Terry and I squeezed ourselves into the miniature desks, our legs jammed against the writing boards. Was he going to make us sing the alphabet song before he plugged us?

Adler staggered to the big desk and plopped down into the chair. Looking down on us from his professional perch, he seemed to feel more in control. He laid the gun down next to a rotten apple—a token from a small admirer a long time ago, now crumbling like Delta Dawn's rose. He folded his hands on the desk.

"I want the truth from you two. What are you doing here?"

I started to answer, but he grabbed up a ruler and *whapped* the desk with it. "What's the protocol?"

Huh? Was that like, "What's the frequency, Kenneth?"

I glanced sideways at Terry and she raised her hand a couple of inches. I got the message and raised my hand to be called upon.

Adler pointed to me with the ruler. "Yes?"

"We were hired by Claude Sterling, Bethany's manager."

"I am familiar with Mr. Sterling, as is anyone who's been watching the news lately. Anyone could throw the name around, pretending to be in his employ."

"Listen, Bethany's disappeared—" Terry started to say.

Adler smacked the top of the desk. *Whap!*

Terry quickly raised her left hand. Adler gave her a sanctimonious nod, pointing to her with the ruler.

"Bethany's run away twice in two days. She's under some sort of duress. Sterling doesn't want to call the police again. It would be the end of her upcoming tour and probably the end of her career."

"One meltdown can be explained as a stunt," I explained. "Two meltdowns means the insurance company pulls out of the tour, and Sterling loses his investment. To say nothing of Bethany's earnings."

He snorted to show what he thought of that. "There are things that are more important than *earnings*."

Whenever possible, I try to humor drunks with loaded guns. "Oh, I agree completely. Education is far more important. And I'm sure that you are a *wonderful* teacher—"

Whap!

"Don't you patronize me, young lady. You have no idea who you're dealing with."

"Why don't you tell us, Mr. Adler?" I fully expected him to recite his qualifications, a resume of his educational accomplishments. But it turned out he wasn't talking about himself at all.

"She's a genius," he uttered with a quavering voice.

"Excuse me?" Terry's eyebrows jumped to her hairline. "Who's a genius?"

"Bethany, of course."

Boy, one of these days I'd have to ask him what he'd been drinking. Everclear? Grain alcohol? Whatever it was, it must have packed a punch.

"Are you sure you're feeling all right?" I started to get out of my seat. "Would you like me to make you some coffee?"

Whap! went the ruler. I resumed my seat.

"You have forced your way into my private residence," Adler said. "You will do me the courtesy of hearing me out."

"Sure, sure," Terry said with a winning smile. "We're all ears."

I raised my hand and got the nod. "So you were impressed by Bethany's intellect, Mr. Adler?"

"Astounded might be a better word," he intoned dreamily; then his voice turned bitter. "Sterling, of course, wanted me to stick to the three R's. He was only interested in fulfilling his obligations to the labor board in the most superficial way. But the girl was a magnet for knowledge. She assimilated information like a sponge. Child actors are frequently highly intelligent, sensitive and intuitive—quick to grasp linguistics. But Bethany was something else."

"Was this just your impression, or something more?"

"I've been teaching for three decades." He peered down his red nose at me. "I think my *impression* counts for something. But to confirm it, I gave Bethany the standardized tests. I told Sterling that she was off the charts, and I thought she deserved to know the level of her IQ. But he forbade me to tell her. The next thing I knew, I was fired."

"What reason did he give you?"

"Incompetence."

"He likes that word a lot," Terry said. "You weren't...?" She made a tippling motion with her hand.

His back stiffened. "Certainly not!"

"Just asking."

"It's true I've been drinking lately, but I became horribly depressed after I was let go. It was the opportunity of a lifetime. Most teachers can only dream of having such a gifted student. Bethany has virtually a photographic memory. We covered algebra and geometry in six months. She was doing calculus before I left."

"What was the problem?" I tried to keep the skepticism out of my voice—*Bethany, a genius*? "Claude didn't want her getting too smart?"

"If she *knew* just how intelligent she was, she might develop enough self-esteem to break away from *him*."

"She's going to be eighteen soon," Terry said. "Then she can do anything she wants. She said she's going to fire Claude the first chance she gets. Maybe she'll even give up performing and be a regular person, have some fun in life."

He gave a scornful laugh. "They'll have her lashed to the wheel for as long as she can sing and dance, as long as she can make them money. They will *not* let her go."

"They won't have any choice," I said. "Slavery's illegal in this country. You can't force a person into performing if she doesn't want to."

"Don't underestimate our dear Sterling." Adler's eyes narrowed behind the bifocals. "He hasn't gotten where he is by being a nice fellow."

No, he got where he is by being a schmuck. But that didn't necessarily mean he was an evil, conniving schmuck.

"Bethany keeps giving him the slip," Terry pointed out. "If she was lashed to a wheel, I don't think that would be happening."

Adler leaned into his desk. "Sterling's got a plan, a backup for whatever happens, believe you me. And for my money, you're playing right into his hands."

"We're only trying to find Bethany," I said. "Whatever they work out between them is their business."

"Better watch yourselves. I've had death threats, myself."

Oh, really? Like people holding guns on you while cramming you into midget desks?

In any case, I'd come to the conclusion that Adler had no intention of killing us. He was drunk and despairing, and we'd been the only human beings available for a little idle chitchat, albeit at gunpoint.

I held up my hand.

"Yes?"

"Thank you for your insights, Mr. Adler, but we have another appointment. May we be excused?"

He regarded me for a long moment, and then gave a woebegone nod. Terry and I inched our way out of the tiny desks. I found that my right foot had gone to sleep, and wobbled on painful needles over to Adler's desk, where I pulled the signature paper out of my pocket.

"Can you tell me if this is Bethany's handwriting?"

He peered at the paper through smudged lenses. "It could be."

"Why would she be practicing her own signature?"

"She has difficulty with writing. Neurological problems that interfere with her fine motor control."

"She doesn't have any trouble coordinating her body," Terry said. "She's a great dancer."

"They're different sets of muscle groups, governed by entirely different parts of the brain. Bethany's schoolwork often looked like it was written by a second-grader."

"Do you have any of her papers or anything?" I asked. "I'd like to compare the writing."

He looked down, ashamed. "No, I...I'm afraid I was obliged to sell them in order to support myself."

"Sell them?"

"On eBay."

Terry rolled her eyes all the way back in her head. "Okay, thanks for the info, Mr. Adler." She pushed me toward the door.

"If you see Bethany," he called after us. "Would you tell her...?" He evidently changed his mind, turning his back to us. "Forget it," he whispered, waving us away.

As I was closing the door behind us, I looked back to see Adler standing motionless in the middle of the apartment, staring down the barrel of his pearl-handled gun.

We said nothing all the way to the parking lot. When we reached the bike, I asked Terry what she'd thought of the exchange with Adler. "I mean, do you think there's anything to it?"

"What? That story about how smart Bethany is?"

I nodded.

"Yeah, and I've got a great bridge for sale. The guy's obviously in love with her. He's trying to make it sound like he has some divine mission to give her instruction."

"But what if she's an idiot savant or something? She appears ditzy, but in actuality she's a genius, like Rain Man?"

"Adler's a drunken nut job, five minutes away from cracking completely. He made up that story to rationalize his own failure. Anyway, you've spent time with her. If she were a genius, don't you think we'd have some indication of it?"

I'd thought about that. "She must have memorized our cell phone number while she was plugging in Claude's numbers in the limo. That means she planned this game of cat and mouse in advance. And she managed to give us the slip at the Pink Spot, and then followed us without our knowing it, and pulled that clever little Webcam stunt. I think all of that shows some pretty wily intelligence."

Terry gave me a scorching look but said nothing.

"You've heard of those kids that have been kept in basements?" For some reason, this genius scenario was starting to grow on me. "They have no social skills, and they can barely speak. I don't know why you couldn't get the same result by denying someone intellectual development, keeping her in a mental basement, so to speak. To the whole world she looks dumb, but there's actually a brain in there that's gone unused, like an undeveloped muscle."

"Sorry. I'm not buying."

Oh well, it was worth a try. "Now what? Do we wait for the next call? Hope she moons a cop and gets picked up?"

"I've got an idea." Terry tapped on her head. "She's gotta stay somewhere tonight."

"Yeah, so?"

"So we go home and call all the motels in the area and ask them if a young Tina Fey look-alike checked in using cash."

"Have I ever told you that you're brilliant?"

"And I wasn't even chained in a basement."

"Only because we didn't have one," I said.

*B*ack at the house, I opened the door and immediately heard Lance shrieking. He stood in the living room, a hand to his palpitating heart. "You scared me again!"

"You know, Lance, you might want to lay off the serial killer shows," I suggested, "or the caffeine."

As he crossed the living room to greet us, a line of baby ducks trailed behind, waddling along in his wake.

Terry and I burst out laughing at the sight.

Make way for ducklings and Herman Munster?

"What's up with the babies?" Terry asked. "It looks like you have them on an invisible leash."

"I know. Watch this." Lance proceeded to walk around the room in a large circle. The ducklings fell in line, quacking and hustling on their tiny webbed feet to keep up. Whenever he moved, they moved. Whenever he stopped, they stopped.

"They think I'm their mother." Lance beamed with pride. "They were imprinted with my image as soon as they came out of the eggs. I feed them, I'm bigger than they are...I gotta be Mom!"

Terry threw out her arms and sang, "I gotta be Mom, I gotta be Mom...! Willing to fly...to waddle or die...I got-ta be Mom!"

I applauded her with my tongue in my cheek. "Where are the dogs?" I glanced around for them.

"Oh, they were a little too interested in the ducks so I tied them up in the kitchen."

"Lance, you have to trust them," Terry said. "They're not going to bother your duckies with us here."

"Oh yeah?" He gave her a suspicious squint. "What about the famous food chain?"

"Don't sweat the chain," I said, heading for the kitchen. "I'm going to let them out, and we'll all keep an eye on them till they get used to the little guys. It's the dogs' house, too, you know."

Lance acquiesced unhappily. "If you think it's a good idea."

The pups were whimpering their little hearts out, tied to the leg of the breakfast table. I bent down to unhook their leashes.

"Now, you have to be very good and let the duckies live."

As soon as I let them go they darted out the door, straight for living room.

"They just want to sniff them," I called to Lance, following them out into the living room. "They'll leave them alone after that."

The dogs scampered around Lance's giant feet, nudging the ducky butts with their noses and sniffing like crazy, creating all sorts of squeaking havoc as the ducklings clambered over their mother's cowboy boots in panic.

"They're going to eat them!" Lance cried.

"No, they're not." Terry crouched down to calm the dogs. "They just want to get to know these little home invaders."

We petted the ducks to show Muffy and Paquito that they were new members of the household. After a few minutes of this, we shooed the pups away to give the ducklings some peace. They sat on their haunches at a respectable distance, watching in fascination as the recently hatched water fowl flapped around on their floor.

Terry said, "See, you just have to introduce them properly."

"What are you guys doing here, anyway?" Lance asked. "What happened to your job?"

"Bethany ditched us at the Pink Spot," I told him.

"No offense, but you guys suck as bodyguards."

Terry shrugged. "So we've been told."

"I was going to heat up some cheese pizza," Lance announced. "Anybody hungry?"

"Sure," we answered.

"Coming right up."

He exited the room with the ducklings trailing along behind him. The dogs fell in line behind the toddling brigade; then the whole procession disappeared through the swinging kitchen door.

Terry and I spent the next two hours calling motels in the search for Bethany, but struck out every time. No one had seen a young girl with dark hair and glasses. Not that they were willing to talk about, at least.

"Hope she's not sleeping in her car," Terry said.

"Nah, she's not that crazy. Unless..."

"Unless what?"

"She really *is* crazy, and she's out there in the life. Buying drugs or turning tricks or something."

"No way, Josefina. She's just hiding out. Probably plans to stay disappeared until her eighteenth birthday."

"And we still don't know why that's so important."

"It's obvious. She becomes a legal adult. She makes her own decisions, including dumping Claude."

"Still, there may be more than what's obvious. Let's go online, see what we might have missed."

We huddled around the screen in our computer nook, the dogs on our laps. A search yielded nothing beyond what we already knew. At one point we got sidetracked by the story of Bethany's alleged kidnapping on Smokinggun.com, along with our own mug shots.

In my photo I appeared pale and gaunt, frizz poking out of my head like live wires, mascara smudged under my stunned eyes. I looked like a raccoon backing into a cattle prod.

Terry's was even worse. She glared into the camera, the braided pigtails sticking out at right angles, looking like Pippi Longstocking had grown up to be an ax murderer.

I moaned, burying my face in my hands. "I can't believe this!"

"Coulda been worse," Terry said philosophically.

"How? I have an online *mug shot!*"

"Yeah, but you look way better than Nick Nolte." She pointed to his picture.

"I look better than a sixty-year-old male Medusa on methamphetamine? Great. No cause for concern, then."

"None at all." She gave me a cheery smile.

The phone rang. I got up and checked the caller ID. It was Claude.

"Should we answer?" I was on the fence.

"We have to give him a progress report, don't we?"

"*What* progress?" I snatched up the phone as Terry got on the extension; then I proceeded to give Claude the rundown on where we'd been. I told him about Kyle the boyfriend and Adler the teacher, but omitted any mention of the "dropping trow" incident on the Webcam. No sense in giving the man a heart attack right then and there.

"We thought we saw her in a green Jeep," I said. "Do you know anyone who has a dark green Cherokee?"

There was silence on the line. "What? Did she steal it?"

"Possibly."

"I suppose she could have rented it," Terry offered.

"With *what*?" Claude bellowed. "She doesn't have a driver's license or a credit card! She's running around in a stolen car. What if she gets picked up? I tell ya, my chest is seizing up...the pain...!"

Terry and I looked at each other in alarm.

"Should we call an ambulance?" I whispered.

There was no answer. Suddenly, a throaty moan came through the speaker. *"Ahhhhhhhh!"*

"Claude...?" Terry said. "Speak to us!"

Another long moment passed, and then Claude returned.

"It's okay. It was gas. Look, I'm giving you girls twenty-four hours to find her; then I'll notify the insurance company and the promoters that I'm canceling the tour. I'll lose fifty percent of my investment, but it's better than losing everything."

Hearing him pronounce the end of Bethany's career left me feeling strangely sad. It was, for all intents and purposes, the end of an era.

"Don't worry," Terry assured him. "We'll find her."

"We'll do our best, anyway." I wouldn't make promises we might not be able to keep.

We listened to Claude's labored breathing on the other end of the line, waiting for him to speak. "You girls are my last hope," he said finally; then he cut the connection without another word.

Later that night we stared at the TV, snuggled up with the dogs and the ducks on the couch. In honor of the newborns, we chose a program about South American birds on Animal Planet.

The ducklings quieted every time they heard their jungle brothers squawking or trilling, after which they'd send up a quacking response. It was cute, but I couldn't enjoy it. My brain was overloaded and in danger of crashing. I needed to defragment my mental hard drive with some sleep.

"'Night, Ma, Pa," I said, rising from the couch. "It's Z-time."

"Paramount tomorrow," Terry reminded me. "We'll check out this Darius Whosit, the choreographer."

"Right. And let's see if we can find Fellows's circus show on the lot."

As soon as I lay down on my bed, I was again visited by thoughts of my romantic dilemma, realizing I was no closer to resolving it. Would I get the answer in my dreams by co-starring in some surreal cinematic epic with one of the men who so preoccupied me? Would it be in color or black and white? X-rated or G-rated?

I didn't know a lot about dream interpretation, but I knew this much: If the same guy keeps popping up over and over in your nocturnal visions, the chances are you're in love with him.

Either that or he's some evil conjurer invading your vulnerable nighttime mind like Freddy Kreuger in *Nightmare on Elm Street*.

I shuddered at the thought, then fell asleep and dreamt about baby ducks.

What were baby ducks doing on Elm Street?

16

Paramount Pictures sits at 5555 Melrose Avenue, on the south side of Hollywood, fronted by an elegant stucco arch. I hadn't been there since we visited our dad on the set of a Bill Murray movie when we were kids. Crewmembers aren't usually allowed to invite guests, but it was bring-your-daughter-to-work day so the director let us hang out and watch the shoot. It was a great afternoon—seeing Dad in his element and lunching across the street at Lucy's El Adobe restaurant with the rest of the crew. We felt like real insiders. It was one of my shining memories from childhood.

Getting past the gates of the studio was daunting even before 9/11. You needed your name on a list, a picture ID, and if they were feeling particularly paranoid, a search of your trunk. We didn't have a trunk, and the guard didn't ask to look in the saddlebags, probably on the theory that no self-respecting terrorist would be caught dead on a hot pink Harley. He directed us down a narrow street to Stage 14, and we parked in a free space next to the stage. A sleek-looking black girl in a skimpy costume was dragging on a cigarette outside.

"Can we go in?" Terry motioned to the entrance. "We're here to see Darius."

"Yeah, he'll break in a minute."

Inside, the place was large enough to house a fleet of stealth bombers. At the far end of the warehouse-type structure was a set lit with blinding klieg lights. A slim Chinese man stood on a raised wooden platform, working with a group of muscled young dancers in harem pants whose faces were painted gold. While canned Bethany music blared over speakers, they leaped across the stage in *arabesques*, crashing to the floor and rolling on their bodies before springing back up to their feet to do that head-whipping thing they always do in music videos.

Darius clapped his hands sharply. "What are you, whiplash victims?" He was like a sibilant drill sergeant. "Put your necks into it!"

The dancers whipped their heads side-to-side so violently I almost slipped a disk watching them.

"Better." He clapped again. "Make-up!"

A woman came running, toting a leather shoulder bag.

"I need to see sweat!" Darius said. "How are we supposed to feel the heat? They're crazed temple priests out to ravish the sacrificial virgin!"

The makeup artist grabbed a bottle out of her bag and ran across the stage, giving each dancer a spritz.

"Don't forget, Bethany's going to be sliding down your bodies. We want to see you mingling perspiration."

"Great," Terry whispered to me. "Seven-year-old girls are going to be mingling sweat with little boys after seeing this."

Darius pivoted on his dance shoe. "Hello?" he said, looking us over. "Can I help you?"

Terry approached the stage. "Claude Sterling sent us."

"Ah, yes. From *Elle* magazine? Any news of Her Majesty?"

"She's still out of sorts."

"Too bad. I thought you brought word of her death. Well...there's always tomorrow."

He gave another quick slap of the hands. "Take five!"

The rapacious temple priests slouched off the set, massaging their back muscles.

"Walk this way." Darius stepped down from the platform and headed for an office at the back, his tiny hips rotating in his dance pants as he glided across the concrete floor. "Do you have any idea what she's doing to my schedule?" he complained. "I'll tell you what she's doing. She's *screwing it up.* I could understand if it were drugs or something, but she'd never do anything so interesting."

"She likes whiskey," Terry said in Bethany's defense.

Darius stopped in his tracks. "Really? That's new. Is Miss Thing out on a drinking binge?"

"No," I said, slapping Terry's shoulder. "Don't start rumors."

"I didn't believe you, anyway." Darius pirouetted and minced away again. "I don't have to say that all my bitching is *strictly* off the record, do I? I take it you're doing a fluff piece, anyway. What else is there to do with Bethany? Fluff, fluff, fluff. A dust bunny of a human being."

He led us into a utilitarian office and plopped down behind an oak desk with a miniature Zen garden, a nano-waterfall trickling through rocks into a pool below. Dust motes swam in the light from windows set high in the walls of corrugated metal.

We pulled up a couple of chairs. "I hear those are soothing for your nerves," Terry said, indicating the fountain.

"Darling, Xanax is soothing for your nerves. This is decoration." He reached up with a rod and opened one of the louvered windows above, and then pulled a cigarette out of the desk drawer, lighting it with a match.

"Do all you dancers smoke?" Terry asked him.

"Is the Pope a Nazi? Yes, we smoke. And drink. And occasionally do drugs. But you can't print that either."

"Look," Terry began, "the bit about being reporters...it's not true."

I was a little surprised she'd come clean with Darius so quickly, but I trusted her instincts. She probably knew we weren't fooling him and had decided that honesty was the best way to go.

"Didn't think so." Darius blew the smoke out his nostrils and up towards the window.

"What tipped you?"

"When posing as reporters, don't get your faces all over the news as kidnappers. It's a dead giveaway." He gave us a Cheshire grin. "So what gives? What's the scoop-skinny-dope-dirt-dish?"

"Bethany's disappeared," I told him. "But she's somewhere in Hollywood. She called us on the phone and then ditched us. Looks like she wants to play hide and seek."

"Oh, dear."

"As you can imagine, Claude's about to flip his wig."

"Well, I hope he flips it into an incinerator. Worst toupee I've ever seen. So, how can I be of assistance?"

"We need any leads you can give us," Terry said. "There aren't too many people we can go to. Bethany doesn't have a lot of friends or associates other than Claude."

Darius trilled a laugh. "Yes, Claude's precious, isn't he? He thinks she's a princess he can lock up in a tower, keeping all the dragons and princes at bay. But he's going to lose control of her one day, and then look out. She sued her own mother into an early grave. Imagine what she'll do to poor Claude." He shuddered as he took another drag.

"We read about her mother," I said. "Were you around when that went down?"

"It was gruesome. First Bethany cut her off financially; then she cut her heart out. The woman died alone in a trailer park. Andie Sue was an alcoholic, of course, and a speed freak. But still, it was a terrible way to go."

Terry nodded. "We read that she got tanked and drove over Laurel Canyon."

"Yes, but that didn't kill her. Probably a good thing she *was* drunk. She walked away with nothing more than a broken collarbone."

"This was during all the lawsuit stuff? I asked.

"Yep. You'd think after a close call like that, she'd clean up her act. But I guess she was too far gone. Or maybe, on some level, she really *wanted* to go."

"And Bethany never reconciled with her before she died?"

"No."

"Strange, though," Terry mused. "She talks about her mother in the present tense."

"Does she? How odd." He let a smoke ring drift out of his mouth, widening as it rose. "Maybe because she feels guilty. If she denies her mother's death, she doesn't have to feel responsible for it."

"It's probably a stretch to call her *responsible*." I don't know why I felt the need to defend the girl.

"Is it?" Darius dipped the ember of his cigarette into the Zen waterfall. It sizzled and he tossed the butt into a metal trashcan. "Andie Sue had nothing but her daughter. No money, no friends, no education. She could have brought Bethany up in some backwater, and the girl would have ended up a penniless tramp, but she wanted more for her. She moved here to Los Angeles when Bethany was three, and spent the next decade working two waitress jobs to pay for singing lessons."

"I haven't followed Bethany's career all that closely," I admitted. "Never cared much for her music. When did she actually break out?"

He leaned forward, arms on the desk. "Let's see, she got her first acting job in *The Girls at Our House* at the age of nine, the standout in a cast of five child actors. She sang on one episode, and after that she was off to the races. Two years later she had a gold record. Another two years and she's the queen of pop."

"And as soon as she gets to the top...?" Terry prompted him.

Darius made a hacking motion with his hand. "There goes the umbilical! They were living in Bel Air by that time. And sure, Andie Sue got a little full of herself. Bought herself a breast augmentation and a facelift, and started driving a BMW. But wasn't she entitled to *something* for all her hard work and sacrifice? Didn't she deserve to share in the success?"

"What was the lawsuit about, exactly?"

Darius pushed himself back from the desk, throwing his foot up on the desk to rub an ankle. "Bethany accused Andie Sue of unlawfully appropriating funds that were supposed to be in trust, or something like that. I don't know all the details. But I ask you, if the woman spends all her time on her daughter's career, how's she supposed to survive? She has to live on the income."

"But she's only allowed to take fifteen percent," I said. "Right?"

"Oh who knows? Look, I've got two elderly parents in San Francisco. I give them a third of my income as it is, but I'd love to be able to set them up in *real* style." He gave an embarrassed little eye roll. "I know, the dutiful Asian son. But they worked their fingers to the bone to bring me up and educate me. Isn't it the least I can do to support them when they're too tired and arthritic to keep their produce stand open?"

"Yeah, I know what you mean," Terry said. "Our parents died, but I would have loved to spoil them in their old age."

"Exactly." Darius sighed. "Granted, all of this was before Bethany was quite as successful as she is now, and there have been cases where the parents blew all the money before the kid knew what hit him. Gary Coleman comes to mind. But there was plenty to go around. Miss Bethany just got it into her pretty little head that it was all hers, and too bad for old Mater. The girl's a mindless, selfish little destructo-bot."

"Mindless?" I recalled Adler's claims. "We heard she was a genius."

Darius stared at me for a second, and then threw back his head and howled. "Hoo-*hooooooo!* Genius, Bethany?"

I gave him a weak smile. "That's what we were told."

"Told by whom? *Teen People Magazine?* She has a serviceable voice and a great body. She can dance, but 'genius'? Someone else writes most of her songs. Someone else produces them. Hate to be immodest, but I gave her all her moves."

"No, I don't mean her musical ability." I pressed forward in spite of his reaction. "Is it possible that she's a genius intellectually?"

This time he almost fell off his chair guffawing. "I love you girls. You should go on the road. You're hilarious."

Once he saw I wasn't laughing with him, he stopped and stared at me. "You were serious about that?"

I nodded.

"What have you been smoking?"

"Her on-set teacher told us—"

"Adler? That pathetic little pedophile? He told you she was a genius, and you believed him?"

"He was pretty convincing," I said sheepishly. "He said she aced the standardized tests. She was doing calculus after six months."

"And *he* was doing cocktails after six a.m."

"Oh. So the drinking isn't a recent thing?"

"Hardly."

Terry took a turn at the questions. "Do you have grounds for calling Adler a pedophile?"

"Uh, *yeah*. He was accused of making untoward advances on our little princess."

"By who?"

"By Bethany herself."

"And they believed *her*? She accused *us* of kidnapping her."

"Hmm. I take your point, but I didn't have any trouble believing it. He was gaga over the girl. His wife left him after he went to work for Bethany. He probably called out her name every night in his sleep, poor old thing."

I wasn't sure why, but Darius's conviction that Adler was guilty rubbed me the wrong way. "Was he officially charged with anything?"

"Nooooooooooo. Would Claude want that kind of publicity? Heaven forbid. He merely threatened to ruin him—did ruin him, in fact—by putting out the word that he was unsuitable, though he didn't go into details. Everybody got the idea."

"Everyone Bethany touches seems to come to a bad end."

Darius held up his fingers in a cross. *"Please."*

"No, I was thinking of her mother and the teacher. Also, Claude says she's the reason he has high blood pressure."

"Well, the triple cheeseburgers and fried onion rings don't help."

"What happens if we don't find Bethany in time for her tour?" Terry asked. "Worst case scenario?"

"Oh, the sky will fall for sure." Darius checked his nails. "It'll be the end of civilization as we know it."

"In other words, you wouldn't mind too much," I said.

"I can always go back to being a sales rep for Danskin."

Darius gave us permission to talk to any of the dancers that we wanted to. We spoke to them in our guise as reporters, but they were wise. They knew Bethany was MIA; I could see it on their faces. They all said the same thing: Bethany was a joy to work with, a major talent. A giving and supportive star, not spoiled at all. Blabbity blah blah. These people knew where their bread was buttered, and they weren't about to dish the girl with the butter knife.

Eventually, we gave up and walked out into the searing sunshine to encounter the same scantily clad girl we'd seen on the way in.

"Psssst." She was waving us to a small alley beside the sound stage, a finger over her glossy purple lips. Ever curious, we followed her as she slipped around the corner into the shade of the building.

"I'm Tenesha," she said, pulling out another cigarette. "You're looking for Bethany, aren't you?"

"Yeah, we were hired by her manager to keep an eye on her," Terry told her. "She gave us the slip."

"She was doing a lot of slipping lately, I can tell you that." Tenesha lit her smoke with a tiny red Bic. "She left the stage one day when she was supposed to be napping. I saw her, all covered up in a cap and a scarf."

Terry nudged me. "That's what she was wearing when we saw her at Fellows's apartment."

"Do you know where she was going that day?" I asked Tenesha.

"No, but I saw someone come in with flowers for her when Bill was doing her hair. Bethany read the note, and then she told Bill she had a headache and had to lie down. When he left the dressing room, she snuck out through the back door."

"Did Bill tell you what was in the note?"

"Uh-uh, he wouldn't say. He only said Bethany started tripping when she read it."

"Where's Bill now?" Terry asked. "Is he on the set today?"

"Bethany fired him right after she got back. Said he poked her in the head with a comb, which was a lie. Bill's a total pro."

"Where can we find him?" Terry pressed.

"You might try the commissary." She looked at her watch. "He's got some other job here on the lot. He has coffee there sometimes with his homies."

"And what does he look like?"

"Looks like Prince. The singer."

That should narrow it down. "Thanks a lot," I said. "This might help us find Bethany."

"Personally, I wouldn't care if she jumped in the lake and stayed there," Tenesha said. "But this is a good-paying gig. I need the money."

I gave her a sympathetic smile; then Terry and I went in search of the commissary and a Prince looka-like.

Bill was sitting at a table with three other people, all of them flamboyant and fun looking—probably hair and makeup crew. Our guy was small, but domi-nated the table with a large personality and booming

Jamaican voice. His delicate hands were in constant motion as he talked, simultaneously sipping chocolate milk through a straw.

The Prince comparison was right on. Flowing black Jerry curls, diamond stud earrings, white ruffles at his neck, black pants tucked into high black boots. He looked like one of the Three Musketeers, if they'd come from the islands and had been more *swish* than *swashbuckler*.

He appeared startled when Terry asked to speak to him privately.

"I didn't sleep with your boyfriend, did I? Was it Josh? How was I to know he was your man? He didn't say *no*-ting about no skinny redhead!"

I flipped open my wallet to the investigator's license. "We need some information. Tenesha thought you could help us."

"Ooooooh." He grimaced at my picture. "You know, I could help you with dat hair. Smooth it out, give you some nice highlights. You look like young Julianne Moore when I done wit' you. Much better than *dis*."

"You think that's bad, you should see her mug shot," Terry said.

Bill rose from the table, giving his homies a warning: "You talk about me when I'm gone, I put de hex on you."

They *ooohed* and waved their hands in the air. "Not de *hex*," one of them mocked. "Any-ting but dat!"

He followed us to an empty table with his carton of chocolate milk, mouthing the straw playfully. "I don' know what I can tell you," he said between sips. "I used to do Bethany's hair. We had fun sometimes, but den one day she loss it and went off like an atom bomb."

"We heard she fired you on a whim," Terry said.

He nodded, eyes wide. "She crazy, dat girl."

"Did you see her get a note the day that she was al-legedly kidnapped?"

"Hey, is dere some-ting in dis for me?" he inquired cagily. "Or I jus' tell out of de goodness of my heart?"

"Goodness of your heart," Terry told him. He sat there waiting for something to sweeten the pot. "Un-less you want a baby duck."

He squealed in delight. "Baby duck?"

"We have five."

"Okay, I tell you every-ting. Bethany got a note wit' some flowers dat were delivered for her. She always gettin' flowers and stuff from somebody. Dey don' let her have de candies or nothin' to eat 'cause they might be poison. Jus' t'row all that fabulous chocolate away. Anyway, de flowers came wit' a note, and de note was not from an admirer, I'm tinkin', because she reads it and starts gettin' all excited."

"Yes?" Terry prompted him.

"So I pull her over to de sink to rinse her—I was givin' her streaks—and I start washin' her hair and talkin' and she says, 'Don' talk right now.' So I say, 'Yes missy,' and I rinse. And den I when I'm dryin' her, I look over at de note—" he stopped and gave us a coy smile. "You wanna to know what it say?"

"You want that baby duck?" Terry said.

"I teasin'. It say, 'I have info'mation pe'taining to yo' mother's death. Meet me at some address on Flower Drive.' I don' remember the exact numbers."

My heartbeat sped up. It was Paul Fellows's street! "That's all it said? That's it?"

"Dat's all." He wrapped his full lips around the straw again. "Now when do I get me ducky?"

Besides knowing about the note, Bill also happened to know where *A Night at the Circus* was shooting. After more assurances that we'd deliver the duckling, he directed us to Stage 20.

"Sounds like Bethany was definitely going to see Fellows," I said as we made our way over to the circus set. "Information on her mother's death. What could that be?"

"Maybe her mother's death wasn't a natural one," Terry speculated.

"Why would Bethany care? Obviously she hated her."

"Yeah, but that doesn't mean she wants to see her murdered."

"Whoa! Wait a minute. What if he wasn't going to convey information, but sell it? What if it was blackmail?"

"It's a possibility. But then it would have to be something that implicated Bethany in something, somehow."

"Yes, so...maybe *she* killed her mother!"

"Come *on,* Kerry."

"Why not?"

"It's a big leap from selfish brat to mother-killer."

"Yeah, but it could explain her erratic behavior—matricidal remorse. And maybe Fellows found out about it and put the screws to her!"

"You're veering into *Murder She Wrote* territory, babe."

"I could see it. She's one destructive little kitty. Maybe she went to see mom in her trailer home and flew into a rage. The girl's got a mean right hook. You saw what she did to the bodyguard."

"But Andie Sue died of liver failure, not a beating."

We walked in silence for a moment. Then I realized we had a problem. "Hey, are we gonna tell Lance we gave away one of his offspring in exchange for information?"

"Not yet, he'll freak," Terry said. "Maybe in another couple of weeks he'll be ready to kick them out of the nest."

As we neared the open door of the stage, I began to strategize. If we didn't get a chance to confront Paul Fellows in person, we'd at least make sure he got a look at us. He'd recognize us after the fight on his lawn and the news coverage of the kidnapping. We'd get the message across that we were on to him. If he ran, we could infer consciousness of guilt.

There was a break in the shooting. We looked inside on a replica of a three-ring circus. A sequined woman filed her nails on the back of an elephant decked out in green satin with gold trim. A clown on ten-foot stilts leaned against a wall talking on his cell phone. Small dogs in tutus wagged their tails, waiting for their chance to jump through fiery hoops. And a guy with a giant shovel stooped behind the elephant doing clean-up duty.

My mind automatically supplied the punch line: "What, and give up show business?"

We wandered in as if we belonged and headed for a group around the craft services table where all the food was laid out. This was the best place to locate a crew-member during a break.

The first assistant director saw our entrance and made a beeline for us, his walkie-talkie bumping against his hip as he scurried across the stage. He wore a headset and carried a clipboard.

"Uh-oh," I whispered, watching him approach.

"Let me do the talking," Terry told me.

He swooped down on us. "Help you?"

"Hey," Terry said in a gruff voice. "We're from IATSE."

Smart move, I thought. Nobody messes with Teamsters.

He did a brow-wiping thing. "Oh, good. I was afraid you were from PETA."

He was more afraid of animal rights activists than Teamsters? What wacky times we lived in.

"How can I help you?"

"We need to speak to one of our brethren," Terry told him. "It's a union matter. Is Paul Fellows here?"

"No, he's been off the show for a week. You didn't know that?"

"Oh right, right." She glanced at me sideways. "We'll catch him at home then."

We had turned toward the door, when the director called out from his chair behind the camera.

"Stop!"

Oh no. He was going to have us arrested for trespassing. I acted like I hadn't heard him and kept moving. But the First AD ran up behind me and clamped a hand down on my shoulder. "Could you hold on a minute?"

"It's okay, we're going now—" I started to say.

"Hey you, twins!" The director trotted up. Short, with a backward baseball cap on his head, he looked all of twelve years old.

Terry leaned over to me and whispered, "Now you do the talking."

Typical. She talks us into trouble; I'm supposed to talk us out.

"Who are you?" he demanded.

"We're from the Stuntman's Association," I ad-libbed. "We had some business with Paul Fellows. But he's not here, so—"

"You're stuntwomen?"

"Uh-huh," I answered, mentally crossing my fingers.

"You're just what I need! My girl threw out her back, and they haven't sent me a replacement. What are you, a size six?"

"Thereabouts. A four on a good day. But I don't think—"

"I have one shot left to do while I have the pyrotechnical guys here. I have to pay them for the whole day anyway, so I didn't let them leave. Can one of you stand in?"

Terry stepped up and thumped her chest. "I'm your girl."

I elbowed her in the back. Saying you're from the union in one thing. Volunteering for a stunt you're not qualified for is a completely different matter. One is a relatively harmless lie; the other could land you in traction.

"Ever work with a wire?"

"All the time," Terry said, wriggling away from me.

"This is perfect! And then if you get killed or maimed—" he pointed in my direction, "we have your replacement right here. We won't even have to re-shoot the footage!"

"Ha ha ha." I felt my stomach clenching.

"Get her in wardrobe, stat," the director ordered the first AD, before jogging back to his red canvas chair.

"Power of the spoken word." Terry gave me a triumphal grin. "I said I want to be a stunt person and see what happens? Next stop, NASCAR."

"We'll do the paperwork later, okay?" the first AD said as he hustled her to the dressing room. "You're sure you've done this before?"

"Yeah, yeah," I heard Terry say. "Dozens of times."

I wandered over to the craft services table and stood in line behind some crewmembers who were making themselves sandwiches. I piled a plate with apples, cheese, and chocolate chip cookies. *Miss Big-Shot Stuntwoman isn't getting any eats. Too bad for her.*

A studio guard sat near the open door on a metal folding chair. He looked up from his paperback and smiled at me.

I moved over to chat with him. "Cookie?" I held out my plate.

He declined. "Your sister's doing the stunt?"

"Yep."

He whistled, impressed.

I frowned at him. "What was that for?"

"You'll see."

Oh, boy.

"She wasn't supposed to do it." I leaned back against the wall as I noshed. "She's just filling in. We came here to talk to Paul Fellows, but apparently he's not on the show anymore."

"Not after what happened." The guard shook his head.

"What do you mean? What happened?"

"You didn't hear? His best friend and AA sponsor killed himself. Guy named Larry Benjamin. It hit Paul really hard."

"Oh, how terrible." *And how terribly, terribly interesting.* "When was this?"

"A week ago. Paul was too upset to work after that."

"I can imagine. What drove the man to kill himself?"

"Paul didn't know or wouldn't say. The guy was as mild-mannered as they come. An accountant with a wife, two kids, a good job with a firm in Sherman Oaks. Then one day he goes home and puts a bullet in his head. Just like the song."

I was about to ask him what song he was referring to, when Terry emerged from the dressing room and took my breath away.

She was outfitted in a sequined leotard and feathered headdress. An ostrich plume rose from her behind like a squirrel's tail. Her skinny legs were encased in red fishnet hose, and her long feet were stuffed into pink ballet slippers.

I'll leave it to you to imagine the expression on her face.

"Love the butt feather, sis!"

She shot poison darts at me with her eyes. They attached a wire to the hook poking out the back of Terry's costume, and then, on instructions from the stunt coordinator, she climbed into the mouth of a cannon.

Terry was cannon fodder?

Suddenly everything on the set became deathly still.

"Rolling," said the cameraman.

"Sound," said the soundman.

"*Death in the Air*, scene five, take one," said the clapboard operator.

Death in the Air? *I thought it was supposed to be* A Night at the Circus!

"And...*action!*" said the director.

The pyrotechnical guy lit the fuse.

The cannon exploded in a stage-rattling...

BOOOOM!

Terry screamed, "*Yeeeeeeeaaaahhhhhhhhh!*"

And shot across the stage, thrashing around like live bait at the end of a fishing line. Everyone on the set stared up at her with mouth agape, as if they'd just seen Superman streak by with his hair on fire.

"Cut!" the director said.

I covered my eyes, cringing. *Oh well. I guess they could always call it* Disaster in the Air.

"What are you doing?" he yelled at Terry.

I looked over and saw her swinging across the room, limbs dangling like a rag doll's, her plume pointed at the ceiling.

"What's the problem?" she said, indignant.

"You're supposed to be an aerialist, not someone at the scene of a nuclear explosion! I thought you knew what you were doing!"

"It's been a while," Terry said, spinning in a circle over his head. "I just got a little scared is all."

"Bring her down," the director ordered the wire operator.

Terry made her descent to the floor, pouncing on her hands and feet. Then she stood up and straightened her tail and her fishnets, trying to salvage some dignity. She licked a finger to smooth out her eyebrows.

"Let's do it again," the director said. "This time, try to look like a circus performer shot out of a cannon, instead of a bird shot out of the air. Okay? Position yourself like you're diving into a pool. And no screaming."

"The screaming was involuntary," Terry mumbled, climbing into the mouth of the cannon again. I thought about ducking out, but it was too late. I was going to have to stay and watch.

"Quiet on the set!" said the first AD.

"Rolling!"

"Sound!"

"*Death in the Air*, scene five, take two."

"And...*action!*"

Fire.

BOOOOM!

"*Yeeeeeeeeaaaahhhhhhhhh!*"

Feathered redhead streaking through the air, screaming her brains out, hands pointed over her head and legs bent out to the side like a frog in mid-leap. Gunpowder settled into the open mouths of the cast and crew, who were staring up again, shaking their heads in disbelief.

"Cut!" The director clapped both hands on top of his baseball cap. "Are you out of your mind? What were you trying to do?"

"I was trying to dive," Terry said defensively, twirling around in circles.

"I said *dive,* not do the breast stroke!"

I turned to the guard. "Would you like to go outside for a couple of minutes? That gun powder's giving me a scratchy throat. I'm afraid I'll cough and ruin the shot."

"You couldn't do any worse than your sister."

We slipped out of the sound stage, and he pulled a crumpled cigarette pack out of his front pocket, Marlboro reds. I wondered if he wore bronco boxers like Lance's.

"So...they don't have any idea why this guy Larry Benjamin killed himself?"

He lit the cigarette from a matchbook and took a deep drag. "It's kind of confidential."

I knew the pressure to gossip would overcome him if I said nothing. The entertainment business runs on gossip. And cigarettes too, apparently.

Within moments, he'd folded the matchbook, replaced it in his pocket, and begun filling the conversational vacuum with no further urging from me.

"He used to be a big-name accountant, personal manager to the stars. But he was drinking heavily and doing drugs, and he screwed himself out of his career."

"You think that's why he killed himself? Because of his professional failure?"

"No, that's the strange thing. He'd cleaned himself up. No more booze, no more cocaine. His wife came back to him, and he got a decent job again. I mean, he wasn't driving around in limos with people like Bethany anymore, but—"

If there'd been food in my mouth, I guarantee I would have choked on it. "Bethany?" I managed to say. "The singer?"

"The one and only."

"So this accountant, this Larry Benjamin, he used to work for Bethany?"

"Yeah, he was part of the big lawsuit."

"Oh, I remember. She sued her mother, right?"

"Right, and Larry was with the management company that handled Bethany's finances. He was a witness in the proceedings. I guess it took a lot out of him. That's when he started drinking and using really bad, and after that he got fired by Bethany's people."

What a scoop! I was about to burst, but worked at keeping my voice sympathetic. "That's really sad—" I started to say, and then I heard:

"Action!"

BOOOOOM!

"*Yeeahhhhhhhhhhhhhhh!*"

"*Cutcutcutcutcut!*" the director screamed. "You're fired! Get her off my set!"

I gave the guard a wan smile. "It looks like we're leaving now."

I'd never seen Terry as shaken as she was when she came out of the sound stage. Her eyes were bugging out of her head, darting from side to side as if expecting an ambush around every corner, and her hands trembled like those of a drunk in the end stages of DTs.

"You look like you could use a drink."

She nodded. "Uh-huh."

I offered to drive, and she let me—a rare occurrence. It's her motorcycle and she likes to be up front. But she sat on the back, slumped against the sissy bar, saying nothing the whole way.

I wondered if she'd ever be herself again, or if she'd remain this timorous, frightened little mouse forever.

And I wondered if that would be such a terrible thing.

I cut up from Melrose and took a quick jaunt past Fellows's apartment, mentally reviewing what we'd learned so far: Fellows had quit his job as a stuntman a week previously when his AA friend Larry Benjamin died, and then Fellows tried to contact Bethany. After the Amber Alert snafu we theorized that he left town, based on the stacks of circulars and the overflowing mailbox on the porch. I slowed down in front of his apartment just long enough to point this out to Terry.

"Evidence of flight."

"But what's he running from?"

"That's the mystery, sis."

I cut back down to Melrose as I pondered it. Why would Paul Fellows, a man who took falls for a living and resided in a skeevy Hollywood apartment, have information about the mother of the princess of pop? Could it have been something he learned from his dead accountant friend, who used to work for Bethany as a money manager? And could that information have had something to do with the man's suicide?

After passing La Cienega on Melrose, I pulled over next to the Bodhi Tree, a New Age bookstore and tearoom.

"Let's go get you some soothing chamomile tea."

Terry was aghast. "Normally when a person says 'drink,' you think of something a little stronger. Like straight vodka."

"Sorry. We still have work to do today."

She climbed off the bike reluctantly and followed me inside the old wooden structure. Crystals tinkled in the breeze coming through the open windows. Customers discussed reincarnation in reverent tones. The place smelled of incense and sandalwood and Yoga enthusiasts who didn't believe in polluting their bodies with deodorant. Terry held her nose none too discreetly.

"We'll get a table outside." I pushed her back out through the door.

Once we were seated, we ordered tea and biscuits. Terry leaned back in her chair and looked out at traffic on Melrose, taking a deep breath. "Ahhhh...car exhaust. *This* I can handle."

I started to fill her in on what the guard told me at the circus set—quietly, so as not to disturb those at the tables around us, who were reading or meditating or having out-of-body trips to other dimensions.

"I got some scoop from the security guard while you were, um, doing your stunt."

"Yeah?" Terry was slowly coming back into her own body, revived by the organic wafers.

"Okay, here's the deal. There was an accountant named Larry Benjamin who used to work for Bethany's management company. He got fired for being a drunk, but then got himself all straightened out in AA and eventually became Paul Fellows's sponsor. He got a new job, his wife came back, everything was roses. Then he went home one day and put a bullet in his head, just like the song."

"What song?"

"I don't know."

"Then why bring it up!"

Yep, almost completely back to her old self. "Sorry. So, let's think this through. What do people do in AA?"

"They unburden themselves to the other people in AA. Tell them about their DUIs and sleeping with their friends' spouses and other stuff like that. Afterward, they're supposed to go to the people they've hurt. Make amends."

"All right. So let's say Benjamin the accountant unburdened himself to Fellows. He had something on his conscience, something he knew, or something he'd done while he was working for Bethany's management company. He unloaded his guilt onto the stuntman before offing himself."

Terry's forehead creased in concentration.

"Later," I continued, "the stuntman sends a note to Bethany, offering to tell her something about her mother's death. He could be making amends on behalf of his sponsor the accountant, who's too dead to do it himself. But Bethany and the stuntman don't connect because of the kidnapping incident; then the stuntman himself goes MIA."

"This amends-making is a dicey business," Terry said.

"Amen to that."

"You think the accountant knew how or why Andie Sue died, and he passed that along to the stuntman, who in turn tried to pass it along to Bethany?"

"Bingo."

"We ought to go talk to someone who knew the accountant when he was alive."

"You up to it?"

She nodded bravely. "I think I'm all right now."

"Good girl. Let's go."

I tossed some money on the table to cover the tea, and Terry got up from her chair, heading for the exit through the picket fence surrounding the patio.

When her back was turned, I thought, *What would Terry do in my place?*

I ran up behind her and yelled, "Boom!"

"*Yeeeahhhhhhhh!*"

She jumped three feet in the air. And when she came down to earth, her fists were pounding my head.

"I can't believe you did that!"

I deflected her blows. "Fearless as all get out? Think again!"

A concerned hippie couple watched us from their table on the restaurant deck. The woman wore a peasant dress. The man had long, gray hair and a headband. "What's her damage?" he wanted to know.

"Post traumatic stress disorder," I told him, and then made a dash for the bike before he could recommend a holistic psychotherapist, while Terry continued to pummel me from behind.

It was the beginning of rush hour, which generally lasts from three in the afternoon until eight at night. We made pretty good time, arriving at the professional building on Ventura Boulevard in just under twenty minutes. Wooten and Benjamin, Certified Public Accountants.

The office was understated and professional. Nothing flashy, just a good, solid business-like atmosphere with pastel-colored couches, a glass end table stacked with back issued of *Forbes* and *Money* magazines, and green ivy trailing from a ceramic pot.

A receptionist with an auburn bouffant and half-glasses looked up from her computer. "May I help you?"

"We're investigators. Kerry and Terry McAfee." I showed her my license.

"Yes?"

"Is there someone here who can talk to us about Larry Benjamin?"

She hesitated. "What about him?"

"I know Mr. Benjamin's passed on," I began, taking it slow and sympathetic. "But it's very important that we speak to someone who knew him."

The receptionist's lip quivered, and her eyes welled up instantly. "We *all* knew him. And loved him. He was a good man."

My attention was drawn to someone in the connecting lunchroom. A young, dark-haired woman hovered next to the door, her pony-tailed head craned in our direction. If she was getting coffee, she was doing it at a very awkward angle. I thought she was probably listening instead.

"We're sorry to intrude on your grief," Terry said in an amazing display of sensitivity, "but it's a matter of some urgency. A young woman is missing."

"Young woman?" the receptionist echoed. "Who?"

"I'm sorry, we're not at liberty to say. Maybe we could speak to his former assistant or something?"

The receptionist's gaze moved over to the lunchroom, and then came back to us. "Oh, I don't know if that would be possible."

Smash! Glass broke in the coffee room. All three of us spun around to look.

"Sorry! Dropped the decanter!" the young woman called from inside. "I've got it."

And then she was in motion, parts of her coming into view as she swept up the shards from the lunchroom floor. The receptionist appeared peeved at her clumsiness.

"The incident we'd like to discuss occurred when Mr. Benjamin was still working at Bethany's management company," I explained, keeping my voice loud enough to be audible to the girl in the coffee room. "But he may have confided in someone here about it."

"Larry was very kind and considerate, but he wasn't a social butterfly." She removed her glasses and pulled a tissue from the box on her desk to wipe her eyes. "He worked very hard, didn't spend a lot of time at the water cooler. He kept to himself."

"Had he shown signs of distress?" I asked. "There must have been something, some indication that he was desperately unhappy."

She blew her nose. "None that I saw. I was stunned that he took his life; we all were. But I thought...I assumed his troubles had come back."

"Troubles?"

"You know, the addictions."

"The county always performs autopsies on suicides victims," Terry said. "Did they determine whether he had drugs in his system when he died? Was his death considered at all suspicious?"

The phone jangled.

"Excuse me." The receptionist picked up the receiver and punched the button for an internal line. "Yes, Mr. Wooten?" She glanced up from the desk, and I followed her gaze to a conference room, which was visible through a glass wall. Facing us was a bespectacled man in a white button-down shirt and tie, a phone clamped to the side of his surly face.

"They're asking about Larry's suicide," the receptionist whispered. She suddenly went white, eyes traveling up to our faces. "Very well, Mr. Wooten."

She cleared her throat, hanging up the phone. "I'm sorry, you're going to have to leave now."

"But—but—" I stammered.

"Now." The receptionist pushed her glasses up on her nose to underscore her authority.

Two keys lay on the counter near the door, with pictograms of a man and a woman. Terry grabbed the ladies' room key and ran to the door. "Just need to use the bathroom," she called on her way out.

"Be right back," I said to the receptionist, who had jumped up to protest.

"*Uh-uh-uh!*" she sputtered, unaccustomed to people ignoring her commands.

Out in the hallway, Terry and I ran to the bathroom. She unlocked the door, and we ducked in.

"Now what?"

Terry laid the key on the shelf beneath the mirror. "Now we wait for the girl with the ponytail and the butter fingers, the one who was so interested in what we were saying."

"Brilliant, baby!"

"Elementary, my dear."

Within seconds, a tentative knock came at the door. I opened it, and an exotic young beauty entered with a furtive look in her large, black eyes. She moved to the sink and began washing her hands, hazarding a quick glance over at us. Terry peeked under the stalls to be sure we were alone.

"No one here," she said to the girl. "Is there something you wanted to talk to us about?"

"I wouldn't want anyone to see me talking to you."

I ducked into a stall. Terry did the same. We closed and locked the doors.

"My name's Arya," she said, continuing to wash her hands. "I worked for Ben. He didn't commit suicide. He wouldn't have. He loved his kids too much."

"What do you think happened to him?" Terry asked from the next stall.

There was a loud knock at the door. I held my breath as the water stopped. I heard the rustling of rough brown paper, then the sound of the door opening.

"Arya?" It was the receptionist.

"Yes?"

"Those two redheaded girls...did you see them?"

"They just left."

"You didn't talk to them, did you?"

"I said hello."

"They took our key."

"Here it is." Metal rattled as Arya returned the key to the receptionist.

"If you do see them again, let me know. We have instructions from Mr. Wooten to call security."

"Yes, ma'am."

There was a pause. "Coming?" the older woman said impatiently.

"I just have to do my lipstick."

"Well, I need to get back to the phones."

The door closed again. We waited another few seconds. I was just about to check if she was still there when Arya stepped up to my stall.

"Ben had committed fraud," she whispered through the door. "He couldn't live with what he'd done. He was going to take it to the Accountancy Board. A woman died because of what he did."

My heart began to flutter. "What woman?"

"Bethany's mother. Bethany, the singer. He wanted to tell the truth about what happened, but somebody made sure he couldn't."

Quick, light footsteps, then the door opened again and *whooshed* shut. Arya the Messenger was gone, leaving our minds blown.

A few minutes later Terry and I stood on Ventura Boulevard staring out at rush hour traffic, trying to put it all together.

"So Bethany's mother was defrauded by the money managers," Terry said. "They made it look like she stole the money."

"But why couldn't she get her own lawyers and counter-sue?"

"She did. She lost. She died."

"And Benjamin wanted to tell the truth about the fraud."

"Then *he* died." Terry grinned at me. "We got us a conspiracy, girly."

Badda bump, badda bump, badda bump bump bump!

I jumped a foot in the air before realizing it was the cell phone in Terry's jacket. "Stow that William Tell stuff, wouldja? It almost gave me a heart attack!"

"Serves you right for 'booming' me." She grinned as she pulled the phone out of her pocket. "Hello? Oh hey, Shotanya. We were just there, but we didn't see you. She *did?*"

Terry pumped a fist in the air.

"And you haven't seen her come out again? Okay, do us a huge favor. Keep an eye on the house..." She laughed. "Yes, this *does* make you an honorary private investigator."

She folded up the phone.

"Shotanya saw a middle-aged woman going into Fellows's house, and she's still in there. Mama Fellows has come home!"

"Let's go!" I said, running for the parking lot.

We found Shotanya camped out on the curb across the street from Fellows's apartment building, filing her nails. She looked up at us with a pained expression. "My butt's gone to sleep. Don't think I can get up."

She held up her hands, and we each took an arm, hoisting her up from the curb. "Urrrr*ugggh!*"

"Thanks," she said, rubbing her backside. "Thought you'd never get here."

"Tell us again what you saw," Terry said. "When did this woman go into the house?"

Shotanya squinted in the direction of the apartment building, concentrating. "Musta been around two o'clock."

"That was hours ago," I said. "Why'd you wait so long to call us?"

"Sorry, I had customers to tend to. And I couldn't find your business card."

Terry glanced at her chest. "It wasn't in your cleavage?"

"Yeah, but I lost it when I was working. You know, some men like to—"

"That's okay!" Terry said, waving her hands in the air. "We don't *have* to know how you lost it."

Shotanya shrugged. "Anyway, I thought it was lost, then a couple hours later I found it again, stuck to the back of my leg—"

"Overshare!" I slapped my hands over my ears.

"Just tryin' to tell you what happened. No need to get all pissy. Anyway, I called you as soon as I could."

"Did you happen to see the woman's car?" Terry asked anxiously.

"Came in a cab."

"What'd she look like?"

"White, middle-aged. Couldn't make out features. She wore a black suit and a hat."

"But how could you know she was middle-aged if you couldn't see her features?" Terry wanted to know.

Shotanya did a sassy head wiggle. "I guess I can tell, bein' a astute observer of the human race. That's what you said you lookin' for, right? A middle-aged woman?"

If she'd been expecting to see someone in middle years, she might have projected that image onto the woman she saw, whatever her actual age.

"Was she slim?" I asked. "Overweight?"

"Oh slim, definitely slim. A skinny ass."

Skinny, possibly middle-aged. On the other hand, a suit and hat could be another one of Bethany's disguises.

"Let's go." Terry waved to me, heading for Fellows's apartment.

"Wait!" I stood my ground. "We're going to confront her?"

Terry turned with an annoyed look. "As opposed to what?"

"Watching and waiting."

"You watch and wait. I'm gonna find out what's going on." She stomped away from me.

Shotanya gave me a sly smile. "Looks like she the boss."

"No, she just thinks she is."

I chased after Terry, catching up with her on the porch. She rang the bell, and we waited. When no one answered, she pounded the door.

"Mrs. Fellows!"

I kicked the mounting pile of circulars and bills. "If it *was* Mrs. Fellows who went in the house, wouldn't she have picked up the mail? Maybe Shotanya got it wrong. Maybe she *thought* she saw someone go in here, but it was next door or something."

Terry suddenly got an idea, pulling the notebook out of my jacket pocket.

"What are you going to do?"

She found Fellows's phone number, the one we'd picked it up at the Stuntman's Association. She punched the number into the cell phone, and after a few seconds, the phone began to ring inside the apartment.

No one answered, but I heard a man's voice on an answering machine. *This is Paul Fellows. I'm not here, but if you'll leave your name and...*

When she got the beep, Terry let the machine have it. "Pick up the phone, lady! Pick it up!"

No one did.

"Okay, this is Terry and Kerry McAfee. We'll be back. You're gonna talk to us sooner or later. And it had better be sooner, if you know what's good for you." She left our number and hung up.

"That sounded like a threat," I said.

"I don't like being messed with."

"Yeah, but threatening is *not* the way to win friends and influence people."

"Depends on the people, doesn't it?"

As we headed back to the bike, a horn honked behind us. Shotanya waved through the passenger window of a low-riding Lincoln.

"Let me know when you find her!" she said.

We waved back, and then I turned to Terry. "Okay, what do we do now, girl genius?"

"Watch and wait. Like I said."

"Like *I* said."

"Whatever."

We watched. We waited. We took turns going down to Sunset for coffee. No one came and no one went. Finally, after two hours, we capitulated and headed back home.

Lance's blue Hyundai was in the drive. This time, out of consideration for his highly strung nerves, we rang the doorbell.

We heard the sound of footsteps; then he pulled open the door wearing an apron, ducks and pups arrayed around his big feet. "Why'd you ring the bell? You *live* here."

Terry shrugged at me, and we bent down to greet all the cute little parasites that had taken up residence in our house, petting various furry and feathered heads.

"You find Bethany?" Lance asked.

"Nope," Terry replied.

"Too bad. You guys up for some dinner?"

I was famished. "Sure. What's cookin'?"

"Tofu burgers."

"Mmmm." I feigned enthusiasm as we trailed him into the house.

Terry picked up the phone in the living room to check voicemail. "Hey, we have a message from two o'clock." She listened for a second. "Kerry! Pick up!"

I grabbed the extension and heard an older woman's voice: "This is the person who hired you. I'm sorry, but I'm not who I said I was. I'm not Deirdre Fellows. There *is* no Deirdre Fellows..."

We waited for the rest of her confession, staring agog at one another. Lance swung his head back and forth between us curiously.

"I...they...they put me up to it. They wanted you to—" She stopped abruptly. I heard scuffling noises. "*Oh no!* How did you—?"

She screamed, and the line went dead.

"What on earth?" I pressed the repeat key again and again.

"Let me hear!" Lance said.

Terry gave him a handset. I watched as his eyebrows came together in consternation.

"Save it," she told him.

He punched a button, and then set the phone down in its cradle.

Terry crossed her arms, declaring, "It's a trick."

"I haven't heard a lot of distress calls," Lance said, "but that sounded real."

I scrolled down the ID log. The woman had called from the 323 area code. The name was listed as Paul Fellows. She'd been calling us from the alleged love nest. She was the woman Shotanya saw going into the house.

"What do you think happened?" Lance asked.

"Don't know." I started to call 911. "We'll let the police sort it out."

Terry ripped the phone out of my hand. "No! Let's think about this for a minute."

"What's to think about? The woman was assaulted! She could have been killed!"

"That was hours ago. If she's dead, she's dead. What's the point of calling the cops now?"

"It's their *job* to find people who kill other people!"

"I don't like it." Terry paced the room. "Something's fishy here. Anyway, why jump to the conclusion that she was assaulted?"

"Oh, I don't know. I don't usually *scream bloody murder* when someone gives me a kiss hello."

"It could have been nothing more than tiff," she argued. "He grabbed the phone out of her hand, and she overreacted."

"What's your problem, Terry? Shotanya saw her go in. She didn't see her come out. She didn't come out because she was prevented in such a way as to cause a blood-curdling scream. So now we need to call the cops."

Terry wouldn't budge. "But why would someone kill her?"

"Yeah," Lance said. "Why would somebody kill her?"

"Okay, try this on for size: Paul Fellows persuaded her to play his wife to get us over there to stake out the apartment. She had a change of heart and called us to confess. He walked in on her and stopped her with violence."

"But *why?* What's it all about, Ker? Shotanya didn't say anything about seeing a man going inside."

"Maybe he'd been inside the whole time! Or maybe Shotanya missed it because she had her skirt up over her head!"

"Who's Shotanya?" Lance asked.

"Our prostitute lookout."

"That would explain the skirt remark."

Terry stood in the middle of the room, biting her lip. "What if it's some kind of hoax?"

I reached for the phone. "The police can determine that for themselves."

She held onto the handset, locking eyes with me. "If it is a hoax, we look like idiots."

"Would you want people to ignore it if you were being attacked for fear of looking stupid?"

"Okay, here's another possibility. It's a trap for *us*."

This was getting ridiculous. "What kind of trap? *Who* kind of trap?"

"Someone could be trying to frame us for murder."

We stood there for a moment, doing the situational math.

Finally, I broke the silence. "If we call the police and it's a hoax, we look like fools. But if we go to the apartment and find a dead woman, we look like suspects. Which is worse?"

"But if she *was* killed, we have an alibi for the time of her death," Terry said. "I was being shot out of a cannon, and you were watching."

"No, I had my hands over my eyes."

"There were witnesses that can place us on the Paramount lot and at the Bodhi Tree, and afterward at Benjamin's office," she insisted. "Come on, let's find out what's going on here before we go to the police half-cocked."

There was no point in resisting. Her mind was made up. "If you're wrong and she's really lying there dead, are you gonna admit your bad?"

"We'll cross that bridge if we come to it."

Oh sure. You never quite manage to cross the I-was-wrong bridge with Terry.

"Let's rummmmmmble," Lance said, rising from the couch.

"Oh no." I pushed him back down on the cushions. "If something happens to us, we need you to take care of the critters."

"You know, I think I'm obliged to respond to that call, as an officer of the law. Or at least to report it to the West Hollywood sheriff's station."

"You do and we'll rip you limb from limb!" Terry said. "Jeffrey Dahmer would cry to see what we've done to you!"

Lance crossed his legs and clasped his hands together on his knee. "Okey-dokey then. I'll keep the tofu burgers warm."

It was Sunset, both the boulevard and the hour. Dwindling light was refracted through the smog, layers of gold and magenta bleeding into the purple of twilight above, silhouetting the palm trees. It was just like you see in the picture postcards from La-la Land. If you didn't know better, you could think it was paradise.

Wish you were here with the thong bikinis and the cool convertibles and the dead woman lying in an apartment in Hollywood!

Terry pulled up to the curb next to Fellows's building. We got off the bike and scouted around. There was no one on the street, no friendly faces to be seen. It was eerily devoid of street people and prostitutes.

The window curtains were drawn at Fellows's apartment. I tried the front door, and it opened.

Open doors are not a good thing.

Typically, they mean that someone left in a hurry without bothering to lock up. For example, when there was a dead body they were anxious to get away from.

"After you." I pointed inside.

"Why do I always go first?"

"Because I came out of the womb first. You're still playing catch up."

"Yeah, but you came out ass-first. And you've been ass-backwards ever since."

I crossed my arms over my chest. "How about this? You go because this was all *your* brilliant idea."

"The brilliant ideas always are." She strode over the threshold, and I tailed her into the sparsely furnished apartment.

Against the far wall was a couch in bright orange vinyl that would have fetched a pretty penny at a retro store on Melrose. In front of it sat a driftwood coffee table, drink rings overlapping on its varnished surface. A multicolored rag rug divided the sitting area from the small kitchen, which contained an old-fashioned refrigerator and stove, and a chrome dinette set. On top of the table sat an open can of Chef Boyardee ravioli, growing mold.

"Mrs. Fellows?" Terry called. "Or whatever your name is?"

No answer reached our ears. However, my nose detected a certain odor, the odor of nature taking its course with a rapidly decomposing body. Bacteria bloating the tissue, gases escaping into the atmosphere. The original recycling policy.

"Do you smell something?"

Terry sniffed the air tentatively. "I think so."

A fly buzzed out of the bedroom and into the living room. We watched as it did a few aerial stunts, and then flew out the open door. Probably a real estate agent, going out to spread the word. *Nice neighborhood! Good eats! Great place to raise your maggots!*

"Let's go call the cops." I was already following the fly to the door.

Terry grabbed the back of my shirt. "We have to check out the bedroom."

"No, I think we should leave and call the authorities."

"We have to look."

"You go. I'll be here." I sat down on the couch, mentally transporting myself to a meadow filled with wildflowers and butterflies and warrens full of fluffy bunnies. I have an awesome talent for escapism when necessary.

"Wimp." Terry clomped down the hallway to the bedroom. I saw the light come on.

Seconds later she ran back into the living room. "You were right. We should go." She streaked out the front door.

After that, I had to go look for myself. I steeled myself for whatever was waiting for me in the bedroom.

Had the woman been killed while speaking on our voicemail? And did that make us somehow complicit in her death?

Maybe she didn't die immediately. Maybe she lay there on the floor, hoping for rescue as the lifeblood slowly ebbed out of her. We'd been idiots not to call the police! Cowed by what had happened with the SWATs and all the rest of it, our fear had interfered with the functioning of our (okay, *my*) moral compass.

The blood left my calves and shot straight up to my pounding heart, making it hard to walk. I took little geisha steps down the hallway to the bedroom and peeked inside. A body was sprawled on the bed.

But it wasn't a woman; it was a man.

Paul Fellows lay on his back, eyes open and crossed upward, as if he had tried to focus on the gun pointed directly at his forehead. The blackened bullet hole formed a perfect bull's-eye.

I whispered, "I'm so sorry we called you a pig."

Then I heard heavy footsteps pounding the floor behind me. I knew immediately what that rumbling was. Sure enough, when I turned around there was another automatic weapon pointed at my face.

"Police!" an officer shouted. "You're under arrest."

I'll spare you every procedural detail of our second arrest in one week, except to say that this time I made sure to smooth down my hair and to give the police camera my best Colgate smile. They wouldn't have Ms. Nolte to kick around anymore.

Turns out the police already knew about the demise of Paul Fellows. They'd had a tip from an anonymous caller in the afternoon. The caller claimed to have seen us enter his apartment, followed by the sound of a gunshot. They'd listened to the messages on Fellows's answering machine and heard Terry's not-so-veiled threat. That's when they sent a car to our house to question us.

The car spotted us leaving home and tailed us. When they saw us heading for Fellows's apartment, they called it in, and the crime scene was cleared. We walked right into their hands.

We found ourselves in the company of a couple of high-blood, pressure-afflicted detectives. But these guys were smart. They took us into separate interview rooms to apply the thumbscrews.

I couldn't bring myself to drag Eli out again, so I decided to take my chances and lay everything on the table. It may have been the arrogance of the innocent, but I was convinced there'd be no way to connect us to this murder. Besides, I was dating a homicide detective from Beverly Hills. Surely that would get me some professional courtesy.

Except that Hollywood and Beverly Hills are like oil and water. Maybe it would be best not to bring up my boyfriend in 90210. They'd probably think he was a wuss.

Detective Howard was tall and white and mean, with a muscular build, prematurely gray hair, and eyes like a hungry jackal. Detective Guerra was Latino and small and mean, with a wiry build and the coiled-up energy of a human switchblade.

Guerra leaned against the wall, arms crossed over his chest. He flexed his forearms continually, the ropy muscles straining against his rolled-up cuffs. I decided to try my charm on Howard, who was sitting across from me at the table and seemed less physically threatening.

"You guys saw my license. I'm a private investigator."

"Yeah?" Howard sneered. "Congratulations on being the lowest form of life."

Off to a great start.

"What were you doing in Fellows's apartment?" Guerra asked in a more agreeable tone. Okay, stamp *Good Cop* on his forehead. "We have witnesses that put you outside his place for several days."

"For a legitimate reason."

"Wait," Howard said. "You were read you your rights, correct?"

"I'm familiar with my rights." I tried to telegraph supreme confidence and blamelessness, hoping he wouldn't notice those little beads of sweat popping out on my upper lip.

"You know that you have the right to remain silent?" Howard asked.

"Uh-huh."

"That anything you say can and will be used against you in a court of law?"

"Yes, yes. I know it by heart. So does anyone who has a TV. Anyway, I'm sure they read them to me when they arrested me." I didn't remember whether they had or not. I was too stunned at the time.

He insisted on reciting the Miranda warning all the way through. "You have the right to an attorney. If you cannot afford an attorney, one will be appointed to you at no cost. Do you understand these rights as I have explained them to you?"

I scratched my head. "What was the part about remaining silent?"

They glared at me.

Safe to say that humor wasn't my best weapon here, but it's always my knee-jerk response to terror. And to tell the truth, I was beginning to be terrified.

INTERVIEW TRANSCRIPT
Subject: Kerry Anne McAfee
Det. Howard: Investigating officers detective corporal Dylan Howard and detective sergeant Jamie Guerra.

Subject is female, twenty-five years old. Do you agree that you've been apprised of your rights?

KM: Yes.

Guerra: What were you doing at apartment number three at 1655 Flower Street tonight at 8:00 p.m.?

KM: I'm a private investigator, which contrary to popular belief, is not the lowest form of life. Everyone knows that Barry Manilow fans are the lowest form of life.

Howard: Is that supposed to be a joke or something?

KM: Yes, I was trying to defuse some of the tension in here.

Howard: I'm not tense. Are you tense, Jaime?

Guerra: I'm not tense.

Howard: Looks like you're the only one who's tense, Kerry. How come you're so wound up?

KM: We were outside Fellows's apartment for the past few days because my sister and I had been hired to investigate an extramarital affair.

Guerra: Who hired you?

KM: I'm not supposed to divulge that.

Howard: (inaudible)

KM: Are you getting this, tape recorder? He just said, "And we're not supposed to hit you in a way that leaves a mark." I want to be sure his threats are part of the record.

Howard: Can't you take a joke?

KM: I will if you will.

Guerra: So who hired you? If you're innocent, you know you have nothing to worry about.

KM: A woman calling herself Deirdre Fellows, who said she was the wife of the deceased. She told us her husband had been keeping strange hours and making weak excuses when she couldn't reach him at work. Then a lady friend of Mrs. Fellows's saw him talking with an attractive young woman outside a bar on Sunset Boulevard. She followed them as they went on foot to the corner of Flower Street. She reported this to Mrs. Fellows, who hired us to look into it.

Howard: She suspected Mr. Fellows of having an affair with the young woman in question?

KM: So she said.

Guerra: How did you conduct your investigation?

KM: We located the apartment and ID'd Fellows from a photograph. We staked out the place for three days, waiting for the girl to show.

Guerra: And?

KM: She never did.

Howard: So you assaulted a pop star, just so it wouldn't be a complete waste of time?

KM: We didn't assault her. She jumped in our car, claiming she was in danger. We took her to a motel to figure out what to do next. And you know what happened then.

Howard: Yeah, then you poured liquor down her throat, forced her to watch porno, and did nothing to administer aid when the girl almost choked on her own vomit.

KM: Distort things much? The charges were bogus.

Howard: Yeah, supposedly it was a stunt. That was real cute. We just love it when people abuse the time and resources of dedicated law enforcement personnel to promote a concert tour.

KM: We had nothing to do with that, but they forced us to swear out a statement so we wouldn't be charged with leaving the scene of the crime.

Guerra: Crime?

KM: We hit a car when we left.

Howard: Let's get back to the alleged client. How'd she pay you?

KM: With a money order.

Howard: Anyone can dummy up a money order. You could have done it yourself to make it look like you had a client.

KM: I didn't do that.

Guerra: What was Bethany doing in that neighborhood?

KM: We didn't have time to wonder about it at the time.

Guerra: Well, you've wondered about it since, haven't you? I mean, a guy got shot right at the scene of Bethany's little caper.

KM: Actually, we had begun to suspect that she wasn't in the neighborhood by accident. And we've confirmed a connection between her and the dead man, Paul Fellows.

Howard: What kind of connection?

KM: He contacted her about her deceased mother.

Howard: Do you have any proof of this connection?

KM: It's something we were told in the course of our investigation.

Guerra: Thought you were investigating an extra-marital affair.

KM: The investigation sort of widened.

Howard: We found your camera in Fellows's dead hand. Want to tell us why he had your camera in his hand when he was killed?

KM: Our camera? Oh, no. Look, all I know is that we lost the camera on the front lawn during the dust-up with Bethany. Fellows probably found it in the grass and took it.

Howard: And you went back to get it?

KM: No, we were going to write it off. We thought the police had it.

Howard: We do have it. It's evidence from a murder scene. I don't know if you'd want it back now. It's got blood all over it.

KM: I'm telling you, we had nothing to do with his murder. We were hired to catch him *in flagrante*.

Guerra: Okay, we believe you. We just need the address and phone number of your client.

KM: I don't have that information.

Guerra: Why not?

KM: It appears she wasn't being honest with us. She lied about who she was and about her reasons for hiring us. I realize now it was a setup.

Howard: People sure spend a lot of time and energy setting you up, don't they, Kerry?

KM: Apparently.

Howard: And why would they do that? Why is everyone out to get you? Are you the center of the universe or something?

KM: I don't appreciate the sarcasm.

Howard: I don't appreciate the bulls—t.

KM: It's not bulls—t! Someone called us pretending to be Deirdre Fellows, and it was a lie.

Guerra: How do you know?

Howard: Don't clam up now, Kerry. We were just about to learn why everybody's out to get you. Don't you want us to know why everybody's out to get you? Maybe we can help.

KM: I doubt that seriously.

Guerra: Hey, take it easy on the poor kid. She's trying to cooperate. Kerry, what reason do you have to believe that the woman who hired you wasn't who she said she was?

KM: She left us a voicemail confession this afternoon telling us that.

Guerra: Out of the blue, she calls and tells you she was faking it?

KM: Yes. She said that she had hired us under false pretenses. She was about to tell us why, when all of a sudden—

Guerra: All of a sudden what?

KM: She said something like, "You...here?" Then she screamed for help.

Howard: And?

KM: And that's all she wrote. I mean, said.

Guerra: And did you call 911?

KM: No.

Howard: Want to tell us why not?

KM: My sister talked me out of it.

Howard: Oh, I thought you were going to say the dog ate your phone.

KM: We had our reasons. Number one, the call had come in several hours earlier. Chances were that if it was real, she was already dead.

Howard: Tell me something, Ker. If you were screaming for help, would you want the people who heard you to sit around wondering if it was real? Or would you want them to call the cops?

KM: That's just what I said! Anyway, we were right, weren't we? She wasn't the one who was killed, Fellows was, and she's probably the one who did it. Look, if we had murdered him, why would we go back there, days later?

Guerra: How did you know he'd been dead for days?

KM: It was obvious.

Howard: Like I said, you went back to get your camera.

KM: But you traced the call made to us from the apartment. If we killed him, why would we call ourselves on the phone, knowing you could trace it?

Howard: Maybe you're not all that smart.

KM: Smarter than that, thanks. The call was made by a woman at two o'clock this afternoon. She pretended to be attacked so we'd run over to the apartment and walk straight into the scene. You were there because you got an anonymous tip about the body, also from a woman. You see how nicely it all fits together?

Howard: So if we checked your messages right now, we'd hear the one from that woman?

KM: Yes! Yes you would! Get me a phone.

Guerra: Here it is.

KM: I'm calling voicemail right now. I'm putting in my PIN. Okay, any second. Hey. What's going on? It's gone! Oh no, Lance! What did you do?

Guerra: Lance?

KM: Our dog-sitter. He's not too sharp. He must have erased the message.

Howard: Lance is a professional dog-sitter?

KM: No, he was just doing it as a favor. He's a rookie in the Malibu sheriff's department.

Guerra: A cop? They're pretty sharp, in our experience.

KM: Not this one! He had to take the police qualifying exam eight times. I know chickens smarter than Lance!

Howard: It's time to stop playing games, Kerry. It's time to stop talking about traps and setups and chickens and mystery women. We know there's something you're not telling us.

KM: I've told you more than I should have without a lawyer.

Guerra: You don't need a lawyer, Kerry. You've got us. We'll hear your confession.

KM: Confession? That's it. End of conversation.

Guerra: We can make you talk, you know.

KM: I'd like to know how, short of beating the tar out of me.

Howard: There are all kinds of pressure, Kerry. There's psychological pressure that's completely legal.

KM: Hit me with your best shot.

Howard: You heard her, Jaime. She said, "Hit me."

Guerra: You want to be careful what you say and who you say it around, Kerry. There are Fanilows in every walk of life.

KM: Huh? What are you—?

Howard: A-one, and a-two, and a-three...

Ramos: (sings) Her name was (redacted)...She was (redacted)*...

* Lyrics redacted due to Stiletto Entertainment's apparent objection to the satirical use of a Barry Manilow song as a form of torture. The Author has no wish to become a First Amendment martyr. For the missing words to the song *Copacabana*, please consult one of the approximately 73,500 pages listing them openly on the Internet. – J.C.

Howard: (sings) With yellow (redacted) in her (redacted), and a dress (redacted) (redacted)...

Ramos: (sings) She would (redacted), and dance (redacted)...

Howard: (sings) And while she (re-dact-dact-dact-ed), Tony (re-re-re-dact-ed)...

Ramos: (sings) Across the (re-*dact*-ed)...

Howard: (sings) They worked from (re-*dact*-ed)...

Ramos: (sings) They were (redacted) and they (redacted) (redacted)...

Howard and Ramos: (sing) Who could ask...for... (redacted)?

KM: Stop! Please! This is cruel and unusual punishment! It's unconstitutional!

Guerra: Don't want to hear the rest? Tony gets shot, and Lola drinks herself blind. It's tragic, but beautiful.

KM: No! I'm calling my lawyer right now. And I'm filing a complaint against you guys.

Howard: I wouldn't do that. The deputy chief is the head of Professional Standards. He's a Fanilow, too. We travel to concerts together.

Guerra: I've been to twenty.

Howard: He's a wimp. I've been to thirty-three.

KM: There's no accounting for taste.

Guerra: You need to do some accounting, Kerry!

Howard: Tell us why you killed Fellows!

KM: I didn't do it!

Guerra: Yeah? Your sister has a different story.

KM: Oh, really?

Guerra: She says you pulled the trigger. You killed Paul Fellows. When you realized you left the camera on the scene, you went back to get it so you wouldn't get nailed. She says she's not going to prison for you, Kerry.

KM: (Inaudible)

Howard: We'll let you think about that for a while.

I sat alone in the interrogation room with my head in my hands, dreading what would happen next door with Terry. Knowing her, she'd worked up a good head of steam, sitting there by herself in the windowless interrogation room, being baked by fluorescent lights.

I just hoped she had the intestinal fortitude to withstand the Manilow torture.

INTERVIEW TRANSCRIPT

Subject: Terry Elaine McAfee

Det. Howard: Investigating officers detective corporal Dylan Howard and detective sergeant Jamie Guerra. Subject is female, twenty-five years old. Subject has been read her rights. Do you agree that you've been apprised of your rights?

TM: Yes.

Det. Guerra: What were you doing at apartment number three at 1655 Flower Street this evening at 8:00 p.m.?

TM: None of your f—ing business.

Guerra: Whoa, a tough one.

Howard: Your sister told us you'd be uncooperative.

TM: Yeah?

Guerra: She said you have impulse control problems. That's why you lost it with Paul Fellows. That's why you shot him.

TM: She did not say that.

Guerra: Want to tell us where the gun is, Terry? It'll go better for you if you tell us where the gun is.

TM: If you thought I shot him, you'd be giving me a gunshot residue test.

Howard: We know you're smart enough to wear gloves.

TM: Okay, then. When did I do it?

Guerra: We'll work out a timeline, Terry. Trust us on that. What we'd like to know is why you did it.

TM: Why don't you get my sister to tell you? She seems to have diarrhea of the mouth.

Guerra: We need to hear it from you. Why did you kill Paul Fellows, Terry?

TM: 'Cause he needed killing? Oh, wait. I didn't know the guy from Adam, so that probably wasn't the reason.

Guerra: So it was murder-for-hire. Who hired you, Bethany? Was he blackmailing her?

TM: Do you have *mierda* in your ears, *pendejo?*

Howard: Yeah, your sister told us you were a racist.

TM: I'm not a racist! I have no tolerance for *estupidos*!

Howard: This is your second strike. You'll be an old, dried-out hag by the time you're released from prison. Maybe we could wangle something with the DA if you come clean.

TM: I've had enough. I want to talk to my lawyer. Get me Eli Weintraub. He'll stick this interview up your a—!

Howard: You're going to regret talking to us like that, Terry.

TM: I don't regret anything. I didn't shoot Fellows and you can't prove I did.

Guerra: Your word against your sister's.

TM: You guys are so lame. Let me tell you something. We're twins. We can read each other's minds, okay? So if you're trying to make be believe she pinned it on me, you're totally full of it.

Howard: You can read minds, huh? What's in my mind right now?

TM: I said I can read her mind, not yours. But I'll take a stab at it. You're thinking I'm a scumbag killer.

Howard: Hey, she's pretty good. What else, Terry?

TM: You think I'm a liar.

Guerra: Keep going. We're impressed.

TM: And you think you can pin this on me, but you can't!

Howard: Why not?

TM: Because there's no evidence! There's no motive!

Guerra: We don't need motive, Terry. But we know you're a drug addict.

TM: Was a drug addict. I'm clean now.

Howard: We know you led the police on a slow-speed freeway chase. We know you'll do anything to draw attention to yourself. You're a hothead, a public nuisance, a sociopath. I've seen a lot of them, Terry. I should know.

TM: A sociopath, huh? Well, you're a disgrace to the force. When I get out of here I'm lodging a complaint.

Guerra: You're not getting out of here, Terry. You're going to prison.

TM: Am not.

Howard: Yes, Terry. Your skinny little freckled ass is ours.

TM: Good luck. I could confess right here and you couldn't make it stick.

Guerra: Is that what you want to do, Terry? Get it off your chest? You want to tell us about it?

TM: Fine. I did it!

Howard: Why, Terry?

TM: You're so smart, you figure it out!

Guerra: Where'd you get the gun, Terry? Where is it now?

TM: You want to nail me? Do your own legwork!

Guerra: Thank you for coming clean with us. I'll talk to the DA and see if we can get you some consideration in exchange for the gun.

TM: The DA?

Guerra: About your charge.

TM: Charge? What?

Howard: You just confessed to murder.

TM: I did not! You, you made me say that! I didn't mean it!

Guerra: I'm sure that will carry a lot of weight with the jury.

hey released me without saying why. Just stormed into the interview room, thanked me for my cooperation, and told me I was free to go.

"We'll be in touch," Guerra said.

I was feeling magnanimous now that I was off the hook. "Anything we can do to help in the investigation..."

"You've done plenty," Howard assured me.

"Could you tell my lawyer that I'll wait for him outside when he's done with Terry?"

"You bet." Then he and Howard were gone.

I went to the property window to retrieve my belongings. There was a roly-poly sergeant behind the gate who looked dangerously bored.

"Need my stuff, please. Kerry McAfee."

He checked his list and came back with a tray containing Terry's wallet and watch, as well as the cell phone.

"That's my sister's wallet and watch, but I'll take the phone." I reached for it, but he jerked it away from me.

"Uh-uh, the name is *Terry* McAfee."

"Yeah, but it's my phone. We look just a little bit alike, huh? Maybe they made a mistake and put my phone in her tray."

He opened Terry's wallet and studied at the picture, and then looked back up at me. "Hey, you're identical!"

Terry would have said, *That's why they call us twins, bright boy!* But that wasn't my style, and besides, I didn't want to alienate him. I needed that phone.

"Yes, we *are* identical," I said with my most disarming smile. "That's why every time she does something stupid, I get the blame."

He chuckled and handed me the phone. "I have a brother like that. A real troublemaker?"

"You have no idea."

He retrieved the rest of my stuff and I signed it out.

"Thanks a lot," I said, waving as I left the precinct. "Toodles!"

He leaned out of the window, waving back to me. "Watch out for that troublemaker sister!"

"I do almost nothing else!"

I checked the voicemail while I waited for Eli outside the station. There was nothing from Bethany. I looked at my watch—eleven o'clock. It was dark and chilly. I slapped my arms to keep myself warm and stomped around the porch, nodding at the occasional officer and malefactor coming up the stairs. Finally, Eli came out the front door toting his briefcase.

"Where's Terry?"

He gave me a strained smile. "We have to talk."

He led the way to the parking lot, walking in silence until we got to his Ford LTD. "Have a seat in my office."

I climbed inside and almost gagged. The windows had been closed for hours, sealing in the cigar smoke. It was like sitting in a humidor. "What's going on? Are they holding her for some reason?"

He nipped off the end of a fresh cigar with his teeth, spitting it out the open window. "She confessed."

"*What?*"

He shook his head in disgust. "They pressured her into it. Her resistance was down, what with two arrests in one week. The poor kid started having flashbacks of prison. Plus, she was rambling incoherently, something about being fired from a cannon. I think she's losing it."

I slouched back in my seat. "No, she *was* fired from a cannon. I mean she was *shot* out of a cannon. But she got fired from being shot out of the cannon on account of she kept screaming and spazzing out. And now she has PTSD."

Eli blinked. "You'll explain that to me later."

"This is crazy! When was Fellows killed, do you know?"

"Last couple of days. They don't have an exact time of death."

"Then she couldn't have done it. She's been with me every single minute for the past three days. I'm her alibi!"

"Sorry, sweetheart, but your alibi won't do her any good." He lit the cigar and the aroma of roasting cow pies filled the air. "In fact, they'll be trying real hard to get her to implicate you, too. They'll probably offer her a reduced sentence if she gives them you."

"She'd never do that."

"Oh yeah? She already asked me how much leniency she could expect."

"*What?*"

"Chalk that up to the strain, too."

"Fine. So what are you going to do, use the *I cracked because I was shot out of a cannon* defense?"

"No, more likely the coerced confession defense."

"Can you prove they coerced it?"

"I'll have to look at the transcript. But knowing their record, it's a good possibility."

"I don't believe this. There's absolutely no physical evidence to support the charge. No gun, no gunshot residue—"

"Yeah, but they can probably find some trace evidence of you in the apartment."

"Duh, 'cause we went in and found the body!"

"Okay, so that's what you need to be working on. Who was this Paul Fellows, and who was this woman that allegedly hired you, and why."

"Do me a favor. Don't use the word 'allegedly' when you're talking about our side of the story."

"Sorry. Habit."

"Anyway, I already know quite a bit about Fellows. He was a stuntman and a recovering alcoholic. His AA sponsor was an accountant who worked for Bethany, named Larry Benjamin. The accountant was fired after the big lawsuit between Bethany and her mother, and now it turns out the accountant's dead, too."

"How?"

"An *alleged* suicide."

Eli raised a bushy eyebrow. "Interesting."

"Yeah, a very interesting, stinking case. So it would be nice if we could get Terry out of jail so we can find out where the smell's coming from."

He stared out the windshield a moment. "You think Bethany killed him?"

"I think she can't be ruled out, although I don't have a motive yet."

He took a bracing puff off his stogie. "They'll want to dig up more evidence before they charge Terry. And they can only hold her for forty-eight hours as a suspect." He smiled at me. "Plus, I got an ace in the hole."

"What ace?"

"She was pretty sure she asked for me before she confessed. That'll show up in the transcript. I'll be happy to point out to the DA that she was deprived of counsel."

"Oh, that's good."

"And I checked into those two homicide dicks. They got a bunch of citizen complaints in their files. Considering that the force manages to filter out seventy percent of the complaints before they even *get* to the files, that's saying something. Those two have been cited repeatedly for denying people their rights, beating the crap out of arrests, that sort of thing. If you had to be arrested for murder, you picked the right guys."

"We're getting pretty good at being arrested, all right."

"Don't worry. I'll have her out in no time."

No time? But surely it would take some *time. Maybe even a day or two?*

"Um, how much time exactly? I mean, your best guesstimate."

"Twenty-four hours, tops."

Plenty of time for me to hook up with Boatwright. I rubbed my hands together and bit my lower lip to keep from grinning.

"We'll just have to live with it, won't we?"

Eli gave my arm an encouraging pat. "That's the spirit!"

Please understand—it wasn't that I *wanted* Terry to have to stay in jail overnight. But she did need to learn a lesson about shooting off her mouth. And I did need to hook up with a hottie.

Besides, she had a demonstrated knack for making lifelong friends behind bars. All in all, a perfect solution to the problems at hand.

Eli dropped me off at the bike, and I drove myself home.

Pulling into the driveway of our little cabin was disorienting. I wasn't used to riding the Harley alone, still less coming home to the pups and the house by myself. I couldn't remember the last time it had happened.

I unlocked the door, and the dogs dove at my feet, wriggling in excitement. They finished with my boots and ran out on the porch looking for Terry. They sniffed the air, whimpering for her.

I bent down to pet them. "Crazy other-mama's gotten herself locked up again."

They followed me into the house with highly suspicious looks in their eyes. They probably thought I'd finally snapped and killed her.

"Hey, Lance!" I called out. "Anybody home?"

"In the bathroom! Come here. I want you to come see something."

I pushed open the door to the bathroom and found Lance on the floor next to the tub, which was full of water. The ducklings were paddling around happily, scooping up water in their bills and flapping their feathers excitedly.

"Their first swim," Lance announced proudly. "They took to the water immediately, just like—"

"Ducks?"

"Guess I'll have to install a tub. I've only got a shower stall at my place."

Did that mean he was planning to keep all five birds? I thought Lance was getting a little too attached to these wild creatures, but I let it go. He could deal with the reality of the situation when the ducks got older and louder.

"So, where's Terry?"

"Jail."

"One day they're gonna lock her up and throw away the key."

"I live in hope—I mean, I live in constant fear of that. Have the dogs been fed?"

"Yeah, and there's still some people food left over. Are you hungry?" He started to get up. "I can heat up the tofu."

"No," I lied, pushing him back down. "I got something on the road."

I wasn't up for congealed bean curd.

"Let me know if you change your mind. Got enough for an army."

"Why don't you feed it to Huey, Dewey, and the gang?"

"Good idea!"

The best I've had all day. Maybe all month. I headed out into the living room and sat down on the couch to check voicemail. Two messages, the first from Boatwright.

"Just wanted to say hi in case you're picking up messages. Give me a call when you get a chance. Sorry about the shooting yourself in the foot remark."

Would he be sorry when he learned that that my feet had giant, self-inflicted bullet holes in them right now?

He'd sounded casual, which meant he probably hadn't heard about Terry's arrest. I wasn't looking forward to telling him. You could argue that Terry and I are separate individuals, as different as night and day. But if Aileen Wuornos had a twin, would you necessarily want to date her?

I'm not saying Terry is *technically* a psycho killer, but it certainly couldn't be ruled out in the future.

Beep.

Another message from Boatwright. "I heard Terry's on death row. How about dinner?"

Beep.

Word travels fast on the cop grapevine. Well, he seemed to be taking the situation in stride. Maybe there was hope for Aileen's twin after all. I called his cell phone.

"Hi," I said.

"Have you eaten?"

"Not really. Have you?"

"Nope, I saved myself for you. Order some pizzas, and I'll be right over."

"Um, Lance is still here," I whispered. "I guess the three of us could spend the evening playing a rousing game of Scrabble or something."

"New plan. I'll pick you up, and we'll go out for dinner."

"Sweet."

"Be there in twenty."

I heard the call-waiting click on the line. "Gotta go. It's probably Terry from lockup."

"Give her my best."

"See ya." I clicked over. "How are things in the belly of the beast, you raving lunatic?"

"Hello?" It was a young female.

I knew the voice. "Bethany?"

"I didn't kill him."

"Kill who? Fellows?"

She hung up without another word.

I told Lance that I would be going out for dinner, and asked him not to let Terry know where I was if she called from the hoosegow.

"Only if I don't have to swear. I'm an officer of the law. My word is my bond."

"Whatever."

Then I went up to the loft to change, wondering what to wear. I wanted to look alluring, but that was difficult when I felt like some sort of human football, bouncing in and out of jail, kicked around by a bratty megastar who may or may not have killed someone in cold blood.

I pulled on a low-cut, green silk camisole, highlighting what passes for cleavage in the McAfee household.

I donned some jeans with holes in the knees, revealing my sexy knobby knees. Next I pulled on my special-occasion boots—black leather with pointed toes, spike heels, and a tiny brass buckle on an ankle strap. I topped everything off with a skimpy black leather jacket, perfect for nighttime here in the desert.

I looked at myself in the full-length mirror. Pretty hot, all things considered.

Bethany's voice suddenly came floating back into my mind:

I didn't kill him.

Isn't that exactly what you'd say if you had killed someone? How many murderers have stood over a dead body, bloody knife in hand, proclaiming their innocence? Your sociopath is a strange animal. He can convince himself he's blameless when he knows he's done the deed. He rationalizes it by saying that the victim deserved it, or he represses the inconvenient knowledge of his guilt because it doesn't fit in with his self-image.

I couldn't be guilty. Look at me, I'm such a great guy!

Great guys like Scott Peterson and OJ Simpson.

The doorbell rang. The dogs barked excitedly, as if they understood the momentousness of this occasion—the resolution of the grand romantic dilemma, once and for all.

"Go time," I said to myself in the mirror, yanking down on the camisole so as to enhance the illusion of boobs.

Then I went downstairs to meet my fate.

Boatwright muttered something about ordering pizza from his place then barely spoke another word as he burned rubber back to his bungalow in Beverly Hills. Needless to say, we never got around to ordering the pizza.

Neither did I get a good look at the window treatments. It was dark, but I could make out a flat-screen TV reflecting the slatted light coming through the blinds. I knew the apartment had hardwood floors because I heard myself clomping across them before he swept me up in his arms and carried me under an arched doorway and down the hall to the bedroom.

I detected the odor Lemon Pledge. *Aha! Premeditated sex.* I didn't think Boatwright had been bustling around cleaning like the Swiffer Lady just for the heck of it. He had been expecting company, had known without a doubt he'd get me back to his place.

So I was an easy mark. So what?

At least I'd made him wait for it.

His lips found mine in the dark, pressing hard, and then he snagged my lower lip between his teeth. We passed under another doorway and he tossed me onto the bed.

I bounced and laughed, silly with anticipation.

I could see him in the dim light, unbuttoning his shirt.

And just then—

Badda bump badda bump badda bump bump bump!

"What's that? World War III?"

"Sorry, it's the phone. I have to get it. It could be Terry."

"What if it is?" His frustration was boiling up into anger.

"She might have been released."

I fished the phone out of my jacket pocket and answered. It was Terry, and she sounded ecstatic.

"Kerry, it's me. They let me go. Come and get me."

"Be right there." I closed the phone and looked up at Boatwright meekly. "Another time?"

"Sure." He began to re-fasten his buttons, nearly ripping them off in the process.

"I hope you don't think this wasn't important to me." I stood and straightened my clothes and hair.

"Of course not."

"Good."

"It's just that your sister is *more* important."

I couldn't deny it. That would be a lie. As crazy as she drove me, Terry would always be my priority. For all practical purposes we were a single organism with four arms and four legs. It mattered little that the two of us act like angry cats stuck together in a pillow case most of the time. We were bound for life.

When I didn't answer him, Boatwright let out a sigh. "Let's get moving. I'll give you a ride to the station."

22

The three of us were uncharacteristically quiet on the way back to Beverly Glen. Terry must have sensed the tension between Boatwright and me because she said almost nothing about her time in jail or her release.

He pulled halfway up in the drive to drop us off. Terry thanked him politely and jumped out of the back seat, running up to the house. Once she was inside the door, I turned to Boatwright. "I can't thank you enough for helping out tonight."

"You're welcome."

I sat for a moment, pondering my hands in my lap. "I'm sorry for interrupting our evening."

He gave me a one-shouldered shrug. "These things happen."

"Okay, so..." I leaned over for a kiss. Again, I got the abridged version. A quick brush of the lips. No passion, no promise.

I dejectedly let myself out of the car, waving to him as he backed down the drive. I couldn't escape the feeling that this was the end. But I comforted myself that I'd done the right thing. If I had to pick between a great man and my own sister, the choice was obvious...

"Hey!" I ran down the drive after him. "Wait, I made a big mistake!"

But his windows were closed and it was dark. He didn't see me. I stood at the end of the drive and watched him coast into traffic, my dream drifting away on Mag wheels.

Slowly I turned and dragged myself back to the house.

When I got closer, I perceived a man in the light over the garage. He was leaning back against the wooden door, his arms crossed over his chest. He had a long, lanky frame, unruly blond hair, and a few days' growth of light brown stubble on his jaw. He wore a plain black T-shirt, faded jeans, and sunglasses.

He saw me and smiled. Was that an overlap in his front teeth?

"Kerry?"

"Yes?"

He covered the ground between us in two sweeps of his long legs, tearing off his sunglasses. And there I was, looking into the eyes of Special Agent Dwight Franzen.

"I don't believe it," I said.

"Surprise," he said.

And then he wrapped his arms around me and laid one on me for the books.

23

"Where've you been?" I tried to sound casual as opposed to completely flabbergasted by his unannounced visit. "And what happened to my Eagle Scout?"

He ran a hand through his long, messy hair. "This is the undercover look."

"It's nice. I mean, for a little variety. You look like a movie star."

"Which one?"

"Like the love child of Brad Pitt and Johnny Depp."

He laughed. "I guess that's all right, aside from being biologically impossible. I'm sorry I didn't call. You know the reason, right?"

"Yeah, you were hunting domestic terrorists."

"Actually, I've been transferred to DEA. I'm doing undercover narcotics work."

"What about the terrorists?"

"That's not something I can discuss."

"Gotcha."

"But I thought about you every night. Did you feel me thinking about you?"

Had I dreamt of him every night because he was sending me psychic signals in my sleep? Was this *The FBI Agent on Elm Street?* That was way too creepy to acknowledge, so I shrugged noncommittally.

"I staked out your house this morning. Saw Lance leaving very early," he said with a teasing lilt to his voice.

Franzen had met Lance on one of our recent cases when we pulled a sting with the FBI. Did he think I was getting jiggy with Lance? Couldn't let him think *that.*

"He was dog-sitting. But he stayed over because he hatched some baby ducks in our living room."

"Baby ducks? Is that what he had in the box?"

"Yeah."

"From the way he was handling it, I thought it was a pipe bomb."

I laughed. "Did you speak to him?"

"No. I was afraid he'd drop the box and blow his foot off. Speaking of terrorists, why did your sister run into the house like that?"

"She was just bailed out of jail."

"Why doesn't that surprise me?"

"Maybe you've been reading the papers."

"You made the news again? What happened?"

"It's a long story."

He arched his eyebrows, waiting for me to continue.

"Uh-uh." I made a zipping motion over my lips. "Top secret."

"I guess I deserved that. Let me make it up to you. I have a couple of days free. Can I take you out to dinner?"

"I'm sorry, I'd like to. But we have a murder mystery to solve."

"Isn't that the job of the police?"

"I don't have a lot of faith in them, since they're trying to pin the murder on Terry."

"Did she do it?"

"No!"

"So how long will this take? When can I see you?"

My eyes darted involuntarily to the street, where Boatwright had just driven away. He caught the eye movement and the conflict behind it.

"It's okay. I was gone a long time. I didn't call. You didn't know if I was going to show. But I'm here, now."

"I—"

"Don't tell me I'm not gonna get a chance because I was off doing my bit for God and country?"

Gosh, when he put it like that, it almost made me out to be a lousy American if I didn't sleep with him. Right?

Wrong! said a self-righteous voice in my head.

Oh, for crying out loud! This moral dilemma stuff is too much for me.

I was going to have to give Franzen the boot once and for all. I couldn't stand being torn between two hot, sexy, adorable men.

"See, there's this guy—"

"I figured that out for myself." He said it firmly, but without any jealousy that I could discern. "I saw him kiss you. Do you love him?"

He's asking me about love?

I certainly lusted after Boatwright, but I didn't know if he was HoverRound material.

I split the difference. "Well, I like him a lot."

"And you like me a lot, I can tell." He pointed to his nose. "Sixth sense."

What could I say? The guy sniffed me out. "I do like you. I was very disappointed when you fell off the planet."

"That's all I wanted to hear."

He walked up to me and stood toe-to-toe. I looked up into his eyes and was suddenly very glad I wasn't a drug dealer. I saw an edge, a fierce cast to his features that hadn't been there the last time I saw him. Maybe my Eagle Scout was growing up.

"I won't always be undercover. It's my goal to one day have a normal life."

"What's normal?"

"A daylight existence, with short hair and decent clothes and a girlfriend. Maybe even a fiancé."

"So I just wait for you to show up in the dead of night? Never knowing when you'll appear, or *if* you'll appear?"

"Unfortunately that's the way it has to be for now. Should I give you something to think about in the meantime?"

I nodded, thinking he was going to kiss me again. But then he did something very strange. He closed his eyes and leaned into me, his nose next to my neck. He inhaled as he moved up my neck and past my hair, moving so slowly it was excruciating. Without even touching me, he caused every nerve in my body to tingle and every fine hair on my skin to stand on end, rippling with waves of goosebumps. It was as if I was being manipulated by some strange, shamanic energy.

I felt as if I had just been ravaged, but the guy hadn't even touched me.

He pulled away and opened his eyes.

"I thought...I thought you were going to kiss me."

He smiled and turned, heading down the drive and into the shadows. I didn't know where he had parked his car, or if he had even arrived in one. Next thing I knew, he was gone.

The door opened just as I reached out my hand for the knob, which meant Terry had been spying on us the whole time. She stared at me with her mouth hanging open, waiting for an explanation.

"Hi." I crossed the threshold and started for the kitchen. "Good to have you back."

She followed close behind me. "Who was *that?*"

We passed through the swinging kitchen doors. I set the kettle on the stove for tea. "That was Dwight Franzen."

She swung around as if to get another look at him through the kitchen wall. "No way!"

"I swear."

"But he looked all biker-y."

"He's undercover. Works for the DEA now."

"Wow." She sat down at the table, staring at me astonished, as if I'd just pulled a rabbit out of my hat.

"How'd you get bailed out so early?" I asked casually.

"I wasn't bailed out, they dropped the charges." She shrugged. "They had nothing on me anyway."

"That was Eli's doing?"

"Yeah, turns out the Deputy DA is one of those civil liberties hard-asses who's always on the lookout for police misconduct." She folded her arms over her chest. "Let's talk about *you* for a second. Been doing a little holding out on the man front, sis?"

"Oh yeah. Holding out *plenty*."

"Is he the reason I was left to rot in jail? So you could get your groove on?"

"Of course not. Boatwright was the reason you were left to rot in jail."

"I knew it! You sold me out for sex!"

"I did not sell you out for sex. No sex occurred. And I did everything I could to *keep* you out of jail, short of confessing myself. Why on earth did you say you did it? Have you completely lost your mind?"

"What can I say? They got my blood up. And I didn't really confess, I just sort of challenged them. Then the next thing I know we're in a shouting match and I'm saying, 'Fine! Pin it on me!'"

"And?"

"They pinned it on me."

I had to laugh, no point in crying. I dropped two chamomile tea bags into mugs and poured hot water over them.

"So the DA didn't like their case?"

"He took one look at it and told the detectives to lay off the steroids. Even called them a couple of cowboys, according to Eli."

"If they're cowboys, they sing Barry Manilow in the saddle."

"Huh?"

"They sang 'Copacabana' till I almost confessed to being OJ's 'real' killer." I handed her a mug.

"I gave it up for a lot less."

"Did you really ask them how much leniency you could get if you turned me in?"

"That was just a stalling tactic."

"Uh-huh." I sat at the table while she drank her tea and regaled me with stories from her time in custody. She'd led the other girls in a round of charades, and then a hip-hop sing-along. Apparently, she'd been a real morale booster among the inmates.

I tried to focus on her stories but I was distracted, still tingling from Franzen's Svengali-like trick.

"Do you think they teach mind control at the FBI?" I wondered aloud.

"*Mind control?* What, was Franzen psyching you into doing it with him?"

I waved the question away with my hand. "Let's talk about the case."

"Fine. Where are we with that? Anything new, aside from the fact that you're porking half the law enforcement personnel in the city?"

"I did not pork Franzen!"

"Then what was he doing here? He just popped in unannounced and worked his mojo on you?"

"Okay, I never told you this. Remember that night in Malibu? The tent, Boatwright?"

"How could I forget?"

"Well, Boatwright got called away, and Franzen showed up."

"And that's when you porked him?"

"I have not porked Franzen! How many times do I have to tell you?"

"Look into my eyes and say it. I'll know if you're lying."

"I have not been with either of them, all right? Let's get back to business."

She wagged her spoon at me. "First things first. Okay, so he showed up in Malibu, and then what?"

"We sat out on the sand and talked. And we... kissed."

"How sweet. You kissed under the Malibu moon. How very, very sweet. And now you're torn between the two guys."

"Right."

"Not to worry. I'll tell you who to go out with. Who knows you better than your sister?"

"*I* know me better than my sister."

"I get a vote, don't I?" I didn't respond, but that didn't slow her down a bit. "Boatwright, hands down. He's a total hottie and a man of the world. Franzen's cute, but do you want to go through life saying 'Do it to me, Dwight'?"

"I don't think I'd be saying that in any case."

"It's funny, isn't it?"

"What's funny?"

"You finally decide to go with one guy, and the other guy pops up in your face. See? The universe likes to mess with us."

"I wish you'd get off of this woo-woo universe stuff."

"I'm just sayin'..."

Finally, she let me tell her about the calls I'd had from Bethany and her enigmatic, one-sentence message: *I didn't kill him.*

"That's it?" Terry frowned. "That's all she said?"

"Pretty much."

"So she found out about Fellows's death, clever dickens."

"Found out or shot him herself."

"Nah. Why would she?"

"I don't know. We can't be sure about a motive until we know what the guy was going to tell her about her mother—" The phone rang on the kitchen wall. "It's probably Bethany. Looking for you."

Terry was perplexed. "Why me?"

"She doesn't seem to want to talk to me. She keeps hanging up when I answer." I grabbed the handset and gave it to her.

"Terry McAfee speaking." I heard Bethany's voice coming from the speaker. "We've been so worried about you. We didn't know where you were, or if you were okay."

She listened for a second, and then nodded.

"Okay. Next to the Taiwanese Siamese Twins. But this time, no running, okay?" She hung the phone on the wall and slapped her hands together. "We got her!"

"Siamese twins?"

"She wants to meet us tomorrow morning at Ripley's Believe It or Not Museum."

"Of course. What else would you do with your time if you were a billionaire megastar?"

25

e parked in an eight-dollar, all-day lot on the side street and bought admission tickets to Ripley's Museum. It's in the heart of Hollywood on the boulevard across from Mann's Chinese Theatre, and contains artifacts and oddities from around the world that were collected in the days before TV brought it all right to your living room, before special effects brought everything from aliens to dinosaurs to life on the screen.

They displayed wonders like "The Lip Plate of the Wild Man of Borneo" and "The Five-Legged Calf from Bangladesh." I could imagine visitors in long coat tails and bustles trembling at the sight of the curiosities from the dark side of the earth. Back in the day, it must have been like walking through the looking glass into another dimension.

"Listen, whatever you may think of Bethany, she's still a suspect in Fellows's murder," I cautioned Terry. "This situation has to be handled delicately. We have to get information without spooking her again."

"I still don't believe she killed him," Terry answered. "But I have to agree with you on one thing. She's very easily spooked."

We found Bethany as promised, next to a set of Taiwanese Siamese twins who were floating in formaldehyde. The twins had seen better days, and so had our little runaway. She was floating in her oversized clothes, having gone for an über-goth disguise with a long, dark wig, white pancake makeup, bangs obscuring her face, and black lipstick. She wore thick glasses with magenta lenses.

Bethany stared at the twins as we walked up beside her. "This could have been you."

"We were actually supposed to be triplets," I told her.

She turned to gawk at me. "Really?"

"We found out when we were thirteen. The ultrasound showed that there were originally three fetuses, but Terry subsumed our sister in the womb. That's what happens when you get in her way."

"Not really," Terry said, "although I may pitch it that way to Fox TV."

Bethany giggled, but the laughter was tinged with hysteria. Her eyes looked unfocused and glassy. She stuck her thumb in her mouth to suck, then yanked it out again, examining her own appendage as if it were a foreign object. Finally, she turned her attention back to us.

"But how does that work when it comes to guys? Being identical, I mean. Do guys fall in love with both of you?"

I smirked. "That's never been a problem."

"Why not?"

"The guys may fall for Terry, but she doesn't fall back. Capiche?"

Bethany was utterly intrigued. "Oh, are you one of those abstinence people?" she asked her.

"No, I'm one of those lesbian people."

"Oooooooohhhhh," Bethany put a hand over her mouth, laughing nervously. "Awesome."

"Glad you approve."

"How about you, Kerry?"

"Me? I'm boy crazy."

"Boy *psychotic*," Terry said.

"But if you're straight and you're gay..." Bethany pointed to each of us in turn. "What would the third sister have been?"

"It scares me to think about it." I gave her my sternest adult face. "We have to have a serious talk, Bethany."

"What about?"

"About Paul Fellows. You knew him, didn't you? You were going to see him when we 'rescued' you."

Bethany shook her head slowly. "No, I did not know him, but I *was* going to see him. He said he had information about my mother."

"What information?"

She scoffed. "I don't know, silly. He's dead!"

I signaled to Terry with my eyes—*Help me out, here.*

Terry asked, "How did you know he was dead?"

"I *saw* him."

"You were in his apartment?" I said too quickly. "After he was shot? Or before?"

"Uh-uh," Bethany said in a creepy singsong, wagging her finger at me. "No more questions from you, bad girl."

Okay.

"What do you know about how your mother died?" Terry asked.

"She's *not* dead."

"Yes, she is. I'm sorry, Bethany, but it's better to face it."

"She's *alive*," Bethany insisted. "She lives in a trailer park in Santa Monica."

Now I know she's nuts. A trailer park in Santa Monica?

"Where did you get that idea?" I asked her.

Bethany reached into her shoulder bag and pulled out some newsprint. From the picture of Bat Boy in the upper right-hand corner, I gathered it was the *Weekly World News.*

The headline read: *Bethany's Mother Living in Squalor.* I took the article and scanned it quickly. It alleged that Andie Sue had been spotted begging for change and eating out of Dumpsters. There was a grainy photograph of a woman who vaguely resembled Bethany's mother, shot with a telephoto lens in front of a mobile home. But it could have been any busty blonde with a past.

"You know better than to believe what you read in these rags. They're the same ones that reported you had a sex change operation."

"Believe whatever you want." She grabbed the paper back from me and stuffed it in her purse.

"She's gone, Bethany."

Bethany hung her head and began sniffling. Boy, could this kid ever turn on the waterworks. Terry glared at me like I'd just tossed a kitten into a sink full of water.

"What happened to *delicately*?" she said in a harsh whisper.

She put an arm around Bethany, who rested her head on Terry's shoulder. Heavy mascara ran down the girl's face, marbleizing the porcelain of her cheeks.

"Come on, let's get out of here." I felt crummy for making her cry. "We'll get you some ice cream, okay?"

Bethany perked up immediately at the prospect of a treat, the tears evaporating as quickly as a toddler's.

"Yay!"

"But you're going to keep it down or no dice."

"Oh, I'll keep it down. I've been wanting to do that for *years*."

We bought cones at Baskin Robbins, and then shopped for tchotchkes in the boulevard tourist spots, wandering around like three regular girlfriends out to see the sights. It was part of our plan to make Bethany comfortable so that she would confide in us. Bethany bought a miniature California license plate with her name on it.

"Look! They have my name."

"It's a very popular now," Terry told her. "Because of you."

"Sweet." She plunked the souvenir in her purse as we wandered back out onto the sunlit boulevard.

The license plate reminded me of the paper with Bethany's signature. I dug it out of my shoulder bag and held it out for her to see. "Hey Bethany, have you been practicing your signature?"

"Huh?" She stared at the piece of paper. "Oh, I could have been."

"You could have been, or you were?"

She licked her peppermint and chocolate chip ice cream. "Sometimes I go, like, spacey, and I do things I don't remember." Her eyebrows came together over the adorable nose. "It's like when I cut myself."

She pulled up her sleeve to display bloody slices all over her forearm. Some of them were scabbing. All of them were fresh.

I grabbed her hand, clutching her by the wrist. "Bethany, honey, you can't keep hurting yourself like this."

"Doesn't hurt," she said vacantly, jerking her hand away.

"Have you seen a doctor about it?" Terry asked, her face pained.

"Uh, *yeah*. But like, the only treatment for it is some brain drug."

This took me aback. "Brain drug? You mean an antidepressant?"

"Yeah." She twisted her mouth as if tasting something foul. "I won't take it."

Terry shot me a sideways look. "The doctor prescribed it, but you won't take it?"

"It made me feel funny." Bethany did a little hop and mimed tossing pills down the tubes. "I threw it down the toilet."

"When did you do that?" I was really trying not to sound too anxious.

"A few weeks ago, I guess."

Oh, man. Going off her meds had probably precipitated this whole episode. I didn't know about the wisdom of putting her on them in the first place, but I did know you weren't supposed to stop taking those drugs cold turkey. It could lead to seizures and who knew what else.

Bethany leaned in and whispered, "They think I don't know what they're up to, but I do. They're following me right now, everywhere I go. They are *out there*."

That was the "what else." Paranoid delusions.

Bethany backed up a step and glanced over her shoulder. "I'm not as stupid as they think. I'm smart. Glen *told* me. I'm *smart!*"

The girl was decompensating before our very eyes. The bars on the windows and the erratic behavior and the running away had all come down to this:

The princess of pop was plumb *loca*.

"Come on!" Bethany said, brightening suddenly. "I want to look at the stars!"

We followed her as she skipped down the Walk of Fame. It was a strip of black and pink granite squares with brass plaques celebrating famous actors, musicians, movie directors, and radio stars, along with a few hard-to-categorize people with dubious talents. Paris Hilton would probably be here one day, and how would we explain that to future generations?

Well, son, she didn't have any talent to speak of, but she was a famous personality. No, she didn't really have any personality either, but every time you turned on the TV or opened a magazine, there she was and so we honor her here because...because her publicist paid ten thousand dollars for a star.

As Bethany studied the plaques, I pulled Terry aside.

"She's supposed to be on some kind of psychotropic drug and she stopped taking it. This is not good."

"No." Terry looked glum. "Not good at all."

"Those drugs do serious things to your brain chemistry. If you go off them all at once, you can have real problems."

"You know what's strange? Claude didn't mention any medications."

"Maybe he doesn't know about them."

"The guy has a security camera in her closet. He's got eyes all over the house so he can make sure she's not cutting herself or running away. He knows, trust me."

We were interrupted by Bethany's squealing a few feet away.

"Marlon Brando! Who's that?"

"We'll tell you later," Terry said. "He takes some explaining."

Bethany hopscotched over the names in bronze. "Ronald Reagan! Wasn't he the president or something?"

"Yep," I said. "Pretty recently, in fact."

"Mickey Rooney! Who's that?"

"He's even harder to explain than Marlon Brando."

We moved over to the prints in front of the Chinese Theatre, sticking our feet into the cement molds.

"They're like little elf's feet!" Bethany was enthralled. "Teeny tiny little movie stars."

"Hollywood stands on the shoulders of those elves," I said. "Look, here's Cary Grant."

Bethany looked down at Cary's smallish footprints. "Who was he?"

Terry took at stab at it. "He was the best, the coolest. A totally handsome, debonair guy who made movies with Katherine Hepburn, among others."

"Who's she?"

I put an arm around her shoulders. "Tell you what. We'll get some DVDs later and show you who these people are. How would that be?"

Terry and I had grown up watching black and white movies with our parents and could probably teach a pretty decent course in classic films.

"But I won't have time once I start rehearsals." Bethany lapped at her ice cream cone.

"We may be coming on the road with you." It was a bald-faced lie—I didn't think Bethany was going anywhere except to a psych ward for a nice long rest, but I wanted to keep her with us emotionally.

"You can go with me in the private jet!" Bethany was jumping for joy. "It's a Gulfstream. You'll love it!"

"Bethany," I began, "we *want* to go on tour with you. We think it would be a lot of fun. But nobody's going on tour as long as you're out here on your own. We want to help you resolve whatever's bothering you, but you have to *help* us help you, okay?"

She made a face, but acquiesced with a small nod.

"Why have you been running away?" I asked, pressing my advantage. "Are you looking for your mother?"

"No. I want to see her, but I'm kinda scared to after everything that happened." She gave us a hopeful smile. "Would you go see her for me?"

"Why?" Terry asked. "What would you want us to say to her if we could find her?"

Bethany looked down at her feet. "That I'm sorry. About the lawsuit and everything. I was a stupid kid."

"I'm sure she knows you're sorry," Terry said, "wherever she is."

I took over the questions again. "What about your father? Have you been looking for him?"

"How could I? I don't even know him."

"If you did meet him, what would you want to say to him?"

Bethany looked up at the sky, considering it. "How about—*Eat lead, creep!*" She broke into a fit of giggling.

Terry and I swapped worried glances.

Bethany spotted a photo kiosk and pointed. "Over there! I want my picture taken!"

I started to object but she was already running towards the cameraman who, for five bucks, would take your picture with Marilyn Monroe and Elvis lookalikes. The actors didn't look much like their impersonees, but the hair and costumes were convincing at a distance.

I paid for a shot of the five of us—Bethany in the middle, her arms around me and Terry, Elvis and Marilyn vamping on the outside.

The photographer was a very large black man. "Smile!" he said.

We did. But we wouldn't be smiling much longer.

"Hey, you know who you look like...?" He peered out from behind his camera. "You look a lot like Bethany!"

"That stupid ho'?" Bethany giggled. "You know who you look like? Biggie Smalls."

"No, you really do look like Bethany. It's something about your eyes."

Uh-oh. I ran to him, whipping the Polaroid out of his hand. All around us were tourists from the Midwest, Europe, Japan, and probably Antarctica. If they spotted our little superstar we'd be mobbed in a second.

"Let's go," I said, waving the photo in the air.

"You sure you're not Bethany?" the cameraman said, moving in closer.

"Wrong!" Terry said, hustling Bethany away.

"Hey, I know who you are! You're the kidnappers. Hey, wait up!"

I grabbed Bethany by the hand, running with her down the Walk of Fame. When I peeked over my shoulder, the photographer was pointing us out to Marilyn and Elvis. The three of them began trotting after us.

"Bethany!" Marilyn yelled out. "Hey, Bethany!"

Heads swung in our direction—people who had crossed oceans and continents to visit the entertainment capital of the world. Brass plaques and concrete shoeprints and false Elvises couldn't hold them with an actual megastar on the scene.

"Oh crap," Terry grumbled as we put on speed.

The group coalesced into a mob, like a maddened colony of bees, buzzing to this flower of popular culture. People are hypnotized by celebrity; their brains desert them in the presence of someone they've seen on TV or films. The crowd continued to move forward like mindless things, reaching out to grab and tear at the object of their fantasies.

"Where's your car?" I shouted at Bethany.

"Parking lot! Over there!"

We sprinted towards the lot with the crowd chasing after us full bore, arms waving, cameras swinging from their necks, screaming Bethany's name. One Japanese guy lifted his Nikon to his face while running, and tripped over a homeless dude who was playing his guitar on a pile of dirty blankets. The Japanese tourist went sailing into the air, landing like a sack of flour blowing apart, lenses and glasses and Mickey Mouse cap flying. What happened next would have been funny if it didn't look so painful.

A woman in the crowd tripped over the fallen tourist. Then, as if it was a speeded-up *Keystone Kops* sequence, the whole lot of star stalkers went slamming into each other, knocking each other down like bowling pins and crashing to the sidewalk, tumbling and rolling around on the Walk of Fame in a mess of arms and legs.

Marilyn was sprawled on the curb, skirt up around her waist. Elvis ended up in the gutter, out cold. The homeless guy crawled out from under the human morass and *konked* the Japanese tourist over the head with his guitar for starting the whole thing.

Once we got to the parking lot, only the photographer was still in hot pursuit, panting and heaving and sweating bullets. He wasn't going to let a little thing like a heart attack come between him and a big payday from the tabloids.

"Hey Bethany!" he pleaded. "How about a little picture without the wig?"

Bethany beeped off the alarm on the green Jeep Cherokee. She tore around the side of the car, jumping into the driver's seat. I reached for the passenger side handle just as the electric locks came down.

"What the—?" I banged on the window. "Bethany, let me in!"

Terry was remonstrating with the photographer, pushing him in the chest. "Back off!" she yelled.

Bethany made an apologetic face at me through the glass. "Sorry!" Then she backed out of the space at top speed and took off, crashing through the wooden barrier next to the parking hut. The Korean parking attendant jumped out of his door, screaming and waving his fist.

As she hooked a right on the street and sped away, I noticed for the first time a busted window in the back of Bethany's ride. She had broken it in order to steal the car.

"Now look what you've done!" Terry said, shoving the photographer again.

"Was that really Bethany?" he panted.

"You didn't even know for sure and you started all this trouble?" I said in disbelief.

"Do you know what a picture of Bethany is worth these days, especially after that kidnapping thing?" He raised the camera to his face. "That's okay. I can probably get something for a picture of you two—"

Terry stepped up to the lens with her teeth bared.

"Or not." He lowered the camera.

The parking attendant stormed up to us. "You gonna pay for your friend's damage! Or I gonna call the cops!"

"Go ahead," I said, sighing. "It's been twelve hours. We're overdue for an arrest."

We gave the parking attendant our credit card to pay for the demolished barrier. When the photographer told him it had been Bethany in the Jeep, the attendant got all excited. He picked up the splintered wood with the solemnity of someone carrying the cross in an Easter pageant and dragged it inside his hut.

"Hey, what are you going to do with the broken barrier?" the photographer asked.

"Sell it, of course!"

Of course.

The photographer snapped away at the attendant and the barrier. There was no point in trying to stop him. It's a free country, and we didn't own the parking lot. The pictures would show up on the celebrity gossip Web sites as soon as they could be uploaded.

Good-bye insurance company, good-bye tour, good-bye stardom.

"You know, Ter? I think I'd like to live on a planet where there are no celebrities. How about we immigrate up to Pluto?"

"How about you immigrate up Uranus?" she replied.

My sister, the comedian.

26

We crossed the boulevard to the Roosevelt Hotel for a drink. After the mob scene on the boulevard, I wanted to be soothed by the Mission-style architecture of the landmark hotel, by its classic old Los Angeles elegance. I wanted to be reminded of the glory years before Bethany was inflicted upon the world, when Hollywood was inhabited by glamorous, tiny-footed, and talented people in black and white.

Terry carried two bottles of designer vitamin water to our table. I took one and clinked with her.

"To Bethany, a force of nature. They should name every hurricane after her from now on."

"It's not her fault people go insane around her."

"*She's* insane, Terry."

I took a swig. "But there has to be some method to her madness. Why do you think she keeps calling us and running away? Why taunt us like that? What's all the game-playing about?"

Terry absently began to spin her bottle between her palms. She was holding something back, I could tell. "What are you thinking? Come on...spill it."

"I think she has a crush on me."

"What?"

She regarded me with a steady gaze. Didn't defend her statement, but didn't shrink from it, either.

"For real?"

She nodded wordlessly.

"Holy moly. How do you know?"

"Gaydar."

"But she's not gay!"

"How does she know what she is? She's only done it once, and she ended up crying in the bathroom."

"Oh, I see what you mean." Then another thought occurred to me. "How long have you suspected this?"

A slow smile spread over her face. "Since she jumped on me in Fellows's yard."

"You knew she was crushed out on you and you didn't say anything to me?"

"Oh, you wanna talk about confiding things? You wanna talk about being honest with each other, Ms. I've-Got-Two-Cops-on-the-Line?"

Busted. "So you think she's acting out because of sexual confusion?"

"Look, I'm no shrink. And even if I were, there's no simple answer to that girl's problems. I'm just telling you what I know."

"What you *think* you know."

"Okay, what I think I know. But I've been at this a long time. I had my first crush at three."

"You did? Who was it?"

She pressed her lips together.

"Tell me!"

"You'll laugh."

"No I won't."

"Swear?"

I held up two fingers. "Girl Scout honor."

"Miss Piggy."

"Ha!" I fell down on the table, pounding it with my fist. "Your first crush was a *Muppet?*" I dissolved into hysterics.

"You swore you wouldn't laugh!"

"The laughter was *involuntary*." I sat up and wiped my eyes.

"She had blond curls," Terry said. "And lots of attitude. Not to mention great bazooms."

"So, given the option at three, you would have porked Miss Piggy?"

"Grow up."

"Boy. The things you don't know about your own flesh and blood."

"You never showed much interest in my emotional life," she muttered.

"I was too busy ducking your fists."

She regarded me thoughtfully for a moment, lower lip caught in her teeth. When she finally spoke, her tone was earnest.

"Don't you think some of my personality problems are the result of knowing I was different, even as a kid? Don't you think some of the poundings you took were because I was jealous? You were everything people wanted you to be—smart, straight, the perfect little girl. I knew I was something else, and part of me knew I would never be accepted the same as you, no matter what I did."

If you'd hit me with a sledgehammer, I could not have been more stunned. The pursuit of self-knowledge is not something Terry is famous for.

"Wow," I said at last. "Pretty amazing insight. So this is the reason you're the way you are? Impulsive and violent and all that?"

"Gotcha! I was born this way, Ker." She smacked my head with an open hand. "Deal with it."

"One of these days." I waved my fist at her. "One of these days, Terry."

"Oooohhh, I'm really scared. That'll teach you to dis Miss Piggy."

"I didn't mean to dis her. I always liked Piggy, too. But of course, not in *that* way."

We clinked, friends again.

"What do we do now?" I wondered.

"I guess we find her mother in Santa Monica."

"Are you bonkers? There's no trailer park there."

Santa Monica is a liberal beachside town commonly referred to as "The People's Republic of Santa Monica." It used to be a funky enclave of apartment buildings, but it was gentrifying fast. Real estate was at a premium. No way a trailer park had survived within city limits.

"There is so." Terry was adamant. "I've seen it. It's near the freeway, just up from the Water Garden."

"A trailer park right in the middle of all that glam?"

"Honest Abe."

"If it does exist, I'm sure Andie Sue would zero in on it like a homing pigeon. She was to the trailer born."

"You know," Terry said thoughtfully, "that could be what Paul Fellows was trying to tell Bethany all along. Her mother really *isn't* dead."

And then, Heaven help us, we were off on a cross-town mission to fact-check the *Weekly World News*.

We took "surface streets," as they're referred to, as opposed to "certain death," as the freeways are known. We passed miles and miles of apartments built in the sixties—two-storied with carports consisting of roofs on stilts. They were boxy, indistinct things, except that most of them had some sort of space-age flourish on the front: a cigar-shaped metal design with prongs jutting out the back; a flame-throwing rocket ship; interlocking acute triangles in seafoam blue, like the emblem on a space nodule; and a mosaic in bathroom tiles depicting Apollo shooting for the moon. I guess people were really big on space travel in the sixties. Of course, they were also big on the Partridge Family and avocado-colored kitchen appliances, so let's just leave it there.

Many of the buildings were dedicated to women whose names were spelled out in wrought-iron cursive above the doors. Muses with names like *Jo Ellen* and *Mary Anne* and *Elizabeth Jane* had evidently inspired these great architectural achievements in stucco.

Naturally, they made me think of another sixties-era babe, *Andie Sue.*

I didn't really think she could still be alive. Then again, I hadn't believed there could be a trailer park in Santa Monica, but as we took a left onto Stewart Avenue, I saw that I'd been dead wrong.

Just east of the new buildings on Broadway Avenue—Sony Music and the Water Garden—just past all the tony new developments that had sprung up to transform the tatty neighborhood into the ultimate in trendiness, was a relic from some distant past.

It sat next to the freeway overpass, between Pico and Olympic Boulevards, a square block of mobile homes like you'd see on any episode of *Cops*, spilling their drunken and toothless residents out into the streets to be billyclubbed and cuffed for the amusement of the TV-viewing audience.

But there was none of that here. It was quiet and well maintained, if completely out of its element.

It won't last long, I thought. *It'll be sold and razed so fast it'd make your head spin, a set of pricey condos built on the spot.*

Terry parked, then we wandered down the narrow private lanes between trailers. We had nosed around for no more than five minutes when we peered around a corner and saw a small singlewide with a rusted green awning at the end of a cul-de-sac.

And there she was in the flesh. The woman from the online news reports, Bethany's mama. She was lounging in a lawn chair, taking in the afternoon sun in her postage stamp of a front yard.

You could have knocked me over with a trailer hitch.

She wore a straw hat and white sunglasses, short shorts, and a halter-top quartering large, conical breasts. The muscles on her skinny frame lacked tone, her skin was saggy. Her face had the texture of a well-beaten drum. Toenails sparkled orange from her gold wedge sandals, the tapering fingernails painted the same. She couldn't have been much more than forty years old, but she could have asked for a senior citizen discount without anyone raising an eyebrow.

She watched us approaching over the top of a frosted tumbler, taking a long pull on her drink.

When we were within a couple of feet of her, and before we could even say hello, she said, "So. The little monster found me."

As it turned out, Andie Sue had seen us on TV after the kidnapping fiasco. She'd taken it for granted that the whole thing was a stunt devised by Claude to garner publicity. When we told her we'd come to convey a message from Bethany, she invited us inside for a drink.

She served us Diet Coke in the can and then freshened her highball. We seated ourselves in chairs across from the floral couch, where Andie Sue sat, curling her legs up beneath her.

"What does she want from me? I don't have any of her money. I never did, not that it matters to her." She took a slug from her drink.

"She wants to see you," Terry said. "She wants to reconcile."

"When hell freezes over."

You couldn't hack through that bitterness with a machete. "We'll tell her that," I said, "if she calls us again."

She squinted at me. "What do you mean, if she calls you again? I thought she sent you here."

"She's in hiding, sort of," Terry explained. "We only caught up with her for an hour before she took off again. But she told us you were alive, and that she was sorry about everything that had happened between you two."

Andie Sue snorted. "Bully for her."

"But that's not the only reason we're here," I said. "We're also trying to solve a couple of murders."

"Murders?" She drew herself out of her slouch, aiming those torpedo-shaped breasts directly at me. "What are you talking about?"

"Two people have died. A man named Larry Benjamin and one named Paul Fellows."

"Don't know—" Andie Sue stopped mid-sentence. "Larry *who?*"

"Benjamin," I repeated.

"Oh yeah," she said, suddenly animated with hatred. "I called him Benji Bizarro. He was with Bethany's management company. Somebody killed him?"

"It was ruled a suicide, but one of his close associates thinks there was foul play."

"Yee-haw!" Andie Sue clinked her glass against my Diet Coke can, laughing as she fell back into the cushions.

"I take it you didn't like him," Terry said.

"He's one of the scum-suckers that made me out to be a common criminal—worse, an animal who'd steal bread from her own baby's mouth. He was the main witness against me."

"How were they able to prove malfeasance?" I asked.

Andie Sue fluttered orange fingernails in front of her face. "Lord, I don't know. I couldn't read that accounting stuff. It was Greek to me. Somehow they made out that I was ripping the kid off."

"Didn't you have representation?"

"Couldn't afford a decent lawyer after they froze all the accounts. No question, I got screwed, but what could I do? I was outgunned." She added softly, "I worked my tail off to give her what I never had. You'd think she could give a little back."

The three of us sat in awkward silence for a moment.

"It looks like Larry Benjamin had a change of heart," I said. "We think he confessed to defrauding you to the other man, Fellows. Then Fellows sent Bethany a note offering to tell her the truth about you."

Andie Sue let out another whoop, waving her glass in the air. "Here's the truth, baby. Right here in front of you. Her mama's living on assistance in a trailer home. You can go back and tell her that." She stopped cackling and looked down. "But what does she care? She's sitting pretty. That's all she cares about."

"She probably believed you *had* died," Terry said, "like everyone else. Benjamin even thought it was his fault you had, apparently, drunk yourself to death."

Andie Sue put a hand over her mouth and giggled. "I'm sorry, it's wicked of me. But him getting killed, don't that strike you as divine justice?"

Or maybe human revenge.

"Why does everyone think that *you're* dead?" Terry asked her.

"I bribed a quack doctor to tell the tabloids the story." Andie Sue smirked at her own slyness. "The idiots never did check for a death certificate, just jumped on the story, and printed it on the doctor's say-so and a photo of me playing dead. You learn a lot about manipulating the media when you're Bethany's mama."

"One of the tabs ran a photo of you recently, saying you were alive and eating out of Dumpsters here in Santa Monica."

"Oh. And that's how Bethany...?"

"Yes," I said. "Why didn't you ever get in touch with her?"

"She was dead to *me*. I wanted to be the same to her. More importantly, to the press. Didn't want them nosing around, asking me questions. Offering me money to talk about her."

That made her downright noble by today's standards, passing up perfectly good green because she didn't want to air her dirty laundry in public.

"But now two men are dead," Terry said. "And we think it's because they were connected to Bethany somehow."

Andie Sue gazed at her for a long time. "That's another reason I wanted to disappear."

"Why?"

She swished some vodka around like mouthwash, then swallowed. "I thought it might happen to me."

"You thought you might be killed?" My surprise was genuine.

"It was a possibility."

"But who would want to do that?"

Andie Sue hesitated. "How much time have you actually spent with my Bethany?"

"Enough to know she's...troubled," I admitted.

"A diplomat, huh?" Andie Sue gave me an ironic smile. "Let me tell you something, you've never known fear until you've looked into the eyes of your own child and seen pure hatred. Cold, murderin' hatred. Try it sometime, and then you come talk to me."

Words failed me.

Andie Sue rose from the couch. "Fresh one, anybody?"

We shook our heads, and she went into the small kitchen, pouring vodka into her glass and plunking in ice cubes.

"We think Bethany may be having a breakdown," Terry called to her.

"She can forget about *me* coming to visit her on the funny farm."

"I can understand your position—" I started to say.

Andie Sue came back in the room, squeezing her glass so hard I was afraid it would crack. "Don't you *ever, ever* say you understand what I've been through. *Nobody* knows what I been through...except maybe Jesus Christ," she added in a whisper.

"We're sorry to bring up painful memories," Terry said gently, "but we've been caught up in this situation in spite of ourselves. We've been arrested twice, and we've suffered a big blow to our reputation as a result. We need to find out what's going on for our own sake, as much as for Bethany and Claude's."

Andie Sue dabbed her eyes with the pads of her fingers. "If you want to continue this conversation, don't mention *him* to me again."

Clearly she was not a charter member of the Claude Sterling fan club.

"We won't mention him by name," Terry said. "We'll call him 'the manager,' okay?"

Andie Sue agreed to that.

"Okay, here's the deal," Terry continued. "Bethany keeps running away. The first time we saw her, when she claimed we kidnapped her..."

Andie Sue erupted with laughter. "He'll stop at nothing to promote his little cash calf."

"Well, on that day she jumped into our car and said she had to get away, to lay low for a few days. We checked into a motel to figure out what to do next, and the SWATs came in and busted us."

"We've been chasing her ever since," I said, taking up the narrative. "And we can't figure out what she's up to, unless...Do you think she could have a problem with Claude—sorry, the manager? With his control over her?"

"She's been running *him* for years. She's the one who talked him into suing me. I used to think he was a decent guy, but he ended up going after me just like the rest of that pack of hyenas."

"There's one other thing that occurred to us, but it's a real long shot," Terry said. "Do you think Bethany might be curious about who her father is?"

"Her father?" Andie Sue gave her a baffled look. "She knows darn well her father was a one-night stand back in Barstow. I never even knew his last name."

"What was his first name?"

"Joe, Jim, Jerry...?" She shook her head, at a loss. "Honey, you try to remember somebody you went to bed with eighteen years ago after a pint of tequila. All I know is he took eighty bucks from my wallet on his way out the door. I never seen him since."

"He might remember you, even if you don't remember him. He might have contacted Bethany himself."

She considered it for a second. "I s'pose."

"If you saw him, do you think you'd know him?"

"Maybe, if he was walking around without his pants on."

"He's got...a distinguishing characteristic?" Terry looked at me with raised eyebrows.

"I don't know how distinguished it is—" Andie Sue rattled the ice cubes in her glass, "But Bethany's daddy only had one ball."

"Oh," Terry and I said together.

"You have no other clue as to what's going on with Bethany?" I asked. "Why she would be running away?"

We waited a few moments for a response, but it was clear there was nothing more Andie Sue could offer. She gave us an apologetic smile and stood up from the couch. "Well, if that's all..."

"Thank you for talking to us," I said. "Is there anything you want us to tell Bethany if we see her again?"

"Sure, tell her happy birthday."

"We will, if we hear from her by then."

"By when? Oh yeah, I always forget. She thinks her birthday is on the nineteenth."

"It's not?"

"No, I lied about her age when she was starting out in the baby beauty pageants. She was five, but I thought she had a better chance in the three-to-four age category, so I fibbed. I never did tell her the actual date, and I'm inclined to forget myself most of the time. It's May fifth."

I could see Terry's stunned reaction in my peripheral vision. "So Bethany is..."

"Eighteen," Andie Sue said. "For four months, now."

28

After leaving Andie Sue to her next bottle, we headed over to Delores's coffee shop on Santa Monica Boulevard to celebrate our new discovery. We ordered chicken salad sandwiches, the best thing on the menu.

"It's all over," Terry crowed. "Bethany's eighteen and she can do what she wants. Even if Claude sues her, she'll have plenty left over for the best shrink money can buy. Happy ending."

"Except for Fellows and Benjamin," I pointed out. "And Andie Sue."

"Yeah." A somber look darkened Terry's face. "But maybe Bethany and Andie Sue will reconcile. Eventually."

We'd left the trailer park with Bethany's actual birth certificate in hand. Andie Sue said she'd thought of burning it along with Bethany's baby pictures, but couldn't bring herself to do it. She'd dummied up a fake one when Bethany was on the pageant circuit, but she'd always kept the real one in a lockbox. The certificate was proof that Bethany came into the world eighteen years and four months ago in Victorville, California.

Terry had palmed one of the baby pictures when Andie Sue got up to freshen her drink. My sister could have had quite a career as a pickpocket. She did for a while, to hear her tell it, but only during the worst of her addiction.

"I can't believe you stole that. Better not be thinking of selling it to the tabs."

"We'll give it to Bethany when we see her."

"What makes you think she'll want it?"

"Just look at it." She gazed at the bucolic scene. "Cute, chubby little baby. Andie Sue all young and hopeful. Those were happier times for both of them."

In the fading Polaroid, mother and daughter were posed on a light blue picnic blanket, surrounded by trees and tall, green grass. Andie Sue was dressed in virtually the same outfit as today, sporting the same big hairdo. But here she was radiant and youthful, not yet the haggard barfly we'd just visited.

"She was pretty, back in the day," I remarked.

"Uh-huh. She might have done all right herself in some showbiz capacity if she hadn't put Bethany first."

"Pole dancer, maybe?"

Terry didn't acknowledge the mean joke. "I think if Bethany sees a picture of the good ol' days, she might soften toward Andie Sue."

"That's unusually sentimental of you."

"If there's anything I'm sentimental about, it's moms. You know that."

I did know it. Our mother had died young, and that was the beginning of all Terry's problems, when she really began to act out. Our dad's death sealed it. After that, Terry went on a cocaine binge that had cost her several years of freedom and almost her life. I had been too wrapped up in getting onto the Dean's list at UCLA to realize she was going to pieces right under my nose. When she forced my hand by getting arrested, I put college on the back burner and made her my first priority. In the end, it brought the two of us closer together.

"So, Andie Sue got screwed over by the lawyers and probably made herself out to be dead so they couldn't attach any more assets," Terry speculated.

"What assets?"

"Maybe she owns the trailer."

"The court would let her keep her home."

"Yeah, I guess so."

"Terry, there's something you're not dealing with."

"Huh?"

"Andie Sue said she was afraid, but not of more legal action. She implied she was afraid of Bethany."

"Here we go again. Bethany the Antichrist."

"Look, we still have two unsolved murders here. And guess who's been at large with a possible motive? Meanwhile, she acts all spacey and crazy like she doesn't know what she's doing—"

"Kerry, that's whack! We don't know where Bethany was when Larry Benjamin was killed, *if* he was killed!"

"She was definitely on the loose when Fellows bit the big one, and she told us she saw him dead. Then, when I tried to ask her about it, she shook her finger at me in that strange way, telling me not to ask any more questions."

"She said she didn't kill him."

"Does this ring any bells: *Eat lead, creep!*"

Terry waved a hand dismissively. "She was being cute."

"Real cute."

"I admit she's crazy. But she's not a murderer."

"Why? Because she has a crush on you?" I paused before uttering the corollary. "Or because you have one on *her*?"

Glares don't come any icier than the one she laid on me at that moment.

I raised my hands defensively. "I'm just saying—"

"Fine, you're right," she admitted, shame-faced. "I wouldn't admit it to myself because I thought she was underage, but now I can legally have the hots for her."

"You'd make a great pair. The PI and the Killer Pop Tart."

Terry laughed in spite of herself.

"I'm serious about this, Ter. Bethany is still a suspect in Fellows's death."

She patted her belly. "The Golden Gut says no."

"Then who's your favorite candidate for the murderer? Want to consult the oracle on Claude?"

She laid her hand on her stomach, closing her eyes. A deep breath, then she opened her eyes again.

"Negatory."

I suddenly remembered Andie Sue's description of Bethany's father, though "father" was probably too generous a word. He was really more of a sperm donor, a wham-bam-thank-you-ma'am kind of progenitor. "Be interesting to know how many testicles Paul Fellows had, wouldn't it?"

"This *isn't* about her father. Look, when we hear from Bethany again, and we *will* hear from her—"

"Because you're such an irresistible babe."

She ignored that. "We'll tell her she's an adult so she can come in from the cold. She can fire Claude and get a lawyer to look into the fraud allegations against Andie Sue or whatever she wants to do. If the police believe she's involved in murder, then they can bring charges. The important thing is that she can make her own decisions now. And my guess is she's going to give up the entertainment business."

"Probably. Hope she gets some serious mental treatment, too."

"That goes without saying." Terry tapped the birth certificate. "But this is gonna go a long way toward solving her problems. No more Claude."

"Should we tell him about it?"

"I guess it wouldn't hurt. He's gonna find out soon enough, anyway. And he *has* been paying us. Besides, it's a matter of public record."

The waitress came by with our sandwiches, setting them on the table. "Enjoy."

"A buck for your pickle," Terry said, eyeing my plate enviously.

"No way."

"Two bucks?"

"Eat dirt."

"Rather eat pickle."

I shoved the whole pickle in my mouth, chomping it to bits before she could steal it. "There. It's gone."

She slapped the table. "I bet myself I could make you eat your whole pickle in one bite. You are so predictable!" She took a dollar out of her pocket and waved it around. "I win!"

"You're predictable, too," I grumbled. "Predictably butt-holey."

"But I've still got my pickle." She nibbled at the end, and then she took a bite of her sandwich. "Mmmm, they go so well together, chicken salad and pickle."

I bit into my own sandwich rather than reveal my pickle envy. I wasn't going to stoop to ordering another one.

Just then the waitress appeared at our table. "Here are your extra pickles," she said, setting down a whole plate of them. "Almost forgot."

I grabbed three dill spears from the plate. "See, all I had to do was think *Big Pickles*, and they appeared. Just like that."

"Don't talk with your mouth full," Terry muttered. "You're ruining my appetite."

After dinner, we decided to call Claude and tell him about the birth certificate. We walked back out into the parking lot to make the call. It was twilight, and the sky was the deep blue of the ocean, four miles away. Terry simultaneously brushed crumbs from her shirt and scrolled down to find Claude's number on her cell phone.

"Hello, Claude? Terry McAfee. No, we haven't found her, but we did find her mother..." She held the phone away from her ear as yelling came through the speaker. "No, she *isn't* dead...We heard a rumor that she was alive and snooped around until we found her... No, Bethany doesn't know yet, we're telling you first... But there's something else, Claude."

She looked to me for the go-ahead. I gave her a nod.

"There's the matter of Bethany's age. Now, I know she believes she's going to be eighteen in a couple of days, but actually she's already eighteen."

More yelling as Terry held the phone away from her ear again.

"Yeah, but it turns out her mother lied about her age for a baby beauty pageant. We have her real birth certificate with us here."

She listened intently for a few moments.

"We thought we'd give it to Bethany when we see her."

More wheedling, cursing, yelling.

"Sorry, we can't tonight. Tomorrow morning at nine? Okay, 'bye." She closed the phone thoughtfully. "He wants us to bring him the birth certificate."

"Why?"

"He wants to give it to his lawyers. If it turns out Bethany was of age when she signed the contract for the tour, he'll have a better chance in a lawsuit."

We stood there a moment, thinking about this.

"We can't give it to him," I said. "Bethany has the right to that document. If we don't own our births, what do we own?"

"I know. That's why I said we couldn't meet him tonight. I wanted to buy some time."

"Why is he so anxious to have it? Why does it have to be tonight?"

"No idea."

"Look, Terry, we don't want to get between these two. This is like a family squabble that's out of control. If he wants to bring suit, his lawyers can do their own due diligence. They can probably get that document off the Internet."

"You're right, you're right. We didn't tell him anything he couldn't have found out on his own."

We stood there another moment, listening to the cacophony of rush-hour traffic on Santa Monica, where motorists were inching their way impatiently to the 405. An ambulance suddenly screamed into the area out of nowhere. The commuters tried to pull over to the side of the road, but the cars were too jammed to give it clearance. The ambulance had to weave in and out them like it was running some kind of crazy obstacle course on its way to St. John's Medical Center.

Terry watched it disappear down the road, its claxon blaring, and then she turned to me with dread on her face. "I hope we didn't just make a gigantic mistake," she said.

We spent the evening waiting for a call from Bethany, watching TV with Lance and the critters. I stared distractedly at the Animal Planet program Lance had chosen until a delicate gazelle was brought down by a lioness with one swipe of her massive paw, after which she ripped into the gazelle's throat with her teeth. I covered my eyes.

Unfortunately the scene was no better inside my head. I kept picturing Fellows's bloated body, the blackened hole in his forehead. I imagined his brains leaking out of that hole, along with his personality and maybe his soul.

Is his spirit wandering around out there somewhere, dazed and confused because his life was so violently interrupted?

Death was coming all too near lately. It was everywhere, even on the show we were watching in order to avoid the serial killer programs.

We humans are just animals, after all. Violent, thoughtless predators, cannibalizing our own kind.

That thought led me to Bethany again. Was it possible for her to have taken Fellows's life? Was she really that vicious? I didn't have a ready answer to that, but I didn't like to think about her out there on her own—friendless, crazy, capable of almost anything.

Badda bump, badda bump, badda bump bump bump!

The ducks squealed, the pups whined, and my heart flipped over in my chest.

"Would you change that ring tone already?" I hollered at Terry.

"You'll deafen the ducks!" Lance said.

Terry defiantly swiped the phone off the coffee table. I knew the call was trouble by the expression on her face.

"Where are you now?" Terry held the phone away from her head so I could hear.

It was Bethany, slurring her words, barely coherent. "I'm...I'm at Glen's."

"Glen Adler?" Terry said.

"Yeah."

"Is he there?"

"Y-yeah."

"Put him on."

There was silence on the line.

"Can't," Bethany finally said.

"Why not?"

"He's dead."

Terry and I both drew a breath.

"I think I'm in *trou-ble*," Bethany sang, before hanging up.

Our first reaction was to call the police. Our second reaction was not to. We told ourselves that the call had been ambiguous. We didn't know why Glen Adler was dead, and we didn't yet know why Bethany was in the dead man's apartment, so we chose to be cautiously optimistic.

Glen could have died of natural causes while Bethany was visiting, a victim of his excessive drinking. Or he could have slipped in the bathtub and cracked his head. Or he could have eaten a bullet to demonstrate how much he loved Bethany.

There was no reason to conclude, at this point, that Bethany herself had visited death upon her former tutor.

We streaked over to Park La Brea, doing fifty all the way. Fortunately the speed trap gods were with us, and we weren't pulled over. As we passed the advertisement for Bethany's tour, I saw that someone had defaced it with paintballs. Bethany's lithe body and angelic face were covered with bright red splotches.

Was it some kind of omen?

Stop thinking that way, I told myself. *Don't get ahead of yourself. One crisis at a time.*

Terry screeched to a stop next to the intercom board at Park La Brea. She jumped off the bike and buzzed Adler's apartment.

There was no answer.

"We should have told her we'd be ringing the buzzer," Terry said, grimacing. "She probably can't even operate the thing."

We heard a buzz and the clunk of the bolt.

"Let's go."

Terry pushed open the door and we ran into the stairwell, throwing ourselves up four flights of stairs. We tore down the hallway to Adler's apartment and saw that the door was cracked.

I shoved it all the way open. We entered cautiously. Last time we were here, a drunken maniac had held a gun on us. This time, it turned out, someone had pulled the same gun on him.

The pearl-handled .22 lay on the floor next to Adler's body. His empty, blue eyes stared at the ceiling. One of his hands clutched his bloody chest, gripping the wound in a futile attempt to stanch the flow. The other hand was at his side clutching his ruler. The ruler itself had been broken in half, probably used in a pathetic bid at self-defense. The room bore no other sign of a struggle.

Bethany sat propped up against the wall underneath the intercom. She was nude, except for a pink satin thong. She smiled crookedly at us and began to sing her number-one hit in a breathy voice. And to punctuate the lyrics, she cut herself with the razor in her hand.

"I ain't..."

Slice.

"No..."

Slice.

"Baby..."

Slice.

"No more."

"Stop!" Terry pounced on Bethany, grabbing her wrist. She squeezed the tendon below Bethany's hand until her fingers opened and she dropped the sticky blade to the carpet.

It was a nightmare vision. Bethany's beautiful, white skin was marked like she'd been the victim of a lashing. There were inch-long lacerations across her thighs, her arms, even her shoulders. Blood was smeared on her face and her breasts and all over her hands. She leaned over and snatched at the razor with a trembling hand. Terry moved quickly, stepping on the blade. Then she lifted her boot and picked up the razor by the corner, flinging it across the room.

"I have to find it!" Bethany's eyes darted crazily about the apartment. "It's here somewhere. I know it is!"

I tilted her face up by the chin. Her pupils were dilated. I was looking into deep, empty blackness.

"What's here, Bethany?"

"I don't know!"

"Who did this to you?" Terry asked her. "Who hurt you?"

Bethany jerked her chin away, petulant. "I *told* you. It doesn't hurt."

Terry looked over at Adler's body. "Did he try to rape you?"

Bethany smiled wistfully. "No. Glen wouldn't do that. He was a good man. He totally taught me everything I know."

"Terry, see if there's hydrogen peroxide in the bathroom," I said.

She ran down the hall. "You call an ambulance!"

I jumped up to grab the phone on the kitchen wall, but something grabbed *me.*

I let out a shriek and looked down to see Bethany's bloody hand gripping my ankle. Her lips were pulled back in a grimace, her front teeth drenched in blood like those of the gorging TV lioness.

"No, don't call them!" she pleaded. "I have to find it! I'll never find it if you call them!"

"Find what, Bethany?" I begged. "Find *what?*"

But her eyes rolled up and she keeled over to her side, unconscious, her hand still clutching my ankle.

30

After the 911 call, we contacted detectives Howard and Guerra directly. (The devils we knew, I guess.) If they were surprised to find us on the scene of another murder, they didn't show it. Neither did they seem to suspect us of committing the crime.

Somehow the paparazzi had gotten wind of the incident. One of the neighbors had probably called them, or perhaps they'd been staking out Adler's apartment to score pictures of the alleged child molester. The story of Adler's advances on Bethany had been leaked, too.

Five additional teams of officers were called out just to keep the photographers at bay. But they still managed to sneak up back stairwells, crawl into windows, and scale the outside walls to the rooftop like the vermin they were. Their flashes went off like smart bombs exploding in the distance.

The paramedics placed Bethany on a gurney with an IV drip in her arm. She roused herself as they were securing the straps and struggled to sit up. When she realized she was trapped, she fixed her wild eyes on Terry and me.

"Help me!" she cried.

But we couldn't help her this time.

She arched her neck and saw Glen Adler dead on the floor, then let out a bone-chilling scream that must have been heard for miles around.

The camera-flashes stopped—the paparazzi stilled for one instant by the sound of sheer human agony—then they started back up in anticipation of the Big Get, a photo of the pop star murderess.

We last saw Bethany being wheeled away, eyes clenched and mouth wide open, the veins on the side of her neck about to burst with the force of her ungodly shrieking.

An hour later, we sat in the back seat of the unmarked police car covered by blankets, the heater turned up full blast. The September heat had suddenly given way to a foggy coolness. Just like that, a new season. But our shivering may have been due to shock rather than the ambient temperature.

We had asked the detectives to question us outside of the apartment. We couldn't stand it anymore—the smell of blood, the sight of violent death, the ghost of a terrified and insane young girl slumped against the wall, cutting herself to pieces.

They went easy on us. If they hadn't, I might have played the Terry role and yelled obscenities at them.

"What do you think she was trying to find?" Howard asked after we'd filled them in on the incident.

Terry and I shook our heads.

"She was slicing herself as she said it," Terry said. "Maybe she wanted to find a vein, to cut herself in a way that would finally end it."

"Not that hard to find," Guerra said, "if you really want to."

"Unless you're stoned out of your mind," Howard argued.

"Some other ideas," I said, "but they're just random."

Guerra nodded. "Shoot."

"Adler told us she was a genius. He'd given her some standardized tests. Maybe she was looking for proof."

Howard and Guerra glanced skeptically at each other, but said nothing.

"Another thing," Terry said. "We found out that Bethany's true birthday is in May. She may have suspected she was a legal adult and have been looking for documentation of some sort."

"How did you find out about the birthday?" Guerra asked.

"We talked to her mother."

"Thought she was dead."

"Everyone did. She staged her death for the media so she could maintain her privacy and keep her distance from Bethany. She wanted nothing more to do with her."

Guerra took notes. "Bethany was high as a kite. She might have been looking for more drugs."

"Did you find any in the apartment?" Terry asked.

Howard shook his head. "No, but we're not through processing the scene."

"It looked like E to me." I recalled the blasted out pupils, the spaciness, and the imperviousness to pain. It all spelled Ecstasy.

"Possibly mixed with something else," Howard agreed. "A near-lethal cocktail."

"It looks like Adler got her high and made a move on her," Guerra said. "Then she killed him. The neighbors said Adler had been unemployed since Bethany's accusations."

There they were again, those unfounded allegations, so difficult to prove, but devastating even as a suggestion. "If he *had* molested her, why would she come here?"

"She came here expressly to kill him," Howard stated bluntly. "She seduced him, and then killed him."

Terry looked at me, and I read her thought—*Impossible.*

I had no idea what to think myself.

"When we saw Bethany in Hollywood, she thought she was being followed," Terry told them. "She was in a green Jeep Cherokee. No one seems to know where she got it, but it's possible someone followed her and set her up for the murder. They could have put a tracking device on the Jeep."

Howard looked over at Guerra, who appeared dubious. Even so, he made a note in his book.

"I wouldn't hold out a lot of hope that someone else is responsible for this," Guerra said. "It looks pretty open and shut. We might even be able to nail her for Fellows, now that we've got her in custody." His deep, brown eyes were filled with sympathy. You never know what gentleness lurks beneath the hard exteriors of some people.

"I guess that's it for now." Howard heaved himself out of the front seat and opened the back door for us. "Would you like someone to drive you home?"

We declined, removing the blankets and tossing them in the back seat as we exited the car.

"Do us a favor?" I asked Howard. "When the medical examiner's done with the autopsy, can you get some information about Glen Adler?"

"Yeah, what?"

"We'd like to know how many testicles he had."

Both detectives blinked.

"Before he died?" Howard asked.

"Right."

"Why?"

"Because, supposedly, Bethany's daddy only had one ball."

31

I'd like to relate that I was snug in my bed dreaming of ducklings, but I'd only just fallen asleep when Terry burst into my room the next morning. My bed looked like someone had been rehearsing the River Dance on it during the night. The blanket was bunched up at the foot of the bed, and I was ensnared in the sheets.

She slapped me on the rear. "Sorry, but you have to get up. You'll want to see the news."

"I got no REM last night," I said groggily.

"Lance's making coffee." She yanked off the covers. "Come on."

I stumbled downstairs where Lance stuck a mug of hot coffee in my hand, and then I flopped on the couch to watch the brouhaha unfolding on one of the cable news channels. The announcer was grim, as grave looking as someone with sprayed hair, a deep tan, and bright white veneers on his teeth could be.

"Superstar Bethany is in the hospital under arrest, suspected in the slaying of her one-time tutor, Glen

Adler. Bethany was under the influence of controlled substances, according to a hospital spokesman, and is being treated for multiple self-inflicted lacerations covering most of her body.

"Police have confirmed that Bethany's fingerprints were found on the bloody gun that was used to kill Glen Adler. Skin tests administered to the pop star were positive for gunpowder.

"Investigation continues into whether Bethany acted in self-defense. She was nude when found, and may have been the victim of a thwarted sexual assault. Her manager and legal guardian, Claude Sterling, made this statement outside the hospital."

The video feed cut to Claude's devastated, unshaven face. His shirt was rumpled and stained with sweat, his toupee slightly askew.

"Bethany is an American treasure. I beg her fans not to abandon her now in her hour of need."

Terry couldn't believe her ears. "Is he asking them to go out and buy her CDs? The guy has no shame."

"We will cooperate fully with the police in their investigation of this tragedy," Claude continued tearfully. "And I can assure you that Bethany will be exonerated of any wrongdoing."

A woman with purple hair in a leather suit pulled Claude away by the arm. But he turned back around quickly to face the cameras once again.

"Pray for Bethany."

A tracking shot followed the woman as she led Claude to his limo, before cutting back to the announcer.

"Wait a minute, wait a minute," I said, rewinding the segment. "That woman in leather. Did you see her?"

"The purple-haired one?" Terry asked.

"Yeah, remember her? She was ushering Claude around when he did the press conference about Bethany's alleged abduction. I couldn't forget that hair color."

Lance shrugged. "So?"

"She's so close to Claude that she's always on his arm when something terrible goes down with Bethany, but we've never seen her in person."

"Maybe she's an assistant or something," Lance suggested.

"An assistant who's never answered his calls for him. An assistant he didn't have when he picked us up in the limo and was fielding ten phones at once. An assistant we didn't see in the mansion after Bethany ran away again, and he was besieged with calls. A faithful assistant that *no one's ever seen...*"

Terry looked at me, wide-eyed. She knew where I was going with this. "Or *have* we?" she said excitedly. "Looking a whole lot different? With white hair instead of purple?"

"And much more white trashy?"

"Huh?" Lance said. "Did she get a makeover or something?"

"We'll explain later," I shouted, as Terry and I sprinted for the front door. "See ya, Lance!"

Not a creature was stirring at the trailer park, not even a street rat. The residents were all inside enjoying their morning beer or watching *Jerry Springer* reruns or doing the *New York Times* crossword puzzle.

Hey. I'm not one to stereotype.

There was no answer when we banged on Andie Sue's trailer door. Terry tried to peer in the window, cupping her hands to her face as she squinted through a slit in the curtains.

"Can you see anything?" I whispered.

"Just the kitchen," she said, moving away.

I knocked again, louder this time.

"She's not home," said a quavering voice to my right.

A tiny, white-haired lady in a lime-green pantsuit wobbled by with a walker. She had bright blue eyes in a face like a tortoise's, folds of wrinkled, white flesh dangling from her skull. Her neck was bent at a forty-degree angle to her spine.

"Do you know the lady who lives here?" I asked her.

"She ain't no lady," the old woman grumbled maliciously. "She's a piece of trash. Good riddance to bad rubbish."

"But is she gone?" Terry asked. "Did you see her leave?"

"Sure did. Took all her stuff and left yestiddy."

"What time?"

"Dead of night," the woman said, inching along with her walker. "Just like a common criminal."

A half-hour later we were back at the Starlight Motel.

The clerk looked up from his computer and curled his wormy lips into a smile. "Got any more celebrity coaches for sale?"

Terry wasted no words. "We need the address for the guy who bought the Chrysler."

He gave her a look. "No way the guy's giving it back. He paid good money for it."

"We don't want it back," I said. "But you said he was Bethany's number one fan, right?"

"Yeah. So?"

"So he may have something that can help us. We need to see some old news footage."

"News footage concerning what?"

"Bethany's bogus abduction."

"I guarantee he's got it. He's got everything on Bethany. Be happy to give you his address for a ten-spot."

Terry jumped up and *bashed* her whole body against the bulletproof glass.

The clerk shot back in his wheeled chair and slammed into a shelf on the back wall. Boxes of rubbers and invoice pads and motel keys flew off the shelf, scattering all over the floor.

"Jeez Louise," he said, rubbing the back of his head. "Don't have a cow. I'll give it to you for free, all right? 'Cause you're special friends of mine."

32

*B*ethany's number one fan lived in deepest, darkest Hollywood just north of the Chinese Theatre, in a ragged, little house with an overgrown yard with a sign painted on the mailbox: "Bethany's Number One Fan."

"At least he knows his purpose in life," Terry said, ringing the bell.

He answered the door, eyes swollen and red-rimmed from crying. He was almost as young as Bethany, probably a fan since the age of ten. His thin frame was draped in an oversized T-shirt with Bethany's smile blazing from his chest.

"No comment, okay? I'm in mourning." He started to close the door.

"Wait." Terry pushed it open again. "We need to talk to you about Bethany. We're trying to help her."

He gave us a blank stare, then gasped. "You're the twins who kidnapped her!"

"We didn't kidnap her." I wondered why I still bothered to deny it.

"The car's out back, want to see it? It's almost paid for itself."

"Thanks, but we don't really care to revisit that time in our lives. I'm Kerry McAfee, and this is my sister, Terry."

He took my hand in both of his and bowed over it.

"This hand has touched, has touched..." He looked up at me with worshipful eyes. "Thank you," he whispered.

"Can we come in?" I extracted my hand with some difficulty.

"I was just on my way out. There's a candlelight vigil at the hospital."

"You may be able to help Bethany in another way," Terry told him. "We just need a few minutes of your time."

"Please, anything I can do." He made a sweeping gesture with his arm, and we stepped over the threshold into Bethany Central.

Collages of her photographs covered every square inch of wall. Speakers played a non-stop loop of her music. A long table was set up displaying Bethany merchandise: T-shirts, children's junk jewelry in pink plastic, Bethany dolls waving from toy convertibles and lounging on striped beach chairs. A Bethany lunchbox. A Bethany makeup kit. A Bethany coin purse. A Bethany *air freshener*.

"What happens if Bethany retires? Do you become obsessed with someone else?" I said.

"I hope that's a joke."

"A bad one, sorry. I didn't catch your name?"

"It's Brad."

"I take it you know what happened last night."

He fell down into a tattered armchair. "Yeah. Did she do it? Tell me she didn't do it."

"We don't think so." Terry said. "But we need your help to prove that."

"My help to prove that Bethany is innocent?" He placed his hands in prayer position and lowered his head. "Make me worthy," he murmured. After a moment, he looked up again. "I am at your most humble service."

"Do you record every appearance of Bethany on TV?" I asked, even as I spotted a shelf full of DVDs.

"Not just every appearance, every *mention.* I don't have to tell you it's a full time job. But it's my life's mission to be her hagiographer."

I wasn't about to admit to this geek that I didn't know the meaning of that word. "What we need is any footage you have relating to Bethany's abduction."

"I've got about sixty hours of it. How much time do you have?"

"Less than that."

"We're especially interested in Claude Sterling's statement right after the abduction," Terry said.

"On the steps of the mansion?"

"Yeah."

"No problemo."

He opened a spreadsheet on a notebook computer, where he'd catalogued all of the broadcast footage of Bethany. The entries had file numbers and descriptions and air times. Within seconds, he was able to put his hands on the carefully labeled DVD. He shoved it into the machine and cued up a picture of Claude, wringing his hands and weeping for the cameras while he begged for Bethany to be released back to the public that loved her.

The monitor wasn't as large as I would have expected, but the heavy investment in dolls and lunch boxes probably prevented him from sinking the necessary funds into a large-screen, plasma TV.

"Hold it there," Terry said at one point.

Brad froze the picture on the screen.

And there she was, the purple-haired woman in a sharks-tooth suit, standing at an angle behind Claude. As Brad forwarded the footage frame by frame, the mystery woman slowly came into view. She wore large, dark sunglasses that obscured her eyes. Her features were good, but time had roughened her appearance. Her skin was artificially tight, tanned, and brittle.

"Is it her?" Terry said, peering at the screen.

I leaned in for a closer look. "I can't be sure."

"Who is she?" Brad asked.

"We were hoping you could tell us that," I said. "Have you ever seen this woman before? Do you know if she's an assistant or something?"

"Yeah, I've seen her. But only twice. Once after the abduction, and then when Sterling made a statement after the shooting. That purple hair's really lame."

Terry laughed. "You should see the big white hair. Can we look at your footage of the shooting aftermath?"

"Sure." That DVD was close at hand, sitting on the end table.

We took a close look at some of the coverage of the previous night's incident. Same problem. The woman wasn't on screen very long, and when we froze the picture, details were hard to make out. She never faced the camera straight on, preferring to keep her head lowered.

"Why are you so interested in her?" Brad wanted to know.

I thought back to the trailer park with no small amount of anger. "We think she pretended to be Bethany's mother."

"Her mother's dead."

Terry cocked her head. "She's *supposed* to be."

"No, she's dead. I went to the memorial in Nashville hoping to see Bethany, but she never showed at her own mother's funeral. Plus, I've got a copy of the death certificate right over there."

He pointed to a scrapbook on the coffee table.

"Mind if we see that?" Terry asked.

Brad didn't want any monetary consideration for his help, but he did have other compensation in mind. Terry and I obliged him by sticking our hands in tempera paint and making prints for him on a piece of butcher paper. Under the palm prints, we signed it *Bethany's Abductors*.

It was the least we could do for the poor obsesso. He said he was going to frame the paper and give it a place of honor in the entryway.

Terry rubbed her blue palms together. "Who says there's no glamour in private investigation?"

"So Andie Sue was a fake. Boy, was she good. She ridiculed the tabloid reporters for being too stupid to look for a death certificate so that *we* wouldn't look into it. Classic reverse psychology."

"So where were we in terms of our master plot?"

"Fact number one: the purple-haired impersonator is someone close to Claude. Fact number two: someone in Claude's household was practicing Bethany's signature, probably to dummy up a contract giving him rights to her songs or something. Fact number three: someone killed Adler and framed Bethany for it. Motive: the 'moral turpitude' clause kicks in, and guess who benefits? Our pal Claude. Everything comes back to Claude."

Terry popped the end of her pigtail in her mouth, chewing it. "But Claude would already have rights to Bethany's songs. The producers always keep the publishing rights. He's got no motive to do this."

"To pump up the sales? Remember that one?"

"But there's no way Claude could have tracked her to Adler's apartment."

"Unless he's been following her all along."

"How?"

"Maybe he's got other people tracking her. *She* thought there were. Maybe we were hired as a blind."

Terry shook her head. "Bethany's too erratic. Jumping from car to car. Probably from room to room. Always looking over her shoulder. How could they follow her, unless...?" The pigtail dropped from her mouth.

"Unless what?"

"Unless her cell phone has GPS." She snapped her fingers. "That's it, she has a GPS-enabled phone that they're able to monitor somehow."

We went back to the house and asked our new friend Brad for a little online time. He was anxious to join the throngs gathering outside the hospital for Bethany's vigil so he left us in the house to use his computer, making us promise to lock up when we left. His trust was touching.

On the Internet, we read all about the GPS-enabled cell phones that were currently on the market. The phones sent a signal to a computer transceiver, and then computer mapping software pinpointed the user's location. It was apparently the bane of teenagers whose parents could always know where they were when the phone was on. If the phone wasn't on, the kids had some *s'plaining to do* when they got home.

They were also used by trucking and sales companies to keep track of their loads and their traveling salesmen.

"Check it out," Terry said, laughing. "Here's a police department that used 'em to catch their patrol officers hanging out at Dunkin' Donuts!"

"Wicked."

Terry pushed back from the computer. "So Bethany could have had a GPS-enabled cell phone and not know it. Claude tracks her via satellite, waits for his moment, and then sets her up for murder."

"You think he's that insidiously brilliant?"

"Won't know until somebody checks the phone." She got up from the computer. "Let's go see our fine friends in blue."

And with that, we locked up Bethany Central and headed out to the Hollywood division.

At the station, we asked the desk sergeant if we could see detectives Guerra and Howard.

"What's it regarding?" The cranky, overweight woman looked more like a postal worker than a cop. Either way, I didn't trust her with a gun.

"It's regarding Bethany's situation," I told her.

"Sorry," she said. "We're all full up on psychic tips."

"We're the ones who found her and called it in," Terry said. "Tell them it's the McAfees."

"Why didn't you say so?" She picked up the phone. "Didn't recognize you without your serial killer masks."

Howard and Guerra ushered us into the same interview room where they had perpetrated the Manilow torture.

"We appreciate what you've done so far," Howard told us firmly. "But you're gonna have to back off now and let us take it from here."

"Did you find a tracker on Bethany's Jeep?" I asked, ignoring his admonition.

"No, but we found its rightful owner," Guerra said. "The Jeep was stolen from a Whole Foods parking lot in West Hollywood. Bethany broke in and found the extra keys under the seat."

"Clever," Terry said.

"Huh?" Howard glared at her. "I hope I didn't hear you call that little killer *clever*."

I tried to deflect him. "What about Adler? You promised to report back on his anatomy."

Guerra held up two fingers. Adler'd had a full set.

"Oh." I was strangely disappointed.

"There's something else," Terry said. "We need to know if Bethany made any calls from Adler's apartment. I mean, other than the call she made to us. We wondered if it was possible she called someone and told them where she was going."

"No calls were made," Howard said. "We checked."

"You checked Bethany's cell phone? And you checked Adler's phone records?"

Guerra squinted at her. "What's your point?"

"We think it was Claude," Terry told them. "And here's how we think he did it."

They sat poker-faced as she rambled on, recounting the bit about the purple-haired woman who might have pretended to be Bethany's mother. She related how the woman had invited us in for a drink, where she provided "proof" that Bethany was eighteen years old. Afterward, she disappeared into the night. Terry set the birth certificate down on the table. The two men gave it a glance.

"Somehow Claude has been tracking Bethany, using us as a blind. That way we could testify that he didn't know where she was, and therefore *couldn't* have set her up. But somehow he did know. Maybe your electronics experts can check the phone to see if it's a GPS-enabled cell phone—"

Howard stopped her. "We looked for that because you were so convinced she'd been followed. See? We gave you credit. The GPS had been disabled."

Terry was momentarily stumped, but she wasn't about to give up. "But *somehow* he knew where she was going. He followed her to Adler's and drugged her to make it look like she killed the man."

I could see their jaws grinding. They were trying to be patient but it was a stretch, especially for Howard. "Why?" he said brusquely. "What's Sterling's motive?"

"There's a moral turpitude clause in Bethany's contract."

Howard sank his chin into his hand. "So?"

"So he can sue her if she murders someone!"

They burst out laughing, unable or unwilling to hide their derision.

Guerra took pity on Terry and stopped laughing first. "He could *always* sue her, Kerry."

"Terry."

He smiled to indicate it didn't matter to him which one she was. We were a *pair* of nuts, as far as he was concerned, indistinguishable one from the other.

"Look," Howard finally said, "we've been doing this a long time. Some fifteen years, right?"

Guerra affirmed.

"And you know how many *master plots* we've seen cooked up by *criminal masterminds?*"

I thought I knew the answer.

Sure enough, he held up his fingers in a big goose egg.

"People are stupid and brutal. They kill for stupid, brutal reasons. They don't sit around plotting and scheming and putting trackers on jeeps and framing people for murder. That's for books and movies. Real killers act on impulse and leave a trail of evidence a mile long."

I beamed to Terry mentally—*This is pointless.*

"We're on the case," Guerra added. "If we need any civilian help, you'll be the first ones we call."

Obviously we'd moved into gadfly territory. They were willing to humor us only so far, and the humor rope had run out. They took turns shaking our hands, the official kiss-off.

"So, what'll you do now?" Howard asked. "What's next for you?"

Terry gave him a wan smile. "I guess we'll go back to duck farming."

33

And so we spent the afternoon in front of the television, dogs in our laps, chips and salsa on the coffee table, watching the drama as it continued to unfold. Thanks to twenty-four hour news programming, we saw the same story repeated at least a thousand times. There were no new developments, but that didn't keep them from reporting the old ones with the same level of breathlessness every hour on the hour.

Bethany's tour had been cancelled. The concert promoters would be refunding the ticket holders' money. Sales of Bethany's CDs, however, remained in the toilet.

"Yes, girly, there *is* such a thing as bad publicity," I muttered.

Terry got up from the couch with a grunt of annoyance. "I can't take it anymore." She carried Paquito over to the computer and snuggled him down in her lap as she logged onto the Internet.

I picked up Muffy and followed her over. "What are you looking for?"

"I don't know."

"What angle are you pursuing, then?"

"Bethany's sales, her business. Following the money, like the man said. There has to be something we overlooked."

We spent more than an hour going through scores of articles spanning the whole of Bethany's storied career. They were mostly fan pages and celebrity profiles, but finally Terry happened upon a headline in *Billboard* that took our breath away: "Bethany Negotiates Unprecedented Deal."

"Snap," Terry said.

She had to buy an online subscription to access the article, but it was well worth the money. The article was dated three years previous, when Bethany's popularity was at its height. She was selling tens of millions of units, and tickets to her concerts were scalped for thousands. It seemed that Bethany's phenomenal popularity had put her in an enviable bargaining position when renegotiating her deal with the record company. Such a good position, in fact, that she was able to obtain the publishing rights to her songs, an almost unheard-of situation.

That meant that every time one of her songs was played on the radio or MTV or licensed for a commercial or even watered down for *easy listenin'*, Bethany got a royalty. Not one based on net receipts, which are squeezed down to nothing through creative accounting practices, but right off the top.

It's how Michael Jackson got to be a billionaire, owning the rights to the Beatles catalog. Bethany would own her own best-selling songs. Only, in this case, there was a catch.

A beautiful, beautiful catch.

The rights to Bethany's library would only become hers when she reached the age of eighteen.

"There's his motive!" Terry yelled.

The pups roused from their naps: *What's all the excitement? Time to throw the ball?*

"Sorry, kids," she said to them. "Mama just got a little excited."

"The timing is perfect. Just as she's going to gain control of her library, she's implicated in murder."

"If Bethany's convicted, I guarantee you those rights remain with Claude."

"How *fiendishly* clever of him."

She gave me a sly smile. "He's not as fiendishly clever as us."

"Well, duh."

34

Claude sounded invigorated rather than distraught when we spoke to him on the phone. I suppose it could have been nervous energy—up for hours beside a hospital bed, conferring with doctors and talking to the police—but I didn't think so.

"What a night! The worst of my life!"

"You doing all right?" I pretended to buy into his act.

"My heart hasn't given out yet. But the day is young."

We offered our condolences, and then told him we expected a second week's pay. He put up no resistance. Why should he? Why balk at the paltry sum of five thousand dollars? If our suspicions were correct, he was now one of the richest men in the world. We planned to confront him about his newfound wealth when we saw him in Hollywood.

The butler answered the door to the mansion, greeting us with that strange, faraway look in his eye.

"Think *he's* in on it?" Terry whispered as we followed him to Claude's office. "He's plenty creepy."

"Stay focused, okay?"

The phones were ringing, but Claude wasn't answering. He sat at his desk with his face in his hands, looking even more rumpled and bloodshot than he'd looked on TV. His state-of-the-art notebook was closed on the desk. He was unwired and by all appearances, coming unwound.

He handed a stack of bills to Terry. She stuffed them inside her jacket without counting them.

"So, girls," Claude said, resigned. "We tried, huh?"

"Yeah." I sat down in front of his desk, as did Terry. "Sorry about everything that's happened."

"I saw it coming, I just couldn't face it. I thought if we could get through one more concert tour—"

I kept my voice even as I said, "If you saw it coming, why didn't you do something?"

He stared at me. "Like what? Throwing myself in front of the train? I did everything I knew how to do. I got her the best shrink money could buy. It wasn't enough, but I did my best."

Terry laid the birth certificate on his desk. "Here's your proof that she's been an adult for four months."

He glanced at the document sadly. "Bad news, if it's real. She'll be tried as an adult. They won't go easy on her."

"Oh, I wouldn't be so sure she'll go to trial," I said.

Claude's eyes flashed angrily. "What do you mean? They got her cold! Her fingerprints, gunshot residue on her hands, motive—"

I interrupted his tirade. "About that motive. Was it Bethany herself who brought those accusations of sexual harassment against Adler?"

He shrugged. "She confirmed it."

"But who actually reported it?" Terry asked.

"The boyfriend."

"Kyle Hearn?"

"Yeah, he saw some funny business going on and told me about it. Adler would brush up against her. You know, with his pelvis. And he'd manage to get his hands on her top when he was correcting her schoolwork. It was subtle, but Kyle was watching like a hawk, and he caught it."

Claude pinched the bridge of his nose.

"I confronted Bethany," he continued. "But she was in denial, big time. The guy had told her she was a genius. Can you believe that? Soaping her up and making out like he was the only one in the world who appreciated her true worth. But I finally got her to admit it."

"She said he'd molested her?" I asked.

"She said maybe it had happened once or twice, but she was sure it was by accident. That was all I needed to hear."

"So you fired him," Terry said.

"And then another man close to Bethany got canned for being too hands-on," I added. "Kyle, himself."

"He was *shtuppin'* her!" Claude roared at me.

"At her request," I pointed out.

Claude looked at us in disbelief. "I see where you're going with this! *I'm* the bad guy?"

"We're not saying that," I assuaged him. "You may have been well motivated, but if you remove everyone from her life that means something to her...it's no wonder she rebelled."

"Rebelling? Is that what you call it?" He leaned in and stabbed the air with his index finger. "She crossed a line. She can throw up her food, she can run away, and she can steal cars. But when she takes a human life—even a scumbag like Adler's—that's an abomination."

He took a deep breath and turned his chair toward the window, gazing out over the lawn.

"So, Claude," Terry said, "just out of curiosity—how does your contract work with Bethany? We read about the deal she negotiated, giving her the publishing rights to her songs when she turned eighteen."

"Yeah." He said angrily, turning to face us again. "Unless she goes and murders someone."

I feigned ignorance. "Oh yeah? You have a moral turpitude clause or something?"

"I put that in the deal myself."

"Way back then, you foresaw Bethany killing someone?"

"I just try to cover my bases. I've been working with musicians my whole life, girly, and I know anything can happen. What if Kurt Cobain hadn't been married? His estate would have been controlled by the government. How would it be if after all my work, the rewards went to someone else?"

"Still, it seems amazingly farsighted of you to predict America's darling going up for murder at the exact moment she would inherit her own publishing rights."

"What did I do to make you think so poorly of me? Am I really that bad a guy?"

I stared back, letting his words fall into the silence between us.

"*I* was the chump, going for that deal in the first place," he said. "But she had me against a wall. I got the moral turpitude clause in there just so I'd feel like I got *something* in the negotiation."

"Who had you up against a wall?" Terry asked. "Bethany?"

"Andie Sue. The woman was a shark. She looked like a truck stop waitress, but she'd been reading the trades and the entertainment magazines her whole life. She knew the business, and she had me just where she wanted me. It was going to be her way or she wouldn't let Bethany sing another note. I gave in. What else could I do?"

"So Andie Sue negotiated this great deal for Bethany, and then Bethany turned around and sued her for emancipation?"

"Bethany was furious that her mother had almost scotched her career. She wanted control of her life so it couldn't happen again."

"But Bethany didn't get control of her life," Terry pointed out. "*You* did. And if Bethany's suddenly out of commission, you control her publishing rights."

"That wasn't the way it was set up at first. If anything happened to Bethany, Andie Sue was supposed to get control of the library. I was in line behind her." He smiled. "Ironic, isn't it?"

"Why 'ironic'?" I asked.

"Halfway through the lawsuit, Andie Sue walked. Said she'd give up any claim she had on Bethany's assets if they would make this one concession. Nobody believed she'd outlive Bethany, so the lawyers let it stand. And twelve months later she was dead, anyway."

"And as a result, the publishing rights come to you."

"Correct."

"What if Andie Sue isn't dead?"

Claude wasn't having it. "She's dead."

"She says different."

"You meet some trailer trash who says she's Bethany's mother and you believe her?"

"Then why are you crediting that birth certificate as real?" Terry demanded. "It *came* from the trailer trash woman."

"Who's crediting? I said *if* it's real!"

"Who benefits if it is?"

"Nobody!" Claude was becoming apoplectic. "Bethany will go to prison for life if she committed the crime as an adult!"

"Because that's what happens to people who exhibit moral turpitude, huh, Claude?" I gave him a knowing smile. "If Bethany's an adult when she commits the crime, there's no question of leniency. No chance of her getting a break as a minor. The pop star goes to prison, and you get the payoff. The rights revert to you."

"What *exactly* are you saying?"

"I'm saying, maybe somebody dummied up a fake birth certificate in order to make Bethany appear to be an adult."

I'd swear I saw his scalp stream, the toupee curling at the edges.

"You know," he said in a tight voice, "I don't think I want you girls in my house anymore."

I crossed my arms. "Gee, and just when we were getting to the truth."

He stood and leaned on his fists, his eyes narrowed into furious little slits. "*What* truth?"

Terry jumped up and faced him over the desk. "You set all this up, Claude, to get control of Bethany's publishing rights. And we're going to prove it."

"Fine!" he bellowed. "Prove it, girly!"

Terry pulled the five thousand out of her pocket and tossed it on the desk. "You know what? We don't want your blood money."

He sank back into his chair, as if his legs were melting under him. "Boy did I ever have you girls wrong. I thought you had class."

"You also thought we were incompetent," Terry said. "And that's gonna cost you, Claude."

Claude stared up at Terry, expressionless. He seemed too weary to respond to her veiled threat.

"She doesn't mean that," I said soothingly. "We're all tense after what's happened. I think we may all be saying things we'll regret."

Claude gave me a grudging nod. "Yeah, sorry about the harsh words. I guess we're all a little *fuhtutzed*, under the circumstances."

Terry and I started out the door, and then I stopped as if suddenly struck by an idea. "By the way, who's that woman who's always at your side when something goes down with Bethany? Your right-hand person who never seems to be here when we come around?"

"What right-hand woman?"

"With the purple hair."

"It's blackberry henna," said a smooth voice behind me. "Sorry to interrupt, but my ears were burning."

Terry and I spun around to find ourselves face-to-face with a woman in a stylish black suit, designer glasses on a gold chain, and a perfect purple manicure to match the mannish hairdo.

"Dr. Marietta Kirby." She held out her hand. "You're the twins I've heard so much about."

I forced my mouth to work. "Nice to meet you." Her handshake was cool and firm.

"Dr. Kirby is Bethany's shrink," Claude explained. "A great doc, but I guess she's no miracle worker. Huh, Kirb?"

"Unfortunately not," she said with a smile full of rue.

Terry shot me a disappointed look—*This woman is not Andie Sue.*

Marietta Kirby was educated, a cultivated woman of the world. Even if she *could* do a mean impersonation of a truck stop waitress, there was no way to mistake her for the woman who'd posed as Bethany's mother.

Andie Sue—or whoever that was at the trailer park—had Bethany's upturned nose, not a strong, aquiline one. Her teeth were not a wonder of orthodontia like this woman's. Nor could her scrawny arms and legs ever be mistaken for Marietta Kirby's well-toned limbs. Marietta's dark, assessing eyes could never be mistaken for Andie Sue's liquid blue orbs.

She let her gaze linger on our faces. I felt like something small and insignificant, visible by dint of a microscope. She was probably giving us an instant mental work-up as we stood there.

"Bethany told us she'd stopped taking her meds," I informed her.

"I feared as much."

"We were hoping you could prescribe more," Terry said. "But it's too late for that now."

"She'd have to be examined first. It's unethical and frankly illegal to prescribe medication without assessing the patient's condition. And her condition would necessarily have changed after she stopped taking the medication. A vicious circle, I'm afraid."

"What's wrong with her?" I asked.

Kirby looked over at Claude before answering. He gave her the go-ahead.

"Bipolar disorder. A rather extreme case."

"Don't say nothin' about that to nobody." Claude waved his hands frantically. "The tabs would have a field day with it."

Why would he care? It would only reinforce his version of events: Crazy Bethany killed her tutor.

"Is that why she shot Adler?" Terry asked Kirby.

"I can't say with any certainty," she began in a detached tone. "But I can tell you Bethany cycles very quickly from depression to mania. If you've been with her since she stopped taking the medication, you may have witnessed some erratic tendencies."

Running away? Baring her butt to the public?

"Disordered thinking, racing thoughts..." Kirby continued.

Plenty of those.

"She may have experienced severe persecutory delusions or suicidal behavior..."

Believing people were following her? Cutting herself?

"Changing her appearance, dressing in a more sexually provocative way..."

More provocative than the nearly nude beaded get-up?

"Or, on the other hand, more disheveled and slovenly. She may have become aggressive, even frightening..."

Eat lead, creep?

Kirby paused, her litany of symptoms exhausted. "Did you observe any of that?" She looked at me for an answer.

"Right on the mark, doctor."

"Even with treatment, she was a danger to herself," Kirby asserted. "Drugs can mediate but not cure the disorder. Untreated, I'm afraid her condition degenerated into full-blown psychosis."

"Psychotics are usually the ones who do the killing, huh?" Terry was evidently not sold on the suave doctor's diagnosis.

Kirby offered Terry a tight smile. "Frequently. Not always."

"Yeah, sometimes it's people with a financial motive." Terry glanced back at Claude, who was toying with his pinky ring. She turned back to Kirby. "Or who are just plain evil."

Kirby stared back with her dispassionate doctor's gaze—mentally clearing some time on her calendar for Terry, perhaps. Or filling out an emergency prescription for antipsychotics.

"Gotta bounce." Terry squeezed past Marietta to get to the door. "You guys take care, now."

"Yeah, good luck with everything, Claude," I added. "Hope it all works out for the best."

He didn't lift his eyes to watch us go. "You, too," he muttered.

"So nice to have met you," Marietta Kirby purred.

As we left the room, I could feel her evaluating us with that brain-penetrating black gaze—yet another predator that would no longer have Bethany's carcass to feed on.

$\mathcal{F}$inally the cable news channels had something new to report on the Bethany affair: The DA was bringing charges.

We watched the news conference in glum fascination as he made the announcement. Howard and Guerra stood behind him at the microphone. The world press was assembled in front of them, broadcasters from Italy, Germany, Britain, France, Hong Kong—identifiable by the placards on their microphones. The foreigners jostled for space with the American journalists, both local and national.

"The office of the District Attorney has charged singer Bethany Jo Kopalski—Bethany, as she is known to the public—with second-degree murder in the unlawful death of Glen Frederick Adler."

The reporters shouted over each other, jumping up and down to get the DA's attention like school kids clamoring for the teacher's attention.

I burst out laughing. Terry turned to me, baffled.

"I was just thinking about how Glen Adler would have handled a press conference. He'd be whacking the reporters with his ruler for talking out of turn."

"Yeah, poor guy. Using his pathetic little ruler for self-defense. Probably thought it was a magical light saber or something."

"It worked on the second-graders, anyway."

The DA began answering questions.

"Ms. Kopalski released a statement through her attorney today, admitting to the shooting Mr. Adler."

"She admits it?" I said. "Well, that's all, folks."

"No," the DA said in response to a reporter's question. "She has not made any allegations of sexual assault. We don't have a motive *per se*, but as you are probably aware, Ms. Kopalski was under the influence of controlled substances at the time of the shooting."

More shouting from the throng.

"No, there will be no trial. Ms. Kopalski has entered a guilty plea to the charges. That is all. Further questions can be directed to our public information officer. Thank you."

He stepped away from the podium and made his way back to the court building. The reporters continued to shout, swarming the poor public information officer, a woman in a conservative gray suit who was soon swallowed up by the crush of correspondents.

Terry said, "We gonna let this stand?"

"No, we're going to spend the rest of our days tracking down the woman who said she was Bethany's mother and trying to piece together this great conspiracy, making it our life's mission until we lose the house and end up declaring Bethany's innocence from a shopping cart on the corner."

"Loser."

"Idiot."

"Wimp."

"Lunatic."

"Well, I feel better," Terry declared, getting up from the couch. Hurling abuse at me always improved her mood. "Let's get something to eat."

She continued to obsess while we munched cheese sandwiches, turning the situation over and over in her mind. I tried desperately to persuade her to give it up.

"Face it, Ter. Bethany's confessed. There's nothing more we can do."

"She was drugged. She could have been hypnotized. We've seen that before. She told us she spaces out and doesn't remember things."

"Doesn't remember someone being shot in her presence? That's a stretch."

"Not if you've been given a date rape drug. It obliterates your memory completely."

I shook my head. *Not buying.*

"Then what about Dr. Purple Hair?" Terry proposed. "What if she and Claude were in it together? She medicates Bethany and psychs her out, then Claude sets up the murder?"

"There!"

"Where?" she said, turning around.

"I'm talking about what you just said. It makes all of this moot. Claude wasn't *there.* He couldn't have known where Bethany was that night. Even if Claude was in league with Dr. Purple Hair somehow, it was still Bethany who pulled the trigger. She was incapacitated, so it's second-degree murder. That's what she's charged with, and that's what she's pled to. If they set this up, they did it so that it's completely airtight. Bethany did exactly what they wanted her to do, *including confessing*, and there's no way to prove a conspiracy. A jury would never buy it as a defense anyway."

"I *hate* it when you're right."

"And you know I am."

"Sore winner."

We heard the front door open. "Anybody here?" Lance called out. "I came to get my stuff."

We went to greet him in the living room. He stood there with his duck box, a symphony of cheeping coming from within. They dogs ran over to say hello to their wee feathered friends, and Lance bent over to let them sniff. "Say bye-bye, little guys."

"You moving on, bud?" Terry asked him.

"Good news, bad news," he answered. "The bad news is they said I can't bring the ducks to work anymore. They're too much of a distraction."

"Aw, too bad," I said. "Want to leave them here?"

"No, because the good news is I found them a permanent home!"

Terry clapped her hands. "Great! A preserve or something?"

"No. A guy I busted for drunk and disorderly owns some property in the hills. He said I could build them a pen on it."

"Drunk and disorderly?" Terry and I exchanged dubious looks.

"He wasn't *that* disorderly. He was just taking a leak on PCH. He's a great guy, really."

"Oh," Terry said. "Does he have a pond or something for them to paddle in?"

"No, but I can rig up a wading pool in the pen."

"What about setting them free? What about letting them live in a natural setting? That's what you said you wanted to do in the beginning."

He stuck out his lower lip. "Yeah, but they think I'm their mother now. They'll be lost without me."

"Sure, for a while," I said. "But it's normal for little ones to leave their mothers and live their own lives. It's the way of things."

Lance's face began to crumble, and tears threatened to come. "But what if the coyote comes back?"

"The coyote *could* come back. You can't control that."

"But how would I even know if they're alive or dead?"

"You'll just have to trust that they'll be okay," Terry said, patting his arm.

He shrugged off her hand. "Oh yeah, easy for you to say, Miss Food Chain! I know what you want! You want to send them out there to be eaten!"

"No, Lance," she said reasonably. "If all ducks were eaten in the wild, there wouldn't *be* any ducks, would there?"

"But I can't just set them loose!"

"It would be cruel to keep them penned up."

"People keep pets all the time!" he said. "*You* keep pets."

I looked over at the dogs. "They're domesticated. Ducks are wild creatures. They like to dive for fish and migrate south. To fly and be free."

Lance plopped down on the couch with the box, wiping his eyes. "I guess you're right." After a few moments, he seemed resigned to a duckless future. "I guess I'll...I'll keep them in the pen until they're big enough to be on their own, then I'll let them go." He petted their tiny heads with the pad of his index finger.

We observed a moment of silence, and then Lance sat up excitedly. "I know! I can put those radio frequency things on them, like they had in the Animal Planet show!"

I'd gone to bed early during the bird show. "What radio frequency things?"

"You know, like when the ornithologists want to track the birds' migration, they put the radio things around their legs, and they know exactly where they are at all times. Then I'd know where to visit them!"

"*Radio frequency things...?*" Terry said slowly, turning to me.

"Or if I couldn't get one of those, I could try those computer chips they use to keep track of dogs."

"*Computer chips...?*" I repeated, turning to Terry.

"Yeah, they insert them under the skin and you can locate your lost dog, just like a GPS tracker for cars."

"Your lost dog?" Terry and I shouted together, *"Or your lost megastar!"*

I ran over to Lance and grabbed his head in my hands, kissing both his cheeks. "Lance, you're a genius!"

"I am?"

Terry slugged him in the arm. "You just cracked the case!"

"I love you," I said, running for the door. "And I'm so sorry about the chicken remark."

"What chicken remark?" Lance turned to watch us from the couch. "What's happening? Where are you going?"

"To the Hollywood police station." Terry followed me outside. "Don't wait up for us!"

36

"Hear us out," I said to Howard and Guerra.

I could hardly believe they'd consented to meet with us. But it was still a grudging consent.

"You do know it's against the law to impede an investigation?" Howard asked pointedly.

"What investigation?" Terry scoffed. "You've got everything all sewn up."

Howard and Guerra exchanged weary looks.

"Bethany said she was looking for something," I began, "but she wasn't up looking around the place. She was on the floor cutting herself."

"Yeah," Guerra said. "She cuts herself to relieve stress. Like the stress that comes from killing somebody in cold blood. It's a well-known phenomenon."

"But what if she was looking for something under her skin?" Terry asked.

"Such as?"

"A radio frequency device, similar to the ones used to keep track of dogs."

Both detectives slumped back in their chairs.

"You've got a wild imagination," Howard said with a derisive laugh. "I'll give you that."

"Maybe you'd have to know Claude Sterling the way we do," I said. "Bethany's his golden goose. He's been controlling her every movement for *years*. He's got everything riding on her. There are video cameras all over the house so he can see what she's doing every minute of every day."

"Lots of people have security cameras in their houses," Guerra countered. "Especially celebrities."

"But suddenly, she gets away from him," Terry said. "And she's out there in the big bad world without her medication and doing who knows what. She's completely out of his control, so what does he do?"

Howard gestured to us. "He hires you two to bring her back."

"Why us?" I said. "Why hire a couple of young redheads who aren't the best at their jobs?"

"Don't put yourself down," Guerra chided me. "You should always be on your own side."

"I'm telling you what *Claude* thinks. He's got these two incompetent girls who are allegedly in charge of Bethany, and she keeps slipping through their fingers. To all appearances Bethany is out on the loose, and Terry and I are witnesses to that because we've been chasing her all over the place unsuccessfully. But then—"

"Yeah?" Howard feigned a gasp. "Is this the exciting conclusion?"

I ignored his sarcasm. "It turns out Claude really *does* know where Bethany is at all times. He knows because one of those times that she cut herself, he inserted a radio frequency ID chip under her skin. That way he's able to track her at all times. And when the time is right, he sets her up for murder. He follows her to Adler's where he drugs her, wraps her hand around the gun, and *boom!*"

"*Yeaaaahhhhhh!*" Terry leaped out of her seat.

The detectives looked at her in consternation. She gave them a goofy grin and sat down.

"My bad," I apologized, turning back to the cops. "As I was saying, Claude puts her hand on the gun and shoots. Adler's dead, and Bethany has gunshot residue on her. She's too stoned to remember what happened, but she feels guilty about the shabby way Adler was treated, letting Claude accuse him of sexual harassment, so she transmutes that guilt into a confession of murder."

Howard and Guerra both sighed.

"It's like something from a bad cop show," Guerra said.

Terry shrugged. "Can we help it if reality is stranger than TV?"

37

Two hours later, Detectives Howard and Guerra returned to the interview room, beside themselves with excitement.

"Unbelievable!" Howard said. "You were right!"

"The doctor used a metal detector to find the chip," Guerra informed us. "It's a passive radio frequency transponder, the size of a pencil lead. It doesn't have its own power source, but someone using a hand-held transceiver can request information from the chip via antenna. That's how you locate it."

"Can we see it?" I asked.

"Had to leave it at the hospital," Howard said. "If we moved it, that would tip him off."

"Oh, right."

"Guess where it was on her body?" Guerra said.

Before we could guess, Howard jumped in. "She's got a tattoo of a Chinese ideogram on her back. It's between her shoulders, impossible for her to reach. Even with all her cutting, she would never be able to remove it."

"Yeah," Guerra said, "we faxed a picture of the tattoo to a translator, and guess what it means?"

"We give up," I said.

"It means 'pure,'" Howard announced.

Terry smiled at me. "How apt."

"This doesn't mean she's off the hook yet," Guerra cautioned her. "But we're getting a warrant to search Sterling's house for the transceiver. It has to be a powerful gizmo because most transponders can only broadcast for a hundred feet or so."

"He probably picked up some ultra high-tech deal from Japan or somewhere," Howard declared. "If it's there, we'll find it."

"Brilliant," Terry said. "Can we come with you when you do the search?"

Guerra gave her a wise look. "Could we stop you?"

"Only if you lock us up."

"Not this time, Kerry," he said, patting her shoulder. "Not this time."

But she didn't correct him on the name. Not this time.

We waited in the back of a cruiser and watched as Howard and Guerra jogged past the stone lions up to the door of the mansion, followed by two uniformed officers.

The butler answered. The detectives showed him their warrant, then muscled their way inside.

It couldn't have been more than two minutes when the radio squawked with the news. Terry and I jumped out of the patrol car over the protestations of the driver. We scrambled up the stairs two at a time and ran through the front door.

The butler tried to block us, but Terry slammed him with the door and he fell on his behind on the marble floor, spinning in circles like a break-dancer in formal wear. We tore through the sunlit living room and around the corner into Claude's inner sanctum.

There we found Howard and Guerra standing over Claude's dead body.

He had collapsed on the floor next to his desk. Foamy spittle had gathered in the corners of his mouth, drying to an unappetizing crust. His face was frozen in a grimace, both hands clutching his left breast.

"I've seen this before," Guerra said. "Massive coronary."

Terry and I stared at Claude, unable to fit his demise into our mental schematic. This wasn't the way it was supposed to end. Claude was supposed to be arrested and charged with Adler's murder. We were supposed to be crowned the master sleuths, vindicated for all the crap we'd been through. The pop princess was supposed to be rescued from the music industry dragon.

"It was all for nothing." Terry appeared numb. "All his planning, all that killing and manipulating—all for nothing."

"Another scumbag bites the dust," Howard said philosophically.

"Wait. Check it out." I pointed to the desk.

On top of the blotter was a contract for the tour, open to the signature page. The slot for Bethany's signature was blank.

And next to the contract was a pad of paper covered with Bethany's signature. Claude had been practicing it himself. He had apparently been planning to dummy up a backdated contract for the tour. I guess a lawsuit for breach had been his backup scheme if the whole murder thing didn't work out.

The coroner's assistant pronounced Claude dead at the scene, declaring him the victim of a "coronary event," which sounded weirdly festive, like disco night at a cardiologists' convention.

Claude's medical records would later reveal that he had four blocked arteries. His doctor had recommended bypass surgery months earlier, but Claude had put it off because of the upcoming tour.

His part in Adler's murder couldn't be proved. No portable data system with a transceiver could be found on the premises, or in his Corvette, or anywhere else the police could think to look.

The chip remained a mystery.

Guerra and Howard interviewed Marietta Kirby but got nothing useful from her. And she was loaded with alibis: out for dinner with friends on the night of Adler's death, at a conference in Geneva during the week of Fellows's murder. She was more than vouched for by all of her peers—a highly regarded physician in good stead with the medical board and everyone else they could think to ask.

No one could determine who had planted the RF tag under Bethany's skin, least of all Bethany herself. She could offer no explanation for its presence.

Nor did she try to defend herself. No abuse excuse, no *I was incapacitated due to cannon expulsion,* nothing. She quietly accepted responsibility for Adler's death, without even a request for a reduced sentence.

The consensus by the legal pundits on TV was that she would be consigned to prison for the entire fifteen years, with possible time off for good behavior.

We couldn't bring ourselves to go to Claude's memorial the following Sunday, so we again watched the coverage on TV. Lots of big names had shown up to pay their respects, names like McCartney, Clapton, Simon, Timberlake, Seal, and Bowie. The photographers and entertainment reporters were in a feeding frenzy.

We sat on the couch, back where we were before it all started. Except now we had no job, no bucks, no ducks.

The celebrities filed into the temple for the funeral. It was just like the Academy Awards, minus the E! Entertainment commentary on the mourning clothes. The paparazzi were cordoned off with red ropes, snapping away at the procession of grim-faced stars. One particular woman stood out of the crowd. She might have gone unnoticed in her designer black leather, blending right in with the rest of the chic crowd, if not for her conspicuous purple hair.

"Look, it's Kirby."

Terry nodded. "So it is."

Marietta Kirby was statuesque and elegant and very distinguished in her grief. But she needed someone to lean on, apparently, and fortunately a very handsome young man was there to do the honors. He gallantly supported her as they went up the stairs arm in arm.

I peered intently at the screen. "Wait. Who's that with her?"

Just then the camera zoomed in on the striking couple. I recognized him at once. The man on Marietta Kirby's arm was none other than Kyle Hearn.

Terry's mouth fell open. "The shrink and the hunk?"

I returned her baffled look. "Why is she hanging out with a disgraced bodyguard?"

"I don't know, but they look very close."

"Almost like lovers."

Terry jumped up from the couch. "Almost like co-conspirators!"

The pair proceeded into the temple. From behind, I could appreciate how slender Marietta was. Skinny, you might even say.

"What's wrong with us?" Terry exclaimed. "It was right under our noses the whole time!"

"Hold on. We don't know..." I was already second-guessing what my instincts were telling me.

"There's nobody left! It has to be the two of them!"

"You're saying we've solved the case through process of elimination?"

"It's better than the police have done."

"If it's true that they're co-conspirators, does that mean we were wrong about Claude?"

She paced the floor. "Not necessarily. The three of them could have been working together. When Claude died, those two followed through on their own." She checked her watch. "How long would it take us to get to West Hollywood?"

"Sunday traffic...maybe twenty minutes?"

"And how long is a memorial?"

"An hour at least. Claude's buddies will be taking the podium to reminisce about the booze, babes, and high times on the road."

"Okay," she said, heading for the door, "the temple is five minutes away from Kyle's place. An hour and five minutes, less the twenty it will take to get there. That gives us forty-five minutes to break into his house and find the transceiver."

"But shouldn't we call Howard and Guerra?"

"On Sunday?"

"Oh, right."

"Anyway, we can't leave it to a couple of wussy Fanilows. This is a job for...*The Texas Chainsaw Twins!*"

The little Spanish house in West Hollywood appeared empty. The curtains were drawn, no lights were on inside. We got off the bike and ambled casually up the walk.

"Go check for dogs," Terry whispered to me.

I leaned against the gate, calling softly, "Here doggies! Here, killer-killers!"

No four-legged death squad appeared. I went back around the corner of the house to join Terry on the porch. She was working on the lock with an illegal pick.

"The dogs aren't there. They could be in the house."

"I've got a plan for that," she said. "We throw the door open wide, and they'll run outside. Then we dart past them into the house."

"He said they're trained to attack."

"When they leap at us, I'll slam them with the door."

"That'll hurt!"

"Stun 'em, is all." She turned and looked at me. "All right, then you run past me and I'll draw the dogs out of the house."

"You'll be torn to pieces! Let's think of a better plan."

She put her ear to the door. "You know what? I don't hear them."

"He called 'em stealth killers."

"He has hardwood floors. I'd at least hear their toe-nails. Even stealth killers have toenails." Before I could object, she threw open the door.

No dogs arrived to tear off our arms or rip our throats out. Were they locked in the back room?

"Look for an alarm," Terry said, ducking inside.

I found an alarm box just inside the door, a red light shining in the lower right corner.

"Here it is!"

She looked over at it. "It's a silent alarm. It'll take the cops ten minutes to get here. Come on!"

Yikes. Ten minutes?

"Look there!" I pointed to two large crates in the dining room. Behind the wire mesh doors were two large shadowy forms. The Rottweilers lay in the crates, heads low, whimpering softly.

"They've been tranquilized," I said. "He's taking them on a plane."

We tore around the living room, looking for some-thing that resembled a transceiver. Bethany peered down at us from her larger-than-life poster. But there was little to see. The place had been emptied, which meant that Kyle was leaving town and not planning to return.

"It's not here!" Terry whispered.

"The bedroom!"

We dashed into the back of the house. On the bed we saw suitcases sitting next to Kyle's ski equipment. There were no clothes in the closet, just a couple of plastic garment bags on the floor. A notebook computer sat on the lone table in the room.

"Here!" Terry stood exultant next to the bedside table. On the table was a small wireless computer. Terry punched a key and the screen lit up with a blinking red light pinpointing Bethany's location on a map.

As far as the computer was concerned, she was still at Cedars-Sinai Medical Center in Beverly Hills.

"Look over here! That's Claude's computer!" I pointed to a shoulder bag folded next to the notebook. The soft leather carrier bore the initials C. S. in gold. Terry scurried over and opened the computer, booting it up.

"Terry, we don't have time for this. Let's take the transceiver and get out of here!"

"It's not enough. We need more evidence. We still have a couple of minutes."

"We'll take the computer with us and get the evidence off it later. Come on, Ter. We have to go!"

"They're not gonna care that we broke in if we get evidence of a murder." She searched the desktop screen; then her face broke into a grin. "Gotcha."

She used the touch pad to select a folder labeled "Bank Accounts." One by one, she opened the files contained inside. Bank of America. First Federal. Chase Manhattan. Deutsche Bank. Crédit Lyonnais.

"Real secure," Terry said, chuckling. "His passwords were saved on the drive."

As she paged through the accounts, we saw that every last one was empty of funds. Millions of dollars had been transferred, probably to a numbered account in Switzerland.

Suddenly, the dogs began to whimper in their cages. I turned my head, wondering what had set them off. But Terry was too absorbed in the screen to notice.

"Holy cow," she said, shutting down the computer. "Who would have ever suspected? That hottie is a criminal mastermind."

"Yes," said Kyle from the doorway. "He is."

40

"You're smarter than I gave you credit for." Kyle sneered at us over the top of the gun. The spaniel's eyes had a cruel glint, and his smile was that of a sadist about to be pleasured.

"Never underestimate your opponent," Terry said.

"I didn't."

He continued to hold the gun on us as he reached into the closet, grabbing what I'd believed to be garment bags. Turns out they were body bags. He tossed them on the bed. "These were for you, in case I was wrong."

"The police are on their way," Terry said. "We tripped the alarm."

"The alarm isn't wired to the police station. It sends a signal to this." He reached into his pocket and pulled out a beeper. "You see? I thought it was possible you'd figure everything out before I caught my Swiss Air flight." He slipped the beeper back into his pocket.

"Why didn't you just leave the country?" I nodded to his suitcases. "You were all ready to go. Why stay for the memorial?"

"If I didn't show up, Marietta might suspect I was cutting her out. She insisted on going to Claude's send-off because she wanted to see all the big stars. Stupid groupie."

"Dr. Kirby? She's your girlfriend?" Terry asked.

Kyle snorted. "She thinks we're going to the Caymans together. I'm sure she's packed her leather thong bikini. Can you imagine a woman that age in a thong bikini?"

"Where does she think you are now?"

"Men's room."

"When she finds out you traded her in for a bunch of Swiss ski bunnies, don't you think she'll rat you out? We have an extradition treaty with Switzerland, you know." I didn't know that for a fact, but I was willing to float it. What did I have to lose? Would he yell *Liar, liar, pants on fire* at me before blowing me away?

"I thought about that. I left her a little good-bye gift. A million dollars in her own numbered account in Grand Cayman. It's not what she was expecting, but it's certainly enough to keep her. Maybe she'll meet some fat retiree her own age and live happily ever after until she dies from skin cancer."

"Yeah," Terry said. "Everybody's happy. You're in Switzerland. Marietta's in the Caribbean. The police think Claude was involved in a plot to set Bethany up, wiring her money to offshore bank accounts in advance of his getaway. But then he died before he could flee. The money managers won't notice the missing funds until tomorrow morning when they open for work."

"Very good." Kyle used his free hand to clap against the one holding the gun.

"They won't be able to trace the money," I said. "You'll have moved it around so many times it would take an army of investigators to find it. Meanwhile, you'll have a new identity."

He took a little bow. "Hans Bücher, first generation American with dual citizenship. *Achtung,* baby!" He swished his hips. "Hans is on the slopes!"

"Suits you to a T. So, what now? You want us to zip ourselves up in the bags? Make it easy on you?" I reached for one of them.

"I thought it would be better if we did this in the shower, if that's all right with you. Then I can put you in the bags, rinse the tub, and dump you before I catch my flight."

Great. We are about to be killed by an anal-retentive.

"And nobody's going to see you doing this in broad daylight?" Terry asked. "Nobody's going to find it suspicious that you're carrying two lumpy bags out to your car?"

"Uh, no offense, but you're not exactly lumpy. You could pass for a couple of microphone stands."

"Then nobody's going to think it's odd when your nice, new Lexus SUV arrives at the dump to drop off some microphone stands?"

"No worries. I've scoped out a construction site in Compton. There's no work there on Sundays. The area's blocked by an abandoned strip mall on one side, a big retaining wall on the other. Even if someone does notice me tossing you into the construction Dumpsters—hey, it's Compton. The only thing that gets *their* attention is a drive-by shooting."

"Excellent planning," I said.

He beamed at the compliment. Why do these criminal types always try to impress before killing? Maybe it's because in order to be a killer, you have to have an enormous ego in the first place.

"From the construction site, it's five minutes to the airport. By the time Marietta gets through slobbering all over the big musicians at the funeral, I'll be on the tarmac sipping my preflight cocktail."

Terry looked over at me and shrugged. "Okay," she said, in a voice bordering on cheerful. "Let's do this."

This threw Kyle off his stride. "Why are you so happy about it?"

"If something's inevitable, there's no point in fighting it." She started towards him. "Let's go."

He jammed the gun barrel into Terry's cheek. "I'll shoot you right here!"

She gave him an exasperated look. "I certainly wish you'd make up your mind. Here, there—"

He pressed the metal harder into her face. "Just shut up."

"Why? Are you afraid if I keep talking, you might find out you're not as *on it* as you thought? Maybe you messed up someplace, and you don't want to hear about it?"

"I did not mess up!" Doubt shaded his face. "Where?"

"We've already called Detectives Howard and Guerra of the Hollywood PD," she told him. "We gave them your description and the dogs'. Even with a fake passport, you'll never get past airport security."

He stared at her a moment. "You did *not* call them."

Terry reached for the phone in her jacket pocket. "You can check the call history on our phone, if you like."

He moved the barrel under her chin.

"Easy," she said. "It's just a phone." She held it out to him casually.

"Open it," he said.

"No."

"Open it!"

"Or you'll shoot me?"

He grabbed the phone, still holding the gun under her jaw. He was awkward, opening the cell phone with his left hand, moving it into position so he could scroll down the call list. When he realized he'd been scammed, the growled and threw the phone up against the wall, shattering it into pieces.

Terry gave him an impish grin. "I lied," she said.

"You die," he said.

"*Booom!*" I yelled.

"*Yeaaaaahhhhhh!*" Terry screamed, jumping in the air and knocking the gun out of her face.

It went off, hitting the ceiling. *Bang!*

A chunk of plaster fell down, hitting Kyle on the head, blinding him with white dust. His hands went to his eyes, and I head-butted him. He slammed against the bedroom wall.

Terry threw herself at Kyle and got a grip on his gun arm, biting down on his wrist. He howled and released the weapon. It hit the wooden floor and skittered away.

I gave Kyle a roundhouse kick behind the knee.

He collapsed to the floor.

Terry dove for the gun, a few feet away. Kyle scrambled across the floor to get to her. I jumped on his back, my arm around this throat, squeezing as hard as I could to choke off his air.

But the downhill racer had incredibly strong legs. He pushed himself up to a standing position with me clinging to his back; then he wrenched my arms off his neck and spun around, flinging me away in the same instant.

I sailed to the bed, bumping my head on the wall as I bounced off the mattress.

Terry was climbing to her feet with the gun, trying to aim it at Kyle. But she stepped on the body bag, and it slipped out from under her. She went down, hitting the floor hard. The gun in her hand went off again just as I jumped off the bed.

I felt the sting on my right arm and looked down to see blood. Then I turned to see a hole blasted in the drywall behind me.

Terry and Kyle wrestled on the floor. He was underneath, she was on top, both of them grunting and growling. He had both hands around her left wrist, trying to wrench the gun from her hand. The fingers of her right hand were digging into his face like a claw.

Then suddenly Kyle arched his back, toppling Terry sideways, releasing her hold on him. He swung up a fist and clocked her with an uppercut to the jaw.

She flew backwards and sprawled on the floor, out cold.

Kyle grabbed the gun and jumped to his feet, eyes blazing, his hands shaking with fury.

"Now I'm gonna be late for my flight!"

He aimed the gun at Terry's unconscious head. Before I could scream, I heard a woman's voice coming from the doorway.

"You are not only gonna be late. You're gonna miss your flight altogether."

I spun around, and the first thing I saw was the big, blond hair. Then I took in the whole picture of her standing there, her legs wide in a firing stance, her high-heeled sandals braced against the doorframe. She pointed an automatic pistol at Kyle two-handed, and it looked as if she meant business.

"Who are *you*?" Kyle's mouth was hanging open, bloody drool trailing from his lip.

"I'm Andie Sue Kopalski." She lined him up in her sights. "And you're the man that made a whore out of my baby."

Kyle whipped up his gun and got off a round.

He missed, his bullet splintering the doorframe.

But Andie Sue's aim was true.

Her bullet caught Kyle right in the center of his chest. He flew back into the closet, slammed his head on the clothes rod, and then slumped to the floor. Blood spread out across the front of his tailored shirt in a bold crimson pattern. His head bobbed and sank, his chin coming to rest on top of his collarbone.

I stared at him in shock, tears of relief flooding my eyes, and I choked on a sob. Turning to Andie Sue, I said, "How did you—?"

"Never mind that now," she said, pointing to Terry. "Better tend to your sister."

The ambulance got there just ahead of the cops. The paramedics treated Kyle before they did me on the basis of triage. I was tempted to say I should come first because he was scum, but I held my tongue. Terry had been revived with a wicked headache and was holding an ice pack on her jaw. I pressed a tea towel to my bleeding arm.

Eventually they got around to dressing my flesh wound.

"You were pretty good in there," Terry said as my arm was swabbed with antiseptic.

"Thanks," I said, wincing. "You, too."

"Will she be able to play the violin after this?" Terry asked the paramedic.

"Should be no problem."

"Good. She never could before."

The paramedic grunted. "I always fall for that one."

Kyle Hearn was conscious when they rolled him to the door on a gurney. Andie Sue stepped in front of one of the attendants to ask about his condition. "Is he gonna live?"

"Probably."

"Good. He's got a lot to answer for."

"Suck it," Kyle muttered, as he bumped over the threshold.

"See you in court, Hans," Terry said, blowing him a kiss.

We helped ourselves to some of the coffee in Kyle's kitchen. It was really rather cozy sitting around the table with our mugs, just like the odd assortment of characters you'd see on some dumb TV sit-com.

The blond, pistol-packing mama.

The wacky redheaded twins.

The two gruff-but-benign homicide detectives.

Well, you crazy girls really saved the day! Chortle, chortle, chortle.

Freeze frame with everybody throwing back their heads and laughing. Roll end credits.

The sound of the dogs' whining reminded me that this was reality, not TV. "What's going to happen to the Rottweilers? Will they go to the pound?"

"I could use a couple of ferocious curs where I live," Andie Sue offered.

"Where's that?" Howard asked.

"Outside Riverside. Got me a real house with a wooden porch and a big back yard. I'm the new care-taker for a trash dump. Those dogs would be happy there. They'd be good protection, too."

Guerra nodded. "Sure, give 'em a decent home. Let the a-hole sue us to get 'em back."

"So," Terry said to the cops, "will the DA drop the charges against Bethany now?"

"Not necessarily. Unless he confesses, we're gonna need proof that Kyle Hearn killed Glen Adler."

I was momentarily discouraged, and then an idea whacked me on the brain like a you-know-what. "Did you collect Adler's ruler at the scene of the crime?" I asked them.

Guerra confirmed, "He had it in his hand."

"I hope the techs handled it carefully. Unless I miss my bet, it's got Kyle's skin cells on it."

Terry burst out laughing. The cops looked at her curiously.

"Adler likes to whack things with his ruler," she explained. "It's his magic light saber."

"He *used* to," I said sadly. "At any rate, it would be a good place to start. Now that we know Kyle was behind everything, you might find other trace evidence of him at the scene."

"We might at that." Howard chuckled as he slapped me on the back. "Thanks to you two wacky redheads!"

He didn't really say that. What he said was, "Possibly."

"How did you three get together on this thing?" Guerra wanted to know.

Andie Sue answered, *"I was minding my own business..."* she gave us a wink. "When these two came by and spoiled my afternoon. They told me Bethany was running scared. I always feared this might happen. I knew how they operated, that pack of hyenas surrounding her, seen them fighting over my little girl like she was a piece of meat."

She looked to the ceiling and wiped away a tear. "They turned her against me, offered her fame and private jets and limos. I offered a reminder of what she'd been—white trash, with a no-count mother and a no-name daddy."

"Why'd you walk after you negotiated that great deal?" Terry asked.

"I didn't care about myself, but no child of mine was gonna have the life I'd had. I would see to that. I wanted Bethany to control her own publishing rights so she wouldn't end up penniless like those great Motown artists and so many others.

"After you showed up, I knew something bad was happening. Bethany's career was in trouble, and it looked like the jackals were cutting their losses. A singer who dies in her prime is worth a lot more than one who lives to a ripe old age, and I wouldn't have put it past them to see that it happened to Bethany.

"I moved out of the trailer park, in case they came after me, and started my own investigation, beginning with that purple-haired people-eater. I guessed that she and Claude had some plot going against my baby."

"I thought you hated Bethany," Terry said. "You sounded so angry."

"It's true. We put each other through so much. But a mother can't stay mad at her own baby. It eats you alive."

"So you thought Claude was working with Marietta Kirby?"

"Yes, at first. But then I saw her coming here to meet the stud muffin and listened at the bedroom window while they went at it like a pair of alley cats. Afterwards, I heard them discussing their plans."

"Why didn't you go to the police?" Howard asked.

"I was supposed to be dead, remember? Anyway, I know what kind of loony birds come out of the woodwork when something happens to a celebrity. If I could even get in to see you, I'd have to waste valuable time convincing you I was who I said I was. Claude knew me. He could have vouched for me. And it looked like he had clean hands. In this, at least.

"I was just about to pay him a visit when he died. I saw the shrink leaving the house that morning with a computer under her arm."

"You're a witness to that? Good." Guerra permitted himself a smile. "The butler was running errands that morning, never saw anyone come or go. I guess in all the confusion, he didn't miss the computer."

"Well," Andie Sue went on, "I watched for a few more days. I followed her and the stud muffin to Claude's funeral. I saw him leave early, then followed him back here. I had just let myself in when I heard a shot go off. And you know what happened then."

"Yeah," Terry said. "Then you saved our lives."

"It was the least I could do. You were trying to help my little girl."

42

*Y*es, Virginia, there *are* criminal masterminds in the world. Marietta Kirby, for one. She began plotting to steal Bethany's money the moment she first treated the girl. During the lawsuit with her mother, Bethany began to exhibit self-destructive behaviors—pulling out her eyelashes, cutting herself, purging. And of course, she had to be treated with pharmaceuticals. Marietta dosed her and dosed her and dosed her, priming her for a breakdown. It was a win-win. While she was on the drugs, Bethany's mental condition deteriorated. When she got off them, the abrupt withdrawal caused a chemical backfire. The poor girl's neurons were fried coming and going.

As Bethany approached the age of eighteen, time was of the essence. That's when Marietta enlisted the handsome and tech-savvy bodyguard. At Kyle's suggestion, she sedated Bethany during one of her sessions and planted the RF chip under the tattoo. The wound was so tiny it could be taken for a bug bite, the transponder so thin it wouldn't show through the tattooed skin. This way Kyle was able to track Bethany everywhere she went.

The accountant Larry Benjamin was the first to die. He had tried to contact Bethany, apparently, to confess to his part in the fraud. The conspirators couldn't let his amends-making interfere with their carefully laid plans, so Kyle shot him after first slipping him a heroin mickey, making it look like suicide.

Next they hired Terry and me to watch Paul Fellows. They were pretty sure Fellows would contact Bethany on behalf of Benjamin, and they wanted pictures of her going into his apartment so they could frame her for his murder, planned for sometime later. Kyle tracked Bethany from Paramount Pictures to Paul Fellows's apartment while we were staking her out, and told her handlers where to pick her up. He didn't want her to stray too far.

After Bethany jumped in our car, Kyle retrieved the camera from the yard. He emailed our picture to the police anonymously. At the same time, he told them they'd find Bethany at the Starlight Motel. Later that day, Kyle went back to the apartment and killed the stuntman, planting the camera in Fellows's dead hand to implicate Bethany. He'd known her prints were on it, having watched the whole scene from a distance.

It was Marietta who placed the call to us from Fellows's apartment a couple of days after returning from Geneva, pretending to be assaulted and drawing us into the trap. But it hadn't been in order to implicate us— she just wanted us to find the body and report it to the police. Bethany was supposed to be charged with the crime. Unfortunately, Terry and I presented a better prospect to the cops. When Kyle and Marietta realized that Bethany might not be accused of Paul Fellows's murder, they conceived of the plan to kill Glen Adler and to frame her for that.

Exhausted from running, lonely for the only person who'd ever respected her intelligence, Bethany eventually did turn to Adler. Kyle arrived at Adler's apartment shortly after she did and told the tutor he was going to intercede on his behalf, recanting the molestation charges. Bethany was delighted and only too happy to celebrate with the mint ice cream Kyle had brought along. It contained a tasteless and odorless drug cocktail, including Ecstasy and GHB, the date rape drug.

Poor little Glen Adler tried to fight Kyle off with the ruler, but it was no good. Kyle shot him with his own pearl-handled .22, using Bethany's unconscious hand to pull the trigger.

They killed Claude, too, of course.

Marietta had ingratiated herself with him over the years. She'd always been there to lend a sympathetic ear whenever he needed to complain about Bethany's antics. Always there with a neck rub, looking over his shoulder when he did his online banking. It didn't take a genius to grasp how it was done and where he kept his passwords. Claude had been such a control freak, he hadn't even wanted an assistant knowing his business. But it never occurred to him not to trust the big-name psychiatrist.

His trust cost him dearly.

She gave him an overdose of digitalis to take when he complained of chest pains, killing him instantly. Then she slipped his computer under her arm and left before the butler got back from his errands. The house-man had never even suspected that his boss lay dead on the office floor until we arrived with the police.

They arrested Marietta at Claude's funeral reception, much to the relief of Eric Clapton. Marietta had cornered him and was blabbing on and on about the public's pathological addiction to fame, boring the poor guy to tears. David Bowie had been too engrossed in his own conversation to catch Clapton's desperate eye signals, so Marietta stayed longer than was wise.

Later, when she heard Kyle Hearn had been planning to flee to Switzerland without her, she spilled her guts. It seems hell hath no fury like a celebrity head-shrinker scorned. She had the additional incentive of a deal offered by the DA for testifying against her lover and co-conspirator, the spaniel-eyed, charming, and very lethal Mr. Kyle Hearn.

43

Bethany was set to be released from the hospital in the afternoon. We sat with Andie Sue in the third-floor waiting area. The paparazzi were downstairs, cordoned off in an area in front of the hospital where they'd been camping for the past week. We'd been sneaked in by the hospital staff through the back entrance, and so far no one had guessed that the pop princess was scheduled to rejoin the world of the living that very day.

"I've been wondering," Terry said to Andie Sue. "How did you pull off being dead? It was more complicated than just putting the story out to the tabs. You had a funeral in Nashville."

"My cousin Tammy Lynne never did take very good care of herself," Andie said, shaking her head. "Too fond of the bottle. After her David died, she came out to visit me. Widowhood did *not* agree with the girl. She drank herself to death right there on my couch."

"So you took her identity?"

She nodded. "Cremated her body and sent it back to Nashville as mine." When Andie Sue saw our horrified looks she said, "It was worth my life to do it!"

"What do you mean?" I asked.

"You heard about my car going off Laurel Canyon Boulevard? I'd had one drink, but I wasn't drunk. Not by a long shot. My brake line was cut."

We gasped in shock.

"Oh, don't be so naive," she scoffed. "You think the management company was gonna let me take Bethany off the market? What's the life of one miserable little woman compared to the millions they got in commissions? Why do you think Larry Benjamin was having so much trouble with his conscience after he got sober?"

"Wow," I said. "Gonna go to the police with this?"

"Uh-uh. No way they're gonna charge those rich guys with attempted murder. It's not worth the effort. They could never make it stick, anyway." She sighed and patted her vaporous platinum hair. "Wonder what's taking them so long? I'm jumpy as a cat. How do I look?"

She was dressed in a toned-down version of her usual couture: faux suede bell-bottoms that laced up the sides, a matching jacket with a bright yellow blouse, and spike-heeled, white ankle boots.

"You look pretty as a picture." Terry reached into her jacket pocket and pulled out the purloined Polaroid, handing it to Andie Sue.

"My goodness. Would you look at this?" Andie Sue took the picture, smiling. "What a sweet baby. And I'm so young!" Then she had a sudden realization, and whacked Terry over the head with the photograph. "You stole it, you little thief!"

Terry laughed. "Sorry, but I thought this reunion might happen one day. Figured you might want to have it with you when it did."

"Excuse me?" someone said.

We turned to see a tall, lean man in dungarees, a flannel shirt, and pointed-toe boots. He wore a cowboy hat and was holding a bouquet of wild flowers. Too old to be a Bethany fan. North of forty, south of sixty. His handsome face was deeply lined from the sun, but he had kind, brown eyes.

Andie Sue stared at him for a minute; then her jaw dropped.

"Jim...Jerry...Joe?"

"Jerry," the man said, pleased that she'd almost remembered. "Jeremiah."

"Wh-what're you doin' here?" Andie Sue sputtered.

He removed his cowboy hat and smiled meekly, showing a missing molar on the right side of his mouth. "Just come to pay my respects."

Andie Sue stared at him for a moment, and then all at once she jumped up and grabbed the flowers out of his hand, beating him about the head and shoulders with them. "Son of a gun!"

A couple of nurses came running but stopped short of interceding with the furious, flower-wielding bowling queen. Jerry ducked the blossoms with his arms in front of his face. The floor was soon littered with petals.

Jerry lowered his arms. "I'm sorry, Andie. I should've known you'd feel this way."

Andie Sue's chest was heaving. She held the bare flower stems in her hand like red-hot pokers. If the man didn't leave immediately, I was afraid she was going to put out one of his eyes.

"I'll...I'll be going now."

"You will *not* be going, Mister. Not until you give back my eighty dollars!"

He stopped and turned slowly. "Eighty dollars?"

"You have some nerve showing up eighteen years later, you sorry, toothless bum! What'd you think, you were going to waltz in and say *Daddy's home!* and that'd make everything okay?"

The hurt on Jerry's face made me want to cry.

"I didn't know where to find you." He spoke softly, worrying the brim of his hat with gnarled fingers. "And I sure didn't know there was no little girl at first. I told you I had to be off with the rodeo the next day, but I guess you were too dru—I guess you forgot."

She narrowed her eyes at him. "So you took my money and had yourself a good ol' time at the rodeo?"

"No, ma'am."

"I had a hundred dollars in that wallet. I know, 'cause I'd just cashed my paycheck."

"You may have been too dru—you may not recall properly, but you lost all your money at the pool tables. I put a twenty in your wallet when I left, just so you wouldn't be without. It was all I had on me. I let you sleep because you were snoring pretty heavy. I figured you needed the rest."

"Snoring?" Andie Sue huffed, hands on her hips. "Well, thank you for that lovely image."

"No. Thank *you.*"

Terry and I stifled a laugh.

"So you figured out who I was after all these years, and you thought it was high time you laid claim to Bethany and her money?"

"No, ma'am. When I came back from the rodeo two months later, you'd picked up and left. I couldn't find you."

Andie Sue's eyes went sideways. "I *was* moving around a lot at the time. Staying ahead of the bill collectors."

"Nobody knew where you went."

"You...you asked after me?"

He nodded. "Years later, when I saw ya'll on the TV, I realized who you were, and I saw what Bethany had made of herself. I didn't know—still don't really know—if she's mine. But I didn't think you'd want some old cowpoke tagging along with you in your limos. Thought you might feel the way you do now."

"Then why *are* you here?"

"I see the news more than I used to, back when I was on the circuit. I was scared your little girl was going to prison for murder. I just wanted to tell you how happy I am for you both. I still have a lot of regard for you, Andie Sue."

She continued to stare him down, but her eyes were softening. "I'm sorry about your flowers."

"That's all right. I hope ya'll don't think I want anything, except to see you happy."

"You don't want any money?"

"I've got me a spread outside Riverside," he said, a little pride breaking through his natural shyness. "Got a few quarter horses, couple of milk cows. I give riding lessons to the kids out there. Some of us have simple pleasures," he added, almost apologetically.

"Bully for you," Andie Sue said, still playing tough.

There was an awkward silence.

"It was sure good to see you. Give Miss Bethany my best." Jeremiah donned his hat and started down the hallway.

Andie Sue stood there, watching him leave with her arms folded over her chest and her foot tapping the ground. She made no move to stop him.

I couldn't let him go like this, couldn't let Bethany's dad disappear into the mist again.

"Wait!" I ran after him, Terry right behind me.

When he turned to face us, I saw that his eyes were wet. "Yes, miss?"

"I'm sorry to ask you this, but it might be important to Bethany. When you were in the rodeo, did you have any accidents?"

"So many I couldn't count 'em, miss. Why?"

Terry came up beside me. "Sorry, sir, but did you at one time lose a testicle?"

His eyes bugged and he looked around to see if she'd been overheard. Finally, he leaned in and whispered, "I wouldn't want everybody in the world to know."

"It's important," she insisted.

He looked at her a moment, before answering in a low voice, "A Brahma bull stomped my groin in Amarillo. Can I go now, please?"

"Just need your last name," I said.

"It's Evans."

"Thanks, Mr. Evans," Terry said. "We'll tell Bethany you came by."

He gave his head a little shake and then ambled down the empty hallway on bowed legs, moving much more quickly than before.

When we got back at the waiting room, Andie Sue was standing motionless, barely breathing, her hands covering her mouth.

A nurse had just wheeled Bethany into the waiting area. She was pale, with purple crescents under her eyes. Her dark roots lay flat on her head; her arms were covered with bandages. Her big, blue eyes overran with tears the minute she saw Andie Sue. Suddenly, she jumped out of the wheelchair before the nurse could stop her and threw herself into her mother's arms.

Mama!" Bethany cried.

"My baby," Andie Sue said in a barely audible whisper.

And they held each other for the longest time.

A helicopter lifted Bethany and Andie Sue off the roof of the hospital, headed for a private yacht in the harbor. Bethany's new psychiatrist had prescribed a mother-daughter cruise along with copious amounts of tranquilizers to ease Bethany out of her chemically induced madness. She'd get a healing rest before her "Farewell Tour," and the two estranged women would have a chance to heal their emotional rift.

Terry and I went to Aunt Reba's house for dinner. She'd gotten wind of what had happened with her fellow truth-seeker, Bethany, and wanted the story right away. Cousin Robert greeted us at the door of their Beverly Hills Tudor mansion.

"Hello, my pets." He gave us each a kiss on the cheek. "Haven't we been busy, stoking the star-making machinery behind the popular songs?"

"Huh?" we said.

"Before your time, dearies." He turned and yelled into the dining room, "Oh Mumsy, the bobtailed twins are here!"

Reba rushed into the marble foyer.

"Where *have* you been? Your friends have been here for an hour, soaking up vodka martinis like there's no tomorrow. Have you no sense of propriety?"

"Huh?" we said again. We hadn't been expecting anyone.

We followed her into the dining room. There, seated around the table, good and looped and having a grand old time, was Bill the hairdresser, gabbing away with John Boatwright and Dwight Franzen!

I turned to bolt, but they spotted me.

"Hi, Kerry!" Boatwright shouted. "We were just talking about you."

I stopped and turned to look at him. "You were?" I heard myself gulp.

"Dwight here was telling me how much you said you'd missed him." Boatwright clinked Franzen's glass. "He said he gave you a real barnstormer of a kiss."

"And John here was just telling me how ready you were to go that night in his bedroom." Franzen winked at Boatwright. "Before you were interrupted?"

"And I was telling dem dat dey're too good for you," Bill said, wagging his head back and forth. "You got no sense of style, you got no boobies, no booty—"

"Help!" I screamed. "This is some kind of *nightmare...nightmare ...nightmare!*"

My voice echoed through my brain, reverberating off the skull bones. I woke up in a sweat, gasping for air; then I heard Terry's feet pounding the stairs, followed by the sound of anxious little claws.

"What happened?" She skidded around the corner. "You were screaming in your sleep!"

"Oh, Terry! I had the worst dream. Boatwright and Franzen were drinking martinis at Reba's, and they were telling stories about me, locker room talk, and—oh, it was horrible!"

"Is that all?" She rolled her eyes at the dogs. They turned around and trotted back out of the room, indignant. "Wish you'd make up your mind, already. We need our beauty sleep." She stomped back down the stairs, calling, "But you're crazy if you don't go for Boatwright!"

I did not recall asking for her opinion.

Epilogue

Bethany got a new manager to go with her on the road, the Rabbi Ibrahim Freilander, who would act as both her career *and* her spiritual advisor, instructing her in the mysteries of the universe while handling the business aspects of the tour. She promised to call Terry for an ice cream date when she gets back. I'm dying to know if Terry was right about our bi-curious little megastar, but I guess I'll have to wait six months to find out.

Andie Sue and Jeremiah Evans are seeing each other, making up for lost time. They live a few miles from each other in the Inland Empire, a ten-minute drive by pickup. Jerry's currently teaching Andie Sue how to ride (and who knows what else) in the saddle.

Terry and I reneged on our promise to give Bill a baby duck after learning that he wanted to use it in a Santeria blood ritual. We told him the ducks flew away, but promised to let him do our hair as compensation.

We figured looking like Julianne Moore was preferable to being hexed.

Reba dropped her study of the Kabbalah when she learned that she was expected to tithe to the temple. "I'll gladly pay ten percent if I actually *get* to the gates of heaven. But I don't really see the point of paying in advance, do you?"

For his part, Eli continues to worship the Lakers at the sports bar. Still single and loving it.

Brad the Number One Fan is now the official Webmaster of Bethany's site. He posted the scores of her IQ test online, and guess what? The girl's a certified genius.

The Hollywood police threw us a little party to celebrate solving the case, to which we invited Eli, Shotanya, Raquel, and Bobbi. Halfway through the party someone wheeled in a huge cake. Barry Manilow burst out of the top wearing nothing but a Speedo, singing "Copacabana."

I almost wet myself when I saw the Barry Man covered in whipped cream, before I realized it was actually an impersonator. But he could really belt out a tune, and by the time he'd done his third rendition of "Mandy" with the cops singing along drunkenly in tears, Terry and I were both confirmed Fanilows.

THE END

AUCTION NOTICE: Green Jeep Cherokee stolen by superstar Bethany. In exact condition Bethany left it, including broken window and discarded ice cream wrappers. Bidding starts today at $30,000.

Author's Note

This work of fiction was completed in 2004, long before any purely coincidental similarities to persons living or dead and their associated public meltdowns may or may not have occurred. If it seems that the story was "ripped from the headlines," they had to have been future headlines.

For lack of a publisher, I submitted *Hellraiser* to the first-ever Amazon Breakthrough Novel Awards. Out of five thousand entries from twenty countries, it finished in the top ten.

Hewlett-Packard co-sponsored the contest with Amazon. HP gave me some really wonderful electronic prizes, and Amazon stepped up with a CreateSpace Total Design Freedom package, which is why you are able to enjoy *The Hellraiser of the Hollywood Hills: A McAfee Twins Novel* in print.

In addition to the excellent work by the CreateSpace team, I'm indebted to my editors Brett Ellen Block,

Alison Kerr Miller, and Mary Whyte. I would also like to thank Keith Border and Aaron Ockman for their notes on the manuscript.

And thank you, Dear Reader, for continuing to support the McAfee Twins.

8227992R0

Made in the USA
Charleston, SC
20 May 2011